I0735258

Satisfaction

a novel

"There is one story,
and one story only..."

LANE JENNINGS

WORKBOOK PRESS LLC
187 E Warm Springs Rd,
Suite B285, Las Vegas, NV 89119, USA

Website: https://workbookpress.com/
Hotline: 1-888-818-4856
Email: admin@workbookpress.com

Ordering Information:
Quantity sales. Special discounts are available on quantity purchases by corporations, associations, and others.
For details, contact the publisher at the address above.

Library of Congress Control Number:
ISBN-13:   978-1-957618-92-0 (Paperback Version)
               978-1-957618-93-7 (Digital Version)

REV. DATE: 20/04/2022

SATISFACTION

SATISFACTION

LANE JENNINGS

A NOVEL

CONTENTS

DEDICATION

To my first draft which was titled

"Bitter Light"

NOTE: This book deals almost exclusively with people and events inside the Purple Valley. To help remind readers what was going on in the wider world while our story takes place, the author offers this prologue made up of selected newspaper headlines from these eventful years:

1962

(Feb)   **LOCAL CUBANS FLOCK TO JOIN FREEDOM FIGHTERS AT BAY OF PIGS LANDING**

(May)   **EX-PREMIER CASTRO FACES FIRING SQUAD**

(Nov)   **Popular Unrest Ousts Hanoi Regime**

1963

(Mar)   **UN Holds Elections in Newly Unified Viet Nam**

(Jun)   **MAO TSE TUNG DEAD AT 69— PRC in Chaos**

(Jul)   **Chiang Kai Shek's Troops Sweep Ashore Near Canton**

(Sep)   **Nationalist Armies Liberate Shanghai**

(Nov)   **JACQUELINE KENNEDY SHOT DEAD IN DALLAS MOTORCADE: Bullet Narrowly Misses President**

1964

(Feb)   **PRC SURRENDERS—Triumphant Chiang Enters Peking**

(May)   **Landmark Civil Rights Bills Clear House and Senate**

(Jul)   **Martin Luther King Named Ambassador to France**

(Sep)   **KENNEDY TO KHRUSHCHEV: "Tear Down This Wall !"**

(Nov)   **KENNEDY/JOHNSON WIN LANDSLIDE SECOND TERM**

1965

(Jan)   **EAST GERMAN RIOTS SPREAD TO POLAND, HUNGARY**

(Jun)   **TWO GERMANIES REUNITE AS EAST EUROPE UNRAVELS**

(Aug)   **WIDOWER PRESIDENT TO WED MARILYN MONROE**

Chapter 1: *Introit*

Seated at the piano, while the crowbars and claw hammers slowly tore the room apart around him, young Allan Ross looked more than twice his age. Later, they would party in the rec room under Baxter Hall; and this night, Allan told himself, for once he was going to get completely drunk.

With apparent unconcern, he began to play: false notes, discordant, out of any measurable rhythm, slurring his right hand fingers off the black keys, while the left remained suspended, hovering, about to fall. He slapped one muddy bass chord down, another, then a third, not even watching where his fingers landed. Yet somehow they pulled the right-hand notes into a recognizable progression. Finally, four sparklingly clear two-handed chords resolved to a repeated B-flat, and he was off and rollicking into the chorus of *Lulu's Back in Town*, in a style that Allan (but probably not many others) knew owed one hell of a lot to Thelonius Monk.

The strike crew laughed and cheered. They'd fallen silent when he sat down to play, afraid it might be something modern, dull, and classical. Now though, with the tension broken, they were obviously pleased, and Allan watched with satisfaction as they turned back with their various implements of destruction to the absorbing work of dismantling the set.

This was a thorough business. The stage was large, and despite one missing wall, and much of the furniture and risers already carted into the shop off right, this spot was still essentially the London drawing room where, for the past two hours, George Bernard Shaw's enchanting Candida had been leading her husband Morell, and her adoring puppy-poet Marchbanks through the paces of that elegant word-dance *love*. But London was gone now, and an already sashless window opened on the huge blue plaster cyclorama towering up into darkness like the empty sky it was supposed to be.

Allan, who had played Morell, the middle-aged, respectable married clergyman, still wore his costume and make up. From the piano, which had been rolled to center stage, he noted with approval how a few of the more rhythmic vandals had begun to time their pounding to his swinging tune. It excited him to see the syncopation of his fingers instantly translated into violence. He ached to be right in there, slugging with the rest. Oh, for something breakable to smash!

Allan's hands were strong. He slammed them down now, and could feel the piano shudder with every chord. The strings screamed back at him, but held. This could not go on long. Reluctantly, he rolled on into the coda, slowed the pace, eased off, and let his left hand slip unnoticed off the keyboard, while the right spilled out one final tinkling trill that sank away like water into sand.

He stood up to scattered clapping from those members of the crew whose hands weren't other-wise engaged. Ordinarily Allan enjoyed applause, but tonight it embarrassed him, set him apart. He nodded; smiled, said "thank you, thanks," closed the piano, and left the stage.

The other members of the cast had already gone down to change. By now, he guessed, they'd be out of the dressing rooms and over at the party. Allan alone had hung around on stage. Closing-night nostalgia? Yes, in a way. He had enjoyed his theatre career and hated to see it end. But facts were facts. As a senior music major with a graded honors recital only six weeks off, he'd have no time to try out for more shows this fall, let alone next spring! Besides, Williams College was a theatre school—there were better actors here than he was, Allan realized, lots of them. This first starring role was pretty sure to be his last as well. He'd never get a chance to play the strong romantic lead. Damn!

Mike Worrell, who was running the strike crew tonight, called over to him.

"Okay Allan, that's it! Got to strike the piano now. Thanks for the tune. Hey, you and the guys playing at the party later?"

"Not tonight. Elroy's walking his bass somewhere up in Harlem this weekend, and our drummer Pete Maynard's got a psych paper due."

"Too bad. Hey, better get that costume back to wardrobe though, or Mrs. Green will kill."

"I'm on my way down now. Catch you later."

An enclosed stairway led down to the greenroom beneath the stage. Allan paused on the top landing to let the metal fire door clang shut behind him, dimming the stairwell and muffling the sounds and voices from above. He descended slowly, grandly; ignoring the torch-bearing guards who stood stiffly to attention in their gaudy uniforms lighting the way.

It was important not to show emotion--lose his dignity. That would not be fitting for a minister of the Queen--even one summoned, as he was now, to sudden conference late at night. Naturally, the guards looked neither left not right. Allan wondered how long they'd been standing there and what they thought about being living furniture.

As they passed from view behind him, one by one the guardsmen turned immediately back into common light bulbs under wire. Only Allan stayed in character. Outside the greenroom door he squared his shoulders, flung the portal wide, strode gravely forward, and beheld . . . the Queen.

It was her whiteness that struck him first: pale skin, ash-blonde hair, hands folded calmly in the lap of her white dress. She was enthroned on a battered high-backed carved and gilded velvet chair that had served generations of college Hamlets, Richards and assorted Henrys.

She looked up, startled, as the door swept shut behind him with an echoing clang. Her eyes met his full on. Instinctively, he bowed to her--deeply, from the waist.

"Hey, Allan!"

He turned. Behind him, by the Coke machine, a lighted cigarette in one hand and two Coke bottles in the other, stood Dave Carter--he of the famous shit-eating grin.

"Allan, you were great tonight, absolutely fantastic!" Dave nodded several times and winked for emphasis.

In his heart, Allan doubted this. But it sounded good.

"Thanks, Dave."

As he pronounced the name, Allan felt its inadequacy. Dave looked more like some late Romantic poet, disheveled hair, wild eyes, elaborate but messy clothes, than a senior at Williams College in this year of DisGrace Nineteen Hundred and Sixty-Four. His name ought to be "Percy" or "Algernon." This was definitely not his century.

Allan turned his attention back to the girl. Her eyes were still appraising him. He returned her look. But neither spoke.

Dave crossed the room, raised cigarette to lips, and transferred one of the open Cokes to his left hand. When he reached the throne, he handed it to the girl. She accepted it easily, nodded her thanks, but never took her eyes off Allan. They went on gazing straight at one another, silently. When Dave finally noticed, he seemed pleased.

"Oh, yes. Allow me to introduce you two. Ann, this is Allan Ross. Allan, I'd like you to meet Ann Ash. Her father's Wooten Ash. Professor Ash? You know? Chairs the astro department?"

"Hello," Allan said.

"Hello," Ann agreed, briefly closing her eyes at the end of the word to make room for her smile.

"You're very . . . convincing as an older man."

Allan laughed. "I've had lots of practice. Somehow, I always end up playing old man parts--no matter what I try out for. Sometimes I think I was <u>born</u> old."

"You were very impressive just now too," Ann went on. "Is that the way you always enter a room?"

He reddened, but smiled. "No. Not always. I didn't think there'd be anyone down here."

She said nothing more. So he pushed on.

"Look, I'd better go change and get this make up off. Nice meeting you . . . uh, Ann. Dave. See you both at the party?"

Dave abruptly hurled the glowing cigarette stub down into his half-finished bottle of Coke, but said nothing. Ann, just sat there, enthroned, watching both of them and smiling.

"Yes, you will," she promised.

Allan turned from her, crossed to the door of the dressing room, opened it (undramatically this time), stepped through, and closed it quietly behind him.

He inspected his face in the mirror. There he was, only partly concealed under the whitened eyebrows, shadowed cheeks, penciled age-lines and brown-rouged lips. He wondered, would he really look like this in thirty or forty years? And what would he feel like then? The painted lips stretched into a wide grin from behind the glass. Spooky.

He could see where sweat had made his age-lines run and smeared the shadows on his cheeks into clumsy blotches. He must have looked ridiculous out there in the greenroom. No wonder that girl had kept staring at him. What was her name again? Oh well.

He undressed, hung up his costume, and began to remove the face paint with mineral oil and cold cream. The white shoe polish in his hair would require a shower—more likely several showers. So he simply ignored it to concentrate on more immediate concerns.

By the time he returned to the green room, Dave and the girl were gone. Allan looked around. The throne was empty. Dave's soggy cigarette floated in a half-empty bottle of Coke beside it. Heavy thuds and footfalls still came from overhead. Allan envisioned risers being stacked and carried, flats knocked apart and barrels of scrap dragged offstage. Did he really want to be up there, straining and hauling? No, he decided. Anyway, they didn't need him. One pair of hands more or less, and his *not* skilled with tools, wouldn't matter. He walked down the hall and stepped out into the fine October night.

Saturday cars came roaring up Route 2, and branches full of dry leaves hissed in the wind like wire brushes over snare drums. Crunching across the gravel parking lot, Allan blinked in the gaudy glow blazing forth from the Sig Phi house across the way. From inside came a noisy mix of laughter, singing, talk, dance records and people moving about, all the fine mild roar of late-night undergraduate life. Allan knew. He had been there himself (at least, physically present) often enough. The place he was bound for now would be much the same.

He cut across the freshman quadrangle—iviest-looking place on campus, Allan thought—and easily remembered back three years to his own first fall. Behind those imitation Georgian walls new generations were discovering alcohol, arguing all night long about sex, sports, and politics, tossing water bombs, even sleeping or studying now and then—just as he had. He smiled, and silently wished them well! *Nunc et semper*—now and always.

*   *   *

The Baxter Hall party room was sufficiently dark when he arrived not to need decoration, though Allan guessed there were probably bunches of sagging balloons and limp streamers of crepe paper pinned to its ceiling and unseen walls. The juke box gave off a poisonous glow bright enough to read by. But no one here was reading.

A few dancing couples shuffled around the floor to a slow number, but most of the shapes he could make out were sitting at tables or booths. Wait, though. Some were in line where a beer keg stood upright in a tub of ice. Allan headed that way.

He would have been happy not to recognize anyone; his walk through the dark had primed him for loneliness. But once in the beer line he couldn't help spotting his roommate, Tom Petard.

"Allan! Hey, Ya made it."

"Tom. Don't tell me <u>you</u> saw the show again?"

"Naw. Just came over for the beer." He grinned, and raised a big paper cup. Dried beer foam crested the lip. Obviously not his first, Allan saw.

"What kept you?" Tom asked, and drank deep.

Allan shrugged. "I helped clean up the stage; no sense in letting the strike crew have all the fun. You know. *Wham! Biff! Pow*! Creative destruction?"

Tom grinned back. "Yeah, I guess." He stepped up to the spigot. But it only gushed foam.

"Oh shit!" said Tom, quietly. Ignoring the air pump most guys would have reached for instinctively to build up pressure inside the keg, he simply tipped his cup and let the foam run off. Allan approved. To his mind, patience and restraint were the marks of an experienced hand, in beer tapping as in life.

"Wouldn't you know," Tom grumbled, "Just when it's finally <u>my</u> turn!"

Allan stepped up, cup thrust forward, to receive his own allotment of the golden liquid.

"Mmmmmmmm," he nodded sagely. "Life is a half-empty beer keg, foamy and over-warm, that makes you sick more often than it gets you high."

"Oh God, Ross! You flame again!"

The flipped spigot closed on cue just when Allan's cup was nearly full.

"D'you bring a date?" Tom inquired.

His head turned to follow a girl in bright red leotard and black skirt--Bennington, from the look of her--brushed by them. Allan spotted the same girl, but only his eyes moved after her.

He shook his head. "Nope, just looking. See you later."

And with that, he moved off, in search of somewhere to be quiet in the dark.

It was no easy quest. The juke box seemed much louder now, all electronic twangs, crashing drum beats, and raw inarticulate voices. At least Allan found he could make out some of the lyrics--for whatever that was worth:

> *"Ah cain't get no-o*
> *Sa-tis FAK-shun.*
> *But ah try . . . and ah Try*
> *and ah TRY . . . AND AH TRY! ..... "*

He grimaced and wished he could turn down the volume, if not pull the plug. Who could hear themselves <u>think</u> in all this noise? He drank instead.

"Allan?"

Someone was tapping his shoulder. He turned to find Dave Carter, this time not grinning. So Allan grinned himself. What the hell?

"David, greetings and salutations!" He gestured grandly, spilling a little beer.

"Allan, I . . ., uh, want to ask you something."

"Ask away. It can only <u>kill</u> you."

The juke box died. Allan's shoulders relaxed. Dave coughed, and then swallowed something large.

"What do you think of Ann?" he asked, finally.

"Your *girl*?" The little left of Allan's beer was warm now. Warm and flat.

Dave looked down a moment, hesitated, then said: "Ann's not MY girl exactly. We're just . . . old friends."

The juke box blared back to life again—same song. Guys were suddenly hand-clapping, foot-stomping, pounding on tables. And there were dancers all over the floor, pumping vigorously. Allan wanted more beer. He ignored Dave, began walking kegward. Dave pursued, looking up at him blankly. Was Dave really so much shorter, Allan wondered? Hard to tell in this light.

It seemed more peaceful, somehow, by the keg. Reverently, Allan began the ritual refilling of his cup.

Dave asked again. "What did you <u>think</u> of her?"

"She seemed nice. I mean, we didn't <u>talk</u> or anything. But, yes. I liked her. She's . . . attractive."

Dave might have winced. It was too dark for Allan to be sure. Besides, the new beer held his main attention.

"You know . . .," Dave began, hesitated, went on, "I think she'd like it if you . . . asked her out." Dave was speaking very softly, drowning in music. Allan couldn't hear a word.

"Sorry. What'd you say?" he shouted.

"We were <u>talking</u>, after you left. From things she said, I know she'd be glad if you asked her <u>out</u>."

This time, Allan heard.

"Wait a minute. She told <u>you</u> to ask <u>me</u> if <u>I</u> would take <u>her</u> ... "

"No!" Dave broke in, "You don't understand. She didn't........She'd like to know you better. That's all. She's over there."

He pointed toward the glowing jukebox. Allan looked, but could see only lighted machine.

"Why me? You been telling her stories about my ...... prowess?"

Allan wasn't displeased at this thought; but wondered just what stories there were to be told.

Dave didn't smile.

"Look, you can laugh, or forget it, or <u>jump</u> in the pond for all I care. I'm only saying she <u>likes</u> you. All right?"

Allan could see this wasn't funny to Dave. And he was already sorry. Rather than meet Dave's eyes, he raised his beer cup again. Nearly empty yet again. Damn!

"Well...sure," he said finally, "Why not? I've never dated a professor's daughter. Who knows? It might be fun."

Dave nodded, and left without another word.

Allan watched him disappear, then he turned back to the keg for yet another refill. Once more the blaring music died.

Peace again, and quiet. Turning from the spigot, he could make out a girl sitting by herself in a booth near the juke box. He couldn't see her face, but somehow he imagined her smiling.

He walked toward her. The music ended and stayed off as he got close enough to speak.

"Hello again. Mind if I join you?"

"No." She shook her head and smiled.

"Do you mean 'No, I shouldn't?' or 'No, you don't mind?'"

"I mean just what you think I mean."

That, Allan thought, was the best he deserved. She was not dumb, this girl. Nor too-shy either. He sat down and slid along the bench to face her across the table. Damn! He'd forgotten her name! Nothing for it now, he'd have to ask.

"I know we were just introduced," he began, "but I'm sorry to say I didn't catch your name. I'm Allan, Allan Ross."

"It's Ann. Ann Ash. Don't worry. I forget names too. Everybody does. Names hardly matter, really."

She looked serious, then smiled at him again. What could he do but smile back at her? It felt good to do.

"I, uh, see you know Dave Carter," he said, still awkward.

Ann nodded. "We were in high school together. Mt. Greylock. Until my family took me abroad."

'<u>Abroad</u>.' Allan relished the sound of the word. It seemed so vast, encompassing not just another country but <u>all</u> countries, the whole planet, many planets, galaxies, who knows--the entire universe maybe! And this girl <u>liked</u> him!

"Something to drink?" he asked, "A beer?" He held his own cup out to her, untasted.

"No. I'm fine. Thanks."

He didn't mind. Who needed beer?

"Dave roomed in my entry freshman year," he went on, "that's how I know him. And we both took Music 301. But we're not exactly buddies. I've run into him working on shows, but he's kind of a loner. I remember he didn't rush a fraternity."

Allan paused. He shouldn't sound too critical. After all, Dave had grown up with this girl. They might be close.

"Of course <u>that's</u> no crime," he added quickly. "Frats are on the way out anyway. So they say. In a place this small you can make lots of friends and have good times without getting clubby."

"I don't think David cares much about 'good-time' friends."

Allan was curious. But Ann said nothing more. So he changed the subject.

"I guess you go to Bennington."

She laughed.

"Hardly. I start at Wellesley next semester as a mid-term freshman. Right now I'm auditing a few courses here. I lost half a year when we were in England. Besides, auditing's one of the privileges they give faculty families. My mother does it too."

"I never knew that. Is it free?"

"No. But it's a lot cheaper than full tuition."

"You like it here?"

"Very much. Especially English . I <u>love</u> Professor Jackson."

Allan grinned.

"I've had him. He was one of <u>my</u> favorites too."

"He's so funny, sometimes. The way he <u>hates</u> some people, like Milton for instance."

Allan nodded, smiling. He did remember He also <u>agreed</u> about Milton.

"So why leave at all? Why not just stay here."

Ann shook her head, and her long hair splashed and glistened in the neon dark.

"I can't wait to get away. Who'd want to live at home all the time? Would you?"

Allan shrugged. Actually, he didn't think he'd mind it. He and his folks got along just fine. But maybe Ann's family was different.

"Do you <u>play</u> an instrument?" he asked on sudden impulse, guessing she did.

But Ann shook her head.

"I dance some. <u>You</u> play jazz though. I heard your trio over at the New Dorm once with Dave. You're very good."

In the dark, Allan blushed, but his smile grew wider too.

"Thanks."

"Tell me though, do you <u>always</u> jump around so much?"

"Jump around?"

"When you're playing. You did that night. It must be exhausting. Or does it just come naturally?"

"No," he admitted, "it's mostly for show. Seems to help people loosen up, get with the beat, enjoy themselves. That's what jazz is all about: relaxing, getting free."

"I suppose. But how do you manage to play the right notes if you never sit still?"

Allan laughed. "Well, you <u>don't</u> always. But people don't mind a few sour notes and slurs. Makes it all sound more 'authentic' somehow. What the folksong crowd calls 'ethnic'. Unrehearsed. Still, I don't recommend it for the concert hall."

"Is that what you want to be, a concert pianist?"

"No," he told her, surprised he could be so frank and open with her, "I want to be a music critic."

"A <u>critic</u>? Why?"

He shrugged. "Well, partly because I never heard of someone setting out to be one. So I thought <u>I</u> would. You know, see if it could be done."

She laughed. And Allan joined her.

"I'm sorry," she said at last, "I didn't mean to laugh. But it just sounds funny somehow, <u>wanting</u> to be a critic."

"I know. Like 'My son . . . the Nurse?'" Allan offered. This started both of them laughing again. He recovered first.

"Okay, yes," he said. "But you see, that's exactly the <u>point</u>. It sounds funny because everyone thinks a critic has to be some old newspaper hack who couldn't make it as a real reporter. They send him to a few concerts as a cub, and he scribbles something witty just to keep his mind alive, and ends up as a permanent music critic. Secretly he hates musicians and concerts and takes his revenge by making nasty comments in print that drive poor struggling composers and performers into early graves."

Allan slowed. He was very earnest now.

"And maybe it <u>is</u> that way today. But I don't think it <u>should</u> be. I think that critics can be creative, too, right along with composers and performers--or like a good professor, one who really knows his stuff and <u>cares</u>. They just need to understand each other's jobs, and be ready to change places--literally. I think a composer should play, and a performer should compose, and a critic should be able to do both--at least well enough to earn the respect of those who choose to do those things full-time. And he should be judged for what he contributes to the enjoyment of listeners too, the same way people rate artists and composers."

A short pause followed this outburst. Ann looked expectant. Allan shrugged, looked down. "End of sermon," he concluded, smiling, and sipped his beer.

Was he impressing her? Perhaps. He realized that he wanted to. But if not . . . well, at least he had meant everything he said.

The beer was beginning to take effect now. Allan caught himself staring at the swell of Ann's white dress where it concealed her breasts. *Dulcitur turigidae, gemina poma* . . . "Sweet fullness, twin fruit . . .," he mused. Jesus!

He refocused his eyes, jerked his gaze back up to Ann's face. Could she tell where his mind had just been? Very likely. Had he offended her? Maybe not though. Was he drunk? Close to. Did it show--to everyone? He didn't think so. Not yet.

"Music means a lot to you, doesn't it." Ann's voice was gentle, understanding.

"Yes," he said. It was half apology, half boast.

They sat together, quiet in the near dark, room sounds lapping against them like small waves on a deserted beach.

Then the juke box exploded once again, louder than ever. More people were dancing. Everywhere laughter and shouting, but no words were clear enough to understand.

The moments of sharing had passed. He felt thirsty again, and awkward in the noisy dark. He would make this short and get back to the keg.

"Want to see *A Hard Day's Night* with me next Wednesday? It's playing all week at the Cinema." He was looking straight at Ann, maybe two feet away from him, but he had to shout to make himself heard above the roar. "What do you say?"

Ann frowned as if thinking. Her lips moved in word-shapes.

"<u>What</u>?!"

"I said <u>yes</u>. I'd love to. But can we make it <u>Friday</u> night?"

Allan pondered. What was Friday? He thought there'd been something planned. But so what. Let it go. This was better.

"Friday's fine!" he yelled, and smiled across at Ann. She smiled back.

Then he cupped one hand to his mouth and shouted: "What do you say we find some other place to sit. This is . . . crazy."

Ann nodded, and they both slid out of the booth. As they stood up, Allan became aware for the first time of their relative heights. The top of her head reached to just above his shoulder. That was nice. And her hands had long, slim fingers. Very nice. Very nice indeed.

They moved away from the jukebox, toward the door. He spotted an empty table and pointed to it. But Ann reached out and held his arm back.

"Do you mind if we stand," she asked? "I'm tired of sitting."

"Sure," Allan said, "if you want to. About Friday. I have a car. I can pick you up at your house around seven. The show starts at seven-thirty, I think. Or if you live close enough to Spring Street we could walk. Where DO you live, by the way?"

"One-Eighty, Westlawn Road. It's a big white house beside the creek. Westlawn Cemetery is just up the hill, if you know where that is."

Allan did indeed. "That's a fairish walk from Spring Street. I'd better bring the car."

"No. Please don't bother." Ann told him. "I like to walk. Or we could bicycle down.

"You know," he confided, "I've never been on a bike."

"Oh, that's too bad. You <u>ought</u> to learn. It isn't hard; and you can bike all over everywhere here. Mother and I pedal all the way into North Adams. Even Cindy, my little sister, comes along sometimes."

"Maybe you could teach me," he suggested.

"Maybe I can," she agreed.

And they shared another smile.

Before he could stop it, Allan's smile opened into a yawn.

"Ohhh, I _am_ sorry."

Ann laughed. "Why _should_ you be?"

"I'm not bored with your company or anything. Just tired."

"Yes. Me too." Ann was yawning now.

Contagious as hell, yawns.

"It _is_ late," she went on. I ought to be getting home."

"Want a lift?" he asked. "I can go get my car."

"Oh, no thank you," she told him, "David here will take me." She nodded to her right, and there, sure enough, stood Dave Carter.

Had he failed to notice Dave come up, Allan wondered? Or had Dave been there all the time beside them in the dark?

"Well then," Allan began, "I guess . . . good night. See you Friday. Sevenish?"

Ann nodded. "Sevenish." She turned away with Dave. Then stopped a moment, and looked back over her shoulder at Allan.

"Good night," she called.

"Good night!" he agreed, and turned his head to follow her as long as possible until she vanished in the dark.

Chapter 2: *Spiritoso*

In the hall outside the door of the dorm room he shared with Tom Petard, Allan paused a beat to listen. No typing chatter or radio blare. Tom must be out, he decided, or asleep.

He opened the door and went in. Looked around. Nobody home. He shed his green corduroy jacket and dropped it neatly onto the hook behind the door. Then he padded over to their battered sofa/ hide-a-bed (picked up for a song from the room's former tenants, who found it too heavy to move) and collapsed full length along it. Allan could feel the room pirouetting gracefully beneath him. He had felt this galactic rotation before. But it never *carried* him anywhere.

For a while it was pleasant to lie there staring up at the ceiling. But the view grew dull, so Allan turned his head to consider the wall. Its washable and inoffensive textured plastic surface framed two posters--one a James Dean photo (Tom's contribution to the decor) and the other (Allan's offering) a neatly framed reproduction of a Japanese print showing two ducks in flight outlined against the moon.

Facing the posters, across the room, were windows, complete with window seats (harking back to the days when this dorm had been luxuriously appointed for young Williams gentlemen of the 19th century). A curtain of dyed red burlap (the joint product of Allan's idea and Tom's labor), split the living room into "work space" (equipped with matching desks and standard college-issue shelves), and "playpen" (containing Allan's stereo, the sofa he was riding now, a tall brick and board bookcase, an old over-stuffed armchair, a marred coffee table, and a ragged Oriental rug that sprawled helplessly, displaying its many rips and wrinkles, over a mottled black and gray rubber-tiled floor). The absence of a fireplace was, to Allan's mind, the only defect in this otherwise cozy and prestigious pad.

When he and Tom agreed to room together after being entry-mates their freshman year, luck of the draw had won them this suite in West College, the oldest building on campus. And they could both appreciate just how lucky they had been every time they passed the dingy grey barracks of Morgan or the antiseptic drabness of the new dorms over by the theatre.

All through their sophomore and junior years, Tom and Allan had gradually reshaped and improved this suite until now it was more than a place to live--it was a place *alive* with their two personalities.

The bedroom they shared was purely functional—'a closet with pretensions' Allan called it. It offered one small window and just enough floor space to fit in two narrow metal-frame beds, two wardrobes, and a double chest of drawers crowned by a tilting mirror.

Over Allan's bed hung a print of Modigliani's *Girl in Red*. He'd chosen this because it reminded him of Sylvia North, a girl he had known--though not as intimately as he would have liked--back in high school, and for whom he still felt pangs of sweet regret. He thought about her now.

High school, high school. So long ago. So many memories! And how many more already lost, forgotten? So much of what he'd said, and done, in those important years was gone now, vanished utterly without a trace, forever, all because he hadn't bothered to record it.

"Re-CORD." Allan turned the word over on his tongue, felt it grow till it became a possibility. As it did, his face slowly stretched into a smile. With a purposeful lurch, he hauled himself upright, crossed the room, and pulled something large and box-like from the lowest shelf in the bookcase. It was heavy hauling, but he managed to muscle the grey-green reel-to-reel tape recorder up onto the low coffee table that squatted shakily before the sofa.

Allan swung the hinged lid open and began unpacking wires and microphone. He had just plugged the power cord into the wall and was threading a spool of tape onto the take-up reel, when his roommate exploded through the door—hair wild and dripping wet from the shower, wearing only a threadbare college towel.

"*Now* what the fuck are you messing with?" Tom rumbled cheerfully.

"Idea!" Allan called, not looking up. "I may not be quite drunk enough yet, but I think we've got the brandy here to do the job. After all that beer, a slug or two of the real thing ought to put me out cold."

Tom's eyes rolled up and his wet face glistened.

"Damn right it will!" he agreed.

"Ee-yeah." Allan yawned. "So how come you left the party before I did? That's gotta be an all-time first for you."

"Yeah, well you know I've got this paper due."

"Dubious, dubious," Allan said. "But if you're really feeling so creative, how about helping me out here? Fire some questions at me while I drink--see how long I can still answer."

"You mean you're pulling all this crap out just to record your fucking 'imperishable thoughts?' Jesus, Ross! Do you know what *time* it is?"

"Maybe one-thirty?"

"That's one-thirty in the fucking *AM* you know."

"Ahhh yes. But tomorrow's Sunday!" Allan countered. "No classes. Besides, who knows when I'll get a chance like this again? Be a sport and help me out. Help yourself, while we're at it." He nodded toward the brandy bottle on top of the bookcase.

Tom scowled and sighed. "Might as well, I guess. But I'm drying off first."

"Don't take too long," Allan warned, "I might pass out on you."

Tom made his "silent-scream" face, but said nothing, and vanished into the bedroom.

Allan finished threading blank tape through the playback head and onto the take up reel. At least he hoped the tape was blank. Better check, play a little first, to be sure. He punched the "fast forward" button, got a few inches in, then switched to "on."

"...Zeeeerrrrrrrp...*we all go about longing for love: it is the first need of our natures, the first prayer of our hearts; but we dare not utter our longing: we are too* zzzzuuuiiieeepop!"

Flinching with embarrassment, he sped the tape ahead. He'd recorded that speech just this September, when he was trying out for the Marchbanks part in *Candida.* No soap, of course. He'd had to settle for Morell--the 'mature' one, the husband, not the young lover-poet he ached to be. How long had it been like this? Since high school? Yes! Cast as Polonius, not Hamlet, in the Senior Class Play; as Poobah, not Nanki-Poo in *The Mikado.*

But, embarrassed or not, Allan wasn't about to erase this tape. Historical? Perhaps. Give his grand-kids a chuckle someday maybe. Or himself. He fast-forwarded a half-inch deeper into the reel before he slowed once more to listen.

This time the tape was clear. More than two-thirds of a reel was still there waiting, *waiting* for his words. An awe-inspiring thought, this. Allan smiled serenely, and closed his eyes. *Mirabile dictu.* Wonderful to tell. The Word would be made Tape. He pressed the "record" and "play" buttons simultaneously and spoke to test the volume setting.

"TESTING, ONE, TWO, Three, four, fIVE..., *clickpop*!" He reversed and played back the section. Level Three would be fine.

That much settled, Allan got up and gathered in the brandy. He lifted down the bottle (not much there) and two snifters (dusty and gummy red at bottom with the unrinsed dregs of ancient party). He gave each a cursory wipe with a Kleenex, then he poured them both about half-full

Back at the sofa, he collapsed dramatically, stretched out, grabbed up the pack of Viceroys lying open on the table, selected one, placed it gingerly between his lips, thumbed his cheap pocket lighter into flame, inhaled luxuriously, then set the lighter down, and took up the microphone again.

Just then, the room-dividing curtain fluttered, signaling that Tom was now emerging from the bedroom, presumably dry.

Lazily, Allan reached out, released the automatic hold button, lay back again, and, balancing microphone on chest, he very solemnly and very loudly burped, several times, with feeling, for posterity.

"*Uu-uuooorrpp*! Did you get that world? *UUUOOOORRRPPP*! Notice the deep-throated roundness of tone, the fruity fullness of timbre, the ripe resonance of bloated gut. *Uuuoorp, Uuuoorp*!"

"You're a lousy burper, Ross" Tom grumbled, from somewhere just out of Allan's sight. "Here, let a real pro show you how."

Ordinarily, Allan would have let him. But he could feel the brandy working in him on top of all that beer.

"Not now. Get on over here and ask me some questions, before I crash.

"Before you 'flash', you mean! All right, I'm coming."

Allan uncurled himself enough to stub out his cigarette on the ashtray, and found Tom, brandy snifter in hand, draped across and into the armchair facing him. He observed with vague disgust the faded blue-striped pajama legs and hairy bare feet sticking out beneath his roommate's frankly beautiful maroon silk smoking jacket. Taste! he thought, some of us have it. And some....

"There you are," he said. "Fire away!"

Tom sighed. "All right. Ahhhh, mmm--tell me, uh, *Mister* Ross, how's your *love life* these days?

"No comment."

"How can I interview you if you won't even answer a simple question like...."

"I refuse to answer on the grounds that you're not being serious. I want you to ask me REAL questions, important ones. So I can find out what alcohol does to my thinking."

Tom tilted his eyeballs upward as if to say: "Sanity! Some people have it. And some...."

But he went on. "All right then. If you're still too sober to be indiscreet about your private life, maybe you'll at least be candid about what goes on around you. Tell me about the music department--like who's the best professor, and why?"

Allan exhaled and nodded, thoughtfully. "That's a very interesting question. Yes, indeed "

"Well, *I* thought so."

"Hmmmm...let's see. There's Markham of course. Very old-fashioned...antique, really. Doesn't like anyone later than Brahms, I'd say. Mozart's his man. Y'oughta read his book! If only he could talk the way he writes. But no. He is dull, dull, dull." Allan fell to musing, and inhaled a long sip of brandy.

"So Markham is a crock, okay. Hmmm? You DO realize this is all going down on tape."

"I didn't SAY he was a crock."

"No, you just said he was '*dull, dull, dull...*'"

"Well, he IS." Allan giggled. "Poor guy."

"So tell me more."

"Hmmmm. Well, there's Forrester. 'Mister piano' around here. Now he really knows his stuff. Works you like hell, but that's what we're all here for, isn't it?"

"Not if I can help it," Tom muttered grimly.

Allan paused.

"You're starting to drift, Ross. Want to quit?"

"Pretty soon. I don't know. There's something's odd about Forrester, though. You don't *trust* him somehow. Maybe he's queer or something."

"God, Ross. You get more reckless by the minute. Now you say Forrester is a fruit. What next?"

"Well what if he is? A lot of artists are. Good ones."

"<u>Musicians</u>, too," Tom agreed, dryly.

"Yeah, well I'm NOT. So don't get your hopes up."

"And how do you <u>know</u> that, exactly?"

"Because," Allan hesitated, "Because, I was approached once and said 'no.'"

"Really? Here? Who by?"

"Not here. Years ago. Summer music camp."

"A teacher?"

Allan shook his head. "A camper. Older guy. Clarinetist."

"Figures." Tom smirked.

Allan ignored him, remembering clearly now.

"We were talking about Bach, and suddenly he just put his hand on my shoulder. He never actually said anything, but I knew what he wanted. And I admit I thought about it, I was a little curious to learn...well...what you DO."

"What DO you do?"

"*You* should know."

"Hoh, hoh, hoh," Tom yawned. "Very funny. So what happened?"

Allan shrugged. "Nothing. I realized I didn't want to; and that if I tried he'd just be hurt when he found out I was only curious."

"Maybe that was all *he* wanted. Maybe he didn't care."

"No. I'm sure he cared. And knowing that made *me* care, too. It isn't fair to play with real affection. At least I know I couldn't do it."

"But what if HE had been a SHE? I'll bet you could be seduced in a minute by the right woman." Tom rolled his eyes. "Jesus, I know I sure could be!"

Allan pondered this.

"Perhaps. But if I thought she really loved me and I knew I didn't love her." He shook his head. "I wouldn't feel right. I'd rather just beat off."

"Blech! It's not the same. Remember what old Lawrence Durrell says: '*For a cast in the bush is worth **two** in the hand! Aboard the Victory, Victory O!*' Ha-ha!" Tom rubbed his hands appreciatively.

"Crass, Petard. Very crass."

Allan swallowed the last of his remaining brandy.

"Awww...fuck yourself, Ross. I'm going to bed." Tom's broad yawn reminded Allan of a hippopotamus.

"Well I'm having one last brandy." He hauled himself up off the sofa and stooped, awkwardly, toward the bottle on the floor. "You too?"

"No thanks. I've got to be up waiting tables by eight. But don't mind me, go right ahead."

Allan did. Though he felt a moment's guilt as he emptied the bottle. After all, Tom had paid for half of it. He thought, too, about his own full music scholarship—how easy it had been to get, and how little effort it took him to keep it. He wondered briefly how many hours Tom had to work each semester to stay in school. Then he stopped thinking, and began to talk.

"Things are hopping up at the house. We're choosing the new pledges next Friday night. Maybe the last group ever. Not that there's much to choose *from*.

He paused to savor the brandy then went on.

"You really should have rushed, Tom, I know you'd have gotten in. Hell, they took ME, didn't they?"

"Yeah," Tom agreed, "they took you."

Allan closed his eyes to clear his head.

"Hell, we sure could use you now. Anyway, it'll be next spring before we can initiate these guys. Funny thing, I'm kind of looking forward to it. You know the ritual's a fake, but somehow you believe it while it's happening. At least I did. I'll be sorry to see it end. It'll mean just one less mystery to be awed by. And I like being awed. You ever feel that way?"

"What way?"

"Awed. Amazed. Left wondering at something you experience but can't explain."

"Sure. All the time."

"No, I mean it." Allan was earnest. "Intellectually. I know that if we just had enough facts, there'd be no mysteries in life at all. We could predict everything, even thoughts and feelings. I mean, we call them 'feelings' but they're really just reactions to stimuli like reflexes only more complicated."

"Bullshit!" yawned Tom. "Not a chance. Not with all the science in the world. Why can't you just accept that some things are unexplainable?"

"You just close your eyes to scientific progress!"

"And you won't *open* your eyes to the things that are too *big* for 'science'."

"Nothing is 'too big' for science! Nothing *can* be. Science just expands to swallow everything it runs across. Then it digests what it swallows and breaks it all down into understandable, useful chunks. Already we analyze words and thoughts, someday emotions too."

Allan sipped his drink.

"Well, anyway that's what I believe. I admit I don't have all the answers but the answers are all there somewhere. We just have to find them."

He'd had this argument with Tom before. They would have it again. It was fun to fight with Tom. Word-wrestling without sweat or tears. But tonight, he didn't feel like going on with it. Instead, he shifted ground.

"Question. For *you* this time, Petard, y'old lecherous bastard, you. Remember that girl from Florida you met last summer?"

"Mary? What about her?"

"What do you feel for her, can you explain it? What does she MEAN to you?"

"What kind of shit-ass question is that?"

"No, I mean do you ever *think* about her or just *feel*?"

"If you mean did I plank her--the answer is no. Not yet."

"You know damn well that's *not* what I mean!"

"Sure I *think* about her. She's not HERE. If she *was* here though, I'd damn sure be 'doing' instead of 'thinking'!"

"Show me her picture again, will you?"

"You want to see it?"

Allan could tell Tom was pleased to be asked. "Yeah, I do."

Tom went into the bedroom, and Allan reached for a fresh cigarette. He fumbled with the lighter, but finally managed. This would be his last tonight. He was very drowsy now. First the show, then the party, and that girl, Ann. They had a date set. Next Friday.

"Here she is." Tom was back.

Allan took the photo from his hand. A pretty girl. Chubby blonde in a not-too-daring but well-filled bikini. *'Round, and firm, and fully packed'*, he thought. Not sexy exactly, but cuddlesome. He smiled, instinctively. He could like this girl.

"She is cute," he admitted. Then he added "You know i-it's lucky she isn't around, in a way, because...well, I think I could go for her myself, if the chance came. And I wouldn't want to do that--fall for a friend's girl. You know."

"Yeah, that could be rough," Tom admitted. "So okay, you agree Mary's cute, and you think you could go for her too. What do you think she's like?"

"Besides cute? Well, she looks intelligent. Is she?"

"Well, yeah, I guess. She reads a lot."

"And she looks kind too, I mean she wouldn't just walk out on a guy; you could depend on her."

"Yeah, well I hope so."

"So will you have her up here some weekend?"

"Winter Carnival for sure. Sooner maybe if I can figure a way to afford it."

Allan nodded.

"What about you?," Tom went on. Got any special girl plans?"

Allan shook his head. "Not really."

"'S funny, though," he added, "I met this girl tonight. Dave Carter introduced us, would you believe? Turns out she's a faculty brat. Her father's the head of the astro department. Professor Ash. You know him?"

"Heard of him. They say he's tough."

"Well, her name's Ann. She's very...quiet, almost strange in a way. But I like her. Anyway, I asked her out for Friday."

"Friday, huh? Hey, that's fast work, for you, Al."

"Huh, yes, I guess it is. Well, I don't know, it all seemed so-ohhh, huuu inevitable. Sorry. Guess I'm fading out."

"Brandy finally getting to you, huh?"

"Yeah," Allan conceded. "And that beer! I think maybe I'll turn off the machine and go take a leak."

So he did. But when he returned, he flopped right into bed with no more than a mumbled "G'night." leaving Tom—who stood by grinning and nodding—to clean up if he cared to.

Allan's last thought before sleep pulled him under was the comforting one that there must still be several hours worth of blank tape left on the reel to use some other time. Still plenty of room to grow.

Chapter 3: *Andante*

Westlawn Cemetery lay on a grassy knoll at the western edge of town. Many of its graves were older than the College itself. Yet no church building stood nearby. Perhaps there had been one once that was later abandoned and pulled down. Allan didn't know.

It was a longish walk from campus, but he often took it after classes to enjoy the fine view from the hilltop—and occasionally at night to enjoy the quiet, and the stars.

This particular evening was too dark for panoramas, too overcast for stars, and too chilly for aimless strolling. But he had another reason for striding westward, pushed by the raw wind: his date with Ann.

He guessed which house would be hers long before he could make out the street number. It was a flamboyant steamboat gothic monster, porched all round and turretted above. It boasted overly ornate knobs and spiderwebs of gingerbready woodwork everywhere, and Tiffany-style glass panels flanking the front door. He had noticed it before on his Westlawn walks, and even wondered idly who might live there. He'd imagined them rich and old, retired city folk settled here in New England to make damned sure they'd never miss high color season again as long as they lived.

He opened the front gate—freshly painted white, like the house itself—only a little nervous about the night to come. He knew for certain that *A Hard Day's Night* was a good flick—he'd seen it already a few months before. And certainly Ann seemed like the kind of girl you could talk to for a couple of hours with no pain at all.

He spotted an ivory button set in a square brass frame at the side of the door. He pushed it and heard, as from a great distance, "SO—mi." He guessed the first note might be G above Middle C, but would not have sworn to this. His ear for pitch was good, but he had never studied to improve it. He was content to leave that to aspiring conductors and piano tuners. The brain was an attic, as Sherlock Holmes once said.

The door opened and a girl wearing black leotards and chewing bubble gum, looked up at him. She must be about ten years old, he guessed.

By way of greeting, she blew a moderately sized pink bubble and burst it at him.

"Hi," Allan said, for want of a better response. "Is Ann at home?"

"Uh huh."

"Well, uh, could you tell her Allan Ross is here to see her?"

"She isn't dressed."

All the better, he thought, stifling a guilty smile, where his roommate would likely have displayed a lascivious leer. But all he actually said was "Then is it okay if I come in and wait?"

The girl stepped back into a wood-paneled hallway. Allan came inside to face a broad staircase leading up to the second floor. He could see the glint of a wall mirror on the landing.

There was a good gravy smell of recent dinner in the air. And there were books all over--even here in the hall. Some were ranged along built-in shelves, others stood in stacks on the floor beside the staircase, and still others lay on a small table close to the door.

"Who is it, Cindy?" a woman's voice asked through the open double doors on the left.

"Some boy for Annndy."

A tall woman, thin, with lightly graying hair, and tired-looking eyes appeared from around a corner. Allan liked her immediately. She looked "homely"—as the English use that word—hospitable, wise, resourceful. She looked, he thought, like everybody's mother ought to look.

He introduced himself. "Mrs. Ash? How do you do. I'm Allan Ross."

"Oh yes. Hello Allan. Ann should be down any moment. We just finished supper. Would you like a cup of coffee?"

"No, thank you. Really. I just ate."

"ANN-DEE your boyfriend's here!"

"Don't shout Cindy! Go upstairs and tell your sister politely that Allan is waiting for her in the living room."

Cindy popped a small but resounding bubble in reply, but did as she was told, attacking the staircase two steps at a time in a ragged gallop.

Mrs. Ash shook her head and sighed. "I don't think that girl will ever learn to walk, she's been running since the day she could stand."

Allan smiled and tried to imagine what it must be like to have a younger sister. As the only child of two only children he had little experience of non-adult relatives--and none at all of siblings.

When Mrs. Ash led him into on the living room, all Allan could see at first were the books. Floor to ceiling all around the room, every inch of wall space seemed to be either a bookcase or a curtained window. But a second glance revealed some other furniture. A leather armchair with a good reading lamp beside it caught his eye first, then a long green Victorian sofa, against the wall nearest the stairwell. Above the sofa, hung, for once, not bookshelves, but what appeared to be a seascape with the colors reversed: a light ocean breaking upon dark sand.

Mrs. Ash motioned Allan toward the sofa. "Make yourself comfortable. Ann won't be long."

As he approached the sofa, Allan examined more closely the seascape on the wall. He could see now that it was not a painting but a photograph, and that the subject was not the ocean at all but stars--a whole galaxy--like a whirlpool made of light.

"Hello. Do I know you?"

A tall man stood in the doorway. Balding, dark, neatly-dressed, he carried a lighted pipe in one hand and an oversized book in the other.

"Hello, Sir. We haven't met. I'm Allan Ross."

"Mmmm. Come to carry Ann off, have you?"

"Yes sir."

"She did say something about a date tonight. Running late as usual, I suppose."

"Actually, I think I'm here a little early."

"Yes, Well, just be patient. It's what they expect. Where will you be taking her?"

"The movies. To see *A Hard Day's Night.*

"7:30 show?"

"That's right."

"She'd better come down soon or you won't make it. By the way, have her back here by 11:00 sharp."

"Uh, yes sir."

"Good. Well, I only came in to find my reading glasses. But they're not here. Enjoy your movie, or whatever else it is you find amusing."

"Thank you. Yes. We will."

Alone once again, Allan couldn't help feeling that he had just been X-rayed. Something about the man's eyes disturbed him and held him spellbound. Any other color, and the effect could have been downright frightening. But these were a soft baby blue, and seemed not so much fierce as luminous. You wouldn't want to have him angry at you though.

He turned back again to the photograph. Most impressive. An engraved brass tag on the frame read: "M-31, GREAT SPIRAL NEBULA in ANDROMEDA." This information was followed,in smaller letters, by details of camera, magnification, and this inscription: "Dr. Wootten Ash, photographer, Pan American Survey Expedition, September 22, 1946. *Sic itur ad astra.*"

"This way to the stars," Allan mentally translated. He'd taken Latin all four years in high school, and two more here. It was his pet language, good for private thoughts, and he was always finding apt quotations bubbling up from the old authors. But if this one was a quote he didn't recognize it.

What was keeping Ann? The possibility that they really might miss the 7:30 show began to bother him. There'd be another show at 9:15 of course, but that would leave barely time enough to get her home. And the wait beforehand would be awkward.

Footsteps sounded on the stairs. He tried to imagine her coming down. How would she look? Would she stop by that mirror on the landing to make last minute adjustments? He listened hard but failed to detect any pause in the quickly nearing steps.

If he hadn't been already on his feet, Allan would have stood as Ann entered the room. She wore a dark green dress of some soft cloth, and her long blonde hair was smoothed back from her face and tied with a deep red ribbon that seemed to glow. He was absolutely dazzled.

"Sorry I'm late," she said, without lowering her eyes.

"That's okay," he told her. "There's lots of time yet." And then, he couldn't help adding, "You look...great!"

This time she did lower her gaze, and blushed ever so slightly. But, he thought, she must have realized it was true.

"We should get going, shouldn't we?"

"Oh, right," he agreed.

Mrs. Ash saw them off, smiling, and gently asked Ann to be back by 11:30. Allan briefly registered the half-hour conflict between this and Professor Ash's deadline of 11:00 sharp. Then he dismissed it. Better not take any chances this first time out. He would get her home early.

*   *   *

The wind had risen as the dark came down, and by the time they were half way up Fraternity Row, Ann had pulled a plaid wool scarf tight around her head, and both of them were leaning into the wind. Over the wind noise, Allan pointed and called, "That's Di-gamma Koppa, my fraternity."

Ann smiled and nodded. "Is that where you live?"

"No, I'm only there for meals and parties. It's mostly theatre types. Things can get be pretty lively sometimes."

"You like parties then"

Allan hesitated. "Well, not just all drinking and dancing. I'd rather be able to talk. Wouldn't you?"

She didn't answer, but he thought he saw her smile. Of course, it might just be her eyes narrowing in the wind. Then he remembered she'd told him she danced "a little." Damn! What had he said? Okay, so he didn't ordinarily like to dance. For this girl, he could *try*.

As they climbed the hill by West College, a sudden gust sent handfuls of leaves swirling right in their faces. Ann shrieked and Allan laughed out loud.

"What's so funny?" she demanded.

"Those leaves must have hung there for weeks, just *waiting* for us to come past. I can't explain exactly. It just seemed strange to me and...kind of *beautiful* I guess. That's all."

Ann smiled at him, and nodded quickly.

"I understand."

Allan was also relieved to find that Ann had the patience for such flights of fancy. Not every girl did. Sylvia, for instance.

He mentally compared the two of them. Ann was better looking. Hands down. What was it about Sylvia that had attracted him so? Would he feel it again when they next met? A week ago he would never have doubted this; now he was less sure.

They walked down the hill and out onto Spring Street. Here, the wind dropped and they could hear their own footsteps ring on the sidewalk. By ones and twos or in small groups, others were hurrying along in their own general direction.

"Yo, Allan!"

"Hi Elroy! What's up? You headed for the film?"

"*Mais non.*"

"Uh, Ann, this is Elroy White. Elroy, like you to meet Ann Ash."

"*Mademoiselle.*"

Elroy bowed cavalierly and, in a perfectly timed gesture, caught, raised, and kissed Ann's unresisting hand.

"*Enchantée, M'sieur.*" Ann replied, her eyebrows arching ever-so-slightly.

The perfect comeback, Allan had to admit.

Now it was Elroy whose eyebrow rose, but just the one. Then, briefly, all his teeth were showing. Ann had a new admirer.

Since Elroy was alone, Allan invited him to join them, hoping he'd say no, but a little ashamed to be hoping it, too.

"I regret that I have other pressing commitments," Elroy explained. "But *merci mille fois* for the invitation. Don't make too late a night of it, *mon ami*," he added, nudging Allan. "We rehearse at 6:30 *le matin* if memory serves."

Allan nodded. "Pete says he's got a new novelty number he wants us to try, and we really need to work on our tempos in the Brubeck thing."

"Brubeck!" Elroy made a disgusted face. "*Ce n'est pas le vrai jazz, ca!*" he muttered.

But before Allan could reply, he had turned his back on them and was moving off into the crowd.

"Elroy's the bass player in our jazz trio," Allan explained, "along with me, and Pete Jackson on drums. That's why the beret and the dark glasses. Likes to think he's Charlie Mingus or someone, I guess. And he plays well enough to carry it off. I sure couldn't do it, though."

"Maybe not," Ann agreed. "But then you're not the token Negro at an all-white northern college. So you don't really have to."

Williams was not an "all-white" college. Not quite. But the justice in Ann's comment startled Allan. Whatever she might think of Elroy he hadn't embarrassed or flustered her.

The usher took and tore their tickets, returning the useless stubs. Allan steered Ann toward a pair of aisle seats half-way down on the right. She slipped off her coat, and he helped her arrange it over the seat back before they settled in.

The room went dark and their eyes woke to previews of coming attractions: Truffaut's *Jules et Jim*; and Orson Wells' *The Trial*. Then they were treated to two rounds of Roadrunner versus Coyote.

Why, Allan asked himself there in the dark, was it always so screamingly funny to watch someone else's pain? The smacking into rocks, the long falls ending in a puff of dust, the flattenings and explosions to which the Coyote inevitably fell victim—it ought to hurt to watch this, but somehow it only made you laugh—even when you knew for certain the poor guy just didn't stand a chance. He listened to the others laughing. Ann was laughing, too.

The feature began. From the opening jangled guitar chord, the entire house roared at the running, the silly disguises, the mop-headed but well-dressed boys pursued by crowds of desperate screaming schoolgirls, the sight-gags and half-comprehensible wisecracks in thick Liverpuddlian accents. It was pure silent comedy with a swinging soundtrack. The crowd loved it. Allan too was swept along inside this catchy, classy dream.

Until he felt Ann nudge his arm and lean against his ear to whisper.

"Allan will you excuse me? I'll be right back."

"Sure, but what's the matter. You feel all right?"

"I-I think so. Not to worry. I'll be fine."

As she made her way up the dark, steep, laugh-rocked aisle, he stared after her, thinking selfishly *"God! My first date in months, and the girl gets sick on me before the movie's half over!"* Then, ashamed of himself, he tried to imagine how much more awkward feeling sick must be for her.

When she came back, he thought she looked pale. But it was hard to tell in the faint gray light flickering from the screen.

"How're you feeling?" he whispered, reaching for her hand.

"Okay." She let him take her hand. It was limp and cold.

"Do you want to leave?"

She hesitated a moment. "Would you mind awfully?"

"No, of course not," he lied—sympathetically.

He was glad they had seats on the aisle. It meant they could leave without getting in anyone's way. He hated doing that, just as he hated having people come in late or leave early in front of him. But by now he was really worried about Ann. That thin soft hand had felt like a lump of ice.

He helped her on with her coat, and guided her up the aisle. In the lobby, the usher looked concerned.

"Are you all right, miss?"

Ann smiled bravely. "Yes thanks. I just need a breath of fresh air. Can we get back in again?"

"Sure. Just keep your ticket stubs."

"Thanks," Allan said, and held the glass door to the street open wide for Ann to pass.

It was colder, but the wind had dropped now and the clouds were gone. A wealth of stars winked overhead as they walked.

"Feeling any better?"

Ann nodded yes.

"Shall I take you home?"

"No. I just felt a little queasy in there. We can walk around for a few minutes, then go back. I'm awfully sorry to make you miss the show."

"That's okay. I like it fine right here," he assured her, gesturing at the shadows and the stars. But his eyes remained on Ann, and this surprised him, till he realized it was not the starry night or the nip of cold that made this moment shine.

"So beautiful," was all he could manage to say. It must sound stupid, he knew. But it was true!

When he looked up toward the stars again, Ann joined him.

"Yes, they're lovely." She pulled the collar of her coat a little tighter.

They had reached the upper end of Spring Street where it meets Route 2. Straight ahead, across the road, the tower of Thompson Memorial Chapel soared above them, its four corner spires deliciously ominous against the star-bright sky.

"Cold roast Gothic" Allan's art professor had described it once. Built far too late to qualify even as Gothic revival, this chapel, of all the buildings on Williams' self-consciously picturesque campus, held for Allan a special aura of age and mystery. If you didn't look too closely or too critically, there was plenty to inspire awe and wonder here.

"Let's duck inside the chapel," he suggested. "Get out of the cold a minute."

"I don't think I've ever *been* inside," Ann told him. "Daddy rejects all religions on principle, and mother can't make up her mind, so we kids grew up heathens."

Allan laughed. He liked the idea of dating a heathen.

"Well heathens need warmth too," he told her. Come on."

Chapter 4: *A Capella*

A lone car, its headlights sweeping the darkness aside as they came, rose blazing over the hill then subsided, gliding quietly past them and away. The chapel's stained glass windows glowed—not brightly enough to mean something going on inside, but enough to suggest the doors might still be open. Allan tried them, and they were! The massive iron-studded oak slab yielded slowly to his pull, and beckoned them to enter.

In silence, they crossed the worn stone portal, passed through the narthex (foyer), and, turning left, proceeded down the vaulted nave along the sloping center aisle. Thanks to a History of Architecture course his junior year, Allan was confident he could identify every feature of the building by its proper technical name, if Ann should ask. She didn't.

Carved stone pillars soared up into shadow. Heavy Tudor-style woodwork brooded overhead. Concealed spotlights illuminated the chancel where a clean new cross, elegantly thin, stood out against a scarlet backcloth.

In contrast to its surroundings, the cross was decidedly modern, consisting of gilded square-edged nails welded together in a free-form lattice structure suggestive of thorns and set into a polished wooden frame. Yet Allan found it wholly appropriate to this gothic hall. Here was skilled construction even a medieval craftsman might acknowledge and admire.

Their footsteps echoed as they walked together down the aisle, each in a separate reverie not yet to be shared.

High on the chancel walls, and along both porches of the transept, were inscribed the names of Williams students killed in wars. The list ended, for the present, with Korea. But, Allan noted, there was empty space still—plenty of room to grow.

Set into the floor in front of the steps up to chancel, and directly underneath the crossing, a large plaque marked the tomb of The Founder—Ephraim Williams. Allan pointed this out to Ann.

"That's Old Father Williams himself, so they say."

"You mean they're not <u>sure</u>?"

"He was killed in an Indian ambush. The survivors buried him on the spot. Later, after they founded this school with the money in his will, some alumni set up a marker at or near the place. And later still, someone dug beneath the marker and found a few bones and hair and buttons, but nothing you could really identify. Still, whatever they found there <u>represents</u> Old Eph and I guess that's what matters."

"I suppose so. Brrrr." Ann shivered.

"Cold?"

"A little. I can feel a draft from somewhere," Ann said, and looked over at him. "But I'm glad we came. This <u>is</u> nice."

"Mmmmmmmm," he agreed.

He led her to the front pew, and, for a while, they both sat silent, glancing now and then up at the pointed windows or at the elegant cross on its rich scarlet ground. When Allan leaned over suddenly and kissed her cheek, Ann didn't break her gaze or pull away from him, but she did smile.

He kissed her again, longer this time, and reached for her hand. Her fingers accepted his, and squeezed back. There was no sound, no word between them. He turned her face to his and they kissed full on the lips. They held together, his left hand braided in her right, through yet another kiss, a hard and lingering exchange.

"Wow!" he whispered appreciatively.

They pulled apart—for fear? For breath?—and Ann, gesturing with her eyes toward the clerestory panes above the cross inquired calmly: "Is all that stained glass real?" Then, without waiting for Allan to reply, she kissed _him_.

"Mmmm-uh huh." he nodded, through the kiss, and went on, once his lips were free, "You can't see the color so well now because the light's inside where we are." This remark too, ended in a kiss; and Allan slid his free hand up across Ann's shoulder to caress her neck.

"Of course," she laughed. How silly."

Ann shook her head, which made his next kiss brush her eyelid. This seemed to please them both, so he kissed her other eyelid too. Then she drew back just enough to let her head sink down onto his shoulder.

So. Just like that.

His mind raced. Steady, now. Think! Ask her back to the room, of course. Tom must be out by now. He pictured the couch, the rug, the bed, the locked door. He wanted to move, but he didn't want her to notice his arousal when they stood up. Think non-erotic thoughts! Like architecture! Like the dead man underneath the floor!

She snuggled closer on his shoulder. Her gentle weight against him made him feel broad and strong. How had all this happened? So far they hadn't even _said_ anything. Maybe she was like this with any guy on a date. He didn't think so but he had to wonder: Why her? Why me? And then...What the hell? Why _not_?!!

Bells in the chapel tower chimed nine o'clock. An hour ago they had been sitting in a crowded movie house not even holding hands, now they were here alone together kissing. And in an hour from now?

"Do you play the organ?" Ann's voice was peaceful, almost drowsy.

"Now and then," he admitted.

"This one here?"

"Every second Sunday, for the early service."

"Will you play it now, for me?"

"What?"

"I'd like <u>so</u> much to hear you play."

"It's probably locked. And anyway it'd make noise. Someone might come."

"Afraid?"

"No, but..., Well...sure, if you really want."

The keyboard was not locked. Allan warmed up the blowers and closed all the stops to keep the volume low. Ann continued sitting in the pew he would always think of now as "theirs."

He tried a simple Bach chorale, sounding faint and hollow in the empty vaulted room. What a way to win a woman, he thought; in a church playing organ music. Ann's eyes were closed now. Was she asleep?

His hands lifted from the keyboard. Hesitated.

"Oh, please don't stop," she called to him. It's lovely."

He began again, but lost the line, and, rather than break off, continued improvising on the chords. Nothing difficult, he wasn't paying any more attention than was absolutely necessary to technique, but as he relaxed and let the music lead him, the rhythm lilted into jazz and his harmonies went smoky blue.

Ann was his focus--Ann with her shining hair, and her quiet—like the quiet of this place. What was he <u>waiting</u> for? He could make love to her right here and now—on the stone floor, before the cross of nails and the windows full of saints; before the names of the honored dead and the relics of the Founder! Would it be sacrilege, or worship to make love here? Something of both, he thought.

It would also be <u>cold</u> and probably damned uncomfortable, not to mention risky. But sometime, maybe, long after midnight, they would come here with the lights dim as candles, or no lights at all, and the heavy doors locked tight, and the watchmen not due to make their rounds again for hours. For tonight though, he would just have to take her up to his room.

Allan ended his improvisation without flourish, flicked the switches off, and closed the keyboard lid. Ann nodded, and smiled up at him. It was applause enough. He felt approved, admired.

He walked down and seated himself on the altar steps facing her. Then, on an impulse, he pulled out from his jacket pocket his cigarettes in their flip-top box, and offered one to her.

She shook her head. "I do, but not right now, thanks."

"You don't mind if I...?"

"Oh, please."

After lighting up, he slipped the silver paper from inside the box, folded it deftly to form a miniature ashtray, inhaled, and flicked a first ash in to christen it. He had never smoked in church before. He wondered if anyone ever had, and whether Ann would think it daring and clever of him, or just uncouth?

"You play beautifully," she told him.

"I like the piano better," he said. "It's less mechanical, lets me feel I'm making the sounds myself. With the organ, you just give signals and the machines do all the work. It's like singing through a typewriter!"

They laughed together.

"Seriously, I'd love to play piano for you sometime."

"And I'd love to hear you."

The smoke tasted fine in Allan's mouth. Releasing it, he watched the vapor roil up through the still air of the chapel. Was this sacrilege or worship? Something of both, he thought.

"Do you have any brothers or sisters?" Ann asked him.

Allan shook his head. "I had a brother but he was born dead. Sounds funny saying it. 'Born dead'. Like a contradiction in terms. Things would have been a lot different, if he'd lived, I know that. Do you have a brother?"

"No. There's only me and Cindy. It's too bad."

"I don't know. At least you've got someone."

Allan stubbed his cigarette out in the foil, carefully wrapped the stub and ashes, and slipped the silvered paper shroud inside his jacket pocket. Then he checked his watch.

"It's after ten. Looks like we missed the movie after all. How about coming up to my room? It isn't far."

"You want to show me your 'etchings'?"

"No..., but I've got some great jazz records."

"Hmm. Thanks, but not tonight. I'm due home at eleven."

"Your mother said eleven-thirty."

"She doesn't count. You don't know it yet, but my Daddy can be very nasty when he tries. He doesn't always say much, but he never ever forgets—or forgives."

"But <u>sometime</u>? Would you like to?"

"Maybe. We'll see. Perhaps."

He held out his hand. She smiled at him and took it. Together they walked up the aisle, and through the echoing dark. He pushed open the heavy door for her again, and they were back out in the ordinary night.

If it was cold now, Allan couldn't tell. They walked the whole way swinging their held hands and stopping every few feet it seemed for another kiss or another moment of looking at oneanother and not saying anything in words.

When at last they reached her front porch, Ann said: "They're waiting up for me, I can tell by the lights. Do you want to come inside?"

"Not tonight," he answered, pretty certain she hadn't meant that invitation quite the way it sounded.

"'But sometime? Would you like to?'" she mimicked his own pleading tone back in the chapel so well that he couldn't help but remember, and laugh.

"'Maybe. We'll see','" he told her, grinning back. "'Perhaps.' How about tomorrow night?"

Ann shook her head. "We're going to my aunt's in Boston."

Allan looked down.

"But I could meet you Sunday night for a while. At the library. Eight o'clock in the magazine room?"

His face brightened. "Great!"

They exchanged "goodnights," and kissed again, but this was so expected, so inevitable, that it didn't count.

Ann hurried up the steps and opened the door. Once inside, she peered out at him, her face stained and distorted by the multicolored glass, and waved.

He stood looking after her till the porch lights went out. Then he turned and began to walk away. At the front gate, he paused a moment, smiled, then headed, not back to campus, but the other way, uphill toward Westlawn—for the stars.

He craved the sound of his solitary footsteps crunching through frosted leaves. His hands fisted tight inside his jacket pockets against the cold. He knew that he was grinning, that he laughed for no apparent reason. Any passing ghost could _see_ his craziness. Well, he _was_ crazy; _wanted_ to be crazy; _had_ to be!

He reached "his spot," at the very top of the hill. Three stones, newly carved but in the old style, stood together here inside a low-walled plot. From here, in good weather, you could see far up the valley, over the trees and mountains, into the sky.

Tonight, a mist hid the valley floor, except where a distant headlight moved along the road to Bennington, or a house window winked through the whiteness here and there. There were fewer stars than he'd hoped for. It was clouding over again—rain driftingin. But he could still make out both the Dippers, and Orion there—his favorite, his friend—climbing the ridge line. It was enough. He pulled out his box of cigarettes and lighted one. It had been a long fine evening--and there would be more.

He sat on the wall and smoked two cigarettes before the chill began to reach inside his jacket. Time to go

But first, he bowed—to the three stones, then to the hills, and lastly to the audience of dead that lay surrounding him, to honor and applaud them.

"*Ave, atque vale!*" "Greetings, and farewell." They deserved this from him. They had been where he was, known what he was just now learning, and had passed the gift along to him. <u>He</u> was alive!

Chapter 5: *Musique Concrète*

It rained hard all day Sunday, and Allan was drenched right through his raincoat when he entered the periodicals reading room of Stetson library. There was Ann, propped in a window seat reading <u>Paris Match</u>. Since they weren't quite alone he decided not to surprise her with a kiss, but he longed to. She was wearing a dark plaid skirt with warm-looking knee socks and a heavy Irish sweater. Just looking at her made him feel rich.

The room had a fireplace that really worked, and Allan hung his raincoat as near the cheery flames as he dared. Then he walked over and gazed down at Ann from across her magazine.

"Hi there."

"Hi yourself." "How was Boston?"

"Awful. Aunt Sally's a dreadful bore. Worse than Daddy! Always running on about what's wrong with everything. Honestly, she can put you to sleep in five minutes."

"At least you're well-rested then.

"No such luck! I'm her favorite. That means I'm the one whose left to smile sweetly, and make "Uh huh" noises every so often, while the others sneak off. It isn't fair!"

"I missed you."

"Oh sure."

"No. Really. I couldn't stop thinking about you all weekend. Do you mind?

"You big silly! No, of course I don't <u>mind</u>."

"Did you think about me, too."

"Sometimes."

"Only sometimes, huh?"

"Aunt Sally says you sound 'promising'."

"You told her about me?"

"Well, I had to say something to stop her. She was talking my ear numb."

"So what did you say about me?"

"Never mind. She likes you."

"How about we go someplace?"

"By 'someplace' you really mean up to your room."

"Well, I've still got those jazz records."

"Huh uh. I've got a lot of reading to do for class."

"*Paris Match*?"

"It's for French Conversation, dummy. I'm taking advanced placement."

"Okay then, we'll play Edith Piaf songs."

"No. Look, I really <u>do</u> have to study. Besides," she added, "I think Daddy followed me over here."

Allan's disappointment showed.

"But...I'll take a raincheck," she offered.

"Oh, all right," he sighed, and smiled resignedly.

Not quite what he'd hoped for, but progress, he supposed. She had told her aunt in Boston about him. That was a good sign, wasn't it?

"So what <u>shall</u> we do?" he asked.

"I suggest we read here for an hour or so, and then, I'll let you walk me home."

"Oh you will, will you?"

Ann cocked her head to one side and smiled in a way that said: You do <u>want</u> to walk me home, don't you?

And the look he gave her back must have revealed instantly that he <u>did</u>, and he <u>would</u>, because she tugged her long skirt more tightly about her legs, and turned back to her magazine without another word.

The rain had stopped by the time they left the library. Once again, kisses and smiles interrupted their long slow walk at intervals, and each one felt better than the last.

When they reached Ann's house, she didn't invite him in. But when he asked if they could meet next day, she simply answered: "Yes." And the smile in her voice told him there was no longer any doubt: they would be seeing each other a lot from now on.

Devising ways to meet was simple enough: walks between classes, lunch dates, "surprise encounters" in the library stacks. Only time at night, and in places where they could truly be alone, was hard to find.

Naturally, Allan's work suffered. He expected this; in fact he welcomed it. He <u>wanted</u> everyone to notice so that he could share with them his grand surprise:

PROFESSOR X

(in a tone of fatherly concern)

"Allan, uh-hummm, have you been feeling
well lately? You don't seem quite yourself.

Been getting enough sleep?"

YOUNG ROSS

(a little shyly)

"Sorry sir. But you see...well, I'm in love."

PROFESSOR X

"In love? Ah yes, Ahem. Hum. Well,
that <u>does</u> explain things doesn't it.

What can I say except...congratulations?"

YOUNG ROSS

(beaming)

"Thank you sir."

...that sort of thing.

But no such scenes were played. The changes in him--if he <u>had</u>
changed--must not have shown. Maybe he bluffed too well, or maybe
his professors just could not believe that he was really unprepared.
He had a reputation for good work, and he traded on it now. It was
a little disappointing actually: his first true starring role as romantic
lead, and no live audience. Well, <u>almost</u> none, he thought. After all,
there <u>was</u> Ann.

By the third week, she was slipping out after supperto meet him in the basement practice rooms beneath the Music Building. They would kiss hello, then she would settle down with a book against the far wall and sit there reading for as long as he could stand to run through scales and finger exercises automatically, his mind less and less on music, more and more on where his hands would so much rather be. Half an hour maybe, forty minutes tops, and he'd be blatantly performing for her.

He ransacked his repertoire for pieces to make love with: like the gentle Brahms *Ballade in G*, and the easier movements of Ravel's *Tombeau de Couperin* suite (leaving out the Fugue and Toccata that really needed the extra work). Often he'd slip in his favorite Chopin *Etude* (Opus 25, #5) with its jumping chords that stretched his fingers achingly—but always seemed to make her smile to watch him. And sometimes, when he felt up to it—which wasn't every night—he'd slam through the wild final movement of Prokofiev's *Sonata #7*, a reckless raggy syncopated flight that he would play at breakneck speed, muddying arpeggios and scattering false notes all along the way.

In the end, worn out by all this passionate noise, he would offer her soft jazz: standards like *Bewitched*, or *'Round Midnight*, or *Spring Is Here*, and sometimes even his own small composition: a little jazz waltz he called *Something for Sylvia*. But of course he never told Ann this tune was his; because that would have meant explaining 'Sylvia.'

And, once or twice, he simply improvised, building chords till he hit upon a pleasing progression, then throwing off lines, which he would chorus again and again stopping only when he could find no more ideas. And as he played this way, inventing for her, his eyes would mist, his throat lump up, and his backbone tingle with a passion that began as music, but was mostly Ann.

When the last chord had died, and there was nothing but the sound of their breathing to disturb the stillness, she might come up behind him and rest her hands on his tired shoulders, or lightly scratch the back of his neck with her long clear-lacquered nails. Or

he might break the silence by clearing his throat and saying "Well..."
and turn to find her sitting smiling at him with her hands folded in
her lap like a schoolgirl waiting to be asked to dance.

One night, as he walked her home from the practice room, Ann
asked him: "Is it really so sad?"

"Is what so sad?"

"What's in your music. You play as if you didn't have a friend in
the world."

"I don't know. I'm usually feeling quiet when I improvise. I just
follow where the notes lead and maybe it comes out sad. But I'm not
depressed or anything, just..."

"...sentimental...?"

"I suppose."

He stopped and turned to face her. "My dad was over in Japan
after the war, helping refugees, and he's told me a lot about what's
different there. He told me there's a Japanese word, *sabi*. It translates
something like 'the sadness and inevitability of passing time.' Quite
a mouthful in English, but it really is a single feeling. I think maybe
that's what I feel in my music. Life's not <u>deeply tragic</u> or anything,
just..."

"Sob-y?"

Allan laughed. "More or less. I don't know—alive today, dead
tomorrow. Grow up, grow old. Build, tear down. Find, lose. That's
all there <u>is</u>, really. So you have to accept it. But you can <u>wish</u> for
something more—something sure and lasting."

"Like becoming famous?" Ann suggested.

"Yeah, that, and maybe having children."

Ann frowned. "That's not so much."

"Mmmmm," Allan thought he understood. "You mean because eventually the children die too."

"No. I mean because you don't <u>own</u> children, or anyway you <u>shouldn't</u>. It's not fair to them."

Allan didn't reply to this. He didn't know how.

At the front steps, Ann told him, "Mother says I should have you over for dinner sometime soon."

"Do <u>you</u> want me to come?"

"Oh sure!" she said, sounding very unconvinced.

"Then, yes," he said. "I'd like that very much. I'm already crazy about your family. 'Specially the eldest daughter."

This was the cue for another kiss; a real one. But Ann didn't smile.

"Hmmm. You don't know much about us yet. You might change your mind."

"I'll risk it."

"Even about me."

"What does <u>that</u> mean?"

"Oh, I don't know." She turned away. "Everything's just so... stupid!"

And suddenly, there she was, the tears squeezing out of her eyes, and heavy choking almost soundless sobs shaking her like a rag doll. Allan took both her hands, and pulled her down to sit beside him on the porch steps. As his arm draped around her shoulder, he was strangely happy for these tears. He could <u>do</u> something for her now, <u>prove</u> his love, reassure her, comfort her.

She leaned into his chest and sobbed. He felt so strong, so proud, to be here, holding her, stroking her long hair as it shone faintly blue in the moonlight.

"I don't know what you're feeling," he told her softly. "But I want to help. I <u>love</u> you, Ann. Does that help? To hear me say it?"

She shook her head. "No."

"Then what <u>would</u>?"

"Nothing. I don't know. You just don't <u>understand</u>," she sobbed.

Allan hugged her and gave her another kiss.

"Look at you," he told her. "What on earth have you got to cry about? You're pretty, and smart, and " He laughed gently. "'You're daddy's rich and your ma is good-lookin.' 'Who could ask for anything more?' I think you're great. I really do."

She sniffed, but smiled. "You sound like a Hollywood musical. Next thing, we'll be dancing."

"Well, why not?" And softly, he began to sing for her:

> *I got rhythm,*

> *I got music.*

> *I got my gal...*

"Stop it," she laughed, "They'll hear you inside."

But Allan kept right on.

Ol' man trouble

I don't mind him

You won't find him....

Ann cupped a hand over his mouth.

"Shhhh! It's <u>my</u> 'old man' you need to worry about," she hissed. But her eyes were gleaming now, and the smile was back.

"All right, so when do I beard this ogre in his den?"

"How about next Saturday?"

"I wanted to take you out."

"Well, maybe you still can. <u>After.</u> But I'm not going to have any peace around here until I bring you in to meet them, so it had better be soon."

"Hummmm. Hoof and mouth inspection."

"That's about it. You're already in my mother's good books—I think she liked your voice or something—but Daddy says he wants to know more about you. So "

"All right. I'll be here."

"Come early, around 5:00."

"Okay. And after, I know a little roadhouse, just over the New York line. We're legal there; and the piano player is hot!"

Ann shrugged. "I'd settle for records," she said. And before he could answer, she blew him a kiss and disappeared inside.

*   *   *

Saturday morning, Allan deliberately cut old Professor Markham's Opera History class, still painfully slogging through the 18th century, and walked instead to the college planetarium to catch a lecture by Professor Ash. He had heard enough to want to see this man in action. Besides, it wouldn't hurt to pick up a few technical terms he could drop if the dinner conversation lagged that night.

The planetarium building had once been an early 19th century observatory constructed of field-stone and wood, with a round domeless tower in the center. The interior had been gutted several years before, and converted from a dusty museum of meteor fragments and tektite globules to house a classroom and the planetarium.

Allan had never actually studied astronomy in school, but for almost ten years, beginning around age 5, he had regularly been to the planetarium shows at the Franklin Institute. Whenever his father's medical practice permitted him to take a Saturday or Sunday off, and the weather made hiking through the woods or a visit to Valley Forge un-appealing, the whole family would drive into Philadelphia to tour an Art Museum, attend a concert, or visit the Franklin Institute.

At art museums, Mrs. Ross would usually tire first and end up meeting "the men" later in the gift shop. At concerts, his father (always a good sport, but completely tone-deaf Allan discovered midway through high school) frequently fell asleep despite his best intentions.

But the Franklin Institute was common ground. The whole Clan Ross enjoyed it. Here there was something for every taste and age group—from the talking statue, whose spoken welcome, triggered by a hidden electronic eye, caught strangers by surprise in the entrance hall, to the hushed inner sanctum of the planetarium chamber itself, with its strange complex projector shaped like some gigantic two-headed metal insect.

The Williams instrument was housed in a much smaller room, and, with no soothing music to mask the eerie acoustic effect of the domed ceiling, Allan quickly found himself growing edgy, disoriented by the muffled silence and dim light.

Students filed in by twos and threes, some with small flashlights for taking notes in the dark. One or two even carried portable tape recorders so as not to miss a single word. Allan admired their equipment. His own machine, though technically able to operate off batteries, was much too bulky for casual lugging around. He wondered if these guys were astro majors, fervent disciples of Professor Ash, or simply lazy— and rich?

Then the man himself strode in, an ominous figure wearing a heavy loden cape, and a dramatic flat black hat (like the one architect Frank Lloyd Wright used to wear). Everyone stirred, and Allan thought for a moment they might all stand up, but there wasn't time. Almost before he reached the lectern with its rows of dials and buttons that controlled the great machine, Professor Ash was speaking. And at his words, the walls and ceiling vanished, it was full night, and all the stars shone out, unwavering, and strong.

"Where are we coming from? Where are we going? These are the great galactic questions."

Allan floated in the dark. Points of light swung slowly past him in formation while the voice— deep, soft, yet echoing—chanted rich, strange syllables:

"The answers come from careful measurement; and that requires points of reference...such as: <u>Alpha Lyrae</u>, <u>Alpha Tauri</u>, <u>Alpha Aurigae</u>, but better known as Vega, Aldebaran, and Capella."

Three of the circling sparks acquired rings of brighter light around them as each name in turn was sounded. Lesser sparks faded away as these three and their rings swelled to occupy a major portion of the vaulted ceiling. By their light Allan could make out the shapes, though not the features, of the students ranged around him—all staring up into the altered sky.

"Yet these three 'guideposts of the night' as they appear to us, are actually moving...shifting, and in time, will occupy far different positions." The voice continued. "Here, for example is a view of the night sky above Williamstown at about ten o'clock on an autumn night in the year 20,000 AD."

Instantly all light vanished, and a whirr of machinery briefly filled the darkness. Then, once again a glittering field of sparks blazed forth. But the three ringed points had shifted.

Allan tried to orient himself, but it seemed hopeless. Familiar constellations were not where they should be--not <u>as</u> they should be. The Big Dipper gaped like an open dump-truck. Cassiopeia's "Chair" was now a lumpy mattress. And where was Polaris, the Pole Star? There <u>was</u> no Pole Star!

Not until he saw Orion still triumphant and unchanged, poised on the horizon, did Allan's ache of bafflement dissolve. So something <u>would</u> survive—even 200 centuries—stay recognizable and whole. The future was not so terrible after all. If you just <u>knew</u> enough. He focused on Professor Ash's words.

"...some other guideposts in the <u>winter</u> sky? The common names will do. Yes?

Several overlapping voices answered in a mumble: "Sirius..." "Rigel". "Betelgeuse." "Procyon...."

"Co-RECT!" the Professor's voice resounded. "Sirius, of course, is the brightest of these, and as it happens the nearest to Earth as well—only about 8.6 light years away. However its 'neighbor' Rigel, alias <u>Beta Orionis,</u> is somewhat further off. Would anyone care to tell us how MUCH further?"

Long seconds of silence followed this challenge. Then a single voice, high-pitched but steady, called out: "Thirteen hundred light years." Allan recognized that voice. It was Dave Carter!

"Close enough! Very good, Carter. I could wish however that one or two of you <u>besides</u> Mr. Carter here might occasionally prepare the reading assignment well enough to answer such an elementary question. But no matter. You will <u>all</u>, I'm sure, have mastered this material thoroughly before next week's <u>mid-term</u>."

Nervous laughter, some coughing, much shuffling of feet and creaking chairs followed this remark.

But for Allan the Professor's spell was broken. The rest of the hour was simply a lecture— informative, dramatic, sometimes captivating, but no better of its kind than dozens of others he had heard in his three years here. Ash obviously knew a lot, but he was over-theatrical, too much the showman for Allan's taste.

He only half listened now to what seemed an endless catalog of relative star distances, followed by several pointless—but admittedly impressive—displays of familiar constellations as they would appear in past or future times, or if viewed from places other than the Earth. Something got through though, because he found himself thinking how this star lore might be turned to music.

The magic of the first few minutes here had given him the sense of what he wanted. A music more quiet than silence itself—and cold. A few bars of clarinet and cello maybe, with a little something odd and modern. Vibraphone! Sure, why not? This piece would not be jazzy though, more religious. Call it *Musica Coeli* which could either mean "Heaven's Music" or just "Music of the Sky." Terrific!

Even though he couldn't see the page he scrawled on, Allan began to write. By the time the lecture ended and the lights came up, he had a twelve-bar theme roughed out on paper using letter designations for the notes. Students filed past him, gesturing and talking. Allan just swung his legs out of the way and kept scribbling. He supposed he must look very studious. Ha! If they only knew!

When he next looked up, Professor Ash and everyone else had gone. He sat there a few minutes longer, savoring the silence. He no longer felt strange in this domed room with its artificial twilight, and its odd acoustics. And now he noticed the skyline frieze that ran around the walls at roughly shoulder height. Black silhouettes created an idealized horizon of familiar shapes. He recognized the seamless rolling outline of surrounding mountains, pierced here and there by shadow profiles of the taller town and college buildings. There was the square chapel tower, the tall spire of the Congregational Church, even the open cupola and weather vane atop his own West College dorm. This was <u>his</u> place, he realized. These shadows marked the borders of a little world he was the center of.

Allan leaned back, smiling, and was content.

Then, slowly, he closed his notebook, repacked it in his green canvas book bag, stood up and walked outside into the sunshine. The booming echo when he closed the door, followed him a long way across the lawn path to the music building.

He stopped in at Professor Markham's office to apologize for having missed opera class. This was polite, but also calculated. Markham was likely to remember a courteous gesture far longer and more warmly than a simple right answer in class. Moreover, this visit enabled Allan to pick up all the reading assignments for the remaining weeks of term. Now, if he and Ann should ever want to go off early some Wednesday or Saturday, or even <u>oversleep</u> (fat chance!) he'd have nothing to fear from a later unannounced pop quiz--Markham's favorite snare.

Chapter 6: Counterpoint

That evening, Allan rang the Ash's doorbell at 5:00 p.m. sharp. Again, Ann's little sister, Cindy, met him. She was wearing rolled up blue jeans and old tennis shoes. Allan noticed a long thin scratch along one bare leg. She was also chewing bubblegum, loudly.

"Hi!" he said cheerfully. "Is Ann around?"

"I guess," Cindy's head jerked to one side.

Allan looked around the broad front porch with its wicker chairs already stacked and covered for the winter, though it was warm today. No sign of Ann.

"She's around back with Daddy, chopping wood." Cindy gestured again with her head. The motion shook out her hair—long, blonde—a lot like Ann's, he noticed.

"You allergic to anything?" she asked. "Cause Mom's making salad."

"I don't think so," Allan said. Then he added "But I don't like tomatoes much."

Cindy considered this. "Me neither. Salads stink."

"Well, don't be too sure. You might change your mind someday. How old are you now?"

"Ten," she answered proudly. "Well, almost ten."

"That's a good age to be," Allan assured her.

"I'd rather be grown up, like Ann."

"Why's that?"

"Cause she gets to wear neat clothes and put on make-up and go out all the time. Stuff like that."

"And you can't?"

"No! Mom makes me stay here and do homework every night."

Allan nodded sympathetically. "That's tough all right. But you know Ann's in school too. When she stays out late it's because she's doing <u>her</u> homework at the library."

"That's diff'rent," the girl objected. "Libraries are neat! And anyway," she paused to look around, then added in a lower voice "Daddy says she doesn't really go there at all! I heard him tell Mom she sneaks off to see some <u>boy</u>!"

So they knew! Allan frowned, but deep down he was relieved. He'd tell Ann, and together they'd face it out with her parents here and now, tonight. Things might be simpler if they were officially 'courting.' Why not? It wouldn't have to be an 'engagement' or anything, just 'going steady.' But still, it would make him part of Ann's life, almost a member of her family. And then this kid would be his little sister.

He gazed at Cindy, and tried to imagine himself in the role of elder brother, teasing her, teaching her, playing games, thinking up jokes and stories to amuse her, looking out for her, kissing her goodbye. The idea intrigued him. How does it <u>feel</u> to kiss your little sister? How would it compare with kissing Ann?

Cindy had stopped chewing gum, and was returning Allan's stare now with a faintly curious expectant smile.

"Forget it, Ross!" he told himself. "She's ten years old. A <u>school kid</u>! Jesus! Do you want to romance every female in the goddamned

<u>world</u>!?" And, with a sudden pang, Allan realized that this was <u>exactly</u> what he wanted.

"<u>There</u> you are!"

Ann stepped out from behind an oak tree by the corner of the house. She was wearing an old army jacket, probably her dad's, and in her arms were the split remains of three or four good-sized logs. She looked deliciously rural.

"I wondered what was keeping you. Then I heard Sissy gabbing away out here..."

"Don't call me that" Cindy protested, "I don't like it! I am <u>not</u> a 'sissy'."

Ann gave her a scornful look. Or was it something else? Allan couldn't say for sure. But whatever kind of look she gave her sister he could tell it wasn't friendly.

"Oh, stop whining and go help mother."

"Why <u>should</u> I?"

"Because," Ann said, with exaggerated calm, "<u>Daddy</u> says so."

For a moment Cindy didn't seem to have an answer for this.

"Well, are you going?" Ann prodded.

A defiant gleam rose in Cindy's eye and her jaw set firmly.

"All right. But if you call me...that name again, I'll call you 'Annnndy' then everyone'll know your name is really "

"Shut up! I mean it, Cindy! Allan, let's go."

But Allan lingered, amazed and amused. What was going on here?

He'd not seen Ann angry before. And he'd never watched two sisters fighting. He looked back and forth from one to the other. They did look a lot alike, especially now: both stubborn, hot, and very child-like—or was it child<u>ish</u>? He tried not to smile, but he couldn't help it.

As he walked slowly over to Ann, he heard Cindy sneer "Daddy calls her ANDY 'cause her real name is..."

"Cindy!" Ann's voice was pitched somewhere between a snarl and a plea.

But the younger girl merely paused as if to measure the full effect of her words on her sister's helpless rage.

"...it's An-DROM-eda!"

"You brat!" Ann howled, and lunged for her, letting her logs drop heavily to the ground.

"Andromeda! Andromeda! Andromeda!" Cindy yelled gleefully, as she ran off inside the house.

"I'll really get you for this," Ann yelled after her, "You just wait!"

Allan reached out and grabbed her shoulders.

"Hey, simmer down! What's wrong with <u>Andromeda</u>? I think it's neat."

"I hate it," she spit out the words. "Hate it, hate it, hate it! It's a bad joke. Daddy's joke."

Allan tried to sooth her but she turned away.

"Look," he told her, "I honestly <u>do</u> like your name. But I'll never use it again if you don't want me to. That's a promise. Okay?"

This seemed to help some. Ann look up at him, and might have been about to smile, when she noticed the logs. She bent to recover them, but Allan stopped her.

"Let me. Where do you want'em?"

"There's a woodbox in the living room. Come on, I'll show you. Then we'd better go around back, to Daddy."

*   *   *

Professor Ash was splitting wood. A long two-bladed axe flashed high above his head and landed with real force in a foot-long bolt of weathered maple. Allan recognized the wood by its bark and color. (He had earned a merit badge in woodcraft as a Boy Scout.) Knowing such things was not exactly useful in daily life, but they made him feel good anyway. Knowledge was power.

The blade sank deep, but did not fully split the log apart. Adjusting his grip on the handle, Professor Ash lifted the axe again and brought it down, wedged bolt and all, with a thunk on the chopping stump. That did it. The log burst in two and the axe bit lightly into the stump below.

The Professor turned smiling toward the newcomers. He wasn't even breathing hard. "Hello," he said.

"Professor," Allan held out his hand. They shook. "Allan Ross."

Ann's father fixed his daughter's latest evidence of lunacy with an appraising glance.

"Yes. I remember. How are you at chopping wood?"

"Out of practice, I'm afraid; but willing."

"Good. Take that sledgehammer over there, and the wedge, and go split some kindling while I finish up here."

"I'll take these in," Ann suggested, picking up another armful of shattered logs.

Allan gave her a frantic "Help! Don't leave me here!" look, but she merely rolled her eyes and shrugged.

Trapped! In a muscle match with Daddy. God, what a fool he was! Allan only hoped he wouldn't smash a toe or something.

He picked up the sledgehammer on his second try. It weighed at least a thousand pounds, he thought, and should have carried a label like: "WARNING! FOR USE BY NORSE GODS ONLY! MORTALS BEWARE!" Then he stooped for the wedge— rust-streaked below and folded out unevenly around the top where bare bright metal showed how crushingly and often it had been used. He grimly upended one of Professor Ash's half-logs, held the wedge midway along the upper rim and began to tap it softly with the sledgehammer head.

"More to the center! Otherwise the log'll fall over when you hit it, and the wedge'll probably come flying loose and brain you."

Professor Ash again had both arms raised above his head and held the long axe poised motionless at highest arc with its blade half hidden in a chunk of wood. As he finished giving his advice he brought all down in one smooth motion.

Just like the movies, Allan thought—specifically, that scene in *The Magnificent Seven*, where Eli Wallach's out behind some farmer's shack splitting wood in exchange for a meal, when Yul Brynner rides up to offer him a real job, south of the border, gunning for bandits.

Allan wrenched the wedge loose, moved it further toward the center of the log, and tapped it into place. When all seemed secure, he stepped back, measured the distance with his eye, lifted the sledge to shoulder height, and brought it down. It was only a glancing blow, but he didn't miss entirely, and the wedge did sink a short way in. Better still, the log wobbled but remained upright. Allan grinned.

In the background he could hear sustained chopping sounds. He guessed Professor Ash was now busy lopping off limbs or breaking up thinner branches. He resisted the urge to turn and look. Again he raised his sledge and swung. This time he hit full center. The wood cracked open—it was very dry—and the wedge fell out on the grass between the fragments. He'd done it.

"Keep it up!" The Professor's voice sounded approving.

Allan flashed a smile across at the old man with his gleaming axe—not really such a bad guy after all—and turned once more to his honest labor.

By the time Ann reappeared, Allan had a respectable pile of hearth-ready kindling, and was working up a sweat. It felt hugely satisfying to strike and strike hard—far better than ripping old flats apart or knocking risers to pieces backstage. Here was _real_ violence. He grinned savagely.

"Having fun?" Ann inquired, coming up close behind him.

"Yes!" he grunted, and launched a particularly vicious swipe at the wedge.

Unfortunately this one missed, knocking over wood, wedge and all, and the unwieldy hammer glanced off into the grassy ground, pulling him off balance after it.

Ann laughed. But when she put a hand on his arm, her touch assured him that she didn't mean to mock. And in another moment, he was laughing, too.

"Ok," he offered her the sledgehammer. "You try!"

"No thanks. I know how it's done. The novelty's worn off for me." She nodded toward her father.

The Professor stood rubbing his hands together and surveying with obvious pride the shattered fragments of what had once been living things strewn all around him on the flattened grass. The sight filled Allan's mind with scenes of aging warriors still fighting hard: Beowulf and the dragon, Arthur pitted against Mordred, Roland at the pass, King Richard on the field at Bosworth. Life was pretty tough on losers, he thought briefly; then shook off the vision of scarred arms and bloody ground.

"Well, if you won't I will," he told Ann, and gripped his sledgehammer again, more tightly.

"This had better be your last." She warned him. "Dinner's in ten minutes, and I think you'll want to wash up first. At least I <u>hope</u> so."

He looked at her tragically. "You mean...?"

"Exactly." She nodded grimly, pinching her nose. And then, to her father: "Daddy, dinner's ready."

The Professor nodded absently, and continued to survey the havoc he had wrought.

*　　*　　*

Dinner was chicken and dumplings, fresh zucchini and the threatened salad. Allan sat facing Ann, and next to Cindy, with the Professor and Mrs. Ash at the ends of the table. Mrs. Ash, he noticed, was quite good-looking--not exactly pretty, but decidedly attractive in a slightly weather-beaten way. She seldom spoke, but when she did, all heads turned to her—as if her attention and approval were the only prize worth talking for. Even Ann seemed somehow less uniquely special in her mother's presence.

Allan watched Professor Ash surgically disjoint a chicken leg. Did he and his wife ever quarrel, Allan wondered? Did he beat her? Did they get on in bed?

"Ann tells me you're a music major," the Professor stated, as if there were considerable doubt— or ought to be.

"Well, actually it's a double major. Music and English." Allan explained. "If I go right on to grad school, I can pick up a Master of Fine Arts degree in music after one more year."

"Hmmm. That would make you a B.A., B.A., M.F.A." Professor Ash said. "Pronounced <u>Bah-bah M-FAH</u>, I suppose. Sounds like some Egyptian god."

Everyone laughed a little. Cindy laughed a lot, and repeated the name "Bah-Bahm-FAH" several times with great delight till her mother restrained her.

Allan squirmed.

"Why those two subjects?" Mrs. Ash inquired.

"Well, because I want to be a music critic, and I figured I'd do best learning what to listen for and how to write about it at the same time."

"But Allan wants to be a composer, too. Don't you?"

Ann said this. And Allan wished she hadn't. It was one thing to admit it casually to her, and, it was true enough, though of course he'd never sold or published anything. But it would sound pretentious here. Too artsy, too insecure.

"Well," he said slowly, "Yes, but I'd never count on making money that way. I think a composer ought to write only music he believes is really good. If he writes for money, there's always pressure to write more and faster than he really can. Do you see what I mean?"

Mrs. Ash nodded. Her husband reached for the salad bowl, and, lifting a generous second helping onto his plate asked: "You mean 'good music' doesn't <u>sell</u>."

"Depends on what you mean by 'good'" Allan parried

"Look at Benjamin Britten, or Darius Milhaud, or Stravinsky— people like that. Their works get played a lot, and I suppose they must do pretty well off royalties. But they've all had to struggle. And I'll bet every one of them would admit they've written too much. Some of it's really pretty awful! Well, maybe not 'awful,' but flat, un-special music. And they're the <u>top</u> of the heap!"

Mrs. Ash nodded and smiled warmly at him. The Professor said nothing but just continued munching.

Allan felt something moving softly up and down his leg. He looked across at Ann. She was sipping from her water glass reflectively, with eyes slightly upturned in innocence.

The little witch! She had her shoes off, and her nyloned toes against his trouser leg were decidedly erotic. He clenched the napkin in his hand, strangled a grin, and reached out with his own foot questingly in search of her.

"More chicken, Allan?"

"No thank you, Mrs. Ash. But it's delicious!"

"Wooten?"

"Couldn't."

"Ann?"

Hah! He'd found her. Or was that just the table leg? Yes, damn it. Too hard and smooth. He eased his foot a little to the right. There! What he touched now yielded ever so slightly to his pressure. And it curved! He must be just behind her knee. Her face gave nothing away, but her eyelids closed.

"Mmmmm. No thanks, mother. This is perfect! Oh, shall I start to clear?"

"Would you, dear? Just stack things in the sink for now. And see how the coffee's doing."

Allan began to get up too. "Here, let me..."

But Mrs. Ash put her hand on his arm to restrain him. It was a firm but gentle clasp, and she held it, he thought, just a beat longer than was absolutely necessary.

"No, no, Allan. You're a guest. Just sit where you are. Men are no use in the kitchen anyway."

"Mom, can I leave the table too? Please?"

"Yes, you <u>may</u>, Cindy. But take your dishes out as you go." Then, to Allan she said: "We'll have dessert and coffee later in the living room."

"Sounds perfect," he assured her. But he felt thwarted. He was aching for a moment, however brief, alone with Ann.

"Coffee's ready," Ann called from the kitchen.

"Thank you, dear. Why don't you join the men in the living room. I'll be along in a moment."

Outside the house it was fully dark now, but within, the shaded lamp glow radiated warmth and coziness. Ann sat beside Allan on the sofa, under the photograph of the Great Spiral Nebula. And there, out of sight beneath the low teak coffee table, their toes and ankles stayed more or less continually engaged throughout the evening. Above the table, though, all was proper and polite.

Mrs. Ash brought in the coffee and dishes of strawberry ice cream on a lacquered tray. Professor Ash set an impressive fire blazing in the grate, then settled back in his wing chair, to fill and light a pipe whose bowl was one large chunk of dark unpolished briar. This was just an evening at home ought to be, Allan thought, and he enjoyed himself hugely.

The talk flowed easily from music to opera to drama to the latest college theatre production, and finally to Williamstown itself and what a perfect place it was to live. Listening or talking Allan felt not at all a stranger. This was a place he belonged in, he was sure of it.

When he finally thought to check his watch it was already after ten, too late, he realized, to go anywhere with Ann. But somehow he didn't mind. Though the two of them were never left alone together, and no one brought up the subject of Ann's night visits to the library, so there were no openings for any public declarations of affection, Allan was confident that time would surely come. From now on, he thought, there would <u>always</u> be time.

If Ann seemed somewhat cool toward him when they said goodnight at the door, he could hardly blame her. After all, her parents were standing right behind her in the hall.

*   *   *

But Ann had other reasons, as he learned the next night when they met as usual in the practice room.

"How <u>could</u> you sit there gabbing with them hour after hour?" she fumed.

"I was having fun. And so were they. So were <u>you</u>—at least that's what I thought. If you were so bored, why didn't you poke me or something?"

"What did you <u>think</u> I was doing with your ankle all that time?"

"Being affectionate?" he offered lamely.

"Oh Allan, sometimes you can be so...dumb!"

"So were you just <u>bored</u> in the dining room too?"

"That was different."

"Well, I'm sorry. Next time I'll pay closer attention to your toe-braille."

"Never mind," she sighed. "At least you passed the audition. I think the phrase Daddy used was 'surprisingly mature for a Di-Gamma Koppa boy'. That fraternity of yours must be a zoo!"

"It's not so bad. I'll show you. Come on."

"Not tonight, thank you."

"But sometime? Maybe?" he implored, in a self-parody of his 'desperate lover' voice.

"You're cute," she conceded, and kissed him, but in a passionless sisterly way.

"I just wanted to be alone with you last night," she went on, "and there's never enough time!"

"I wanted that too, but it didn't seem so...crucial after a while. I mean I think we'll have all the rest of our lives now to be together in."

Ann looked at him seriously, sweetly.

"I hope so," she answered. "But once I go off to Wellesley all sorts of things could happen."

"Such as?"

"I don't know. You could find another girl."

"Here at Williams? Are you kidding? Bennington's out on Non-resident Term from Christmas till March, and there's not another datable girl within fifty miles. Believe me."

"You can always drive down to Smith or Holyoke or someplace, and besides you all have girls up here for weekends, don't you?"

Allan couldn't deny this, so he took another tack.

"Well, it's a lot more likely <u>you</u>'ll find another guy," he countered. "Tootling into Boston, with all those Harvard millionaires enticing you into their sports cars, and MIT brains crazed with lust after six weeks locked in a lab. <u>I</u>'m the one who ought to worry!"

Ann laughed, but didn't answer, and the question of who had reason to be worried about who was dropped—for now.

Chapter 7: *Crescendo*

But Ann was right, he found. There was never enough time. And as the nights grew colder, meeting in the poorly-heated practice rooms beneath the Music Building grew less and less appealing. So he suggested the library, and Ann agreed. It was where she always <u>told</u> her parents she was going anyway.

Allan wondered why she bothered trying to conceal their meetings. They were dating every weekend now, he had been invited twice for dinner, and both times he had enjoyed himself and felt at home (although, after that first time, there was no mistaking Ann's eagerness to get away as soon as possible).

He supposed it must embarrass her to have her family around when it was obvious that she and Allan liked each other. He felt no such shyness though--in fact, he couldn't wait to 'show her off to <u>his</u> folks.'

So most nights Ann walked to the library and Allan would meet her there after his piano practice—sometimes at his carrel in the stacks, but more often in the reference room. The stacks were quiet and secluded, but he really preferred the ref room with its Victorian woodwork, white marble floors, hissing radiators, intimate lighting (others called it <u>dim</u>), broad leather-inlaid tables scarred by generations of use, and black-lacquered Morris chairs emblazoned with the College Seal in faded gold.

On Sundays, or whenever his class schedule let him practice early, Allan would hit the library right after dinner, and just browse along the reference shelves, picking up a dictionary or a random volume of Encyclopedia and letting one bit of information lead him on to others, until Ann appeared. It was a great way to learn: letting curiosity take over, brushing into facts and dates and commentary without any conscious effort to master them, never knowing though when something might stick fast to his memory like burrs along an uncleared trail cling to your jeans.

It was a Wednesday night in mid-November when he found the *Thesaurus of American Slang*. He happened to start reading under DRUNK, and was soon silently mouthing each new word, savoring the syllables in disbelieving ecstasy. Halfway down the first page he was already heaving with heavy chuckles and laugh-tears blurred his eyes.

When Ann arrived she found him utterly collapsed, convulsed, gripping the chair arms with both hands and gasping out words in a voice as close to silence as he could manage in his condition: *"...lit up, muzzy, squiffy, gilded, ripe, lushed, potted, soaked, boiled, fried, canned, blasted, honked, sozzled, blind, blotto, <u>gone</u> "*

"Allan! What <u>is</u> it? What's wrong? Allan? Look at me!"

He couldn't. He just pointed down at the page and burbled *"honked*!" again, then gasped as if in pain.

Other readers in the room looked up. Chair legs grated on marble. Someone hissed "SHHHH!" Even the reference librarian (an ex-WAC sergeant by repute) was aware of some disturbing element in her hushed world, and fixed him with her glare.

"Al-LAN," Ann whispered fiercely, "People are looking!"

Allan struggled to his feet, keeping his mouth pressed tight against the sobs of laughter churning inside him. Somehow they made it to the entrance hall, past the card catalogues and the check-out desk, through the enormous wooden doors, and out into the frost-sharp air. Then he exploded.

His laughter echoed off the brick wall with its empty birds' nests and its nets of withered ivy. The bare trees shook with him as he roared and whooped. The wire-stiff grass caught his echoes and quivered sympathetically. The steam of his great laughing fogged the stars.

Utterly helpless, he stumbled down the steps and flung himself arms outstretched, panting against the broad trunk of the nearest convenient tree, digging his fingers into the bark to keep himself upright.

He could hear Ann's voice: "Allan, what on <u>earth</u> is so funny?" She was smiling too now, he could hear it in her voice, though he couldn't <u>see</u> her yet through the laugh-brine that still brimmed his eyes.

"Oh,.I-hye, can't...those words...they-hey, I just, uhhhh..." He shook his head. The grip of lunacy was subsiding in him now as he sucked in brittle air. He looked over at Ann: her questioning eyes, the half smile on her lips. Why was it so unbearably painfully wonderful to see, that face of hers?

"Are you really all right?" she asked.

"I'm fine," he shook his head. "Words just <u>get</u> to me sometimes. Like music. And I just...let go!" With an effort he pushed off the tree and held out his hands to her. She took them in hers and held them tightly, warming them.

"What <u>were</u> you laughing at in there?"

"All these wild words for <u>drunk</u>. I just started reading them, and suddenly I couldn't stop laughing. It was like <u>being</u> drunk, only better."

She seemed unconvinced.

"I guess I get a little crazy sometimes," he offered.

And she didn't disagree.

Allan shivered. "It's <u>cold</u> out here. Let me run back and get my coat. Then maybe we can hit the snack bar for some hot chocolate. Sound good?"

Ann nodded.

*   *   *

It was barely half past eight, so the snack bar wasn't full. They got their cups of chocolate and found a booth to themselves by the window. They talked about classes, and assignments, and the Thanksgiving Break.

"You'll be going home, I guess." Ann said.

"Yep," Allan sighed with exaggerated pathos. "Four empty days—three endless nights. But I'll be back before you know it."

Ann shook her head. "I'll know it."

There was a short sweet silence.

"Thanksgiving is one time you really appreciate a family," Allan mused aloud. "You know, my folks and I get on so well, I actually miss them up here sometimes. It'll be good to see them again, and home. For a few days anyway."

But Ann only sipped her cocoa and looked glum.

"Wish I could take you <u>with</u> me," he added.

"Really?" She brightened a bit.

"Sure. Well, I mean, I know it's impossible. But hey, wait! Maybe you <u>could</u> come down at Christmas? And we could drive back here together. What do you think?"

"Okay, I guess."

"You don't sound exactly overjoyed."

"No. I'd like to come. It'll be fine."

"Then what's wrong? You're not still mad about me laughing in the library are you?"

"No."

"Well <u>what</u> then?'

"I don't know. I guess I just hate <u>holidays</u>!"

"Why?"

"Oh, because I'm on display every minute and have to spend hours with all my boring relatives, and pretend to be impressed when Daddy or Uncle Charlie or someone starts telling us all how wonderful they are."

"It can't be <u>that</u> bad?"

"But it <u>is</u>! You just don't <u>know</u>! Cindy's still small enough no one cares if she sneaks off somewhere. And mother's so dead to everything she just smiles and doesn't listen any more. But I've got to stay there and pretend its all fascinating and...I just hate it—and there's no <u>escape</u>! Don't you see?"

"I guess...a little. But I don't know...I mean your father really <u>has</u> done a lot and...well, you know, for a professor I think he's pretty interesting. It's not like he were babbling on about Victorian poets or jungle beetles or something. Stars, galaxies, space... all that stuff is exciting! That's where the <u>future</u> is, you know. It makes you think makes ME think—anyway."

Ann was not responding. He tried a different approach.

"Okay, why not say you're going to the kitchen to check on the oven or something, then you just hide out for a while? Or maybe go outside and chop some wood? That'll take out your frustrations fast!"

"Oh, you <u>don't</u> understand!"

She was sulking now in earnest. It annoyed Allan to see her do that. Sulking wasted time, and he <u>hated</u> waste.

"No," he sighed, "I guess I <u>don't</u>. "I don't understand what it is you want that you don't already <u>have</u> right here—or <u>couldn't</u> have just for asking. You're living in this gorgeous place, surrounded by mountains and history, and the College and all. You've got a great home, and clothes and books and stuff from all over world. But you don't seem to care. You don't even act <u>grateful</u>. And that I <u>don't</u> understand. Not at all."

"<u>Grateful</u>," she sneered. "That's a laugh! You can't imagine what it's like at home when no one from outside is around to see."

"Okay, then tell me about it."

"What's the point? <u>You</u> don't care."

"I <u>do</u> care, Ann. I just can't read your mind, and what you say you're feeling I can't <u>see</u>."

She glowered at him, but he went right on.

"Every time I'm over at your house you can't wait to get away. You'd think they were <u>torturing</u> you. And this sneaking out nights to meet me. Who are you fooling? Your folks must know."

"Oh no they don't! Mother might suspect, but Daddy doesn't have a clue. Otherwise, he'd never let me out of the house!"

"Look. Will you listen to me? He <u>knows</u>! I'm sure of it."

"Why? What did he say to you?"

"Nothing. But...Cindy said he told your mom you weren't really studying at the library like you said "

"That's just his way of prying. He was <u>testing</u> her. He doesn't know a thing. He only <u>thinks</u> he does. He's such a <u>fool</u>!"

Ann's bitter outburst shocked him into silence. He sat and waited for her to calm down. Who'd <u>started</u> this fight, anyway? Well, all right maybe <u>he</u> had; but he wasn't about to say he was sorry!

"Hey, Allan!"

Tom was coming toward them from the counter with a cup of coffee in one hand and a fried honey bun on a paper plate in the other. He wore jeans and a scarred brown leather jacket with scruffy-looking wool trim. His hair looked as if he had just woken up. But Allan was glad to see him.

"Okay if I join you two?" Tom looked around the room as he said this, and Allan, following his gaze, saw how much the snack bar had filled up since they'd arrived. There were places to sit, but no entire tables free. Tom would have to join somebody's party. So why not theirs?

"Sure," Allan said. "Come on. Ann, this is my roommate, Tom Petard."

"Hello."

"Hi." Tom flashed Ann a grin as he slid into the booth. Allan moved down the bench toward the window to make room.

"Slept through dinner," Tom explained.

"I wondered where you were," Allan said. "I ate over here tonight, with Pete and Elroy. Pete's booked us a gig up at Bennington this

Saturday. We were downstairs rehearsing all afternoon." He paused for comments or questions. But none came.

"'Shouldda woke me," Tom complained through a mouthful of honeybun.

"Yeah, I'm sorry. But we never stopped till it was so late we had to run upstairs to eat."

"'s okay." Tom shrugged and munched.

Allan looked across at Ann. Her eyes avoided his and fixed on Tom. She wasn't a staring exactly, just appraising. Allan wondered if she was purposely trying to annoy him now? If so, it was working.

He decided to try conversation again.

"Oh yeah, Ann, about Saturday. We'll just be playing three twenty-minute sets in one of the Houses between five and seven. Cocktail hour for visiting parents and rich alums or something. But hey, for sixty bucks why not?"

"Anyway," he reached over to squeeze her hand, "I thought maybe you'd like to come too.

She pulled her hand away.

"Are you sure you really want _me_ there? Maybe you'd rather invite my _parents_."

"What's that supposed to mean? Of course I want _you_."

Ann was gazing off into space, vaguely in Tom's direction.

"I _always_ want you with me," Allan said.

The minute the words left his mouth he was sorry. It was too much the romantic tragedy line. Who had he said them to impress? Ann or Tom? God damn it! He was being an ass!

"Somehow," Ann said, "I don't see myself standing around all night at Bennington."

"Oh, come on, Ann! You won't be 'standing around all night'. Besides, there'll be time between sets. We can stroll, and talk…"

"Oh, yes; I forgot. You do love to <u>talk</u>, don't you? Well, I'm sorry, Allan, but I'm just not all that fond of <u>listening</u>!"

Tom went on eating as if couldn't hear a thing.

"Well okay then. Fine. Great. You won't have to listen to <u>me</u> any more tonight!"

Allan slid out of the booth, on the window side, and stood up.

"I'll call you tomorrow. Maybe you'll feel more like listening then."

And with that he strode away. Well, actually he had to edge out sideways around two other booths for the first few yards. But effectively he was striding forth from the chamber, leaving his shattered and (he hoped) already repentant lady aghast.

Outside, in the night air, he felt even more self-righteous. <u>Damn</u> the girl! What did she <u>want</u> from him? Glancing in through the snack bar window as he passed, Allan was disappointed to see Ann peacefully sipping her cocoa. He kicked a clump of frost-hardened leaves, and trudged along uphill toward West College.

The room door was locked, as usual when both he and Tom were out. He dug the key ring out of his pocket, and saw his car key glitter. Go for a drive? Nice moon tonight. But no.

The fact was, he wanted a smoke, and his cigarettes were inside. He could handle some port too. Too bad he'd killed off the brandy gabbing into his tape recorder that night last month—the night he'd first met Ann.

Propped on the sofa, with a cigarette drooping from his lips and a half-empty tumbler of ruby port in his fist, he felt better. If there'd been a piano near he would have played, but there were only his records, so he listened.

He put on Carl Orff's *Catulli Carmina*—a sort of erotic opera in Latin, based on texts from the ancient Roman love poet Catullus. This piece had been a favorite since high school, and tonight he took a special delight in the repetitions of its passionate choruses and raw percussion. Though worn and scratched from many, many listenings, the familiar words and rhythms still grabbed, still soothed him.

"*Eis aeona...*" the young lovers chanted, for all eternity, I am yours"; while the chorus of old men chuckled and called them fools. "*Eis aeona (ha-ha, ha-ha-ha).o vos stultos! vos stolidos! vos stupidos!*"

Further on, the betrayed disconsolate lover shrieks his anguish at the faithlessness of all women and of his sweetheart Lesbia in particular: *O mea Lesbia...*, (oh, my Lesbia...), *Nulla potest mulier...* (no woman was ever loved so...)... *nunc, jam, illa non vult...* (now she is no longer willing...), *Vale, puella! Vale...* (Farewell, mistress! Farewell!), and so on.

Allan could understand now what that poor guy must have gone through. He really could!

As the side ended, and the stereo's automatic shut-off quieted the room, Allan gazed idly down the Latin text on the record jacket with its partial English translation in facing columns. (The really sexy passages were left blank on the English side, but of course he'd looked them all up long ago and knew them now by heart in both languages.)

Was Ann to be <u>his</u> Lesbia—the grand passion of his life? Or would she just be Sylvia all over again—a possibility never realized, a dream? Allan smiled in sad remembrance; he was actually starting to <u>enjoy</u> his gloom.

Pennswood Academy, Swarthmore. Allan had transferred in from public high school his sophomore year, and the very first week there he had fallen for a junior girl: Sylvia. She'd noticed, and, while she never really led him on, she didn't exactly chase him off either. After all, he was flattering—and harmless.

They'd dated a little (mostly to movies or concerts with one or two other couples along), they'd acted in two school plays together (never a love scene though), and ended up co-editing the yearbook. That first year, they were both taking Latin and Geometry. Her math was better than his, but he had an ear for languages. So they began to call each other up at night for help with homework. This gradually led to talking for hours on the phone, and formed the basis for a kind of arms-length over-the-wire romance.

Allan solemnly made her his muse. And she enjoyed the game. His first improvisations on the battered upright piano in the gym were done for her; and it was to her he dedicated his first sonata. He winced even now at the thought. What conceit, what stupendous idiocy to have called that three-page pseudo-Debussy mush a <u>sonata</u>! But he had done it for her—and played it for her too in the darkened auditorium the night of her senior prom. There had been real tears in her eyes when he finished, and she had kissed him. That much had been real.

She went to Stanford after graduating, and Allan would have followed her next year. But Stanford was so far away, and she'd stopped answering his letters after the first month. And the recruiter from Williams had been so persuasive, even offering a scholarship, and Oh well. So much for the staying power of young unrequited love. *Sic transit Sylvia.*

Now, here was Ann, a miracle at first, but already tiring of him at the very moment when it seemed they might become really close. Possibly even lovers.

<u>Lovers</u>. That was the difference, he realized. This time the prize wasn't just a stolen kiss or a last dance, but going to bed and living together and facing the world forever side by side.

He wished Tom would get here. He could use a friend just now, someone to talk to. Tom would understand how important Ann was to him, how much it meant having her as his girl—no, his <u>woman</u>. Well, almost anyway.

It hardly mattered <u>when</u> they took that last long leap into bed. What <u>was</u> sex after all? A symbolic rite, a ceremony, the last and best-kept secret of adulthood, hidden from children until they learned enough about the rest of life to put the power of passion in its true perspective—just as he could now.

Allan recalled how carefully, even methodically, he had set about unlocking each of life's Great Mysteries, one by one: learning to drink coffee, and smoke cigarettes, learning to drive a car, opening a bank account, travelling cross-country alone. He had done all these things by the time he left high school.

There had come a night early in his freshman year at college when he sat down with a friend on either side, and began slowly sipping—not gulping or chugging—tumbler after tumbler of straight cheap atrocious-tasting scotch until, to his wonderment, he found there actually <u>was</u> such a thing as drunkenness. He still remembered his surprise at suddenly knowing that those funny drunks in the movies or the less funny ones out on the street in certain parts of Philadelphia weren't just putting on an act. You actually <u>did</u> stagger and blur words, and feel first relaxed, then dizzy, and finally sick. He could still recall how calmly he had climbed the three long flights up to the top floor bathroom and the welcome bowl that gaped there consolingly as if for him alone.

Even barfing had been good that night. Every surge, every globule had splattered safely into the wide white bowl he had knelt before as if in prayer. And he recalled looking up out of his sickness only to meet—gladly, and gratefully—a bright full moon grinning in through the window they always left open to let steam escape from the showers. How he had laughed for pure joy at it all—the moon, the clotted bowl, the ache of his knees on the gritty tiles.

That left only sex—the ultimate unknown. He had kissed and fondled enough girls to know for sure it felt good and he wanted more. Then, last summer, he had learned just what that _more_ he wanted was.

Now here was Ann, desirable, liking him as much as he liked her. And there was nothing to stop them from becoming lovers. Nothing that is but Ann's own maddeningly unpredictable moods.

From his sofa of reflection, hidden by the book-case, Allan heard the front door open, and gently close.

"Hey, Tom! Get in here. Grab a drink," he called.

But the voice that answered him was Ann's.

Chapter 8: *Pas de Deux*

"It's me."

"Oh."

Allan wanted to sound hard and unforgiving, but surprise and pleasure so overwhelmed him that he couldn't manage it. He bent his head to the record jacket to hide his smile; and when he looked up she was there.

"What were you doing all this time?" she asked.

"Playing music," he picked up the album cover.

"May I see?"

"Sure."

He handed it to her, face up. The illustration, purple, pink, and red, showed a pair of angular, medieval figures dancing and playing. The woman was naked but not what you'd call voluptuous— skin like a plucked chicken, and scrawny. The man wore skin tight motley, and a cap with ass's ears—a fool. Allan watched Ann flip to the liner notes on the back and begin to read. He wondered if she knew Orff's music, or the poems of Catullus, or could read the untranslated Latin lines.

> *...O vos papillae horridulae!*
> *Mea manus est cupida, cupida, cupida,*
> *Illas prensare, illas prensare--*
> *Vehementer prensare...*

She stood there a while, maybe reading, maybe not.

Then she said: "I'm sorry. I was hateful to you."

"No," he shook his head. "It was my fault. I should never have gotten sore."

"Oh, Allan..."

He got up and put his arms around her, just like in the movies. And it worked. He could feel her change as he held her. Something other than sorrow entered her eyes.

His fingers stroked her hair. Her face turned up. Her smile became a kiss full on his lips. He responded with several gentle kisses down her cheek. Then suddenly, rising on tiptoe, she reached up and gave his earlobe a savage bite.

"Ow! What the...?" He recoiled, shocked by genuine pain.

Instantly she was apologetic. "Did I bite too hard? I didn't mean to. Oh, your poor ear!"

Allan winced, and rubbed his dented earlobe experimentally. But he was laughing.

"Still attached. You never told me you were part beaver."

She began to laugh too. And they kissed again, longer this time, just for fun.

It was Ann who finally stepped back, took Allan's hand, led him into the next room over to a bed—his own—and sat down on it, the relatively-fresh laundered sheets and blanket wrinkling beneath her.

He couldn't believe it.

"Tom'll be coming back any minute now," he warned.

She shook her head. "I asked him not to."

He looked at her amazed. She was serious.

"What's more, my daddy's away in Boston tonight, and mother never waits up alone."

"Ann...I...don't know what to say."

"Then don't say anything," she whispered.

It should have been like being pushed on stage without rehearsal, his surprise was so complete as he sat down beside her on the bed. Was she amused? Excited? He was definitely both. And somehow that turned everything they did to music.

His left hand fumbled with the buttons of her blouse while at the same time his right raised lightly off her shoulder and hovered close, barely touching her hair. As the soft cloth parted to reveal her white brassiere, his right hand fingers trilled along her cheek and neck, while with his left he moved around to press the warm skin of her back with the heavy sprung chords that would, on ivory keys, have been his Chopin *Etude*. But he quickly lost the fingering, forgot the beat, and had to improvise—slipping from concert into jazz—from romance into passion.

They were making music, making love. Playing each other like instruments, performing variations on an intricate duet to please an audience of two. And not a critic in the house.

As his fingers moved to cup the thin but surprisingly rough fabric that contained her breasts, Ann's eyes closed and she nuzzled at his ear a moment. Then, before his hands could leave her, she shook free, and, reaching easily behind her, undid her bra for him and slipped it off. His hand replaced the cloth, sliding, questing.

The bedsprings didn't squeak, the blankets didn't scratch, and though they several times heard footsteps and voices passing in the hall, no one tried the door and they were not disturbed.

Because it was their first time, there was a special eagerness in the way they touched and kissed and shared eachother, and a certain hesitation too—that arose, on Allan's side at least, not so much from shyness, but from his own surprise that he <u>didn't</u> feel shy.

For one moment, when they were horizontal and quite bare, her nipples pressing hard against his chest, and his cock a polished tower questing along her thigh, awkwardness overcame him. He felt suddenly afraid—afraid of hurting her, of doing something wrong, of failing to please. But she reassured him, with gentle fingers teasing his own nipples rigid, and flicking her tongue in and out like some lithe serpent hissing at the doorway of his ear.

Her legs eased apart, he found her moistness, drew closer, centered on her. Her hand guided him inside, then slid down moving along his flank. She was not a virgin. He had not expected her to be, and felt no disappointment.

A sudden gust of wind blew leaves against the partly opened window. One slipped inside and danced across the smooth bare floor. On and on they rocked and cradled, till at last the bough broke and he fell. Did she fall with him? He couldn't tell.

Her fingernails bit tiny crescent moons into his arms. He held on, wanting nothing different, nothing more, until her breath slid out beneath him in a long low sigh. And for a while they lay unmoving, moved. A faint echo of sad music, like his own improvisations in the practice room, entered his mind.

When they unpaired at last, Ann asked if she could use the other bed. Not exactly romantic, but he had to admit that for actual sleeping it made more sense than cramming the two of them into his narrow college-issue single.

They shared his best pajamas. She wore the tops, he wore the bottoms. A perfect fit, he thought. Ann seemed to think so too.

*   *   *

The room was warm and quiet. Allan lay contentedly awake, listening.

"Ann, are you awake?"

"Huh-uh. Sound asleep."

"Well, you don't _sound_ asleep to me."

"That so? How do I 'sound' asleep?"

"You go 'Honnnk-kweee, honkkkkk-lweeeee...'"

"I do _not_!"

"Wanna bet?"

"Do I snore, really?"

"Uh-huh. A little"

"Well I'm sorry. I'll try not to. Now what's wrong? Why are you laughing?"

"The thought of you trying _not_ to snore."

"You shouldn't laugh at me."

"I'm not laughing _at_ you, I'm just...happy."

"Oh."

"When do we need to get you home?"

"Five-thirty. Six. Mom is never up much before seven.

"Well it's just 3:30 now 'according to the ancient pyramidic scrolls and me Ingersoll watch'."

"Come again?

"Forget it. Just a quote. G'night."

"G'night."

*   *   *

"Allan?"

"Uhngg, mum? What is it? What are you doing out of bed?"

"I came over to listen. Know how <u>you</u> sound, asleep?"

"No. How do I sound?"

"You go 'Lub-dub, lub-dub, lub-dub...'"

"That's nice."

"Mmm-hmm, <u>I</u> think so."

Somehow he managed to laugh and yawn at the same time without strangling.

"Hey," he said reaching up to her. "C'mere."

And she did.

He came hotly, quickly, holding nothing back for courtesy or style. She was here for him and he wanted her. That was what mattered; that was all that mattered in the world.

This time after they quieted, they lay compactly close, with his arms around her and his blanket up to their ears. If it felt cramped neither of them said so.

*   *   *

He came awake abruptly to the sound of footsteps, and a whisper close to his ear.

"Allan!"

"Ungh-mmm? Wha's it?... Ann?"

"I'm leaving."

"'kay. Just lemme get my pants on. Be right there."

"To do what?"

"Well, to see you home."

"You will <u>not</u>! I might just possibly explain away a solitary pre-dawn stroll. But if anybody spots the two of us together it's all over."

"I know some ways. We'll get you home safe."

"Oh great! And if my <u>daddy</u> catches you gallantly kissing my hand on the kitchen doorstep, what then hmmm?"

"You said he was out of town."

"Well maybe I lied."

That woke him up, <u>fast</u>.

"Wha...? Why did you <u>say</u> that if he was really .."

"It doesn't matter. <u>Anyone</u> might see us..Cindy even. The point is we'd both be in deep trouble fast, and you know it."

"Well, I can't just let you walk all that way alone "

"I'll be perfectly safe. In fact, I'll be a whole lot safer without <u>you</u>!"

This was true, and Allan knew it. Still....

"I'll be careful, I promise. When I'm safe I'll call you. Just one ring, so you'll know. Okay?"

"I still wish you'd let me "

"No!" She silenced him with a quick kiss, then straightened up— he saw she was already dressed— and started toward the door.

Before she reached it, he called out to her:

"Hey. Tomorrow night?"

"We'll see. I'll let you know."

"All right. Hey!" he called to stop her one last time. "You're really fine. You know that?"

"Shhhh! Go back to sleep."

The door opened softly and closed again. He was alone.

He waited until he guessed she would have made it downstairs and out the door. Then he got up, and moved to the window.

There was no moon. The first grey light of pre-dawn filtered through a faint mist. He couldn't see Ann, but he could hear her shoes click on the sidewalk, walking quickly, determinedly, away.

Allan shook his head and sighed.

Now that it was over—and something <u>was</u> over—he felt strangely detached. Not <u>indifferent</u>; not at all! He cared for Ann more than ever now. This was more a heaviness—not exactly sorrow, but sobriety.

Abstractly he had known there was a secret beyond sex: a deeper sharing to be had than mere physical contact—call it <u>love</u>. And now, tonight, he thought, he had finally experienced it himself.

He wondered what came next. Now that he and Ann were 'lovers' he was certain they would find ways to be together often. They would need to hide from her parents of course, and from the guys in his dorm—maybe even from Tom. This was no conquest to boast about or snigger over. This was <u>real.</u>

And all at once Allan realized he felt <u>married</u>. Ann was a responsibility now, not just a promised joy. She was his <u>woman</u>, no longer just his girl.

This was what he'd longed for; and now he had it. The simple fact of changing what they had <u>wanted</u> to do into what they <u>had</u> done made them a couple. They were Allan-&-Ann now; practically married in everything but name. He supposed he was happy. He <u>knew</u> he felt tired—and proved it with a yawn.

He sat down on Tom's rumpled bed. Felt the pillow. Sadly, it wasn't still warm as he'd hoped. But <u>her</u> head had rested there. From now on, this bed would hold her memory for him whenever he saw it empty and disarranged like this.

But he wanted his own bed. His pajama pants stuck to him a little as he moved. The tops lay folded neatly over on the seat of his desk chair. <u>She</u> had done that. He shivered with joy at the thought of it (or was he just cold?).

The window was still partly open. He picked up a leaf from the floor. Maple. Already curled and brown. Not worth a second glance ordinarily. But now he laid it tenderly inside his top desk drawer. It would be their *Memento Amoris*—their love souvenir.

He buttoned the pajama jacket on. It smelled, he thought, very faintly of perfume. He wondered what her special fragrance was. He would find out and buy her more. How much could he afford? A lot, he hoped!

The telephone rang. Just once. Ann was safely home.

Allan slid into bed, pulled up the sheets and blanket, lay on his back a minute, staring upward, smiling, then said aloud in a calm but quiet voice: *"Deo gracias!"*

Was it worship or sacrilege to credit the deity for this particular blessing? Probably a little of both, he suspected.

He closed his eyes and slept. Well! Well enough, in fact, to miss Professor Markham's opera history class <u>again</u>.

Chapter 9: *Accelerando*

Allan sat up in bed. Sunlight was streaming into the room. He could hear movement outside the door. He looked over at the other bed. Empty. He called out "Tom, you out there?"

"Yo!" There followed a flurry of typing.

Allan sat up in bed and reached for his wristwatch. 10:45? God! How did that happen? Then, he remembered how, and grinned, and was glad.

He wrapped himself in the yukata robe he had bought in Tokyo last summer, and checked his image in the mirror. Hair like the Wolf Man; otherwise, Oliver Cool. Ah, so! He bowed politely to his image. The image bowed politely back.

He shuffled out to the living room in search of eats—stale Oreos, a wrinkled apple, soggy crackers, anything! Tom didn't bother to look up. The typewriter clacked on.

"What are you working at so hard?"

"Poli-sci paper. And tomorrow there's a fucking English midterm!" Tom pecked away savagely, still without looking up.

Allan scratched his stomach, unselfconsciously since he knew Tom wasn't looking, and munched contemplatively on an Oreo. Only two more in the bag. Well, he'd leave <u>one</u> of them for Tom.

"Thanks for, uh, stepping out last night."

Tom grunted.

"Where <u>did</u> you sleep."

"Over in the new quad. Dave Carter's room."

Allan was surprised. "I didn't know you <u>knew</u> Dave."

"I didn't." Tom snapped. "But your girlfriend does. Hey, she asked me to go.. I went. No sweat. Okay?"

"Look, Tom...I'm sorry if Ann embarrassed you. I had no idea she was going to..."

"Didn't you? That's funny. Dave sure did. He even knew my fucking <u>name</u>! Couldn't do enough for me, said I was welcome to sack out on his couch any time. Don't worry. It was great."

"No, I mean it, Tom. I'm sorry. I'll do the same thing for you some night."

"Yeah, yeah. Fat chance. Two fucking years I'm trying to get some chick up here for a lousy quick lay! Now you, just a couple dates with this little towny and she's so hot she can't sit down! Jesus, Ross, what do you use, Spanish Fly?"

"Cut it out Tom! I said I was sorry. Hey, it's not like this ever happened before, right?"

"Yeah, yeah. But the next time you two plan to spend the fucking night together (or vice versa) get a motel room, huh?"

"Well, look man, this <u>is</u> my room, you know."

"Uh huh, just like it's <u>your</u> tape recorder, <u>your</u> fucking stereo, <u>your</u> rug, <u>your</u> goddamn bookcase..."

"Hey, I let you use them too, don't I?"

"Oh right. Any time I like. Except when <u>you</u> want 'em yourself that is. Thanks a bundle, man. Big fucking deal!"

Tom banged his heavy fist on the desk. Painfully, Allan thought.

"Look, I'm taking a shower. When I get back, we'll talk. Alright?"

Tom shrugged.

In the shower Allan turned the water full on, feeling each jet like a thin blunt metal rod push into his chest, and back, and shoulders. He raised the palm of his hand to his nose for one last whiff of Ann's perfume. But there was nothing there. Then ruthlessly he lathered all away.

He took a good long time in the shower. When he got back to the room, Tom was standing looking out the window.

"Feeling better?" Allan asked.

Tom looked up. "Sorry to sound off like that. But shit! Sometimes it all just piles up, you know? All the fucking classwork, no chicks, and then <u>her</u> asking me to 'leave you two alone' last night. Christ, Al! How would <u>you</u> feel?"

"Pretty fed up I guess," he admitted.

"And that Dave character! I couldn't believe it. All he could talk about was how <u>great</u> Ann is. And crazy things they used to do in high school—on and on like she was his fucking kid <u>sister</u> or something. I mean who really gives a good God damn about his beautiful fucking childhood!"

"What kind of 'crazy things'?" Allan asked.

"Aw, I don't know, cutting classes to go dance in the woods, stuff like that."

"Dance in the <u>woods</u>?"

"Yeah, and he's got these pictures of her up on her toes like a fairy princess. When she was <u>ten</u>! I tell you that guy is a <u>nut</u> case. I couldn't shut him up!"

"You won't have to do it again, Tom. We'll figure out something."

"You sound sorry I stayed away."

"Hell No! I'm only sorry you <u>had</u> to."

They looked at each other.

Outside, the sky was bright blue. Allan could hear a car chug up the hill. Leaves were fluttering against the wall. A few whirled by the window too fast for him to see. More maples?

"You had breakfast?" he asked Tom.

"Yeah, I ate in the line at the new quad."

"Well I'm starving. How about coming with me to the snack bar?"

"Sure, why not? I'm not getting much done here, God knows."

As he dressed, Allan wondered exactly what Ann had said to Tom. Just how had she phrased her request? He wondered too about Dave Carter—how he had known to expect a visitor, and what was his interest in Ann? Well, he'd just have to ask her about that, wouldn't he?

*   *   *

She phoned that afternoon. She was sure no one saw her coming in, but her father (yes, he HAD been home) knocked on her door very early— supposedly to get her up for breakfast. She thought everything was fine. But to be on the safe side, she thought she had better stay home tonight, and maybe (would he mind awfully?) tomorrow night too. Then they could go out again on Saturday.

Allan minded all right, but he could see the sense of what she said. Still, wasn't there <u>some</u> way they could spend a <u>little</u> time together before Saturday?

She smiled then; he could <u>hear</u> her smiling right through the phone. Well, she offered, he'd said something once about wanting to learn how to ride a bike. If he came over Friday afternoon she might try and teach him. He could even use her daddy's old bike. But it could only be for an hour or two. Tomorrow, say four?

An hour or two was better than nothing. He'd be there.

*   *   *

When Allan arrived, Ann was standing at the front gate holding a bicycle. She welcomed him by nodding in the direction of another bike that leaned against the gate post.

"It was Daddy's," she explained, "But he got a new one last Christmas."

Ann was already wheeling her machine out to the road. Taking his own bike by the handle bars, Allan kicked out the support, and followed her. As he walked, he examined the battered contraption with its rusty handle bars and badly torn seat whose saddle horn seemed purposely designed to make a eunuch of him if he even once leaned too far forward.

Running his hand along the leather saddle, narrow, hard and smooth, he wondered whether girls got sexually aroused riding a bicycle? He imagined Ann mounted and riding, rubbing rhythmically back and forth along the saddle, perhaps twitching now and again from side to side to intensify the pleasure as she raced and jolted. Hmmmm. Possible, possible.

But this train of thought was beginning to get <u>him</u> aroused, and it was <u>not</u> a convenient time. In fact, it was a <u>terrible</u> time. Have to think about something else. That was easy. He imagined <u>himself</u> on the bicycle. The thought alone was painful, and it had the desired effect. By the time they had crossed the bridge and walked uphill to the parking lot of Westlawn cemetery, he was sober of mind and decent in appearance.

"So how do I get aboard this thing?"

"You jump," she called over, "like this."

She made it look quite easy. Still, he hesitated watching her circle lazily around the empty asphalt.

Late autumn sunlight dazzled in her hair. The slight breeze of her riding, the slow up and gentle down of her knees beneath her red and green plaid skirt, the calm assurance of her balance--all charmed him. How could she <u>be</u> so dignified, so graceful in slow flight, while he, still firmly planted on the ground, was just plain scared?

"Come on!" she urged him. "Try it!"

He made an effort, but, as he expected, didn't get far. Setting his right foot on the pedal, he pushed off with his left, and felt the bicycle, propelled by this effort, roll ahead unbalancing him. In an instant his left foot was back on the ground, dragging man and machine to a bumpy halt.

"Not like that! You've got to jump <u>up</u>! Like this! See how easy it is? Come on won't you? Try it again."

Reluctantly he did. And this time the results were better. He actually got his rear end up on the saddle, and was about to put his left foot into contact with the pedal, when the momentum of his first push-off gave out and he skidded down sideways onto the asphalt with the bike on top of him.

"Ouch!" he complained.

"Don't give up." She was cruising past, weaving in and out around him. He supposed this must be meant for inspiration. She was taunting him, teasing him to catch her as she passed just barely out of reach. But he could never catch her on foot; he would have to ride.

And her method worked. He tried and kept on trying. In less than half an hour he was actually able to maneuver fairly competently over the level pavement. He still wobbled slightly, and the low curb on the edge of the parking lot nearest the graves loomed up like a mountain range whenever he came within three feet of it. But somehow he stayed upright even there, and felt besides his fear the first faint thrill of a new freedom that he sensed in time could swell into a wild and soaring joy.

Ann rode beside him now, in parallel, encouraging, praising, warning of upcoming turns, or just cruising silently near, letting the wind they raised between them do the talking. Whenever Allan dared to call across to her, he felt they were flying together, two birds exchanging sounds that were really kisses you could <u>hear</u> instead of feel—two ducks in flight across the pale full moon.

Finally she said, "Time to head for home. Think you can follow me?" "I can <u>try</u>," Allan called after her—and immediately wished he hadn't.

The public road was rougher than the parking lot and much, much steeper than it had seemed to him walking up. And, to make things worse, his bike had no hand brakes. Ann had shown him how to back-pedal to slow down, but up on the level parking lot his problem had not been how to stop but how to keep moving.

Throwing every caution to the winds—as it seemed to Allan— Ann headed straight downhill, not braking at all, just letting gravity whoosh her along ever faster toward the bridge. Gamely he followed, but as the bouncing over the uneven pavement got to him, and the inertia of his downward rush increased, he found himself gripping the handle bars for dear life. Gritting his teeth in what might not be full-blown panic yet, but was fast approaching it, he applied ever greater backward pressure to the pedals.

Ann shot across the uneven wooden planks of the bridge with blissful unconcern. But Allan was coming too fast. He could feel that the first bounce would knock him over the handle bars into the stream. Fiercely he applied his full weight to the pedals. They froze, and just at the base of the hill, his bicycle came to a dead stop, and he toppled into the road—this time with the bike beneath him.

Aware that he had received only minor cuts and scrapes, and pretty certain the bike itself had not been seriously damaged, Allan's first concern was for his clothes. The thought of stumping up fraternity row with a huge hole torn in the seat of his pants did not appeal. But a quick inspection showed no damage in any vital places. One knee burned some beneath the trouser cloth, his shoulder had been scraped, the flat of his left hand was black with dirt and satisfyingly blood-streaked, but otherwise quite presentable.

It had not been a very graceful descent, however, and the sound of Ann's laughter from across the bridge did little to build his confidence. Still, dignity could be repaired. He'd show her!

Stiffly, but carefully, he remounted, pushing off with just the right amount of force to let him ease up into the saddle and pedal steadily across the bridge and up the gravel path to Ann's feet.

"Bravo," she laughed and clapped as he slid off, just inches before he would have run into the front porch steps. "You didn't hurt yourself did you?"

"I'm fine."

"I was sure you were heading for a fall when you hit the bridge. It was very smart of you to stop before you got there, even if you did do it too fast. You're learning."

"Yes," he agreed, "I guess I am."

"Well, I've got to go in now."

"Kiss?"

She looked around quickly. No one in sight.

"All right. But just one."

He was coming for dinner again on Saturday and they agreed to go back to his room right afterward. He must have her home by 11:00, but Tom would be down at Smith that night, so the bedroom coast would be clear.

Walking back to the dorm, Allan felt distinctly proud. He was no hero, and a long way from perfect in Ann's sight he knew, but he was game. And it pleased him greatly to have added one more to his list of first times: cigarettes, alcohol, riding a bicycle, love Ahhh, it was a full life!

Chapter 10: *Cantabile*

Allan drove west through the city, passing places his parents no doubt knew well, but that he scarcely recognized.

Allan's father was a true "family doctor"—the kind everybody wants, but can never seem to find these days. Born and raised in Philadelphia, he had set up practice right out of medical school in the depths of the Depression. The rented garage and servants' quarters of a down-at-the-heels Main Line estate was his combination office, home, and lab. The practice grew, and by the mid-1940s, Young Doctor Charles Ross had a sizable clientele.

In 1939, he married his nurse, Margie Dawson, and moved with his new bride into the Swarthmore house where they still lived—the only home Allan had ever known. Being a Quaker, Dr. Ross's war service added nights and weekends in the local military hospitals to his regular civilian practice, but never took him to the front lines. In February 1943—the same day Stalingrad surrendered—Allan was born.

With his mother a nurse and his father a doctor, it should have been like growing up in a hospital, but it never was. And somehow, the idea of becoming a doctor himself had never captured him. The only patients Allan remembered seeing in his father's waiting room had little things wrong, mostly colds and fevers, sprains and broken bones, measles or the chicken pox. He wondered how many other patients he <u>hadn't</u> seen. His parents had never pushed him, but, as an only child, he suspected they might have shielded him—a lot.

It was full dark by the time he pulled up the familiar driveway this Thanksgiving Eve, and, as always when he was expected, the porch light was on. Its yellow glow reminded him now of the light on <u>Ann</u>'s front porch. He compared their shapes and colors, pleased to find the two so much alike. Later tonight, he told himself, he would stand here, close his eyes, and imagine Ann beside him.

The front door opened and he saw his parents standing there as he climbed from the car. His mother looked the same as ever, but his father looked noticeably older than he remembered. Well, they <u>were</u> older, both of them. Had to be. It was three whole months since he'd been home.

His mother hugged him.

"Oh, it's so <u>good</u> to see you!"

"Welcome home. You look well, son." His father nodded, grinning.

From inside his mother's embrace, Allan nodded back. "You, too, dad."

His mother partially released him, holding him at arm's length for a better look.

"Why, you've lost weight!"

Allan blushed and looked down.

"I don't know. Guess I've been getting more exercise." He didn't specify what <u>kind</u>.

His father offered to help with the bags, and Allan let him carry his guitar. He was afraid the suitcase might be too heavy, though he didn't say so. After all, the man was over 60!

His bedroom hadn't changed. There were his plastic model planes and warships—not even dusty, and his set of miniature flags for all the U.N. countries up to 1960, and the shelves of children's books and records (mostly classical), and the catcher's mitt he'd hardly ever used. It all felt right, and smelled right. All still his.

He stretched out on the bed and stared at the ceiling. All nine planets were there, painted for him by his mother when, as a little boy, he had been sick enough to have to stay in bed for ten whole days. Each morning he would wake to find another planet in position. Later he realized she'd painted them on paper and only pasted them up while he slept, but at the time he'd imagined her working like Michelangelo on the Sistine ceiling, never spilling a drop or waking him once with light or noise. On the morning of the last day, she had added Halley's Comet as a final touch.

The planets seemed to float above him. The old unanswered comfortable questions rose again in his mind. What made that great red splotch on Jupiter? How were Saturn's rings formed? Why was Uranus rolling on its side? And was Pluto really just a moon of Neptune broken loose to steer its vast erratic arc around the light bulb sun that marked the center of his indoor sky?

Professor Ash might tell him if he asked. But he didn't really <u>need</u> the answers. After all: *"The less one knows, the more one has to marvel at."* Still, he might casually inquire some night over dinner at Ann's if he needed to make conversation.

He imagined her whole family gathered for Thanksgiving. She had told him of a grandfather and two grandmothers, plus a gaggle of aunts and uncles coming down. The site of the gathering varied from year to year. This time, it was her mother's turn to play hostess. What were they like, these relatives? What would they <u>hear</u> about him and Ann? And what would they <u>say</u>?

"Really!? You don't say!"

"Nice looking boy, from the college. And talented, plays the piano beautifully, she says."

"What that, Sally? Yes, I know Ann told you he plays jazz, but surely that's just for fun now isn't it? I mean after all he is a college man."

"Well? So don't stop! Go on! Tell me all! Has he...well, you know..."

"Oh, I don't think so. Ann darling, has that boy officially . . . proposed yet? Now where did she disappear to?" Honestly, that girl!"

"Seems like only yesterday we were changing her diapers! I don't know where the time goes "

words to that effect.

Allan only wished he could be there to overhear.

But he wished even more that Ann were here with <u>him</u>. In <u>this</u> bed, where he had slept alone so many nights, had woken up to start so many mornings—happy and sad, ordinary and special. He wanted to show her this—his family, his house, his city—and make them <u>hers</u> too.

He'd only gone upstairs to unpack and wash his hands. But instead here he was on his old familiar bed feeling lonely—lonely for Ann. Even at home now he would be homesick, if Ann wasn't there. That's what love <u>does</u> to you, he thought, makes you feel lonely anywhere apart. He was smiling sadly at this insight when his mother called him down to supper.

As soon as the meal was over, he pleaded tiredness and excused himself. He wasn't really, but he wanted to be alone and think more about Ann. He promised himself he would make it up by spending as much time as possible with his parents over the next three days.

That was Wednesday night. On Saturday, a letter came from Ann.

Williamstown, Thanksgiving Eve

```
Dear Allan,

The yard outside seems empty with all the
leaves raked up, and the trees so bare and night
almost here. The wind is blowing hard, and it
started to rain when we were coming in, but all
```

I can hear now is the wind, and that sounds
very bleak and lonely.

Like this letter I suppose. If you were here
right now, we could sit beside the fire and read
to each other. Do you know *The Bear That Wasn't* by
Frank Tashlin? I hope not, because I'd so love to
read it to you for the first time. And what would
you read to me? Latin love poems? Hmmmmmmmmmmm?

I've been playing the piano tape you recorded
for me over and over. Your music sounds so
sad. Is that really how you feel? If so, you
shouldn't. You have so much to be happy for.

I'm inventing dances for your music. Your
jazz waltz is especially nice. I only wish you'd
keep the tempo up and use a little less *rubato*.
I can tell you've never played for dancers.

Stuff yourself tomorrow. Mother and I are
baking pumpkin pies today. I don't even <u>like</u>
pumpkin pie! But I'll save you a big slice
anyway—maybe the whole pie.

You'd like that, wouldn't you? I do so want
to make you happy. Do I? No, don't answer that.

What a silly letter this is becoming. It must
be that awful wind. Promise you'll never let me
make you sad, or at least not hate me if I ever do.

Take extra-special care of my very favorite
music maker.

Hugs and kisses,

Ann

Allan put the letter down feeling empty. He wanted to find Ann, tell her everything was fine, that of <u>course</u> she made him happy, that he loved her and always would. Her words disturbed him more because he heard her voice in them so clearly. He didn't mind so much that she felt lonely—he was lonely too. But she sounded more discouraged and even strangely self-accusing. How could she be afraid that she would ever make him sad, or even think that he could possibly come to hate her?

He must call her, talk with her, console her. Would she cry on the phone? He <u>wanted</u> her to cry; so he could caress her with his voice into releasing all the stored-up hurt and doubt whatever it might be, let it all run out and away.

But he needed some important news, something to justify a call to her—in case her mood had changed; in case her parents answered; and in case his own parents asked why he was calling someone he'd just left and would be seeing again in a day or two. It was time to tell them about Ann—at least <u>some</u> of it.

He brought the subject up at lunch, and rather formally. He wanted them to know that he was serious, and so he chose his words with care, inserting maybe just a hint of bashful hesitation.

"Mom, dad...look, there's something I've been meaning to tell you but, but I wanted to find the right moment. And I guess it's now."

"Is something wrong, dear?" his mother asked. "Trouble at school?"

"Nothing like that. It's just...you see I've met this girl...and she's kind of special. And, well...I wanted you both to know."

"How old is she, Allan?" his father asked.

"Nineteen next summer. She'll enter Wellesley at mid-term in January."

His mother smiled encouragingly. "What's her name, dear?"

"It's Ann. Ann Ash. Her dad's Professor Wooten Ash, from the astronomy department. Her mother's name is Susan, and she's got a little sister, Cindy, who's only around ten, and "

"And you say you're serious about her?"

"Yes, dad I am. I think .... I want to marry her."

"Mmmmm. And what does <u>she</u> want, Allan?"

His father's question was so practical and to the point, as always. Allan blushed to realize he had never once stopped to ask it himself— only 'what does she want from <u>me</u>?'

He shrugged, "Well, I haven't asked exactly her that yet. Not in so many words."

His father chuckled, folded his napkin and set it down beside his plate.

"Well I suggest you do. Eighteen's a little early to be settling down for life, it seems to me. Suppose your 'Ann' has something else in mind? As I recall <u>you</u> did at that age, Margie."

"Oh, now Chas." Mrs. Ross sighed, pulling her glasses down so she could look at her husband over their rims. "I was only waiting because I hadn't met <u>you</u> yet. Mamma was married at seventeen, and after I hit twenty, pop-pop was convinced I'd die an old maid. A girl is ready when she's ready, and she'll know when that is. But your father's right, dear, don't be making too many plans until you're sure you know her mind—and that she knows yours."

"I didn't mean we'd actually <u>marry</u> right away. I'll have to get through grad school, and I'm sure Ann'll want at least to graduate from Wellesley before we...make things formal. I just wanted you to <u>know</u>."

"We appreciate that, son," his father assured him.

Then for a while no one said anything.

His mother picked the conversation up again, just when it seemed no one was going to.

"What is she like, Allan?"

"Well," he grinned, "she's five foot six, and has blonde hair, kind of long down her back you know, and she likes the outdoors a lot—more than I do really—she actually taught me how to ride a bike! And she dances (modern dance, not classical ballet), but she's going to major in history at Wellesley. And she lived in England all last year with her family while her dad was on sabbatical (that's why she's late starting college), and we share lots of interests— music and... other things."

His voice trailed off. His parents still smiled expectantly. He longed to tell them more, but he didn't know how. So all he said was: "I wish you could meet her. You'd like her a lot."

"I'm sure. She sounds lovely."

"Actually, maybe you can. Before I left, I asked her if she'd like to come down here for a couple days over Christmas break, just before New Years. Then she could drive back to Williamstown with me."

"Of course we'd love to have her," his mother said.

"You don't mind?"

"If her family agrees, then by all means."

"Wow! Thanks, mom, dad! That's great! Is it okay if I call right now and tell her?"

"You mean this minute?"

"Well, I guess I <u>could</u> wait until the rates go down after five."

"No, no. Go right ahead, son. Use my office if you want some privacy."

From the padded leather swivel chair behind his father's desk, Allan dialed long distance for Williamstown, Mass. The connection was weak, but he recognized the voice that answered.

"Hullo?'

"Cindy?"

"Uh huh. Who's this?"

"It's Allan. Allan Ross. Is Ann there?"

"Just a minute."

The receiver dropped on something hard. Allan winced. He could hear muffled house sounds— footsteps, voices, water running (was this the kitchen phone?) then more footsteps, growing louder and at last another voice:

"Hello?"

"Ann? It's Allan."

"Allan! Where are you?"

"Down in Swarthmore, at home. Surprised I called?"

"Well, yes, a little. Are you all right?"

"I'm fine. Your letter came. I read it, and... How <u>are</u> you, really?"

"Oh, you know. All right."

Her calm voice disappointed him. He'd hoped she would sound more excited, pleased to hear his voice. But of course—he should have realized—she was at home, with her parents and Cindy and who knows how many others probably all within earshot. No wonder she sounded remote.

"Did you get <u>my</u> letter?" he asked.

"Yes. It came this morning. That's why I didn't expect to hear from you so soon."

"Look," he said, feeling rude and selfish now, a real fool. "I just asked my folks if you could come to visit for a few days after Christmas, and celebrate New Years Eve with us, you know, like I'd suggested?"

"Oh, you did?"

"They said it's fine! That is, if <u>your</u> folks agree."

"Well," Ann said slowly, "I asked mother; and she said she'd like me to be invited formally, you know, in a letter, but that it would be alright with her; and that she'd persuade Daddy."

"Really? You mean you already asked her?"

"A couple days ago," Ann admitted.

"That's great!. I was afraid you'd be...surprised when I called this way."

"Oh, Allan, it <u>is</u> a surprise, a lovely one. But you really didn't have to call. I hadn't forgotten."

The phone wires hissed and mumbled, covering their silence with the living noise of far machines and other people's talk, all mixed together—background music, there but not any part of them.

Ann broke the spell: "Look, I'd better get off now. This must be costing your folks a fortune."

"I suppose. But I don't want to let you go."

"Oh Allan. Don't be silly. I can hardly hear you anyway. When are you coming back?"

"Sunday. Pretty late I guess."

"Well...I'll be in the library till ten...so if you're not <u>too</u> late..."

"I'll top 70 all the way," he grinned. One little phrase from her, and his world was beautiful again.

"Don't you dare! You're no good to me in pieces! Look, I really must hang up. Drive carefully."

"I will," he promised. "And I'll have my mother write yours first thing tomorrow morning."

"That'll be fine."

"Sweet dreams," he whispered.

"Musical ones," she promised, and blew him a kiss. Then he heard the phone click shut behind her.

He laid the receiver down, and readjusted to the room around him. He had felt himself up there, imagined Ann's front hall while they were talking. Now he had just been whisked miraculously—or maybe cursedly—back from Williamstown to Swarthmore and it took him a moment to focus.

When he told his mother about the invitation letter she seemed pleased. It was a sign to her that Ann's family were good people, concerned and polite. Allan was glad. He wanted his mother to like Ann's folks, just as he did.

*   *   *

It was a little after 8:00 Sunday night when Allan turned into the unloading area behind his West College dorm. Looking up, he saw that the lights were on in his room. That must mean Tom was back already. Damn!

He had counted on arriving first so that he and Ann could get together right away. He ached to hold her. Double damn!!

He slammed the car door angrily, and stalked on over to the library without unpacking anything or even bothering to wave up at Tom, though he thought he saw him up there peering out the window.

Ann was in the reference room. She looked tired, and a little sad. Saying "hello" was awkward. Allan led her into the stacks where they embraced tightly, urgently, in the narrow twilight between dusty shelves. His hands caressed her body through a heavy Irish sweater, reassuring him that she was truly here, and willing to be his if only time allowed. Footsteps approached.

They quickly pulled apart. Ann turned away from the main aisle, keeping her face in shadow; Allan knelt down to scan the titles on the lowest shelf—and to hide the erection that just now was killing him.

Someone, too old and slow to be a student, looked right at them both in passing but said not a word.

Even before the footsteps faded, they embraced again, but the mood was broken. He apologized. So did Ann.

"I don't know what's wrong, tonight," she said. "It feels so cold in here."

"Yeah," he agreed. "It _is_ cold. Maybe we could try the music building or the theatre..."

"I can't. Daddy'll be here to pick me up any minute."

"What?"

"I couldn't get out of it. He just insisted that I wait for him here."

"It's okay. I guess."

"There'll be other times."

"Sure. I know that."

"Are you awfully disappointed?"

His only answer was to take both her hands in his, and squeeze them hard.

"You really <u>are</u> cold," he murmured. "Come on, let's get you back to the ref room where there's a radiator at least."

He wanted to stay with her till her father came, but she asked him not to.

So he left her sitting alone at a long leather-covered table by the wall.

What a homecoming, he thought, as he walked alone back to his dorm room, only to find that Tom was <u>not</u> back after all, or else had gone out somewhere. What a waste of a welcome!

Chapter 11: In Concert

The weeks between Thanksgiving and Christmas vacation were full ones. Classwork took up more of their time now—Ann's as well as his. Most nights they really <u>did</u> study in the library.

Allan and Tom didn't interact much either. In fact, they seldom met, let alone talked. Tom went off somewhere to study most nights, and Allan understood. He knew Tom had received midterm warnings in two courses and that it bothered him.

Any other time, Allan would have tried to help somehow—not that there was much he could do. Tom was a poli-sci major, a subject about which Allan knew next to nothing. Coaching from a Music history and English lit guy wouldn't do much for a future lawyer or prospective politician.

Besides, he was leading a double life right now—or felt like it. First he had his end-of-term recital to prepare for, which required many extra hours of practice, plus the usual classes, tests, and papers. And then there was Ann. It was just too much. He felt sorry for Tom; but damn it, the guy was always goofing off. He had the smarts if only he would apply himself, and get his priorities straight.

*　　*　　*

Allan's recital program was a compromise. Since he wasn't aiming at a concert career, he didn't need show pieces to display spectacular technique, and frankly he didn't care to work that hard. But because this <u>was</u> being graded as his Senior Honors Project, the selections had to be special.

His piano coach, Professor Forrester, originally proposed Stravinsky's *Serenade en La*, Aaron Copland's *Piano Variations*, and the Prokofiev *Sonata #7*. But Allan persuaded him to accept a program containing only works by American composers: Samuel Barber's *Four Excursions* (light and swinging variations on American folk themes); then the Copland *Variations* (too dissonant and technically demanding for Allan's taste, but Forrester had <u>insisted</u> he must play something "really modern"); followed by Gershwin's *Three Preludes* (easy but practically guaranteed to please a crowd). And last, as an exercise to gauge his skill at both harmonic theory and inventiveness, he would be handed a surprise theme on which he was to improvise five variations. Assuming he survived this and the audience offered anything approaching warm applause, Allan planned to offer as an encore his own little jazz waltz *Something for Sylvia*, which, if the moment seemed right, he would rename on the spot and publicly dedicate to Ann.

Ann accepted his need to put in extra practice hours without complaint. Remembering her outburst the week before Thanksgiving, he was surprised but pleased to feel that she understood his reasons and was not annoyed. It meant she was coming around to think as he did in terms of the long haul: their future together.

Now when he had to practice late, he would generally join Ann in the snack bar afterward and walk her home. As it happened, Tom was a snack bar regular. So, often as not, Tom would show up at some point and sit down with them. Some nights, he would even get there before Allan, and gallantly keep Ann company, till his roommate arrived. This was pretty nice of him, really; but somehow Allan always felt a little guilty when he saw the two of them together waiting for him. In fact, he felt doubly guilty: first for making Ann wait, and then for keeping Tom busy being polite to her at the very time when he was struggling so hard to hang on here at Williams. Life just wasn't being fair to any of them!

Ann knew some other students too, of course, so it wasn't <u>only</u> Tom she talked with. There was Dave Carter, for one. But the truth was, Allan didn't really <u>approve</u> of Dave. The guy was just a little too <u>arty</u>, too self-consciously <u>romantic</u>. And that story Tom had told about Dave and Ann being friends back in high school and going off alone to dance in the woods and all. It sounded odd.

No, on balance, Allan was grateful Tom was there to be with Ann when he couldn't be himself. She must be lonely. After all, she was not only a professor's daughter, but practically the only girl on campus. And while that made her the natural target of many approaches, it must also make her feel at least a little defensive.

Allan wished, not for the first time, that Williams were co-ed. He himself was done roaming now, of course. But there were all the other guys to consider. He honestly wished them the same chance to find pleasure and contentment, to love and be loved, that he now enjoyed with Ann, Besides, having other girls on campus might give her more chances for companionship, and gossip, and innocent fun.

As for not-so-innocent fun, the two of them were managing pretty well, considering. With term papers due and exams closing in, guys were always around the dorm studying and typing to all hours—so no more overnights. But there were other places, and other times.

It surprised Allan how much fun they both could have without fully stripping, or even noticeably mussing their clothes. Ann had helpfully begun wearing wrap-around skirts ("_un_wrap-around skirts" he liked to call them), and a brassiere that conveniently opened from the front. She had bought this in Pittsfield, just for him she said, and her saying so pleased him enormously.

One night she actually seduced him right on stage at the grand piano of the small rehearsal hall in the music building. Tired of waiting for him, she had left the snack bar, slipped in a side door, past the practice rooms, and surprised him halfway through the Prokofiev _Sonata #7_. (It wasn't really on his program now, but it challenged him at least as much as the Copeland and he preferred it by miles.) Before he could speak, she had dropped her coat, hiked up her skirt, and slipped around to straddle his lap with her bare arms draped about his neck.

"Oh, don't let _me_ disturb you. Please, go on."

And he <u>had</u>! Somehow, he had managed to play through that entire third movement with Ann, her legs wrapped tight around his waist, teasing, and kissing, and fondling him mercilessly. After that though, there was no hope. The best he could do was struggle free, switch off the lights, lock the door, and spread his overcoat out for them both on the floor. Hmmm, he wondered, was <u>this</u> perhaps what Sir Walter Raleigh had really done for Queen Elizabeth?

*   *   *

On the night of his recital, Ann came backstage and adjusted Allan's black bow tie for him, just before he went on. (It was a real one her father had loaned him, not the clip-on job that had come with his old Glee Club tux.) He found this wifely gesture enormously on-turning, and was still grinning broadly as he walked on stage to play.

He stumbled early—in the Barber of all things—getting his fingers tied up in the cross-over passage of the syncopated Number Three *Excursion* (his very favorite), and slurring a few of the runs in the final "Barn Dance" movement. These lapses started him sweating with embarrassment; but they seemed to steady him down, too. Copeland proved endurable after all, and the Gershwin *Preludes* really pleased him—as bluesy and pert by turns as a Fred Astaire tap-dance.

He was still breathing with relief, when professor Forrester came out from the wings and presented him a note card with but a single word printed on it: *Greensleeves*.

So <u>that</u> was to be his improv theme. Allan nodded thanks; shook his head to clear it, then turned to the audience to announce five original variations on a theme they really <u>ought</u> to recognize. It pleased him to keep the listeners guessing just a moment longer, and of course it also heightened the suspense.

He started with the melody alone, right hand only. Hey, Forrester hadn't said he couldn't, and this meant that adding even basic harmony would now count as one variation! He did that next. So four more still to go. The next variation was stronger, more adventurous; not fast but fuller—as he might have played it on the organ. With number three he began to swing, go lyrical a little, but still holding something back. By number four he was safely into his own world—voicings all Debussy, but with achingly sweet harmonics borrowed from the blues; and slow, as slow as if the song itself were dying.

On his own, he would have rather stopped there. Nothing more to say—just the need to take someone in his arms—and Allan knew exactly who that someone was. But he'd agreed <u>five</u> variations, so he just went loud, building chords as wide and grand as his hand-breadth allowed (Brubeck was so damned lucky to have those monster paws of his!), and ended with an impressive crash of sound.

He got applause—even some whistles of enthusiasm from the few dozen listeners in the hall (not a full house by any means, but then classical music wasn't exactly a big draw on campus—even when the concert was free). So he did come back to play his Jazz Waltz; but without the dedication.

At the last minute, his resolve failed him. It seemed too much like bragging to claim Ann as his inspiration—particularly when, in this case, it wasn't strictly true. He didn't even mention that the piece was his; just called it "*Something of a Waltz*."

Besides, he decided, Ann deserved a waltz of her very own, not a hand-me-down. He would write her one for their wedding—maybe sooner, if there was time.

Backstage, he accepted congratulations limply. He was sweaty and tired, and woozy with relief that the ordeal was over. He had no idea what he had really sounded like, he only hoped he had played well enough to keep his honors grade intact.

Professor Forrester, as usual, was blunt to the point of gruffness. "Uneven, but competent," he began.

"You lost your concentration badly in the Barber, but I don't think many people will have noticed. Interpretation is no substitute for sound technique, but it's fair to say you played with feeling."

He paused.

"Don't look so glum. It was a professional effort and I'm judging you accordingly. We'll go over the details Monday morning. Frankly, I'd say you saved your best playing for the encore. Slight, but endearing. You should pay more attention to composing. I'll help you—if you're willing to work at it. Writing clearly matters to you more than concert playing. Overall, a decent job." And he shook Allan's hand.

Damn! Allan thought, guiltily. Forrester always could see through him like a piece of glass. But at least it was over now.

He got away as quickly as he could and phoned his parents. At the last minute they hadn't made it up to hear him—even doctors sometimes get the flu, and his mother didn't drive—but with the help of Forrester he had arranged to tape-record the whole performance and would send it down to them.

His dad seemed better, though he still sounded hoarse, and the glow of pride in his mother's voice when he told her how the concert went was wonderful to hear. All his life, it seemed, he had been making his parents happy, and they had done the same for him. Not a bad exchange, he thought, not bad at all.

He hung up the phone and looked around for Ann. It was unfair, he knew, but he felt just a little irritated that she hadn't been right there waiting as he came offstage. After-performance let down had hit him full-force by now. All he wanted was to go off alone with her somewhere and get the sex need in him out and down so that he could really, really sleep. No tender play tonight. He would just possess her. He had earned the right. And she must be eager too. It was almost a week since they'd last...

"Allan! Over here!"

There she was, smiling and waving. And Tom was with her.

"Damn it to hell," Allan thought behind his smile. Why does <u>he</u> have to be here? Tonight of all nights! <u>Now</u> what are we going to do?"

What they did, it turned out, was to all pile into Allan's two-door Ford and drive across the New York line to a roadhouse where he and Tom could legally order drinks and even Ann could have a beer. She ended up taking sips of Tom's rum cola and Allan's vodka tonic too, since it turned out she didn't care much for beer.

The piano player in the bar was a Negro, grizzled and gap-toothed, but with tireless hands. He could been around since the 1930s Allan guessed, brought up on stride and boogie-woogie, already set in his ways before bop came along. Nothing cool or intellectual about him. His sound was rough, direct, powerful and gutsy. He didn't announce his songs, or take requests, or chatter with the customers. He played.

Now and then he'd nod when someone dropped a couple quarters or stuffed a dollar bill into the highball glass on top of the piano. He smoked constantly without ever seeming to drop an ash or remove his hands from the keyboard to tend his cigarette. For all Allan knew, the man might have been blind. But he could play. God, he could play.

"Yeah, not bad," Tom conceded as they drove home, leaning forward over Allan's shoulder from the back seat. "You really dig that old time music, Ross?"

Allan looked across at Ann on the front seat beside him. How, he wondered, did other guys in cars always seem to have their girls snuggling up beside them as they drove? Maybe the kind of girls he'd dated were just too safety-conscious (or was it too sex-cautious?) to risk distracting the driver of a moving vehicle. Oh well....

Ann caught his smile and passed it back, squeezing her eyes shut for just an instant as she did so. He felt sure that she had meant this for him alone, knowing the darkness would hide it completely from Tom.

When they reached Ann's house, Tom at least had the decency to wait inside the car while Allan walked her to the door.

"I'm sorry about tonight," she said.

"Me too," he agreed. "I want you so badly it hurts."

"I could tell," she said. "But we couldn't have...not tonight. My period's started early. Tension I guess. It always happens like this."

Allan honestly tried to be sympathetic. "You should have told me you weren't feeling well. We didn't need to go out at all. I could have had you home hours ago."

She laughed. "Don't be silly. It's only a period. I'm fine, really. It's just a nuisance."

On the porch they kissed, tightly embracing. He turned her head slightly to bite her ear. He bit hard— from desire <u>and</u> frustration, and as she twisted free he blurted "I just want to be inside you so damned badly "

She brushed a hand over her hair and said in a helpless voice: "I miss you, too. You just don't know! Maybe tomorrow night. We'll see. I've got to go in now, it's late. I'll call you. Take care. Please?"

She kissed him one last time and was gone.

Back in the car, Allan didn't speak to Tom. He resented him having tagged along tonight but why say it? The guy had meant well. Hell, he and Tom had been friends for almost four years, and this was a big night for Allan. Of course Tom would want to be there. Besides, knowing now that he couldn't have taken Ann to bed anyway made it all pretty academic.

He parked behind the Di-Gamm House and the two of them walked up Main Street to West College. There was a live wind blowing, and the flat black starless sky suggested snow was coming. Allan turned to comment on it. But he stopped when he saw Tom's face, set hard against the wind, and scowling. Somehow, he didn't seem to be in a talkative mood.

Once they were up in the room, Allan proposed coffee. Tom shrugged agreement and set about getting cups out while Allan went down the hall to fill up their old metal coffee pot from the drinking fountain. As he returned, Tom was ladling spoonfuls of instant into their chipped mugs of glazed red clay.

"Don't give me too much," Allan warned, "or I won't close my eyes all night long."

Tom muttered something in reply.

"What'd you say?"

"I said no need to worry about that."

"Oh." Allan nodded. Guess he meant there wasn't that much coffee left to share. Well, he'd buy a new jar tomorrow.

Tom thrust Allan's mug at him so hard some hot coffee sloshed over the rim and burned his hand.

"Ow!"

"Sorry."

"Something eating you?" Allan asked, rubbing the scalded patch between his thumb and index finger dry against his other sleeve.

"Should there be?" Tom looked straight at him, unsmiling.

"Nothing I know about. That's why I asked."

"Then no. Nothing's wrong." Tom screwed the lid back on the coffee jar.

Allan sank down on the sofa and closed his eyes. He wanted to see Ann, to visualize her smiling at him, kissing him. But it didn't work. He only heard her voice. He couldn't picture what she looked like at all; not her face or hair, not her legs, not even her eyes. He could remember sounds— whispered words and laughter—and the texture of her skin beneath his fingers—so incredibly soft and smooth along her cheek. But what did she <u>look</u> like? The picture simply wouldn't form.

Tom went into the bedroom, and came back a few moments later wearing his rich-looking smoking jacket over jockey shorts and a rumpled T-shirt. *Vestimentum hominem fecit*—"clothes make the man." Allan shook his head and failed to totally suppress a chuckle.

"What?" Tom asked.

"Nothing," Allan said. "Just thought of something funny, but it isn't worth explaining, the joke would be gone."

Tom shrugged and picked up a copy of *Playboy*, the latest issue. It was Tom who subscribed; though Allan glanced through every issue at least once, just for the nudes and cartoons.

Allan was frowning almost before he realized that he resented Tom reading *Playboy* tonight. And why? Crazy reason. Because when <u>he</u> had looked at this month's Playmate, she had made him think of Ann. And now Tom was looking at the same girl and thinking of somebody else. Maybe "Mary" or whatever the hell his girl's name was.

Then he shook it off. Hey, what did it matter! He and Tom were just <u>different</u> people that's what had made them friends.Each of them was himself and there was no need to compete—at anything. Allan was modern jazz, Tom was rock and roll. Allan was Swarthmore, Tom was South Boston. Allan was a frat rat, Tom a swinging non-affiliate. Tom never talked about wanting a steady girl. But Allan did and now he finally had one. So great. Fine. Where was the problem? Yet there <u>was</u> a problem.

And the problem was himself.

Here he was, everything going his way, and still he felt so damned insecure that he didn't even like his own best friend around when he was with Ann. He felt ashamed to admit it, but there it was. Allan Ross was jealous of Tom Petard!

Tom turned a page.

Allan decided to say nothing about tonight. Tomorrow would be different. This time tomorrow night he and Ann might be lying right here on this sofa—together. He rehearsed with his body just how he would roll to one side to give Ann a little more room, and then roll back tight against her. He wanted her to be comfortable. He always wanted that. He was proud of wanting that. Even when his own passion was raging, he still cared that Ann should be comfortable. He would always care.

*   *   *

The note from Allan's mother inviting Ann down to Swarthmore after Christmas arrived next day. Ann wrote back accepting with pleasure, and added that her own mother would be writing soon.

Allan had already planned how they would spend their days together. He reviewed the places he would go with her: Valley Forge, and Independence Hall because she liked history; then maybe shopping at Wannamaker's, and of course the Franklin Institute—especially the Planetarium. But anywhere they went it would be together, and that alone would be enough to make it fun.

Best of all, if they were ever left alone in the house, they would have their choice of bedrooms: his parents', his own, the guest room. Hell, why not cushions on the rug by the living room fireplace?

Allan spent far less time with Ann than he'd have liked in the days before Christmas break. But they both had exams, and Tom seemed somehow to be always either up in the room studying or trying to get some sleep. The music building too, was humming with activity (no pun intended), and the library so crowded now that even there they could seldom find space to themselves.

The day he left for home, Allan could sense in Ann the same tense nervousness he felt himself.

"Don't worry," he assured her, smiling. "Things'll be fine once we get down to Swarthmore!"

Chapter 12: *Recitative*

180 Westlawn Road
Williamstown 26, Mass.

To: Mrs. Charles Ross
2340 Fernold Drive
Swarthmore, Penna.

December 21, 1964

Dear Mrs. Ross:

Just a brief note to wish you all the best this holiday season; and to reconfirm that Ann will arrive in Philadelphia's South Station at 6:45 pm on December 28. I understand that Allan will be meeting her train.

Inviting my daughter into your home was a lovely gesture. Children take so much into their own hands these days. Ann thinks I'm terribly old-fashioned to have asked you for a formal written invitation. But your letter was so warm and gracious that I sense you understand and share my feelings.

You must be very proud of Allan. In all the years my husband has been teaching, I cannot remember meeting a more charming and talented young man. His playing makes even our battered old spinet sound beautiful, and his recital last week was an absolute delight. I'm so glad he recorded it on tape for you.

```
I hope you won't think this too forward of
me, but Allan mentioned you and your husband
might drive up here a day or two early for his
graduation in June.If you do, Wooten and I
would like very much you to join us for dinner
one evening during your stay. Do say that
you'll come.

   Best wishes from our family to yours for
Christmas and the New Year,

Cordially,

Susan Ash
```

*   *   *

22 Dec. 1964

Tom!

You'd cleared off by the time I got back from taking Ann to lunch, so I leave this to greet you after Christmas Break. HAPPY NEW YEAR! I would order up a full peal of bells to celebrate your coming, but I think Rev. Jones is still sore at me for pounding out the "St. Louis Blues" this noon on carillon instead of "The Old Hundredth" originally scheduled for that slot. Ann, who was up there with me (hands over ears most of the time) dared me to do it. So of course.....

We both about died laughing. You'd have too if you'd seen Jones's face after running up all those stairs to get us down out of there. He was, shall we say, "pissed off?" Yes. Let's say exactly that. Anyway, considering all the times you've been after me to break some rules and let go once in a while I assume you approve of this little action heartily.

Now then, to business. For your enlightenment (and because I still have half an hour to kill before my three freshmen come running up here looking for their ride to Philly) I shall set down a list of New Year's Resolutions for the two of us. Naturally, you can ignore them-at least all but the last one, which is kind of an all-or-nothing proposition. But otherwise I'm willing to abide by them if you will.

<u>Number 1</u>—I will stop lecturing you about your taste and opinions, if you will stop lecturing me about mine.

On second thought, if we stop criticizing each other, we might have nothing left to talk about. But what the hell, just for variety, let's give it a try. Seems worth the risk to me.

<u>Number 2</u>—I hereby solemnly resolve NOT to play my <u>Highland Pipers on Parade</u> album after ten o'clock on weeknights if YOU agree not to play your Rolling Stones <u>Out of Their Minds</u>, which they must be to sound like that in public (Whoops, sorry. Well, so much for Resolution Number 1...) before nine in the morning on weekends. You know it drives me figuratively up the wall, and literally out of bed. A man's bed is his castle, or should be. Let's keep it sacred. Okay?

<u>Number 3</u>—Your best friend might not tell you, but your roommate will: GET A HAIRCUT! You don't look "tough," or "beat," or even "cool." You look like a wet cocker spaniel. The Beatles get away with it, but at least they have straight hair and it looks well-groomed (if a little oddly shaped). But you cannot—you really look like "the night they burst the mattress," and what's more, you are not making X million dollars per record, and <u>you</u> can't sing. (Aha, you say. Does that imply that the Beatles CAN? Well, all right, yes. I'm willing to concede the point. Chalk it up to Christmas spirit if you like. Not that their voices are that GOOD, mind you, but they <u>are</u> pretty clever at what they do. How you can put your Rolling Stones anywhere near them is beyond me. The Beatles are artists; the Rolling Stones are freaks! But I digress.)

A haircut costs $2.00 maybe twice a month plus a half-hour wait at the barber's. But in return, you get "respectability." Yes, this is phony and superficial and I know you despise it, but trust me, Tom, you <u>need</u> it. It lets you talk to the people you need to reach: deans and professors and job interviewers and grad school reps and what not. It means you can go anywhere you like, high-class or low, Village coffee house or Club 21. Sure, if you get drunk and start wrecking the place, or can't pay your bill, they will still chuck you out—but at least they let you <u>in</u>. The way you look today, they won't. That woolly badge of freedom you peer out from under is like a signboard around your neck with a message in big black letters reading: "OCCUPATION: REBEL. KICK ME HARD!"

You don't have to take my word for this, but please, man, try it just once. Give up the "symbol" of defiance and behave exactly the same way you do now, and I'll bet you a fifth of Seagrams that in two months you'll find you have done more and made a bigger impact on everyone around you—from profs and deans to campus clowns and (hem, hem) girls—than you ever did before.

Interruption. Dean Berkley just phoned. Seems Jones went storming in there asking to have me permanently banned from the belfry. Our Mutual Friend managed to soothe him down, but suggests that I be a bit more conservative in my choice of spontaneous improvs from now on, or better yet, stick to the scheduled program.

You see, Tom, this is just what I mean. I have "lived right" for so long now, that I don't get treated like an outlaw even when I'm caught red handed. When I TRY to break the rules, they simply stretch themselves around me. And it could happen to you!

<u>Number 4</u>—Not so much a resolution as a request, and a pretty serious one. I know I've got no right to ask this, and believe me, I wouldn't if there were any other way, but I just don't see one.

You know Ann starts at Wellesley just three weeks after Christmas Break. Between my prepping for exams and her packing for college, we won't have much time to be alone together at best. But I want to make the most of what little time we do have, and frankly, old buddy, I can't do that if you're always hanging around.

I guess I don't have to tell you how much Ann means to me. You've been in on our little secret from the first night. You've seen me come stumbling back from taking her home with the glazed, crazed look in my eyes and that slap-happy grin on my face. I am nuts about the girl, absolutely loopy. You used to warn me love was dangerous, and boy, were you ever right! It is a blind obsession, totally irrational, and absolutely a blast and a half!

Whenever she's around I change inside. What I did in the belfry today shows it. You've been after me to loosen up, break out of my quiet image and let things go to hell a little now and then. Well, what you couldn't persuade me to dare in three years, Ann has bewitched me into in under three months!

Whenever we're alone I just can't keep my hands off her. Even when we're not alone it's gotten so I hardly care what anybody sees. I know she feels self-conscious sometimes, and I can't exactly blame her. She is the "Professor's Daughter" after all, and everybody in town knows her and watches her (or so she thinks). Besides, a "nice" girl is supposed to keep up appearances even during the courtship.

Courtship...that's what it really is, Tom. I've felt married to her almost from the start. But we're _not_ married yet, and God only knows how long we'll have to wait yet till we can be. Until then, there just never is or can be enough time for us to be alone in.

And so I get jealous. I feel guilty as hell about it sometimes, but it's true. I'm jealous of her professors because they keep her in class when we could be off somewhere alone. Jealous of her parents because they know so much more about her than I do yet and there's so much I _want_ to know. I get jealous of YOU sometimes, because you don't just ignore us when we come into the snack bar, or don't make up some excuse to leave us alone the minute Ann comes in here. Hell, I'm jealous of her bath tub because _it_ gets to hold her naked every night and I can't--yet.

This is crazy, Tom, just crazy, and I know it. But knowing doesn't help. I'd always read it was the _girl_ who was supposed to feel this way, but I want to give up my whole life for her—nothing I am or can be seems to matter without <u>her</u>. I want to build a future with her, a home, children, everything. I want to play for her, write music for her, become famous just so SHE can be proud knowing I belong to her.

Imagine WANTING to be a husband! The guys at Di-Gamm would laugh me out of the house if they knew. But that's what I feel! I get such a kick out of courting her. I don't even mind the "official" dinners—making conversation with her folks—and her little sister butting in to tease us every few minutes. Trying to keep a straight face and look calm, while our fingers are groping for each other beneath the table, or we're playing footsy and praying we don't kick somebody else's shin—all that's fun, too, in a way. But it's also been wearing for both of us, and somehow it's just not enough any more.

When Ann comes down to Swarthmore over New Years I'm going to propose to her. Her parents will probably say we're too young (and if they didn't say it, MY parents WOULD). I suppose they're right too, as far as earning a living and setting up housekeeping goes.I need to graduate, and I don't intend to ask Ann to give up college either. So we're looking at a four or five year wait—maybe 1969 or'70. But we can use that time to plan once we're formally engaged.

My first freshman just showed up. I've parked him in the corner with a book while I finish this letter. It's become a massive missive, which is not at all what I planned. But, since Ann came along, lots of the things I planned are working out a whole lot differently.

The point of all this is, that once we <u>are</u> "officially" engaged, with ring, bell, book, and candle, and the works, we really <u>will</u> be married in every way that counts. But since we can't start living on our own until at least next summer, we'll just have to go on somehow as we are now, stealing time to be together in. Only then it will be real—not just two kids making out, but two adults in a full-on love affair.

I guess we'll still be hiding some of the truth from her parents and everybody else except our closest friends—you, of course, and probably Dave Carter (who seems to know so much--he must have his own crystal ball). I'm counting on you to help us, Tom, by simply—I know this sounds crass, and I AM sorry—by simply keeping out of our way.

What I'm asking amounts to working till midnight or so every night at the Library rather than using the room, and if you see the shades drawn when the library closes holing up somewhere else for the night.

That's a hell of a lot to ask, I know. But it's only for three weeks. Then she'll be off to Wellesley and however we manage after that will be up to us. I've toyed with the idea of renting a room in or near Boston and letting guys from the house use it when Ann and I can't be there. I've even got some high school friends at Harvard now, and maybe they can help us somehow. We'll see.

To make this a little easier, here's a belated present for you: an extra set of keys to my car. Merry Christmas! Take it any time you like to drive up Bennington, or Holyoke, or anywhere. And I promise you, Tom, once Ann is gone, I'll do the same for you and Mary, or whoever you may start dating, any time you ask. So <u>will</u> you do this for us? It means so much.

But you'll have to be discrete. So long as Ann doesn't know I've asked you to stay out of our way, I think she'll just accept our good luck and relax. But she's awfully down on being "unfair" to anyone. It's one more thing I love about her, really. So let's just keep this between us, okay?

The truth is, I think you scare her a little, Tom. She almost never mentions you when we're alone, and whenever I say something about you she gets all tight and nervous. Maybe she still feels bad about sending you off to Dave's that very first night. Or she may worry that you'll let on to someone who might tell her folks about us. I don't know.

So far as I'm concerned of course you COULD tell her parents or shout it from the cupola of West College! I'm not ashamed of anything. If it were up to me I would have told them long ago. But Ann won't hear of it. At least not now.

Hope you're not sore at me. It's not that we don't enjoy having you around. We <u>do</u>. But with so little time left now, we'd rather spend it alone together than with anybody, even our best friends.

Another freshman has arrived, and I'll bet the third is wandering around helplessly downstairs somewhere trying to find me. Everybody's getting restless to leave, even me.

God, Tom, you should see them! Freshman Number 1 has hair as long as yours but kinkier and less clean. Whatever I said about your mop, at least you wash it! Number 2 is toting a rolled up copy of some rag called <u>Ramparts</u> and tells me that he's in a big hurry because he's got to hitch on down from Philadelphia to Washington to join some crazy demonstration. "Merry Christmas and a Happy Revolution to all!" I shudder for the younger generation.

Thomas, I close. Indulge your Christmas fancies, and in the New Year—oh, it is a roommate's parting prayer—I wish that you may fall in love as wonderfully and crazily as I have and come to know the same joy with your girl that I know with Ann.

All right, ye rabble. Hyah! Head 'em up, Moooove 'em out!

Take care,

Allan

P.S. Excuse this scrawl, my Smith-Corona was already packed. The two bucks I owed you for cigarettes are in the lower right hand drawer of my desk, right beside a supply of what are known in the trade as "reservoir ends." Help yourself. And do nothing I wouldn't do given the same chance. Ho. Ho. Ho. See you sometime late Sunday, January 3, 1964--no 1965!!

—A.R.

*　　*　　*

Williamstown
December 24, 1964

Dearest,

Christmas Eve? Bah, humbug! This time two days ago I was curled up on the couch beside you feeling so warm and cozy and at home. And now I AM at home, and you are miles away, and I feel like a lost dog in the snow—all cold and frightened and confused and miserable.

Officially I've got a headache. Mother and Cindy are last-minute shopping, Daddy looked in a little while ago, mumbled something cheerful at me in that maddening way of his, and charged upstairs again to grade papers.

I dread the next few days. We leave tonight for my grandmother's where I can look forward to being paraded and teased and hugged and fussed over and talked at for hours and hours by sticky-sweet aunts and frowsy married cousins and expected to help in the kitchen or change smelly diapers for somebody's squalling brat, and always to smile and be a "lady" when I'd rather be practically anywhere else in the world!

It's awful to be a girl. Simply nothing you can do except put up with being bossed around and lectured to and warned about doing this or scolded for wanting that. Boys have it so much easier. You just don't know!

No use being cranky I suppose. But when I'm alone—really alone like now—I just start hating everything and everybody in the world

and wishing I could just for once stop having
to be ME all the time. This is sounding worse
by the minute. I will stop it.

Whenever Daddy gets impossible—and that's
pretty much all the time these days—mother goes
and DOES something, like wash blinds or bake
cookies or dig up the garden. It must work. At
least she's still alive and reasonably sane after
all these years of being married to him.

I think I'll try her method. I shall go out
to the kitchen right this minute and bake a
loaf of banana bread just for you. Would you
like that? I hope so. I hope too that baking
you something will make you seem less far away
and take my mind off miserable me for a little
while at least.

I know what you are going to say—would say
to me right now if you were here. But please,
don't. Let's not tell them anything until after
I'm away at school? Maybe not even then. Not
your folks, and certainly not mine. Please
promise me. Please?

And promise me too you'll sit down the moment
you get this letter and write me back? I worry
about you. And I miss you. Dreadfully.

Be very good to yourself for me,

your

Ann

* * *

January 2, 1965

You poor Kid!

I got your letter but there wasn't time to write before my bus left. It must be hell for you, all those relatives and then to top it off Swarthmore hanging over you. You're a lot braver than you think. Don't kid yourself.

One thing you wrote really bugs me though. Stop worrying so much about what people think. It's you and me that count, right? There's nothing to feel guilty for. We wanted each other, that's all. And we were strong enough to not pretend it didn't happen. That's the truth and you know it.

You can't live your whole life being "grateful" because someone's "good" to you. Sure he's a nice guy, and you're flattered that he cares, and you don't want to hurt his feelings. That's swell. But you don't <u>love</u> him. And it's no good pretending you do. Especially not to him.

Stop punishing yourself. Look, you are not "his" girl, or anybody else's— not even mine. You're your <u>own</u> girl, for as long as you want to be, and nobody can change that unless <u>you</u> let them. Got that?

You want more? Wait till you hear this. When I get in the room I find this note on my desk. And you know what it says? That he thinks maybe you're <u>afraid</u> of me, and won't I be a pal and leave you two lovebirds alone together more. Can you <u>believe</u>!? It's a riot. I don't know if I should laugh or cry.

I told you he didn't know. He doesn't even <u>suspect</u>. Remember I've known the guy for three years. But he has to find out sometime, so come on; let's you and I tell him. Now.

You're not the only one who's sorry for him. Hell, you think I LIKE sneaking around behind his back? It makes me feel like shit!

But how do you think I feel when I come back to the room and find the door locked and know it means you're in there with him? And how do you think I like hearing him go on about all the cute little things you do for him, and how he's buying you something sexy for a surprise? I want to bust his head open for him, and so help me I'll do it too if this goes on.

I'm sick of lying, and hiding, and I'm goddamned sick of waiting till he's asleep then hanging around in the dark till you can sneak out of your house so we can drive up some dirt road in <u>his</u> car for a quick fuck. I want some <u>real</u> time with you, baby. In a real bed.

And a little respect wouldn't hurt any either. It's degrading never to be able to phone you or come around the house in daylight. Do you ever think of that? Do you?

Look, if you won't tell him, I will. There's just no other way. Deep down you know I'm right.

About our overnight in Boston; you didn't need to worry. My folks weren't sore about me staying out. I think they guessed I hadn't been staying up here to work on a school project like I told them. But they don't pry. Hell, half the time they don't even <u>notice</u>.

You'd like my Mom if you met her though. And she'd like you just because you were a professor's daughter. That's typical I guess. Both my parents are very class conscious--they know they're lower-middle and they hate it. But, what the hell. That's their problem not ours.

Once you're at Wellesley, you can get to my part of town by bus pretty easily. So between your coming here and my going there we ought to do all right, on weekends anyway.

The minute Allan drops you home, I'm betting he'll go off to practice for a couple hours at least. So that means right now, while you're reading this, I'm up here waiting for you all alone. Don't think, don't call, just come.

I'll pull the shades down so you'll know he's not here. If he is, they'll be up and I'll have his car and meet you at the snack bar. He left an extra set of car keys tucked in with that note, as a present. "Merry Christmas."

Stinks, doesn't it? But until you tell him, or I do, we've got to take it any way we can get it. That's life, baby. At least it is where I come from.

So do whatever you want. Only just remember you're <u>free</u>.

I mean it!

Tom

Chapter 13: *Tremolo*

Ann's train was an hour late pulling into South Station, and the snow was falling hard. She had called up two nights earlier to say she'd be staying an extra day in Boston with her aunt before coming down. That had been bad enough, but this unexpected hour's delay in the heavy snow somehow hurt Allan worse than the whole day without her he had been warned about.

His eyes ran down the line of drab silver snow-topped coaches slowing to a halt in the noisy station shed. Passengers swarmed out like ants from a hill, bemusing his cold-numbed mind still further by their energy and numbers. Then he saw her.

She was lugging a worn brown suitcase down the platform. He struggled toward her through the press of passengers--the way a salmon fights his way up-stream, and with the same ambition. He called out to her. No use, too much noise. But she had seen him now, and was striding toward him briskly, stiffly, smartly.

She was so cute it made him ache to look at her: camels-hair coat flapping open, green skirt patting her dark-stockinged legs. She came nearer, smiling, raised a hand to wave. He waved back at her wildly. She was so rich, so perfect. God, it hurt to see her!

She wore no hat and the long bright hair poured down to her shoulders. She looked like someone else, he thought, someone magical, and impossibly remote. Who <u>was</u> she?

Then he remembered: Lauren Bacall in *Key Largo*! Except that Ann's hair was blonde— ash-blonde to match her name.

Face to face now, she set the suitcase down, and looked up at him, smiling. (Or was that a smirk? She must think him an idiot staring at her this way!)

"What's on <u>your</u> mind, hmmmmmmmmmmmm?" she asked pertly.

"Rape. Right here on this freezing station platform; with everyone watching and cheering us on. And for hours, and hours," he thought. But all he said was:

"You."

They kissed each other hard enough and long enough to lose their breaths. Then he picked up her suitcase, offered her his free arm (which she declined), and they walked off together toward the escalator, trying at first to talk above the crowd and the roar of the train that was now pulling out toward other destinations.

"How was your TRIP?" he bawled.

"FINE. I SLEPT the WHOLE WAY. Were you WAITING LONG?"

"HUH?"

"DID YOU HAVE TO <u>WAIT</u> LONG?"

"HUH-UH," he lied to her (smoothly, he thought) "I JUST GOT HERE. But it's REALLY been SNOWING."

For a while then they were silent, gliding up the narrow escalator, and clicking heels across the marble floor in the echoing cavern of the terminal. At the door, which he gallantly held open for her to pass through, she smiled a complacent "thank-you." This led effortlessly into another kiss as the feather-flaked night air hit them full, and she started to pull up her black velvet collar.

"Car's over this way," he gestured. "Not too far."

"Brrrrrrr. It's freezing! Let's run!"

They broke into a trot, Allan leading the way. He found it hard to keep his balance in the slick snow with Ann's suitcase weighing him down on one side—but as always, her presence inspired him and he managed. Soon they were safe on the front seat of his car, and warming nicely.

He held both her hands and looked long into her eyes and told her how much he'd missed her, how glad he was that she'd come, and what a long time it seemed since they'd last been together. The usual things.

She ruffled his hair, said "Awwwww," and looked mock-sorrowful just to tease him and make him laugh. But he wanted, needed, more and tried for it.

She pulled away and warned him gently to be patient. He said that was okay, he understood, as if it didn't matter much. Only he hoped they could maybe do something--that night, he wanted her so badly. But, he added quickly, he was just so goddamned glad to see her! She looked great!

When she put her ungloved fingers to his cheek, he caught them up and kissed them. And they looked at one another for a while. He had to climb out and brush the windows clear again before they could drive away.

As they pulled off, snow was falling fast and despite the darkness overhead, the streets blazed white and yellow under lamp glare.

Philadelphia was a maze of one-way streets and there had been much building in the three years Allan had been at college. It was hard enough spotting street signs through the falling snow, let alone making out house numbers. And before long, he was totally lost.

For a while he drove on, trying not to let Ann know. He wanted so much to be perfect for her. But at last he pulled into a filling station and asked the way to Swarthmore. The attendant told him he just needed to keep going straight. He had been right all the time and never known it. Typical! Damn!!

Snow perched in the crotches of trees, capped every fire plug and lamp post, muffled traffic signs and billboards, and swirled dizzily across through their headlight beams. And Ann was here beside him. Both Allan's hands stayed on the wheel, even when her re-gloved hand reached over to rest comfortingly on his thigh. But oh, he longed to let go, turn, and just fall with her into some deep snowdrift white, and warm, and never-ending.

Finding his house on the trafficless snow-bright street was so easy that Allan wondered why he had ever worried. The porch light went on as they turned up the driveway, and he saw his father step out through the open door to greet them, with his mother just behind—two silhouettes, framed by the glow from the living room, just out of sight, where a Christmas tree silently twinkled, and presents, both wrapped and unwrapped, were waiting to please.

Ann shook hands with Doctor Ross, as Allan introduced them. His mother held out both hands to the girl, and squeezed them smiling.

Once inside they sat down to coffee and devil's food cake with orange icing freshly baked for the occasion by Allan's father. Baking had been one of Dr. Ross's hobbies from his bachelor days, or, as Allan liked to tell the story, since medical school where he'd learned to compound pharmaceuticals. Allan insisted his father's chocolate cake had curative properties unmatched by any over-the-counter drug, and most prescriptions.

Looking across at Ann, he tried to guess what she thought of his parents, and what they might think of her. Her attractiveness, her quiet but lively talk, and, not least, the little jar of home-made blackberry preserves she had brought as a hostess present, all won quick approval from his mother. But his father seemed unusually quiet

Ann politely declined a second slice of cake; but of course Allan took one himself. She seemed a little stiff, he thought, withdrawn somehow, almost apologetic. Had she been that way at the station? In the car? He couldn't remember. But he had her safely home now, and that was one goal achieved.

*   *   *

The next two days passed pretty much as Allan had imagined, except that he and Ann somehow never quite managed to spend even part of a night together. The best he could do was to tiptoe down the hall to her room twice in the early dawn for a few brief moments of drowsy endearments, fondlings and spooning. Still, he could afford to be patient. There was Williamstown ahead, and three whole weeks before Ann had to leave for college.

He took her downtown to shop, and to the planetarium. They saw the Christmas show, about just what the Star of Bethlehem might have really been—assuming that it <u>had</u> a natural explanation. And he showed her his old high school. And, on the afternoon of New Year's Eve, they drove out to Valley Forge, and played in the snow.

She began it, smacking him from behind with a snowball as he was bent over, brushing snow clear to read the bronze marker beside a row of cannons. She made good time escaping through the deep drifts and into a clump of trees. But he stalked her, molding an arsenal for himself as he came on. He flushed her out of hiding with a well-planned barrage, then charged in to grapple at close range, pushing handfuls of loose snow mercilessly down inside her collar while she squealed and pleaded.

"Give up?" he asked breathlessly, when he had her pinned by the arms on her back in the snow.

"Yes! Yes," she shrieked, "I give up! Let me go!"

"I will," he puffed, "if you say you'll <u>marry</u> me."

Her laughing stopped, but her eyes still shone with it.

"No. Seriously, I <u>mean</u> it. Marry me!"

She looked up at him, tenderly now.

"Oh, Allan.. "

"If you tell me 'no', you might just have to stay here."

"Allan. Don't. Don't ask me that."

"Ha. Then suppose I <u>tickle</u> you? Hmmmmm?"

"Ha, ha! No! Please stop, Allan. It isn't funny anymore."

He could see that. Feel it, too. She lay there, bedded in stiff white, cheeks flushed and snow-blotched, strands of limp wet hair pasted down across her nose and forehead. She had lost that aura of controlled perfection that had so enchanted him on the station platform. She was sweaty and damp and disheveled. But it only made her seem just that much more <u>alive</u>, more desirable.

It was his cue to laugh now. So he fell on his back beside her, staring up into the closed gray sky.

"Okay, okay. But you can't blame a guy for asking, can you?"

*   *   *

All through that last long evening of the year, Ann avoided Allan's questioning eyes. Even when the bells rang out, and they kissed and sipped champagne, her gayety seemed borrowed like a dress for a costume ball. Allan danced with her, eagerly but badly, to the music of his parents' day--Glenn Miller, Artie Shaw, Shep Fields and his "rippling rhythm." The ancient 78s Allan had found and rescued for this special night after years of silence in their sun-faded paper sleeves, hissed with static and popped out a complex counter-rhythm from scratched grooves. *"We are old, we are old, we are old,"* Allan heard them whisper, *"but we do not die!"*

Allan wished he were a better dancer, for Ann's sake; just as he wished that she would end her baffling evasion for <u>his</u>. He had been planning to announce their engagement just at midnight, and then to call her parents with the news. It had seemed the perfect plan: to seize that single moment of the year when memories of past romance are closest to the surface, and then add to it the joy of new romance, restart the cycle of life with the newborn year.

Maybe she'd been embarrassed by the way he'd asked. But he had so wanted that moment to be memorable--something to tell their grandchildren about if only to hear them say "Ohhh Ick! That is so corny!" or whatever the 21st century equivalent of those words might be. Instead, he had only kissed her and let her go.

*   *   *

It was two days later, and they were alone in his car driving back up to Williamstown before he was able to ask her again:

"You know, I wasn't kidding about asking you to marry me?"

She didn't speak right away. They were turning onto the New Jersey Turnpike and Allan was desperately trying to stay looking calm while he maneuvered the car carefully through the heavy traffic. Still, he could tell that she wasn't looking at him when she gave her reply.

"I don't know, Allan. Not yet."

They drove on a while.

"That's not much of an answer," he complained.

"Then I'll just have to say 'No'. Is that better?"

It wasn't, and she knew it; but all he said was : "Well, at least it's clearer. Mind telling me <u>why</u>?"

"Please, Allan. Let's not talk about it now. I <u>do</u> like you, a lot! You <u>know</u> that. I'm just not ready to make promises. Why can't we just go on the way we are?"

He was sorry he'd asked at all, now. In a flash he could see how wrong he was to try and force things. He should have waited for some time when they were both on familiar ground, undistracted and already passionate. Then he could have asked and she <u>would</u> have thrown her arms around him, and hugged him, and cried for joy, and done all the silly wonderful things he wanted and expected from her. He'd just been too eager to show off for their two families, secure her formally, forever, and give himself to her.

"Sorry," he said. "I didn't mean to put you on the spot. Sure, we can go on this way for as long as you want. I just wanted you to know that if you ever want something more, well, so do I."

"I knew already," she told him, gently. And they left things there for the next few hundred miles.

*　　*　　*

Half way up the Taconic Parkway, he pulled over to let Ann drive. She'd been taking lessons all fall, and finally passed her driving test on the second try. It was worth his nervousness as an unaccustomed passenger to share her excitement, and her pride. She did just fine, of course, and they arrived right on time.

Professor Ash opened the door in his slippers, with folded newspaper and aromatic pipe in hand, looking altogether fatherly. Mrs. Ash asked Allan in for coffee, but he politely begged off, saying he needed to get right over to the practice room. She said she understood.

Allan kissed Ann goodbye right there in the front hallway, ignoring Cindy, who stood munching an apple all through the tender scene, her head cocked slightly to one side like a curious bird.

He was delighted when Ann agreed to join him for lunch next day at the Di-Gamm house. He'd been aching to show her off to his fraternity, and vice-versa--if only to prove to her that it wasn't nearly as rowdy as some of the others here.

Allan turned one last time in the doorway to call goodbye. Ann was already opening mail from a pile on the hall table. When she hurriedly glanced up from what she was reading, he thought she was about to cry. Instead she smiled and blew him a kiss. So he smiled back and left as her sister closed the door behind him.

He drove straight to West College to unload, and, looking up, observed that a light was on in his room and the shade was drawn. So Tom had come back early. He thought briefly about going up, but decided to wait until after he'd practiced. His fingers were itching to get at the keyboard.

And besides, the note he'd left for Tom said enough. Tom might have just this minute arrived and be reading it through even now. Why interrupt him and have to explain face to face? Far better to let his written words do that. Besides, *"He who takes no needless chances loses fewer teeth,"* sayeth the preacher. He locked his car and walked off to the Music Building through the January dark.

He stayed late in the practice room, seriously working at pieces that had long given him trouble: Ravel and Prokofiev, and Stravinsky. He would lick them now. He was determined. He played on and on until he was tired enough to feel really proud of his effort, and ready for sleep.

Stars stabbed down at him, as he walked home in the clear cold night. There were just too many to pattern easily. The Milky Way was a river in flood tonight, not a mist, and the glory of it twisted his heart like love.

But when he reached West College, his car was gone. This shocked him for a moment--until he remembered that Tom had his own set of keys now. Still, the guy should have known he'd be over in the Music Building. He might at least have stopped by to say "Mind if I take the car?" Damned impolite just driving off without a word! On the other hand, the note he'd left him <u>had</u> pretty much invited Tom to do exactly this. Then too, maybe Tom was sore. And he had some right to be. After all, he was practically being asked to vacate his own room for the next three weeks.

Too bad though, Allan thought, that his suitcase was still locked inside the trunk with his books and pajamas and shaving kit and all.

He climbed the stairs feeling--yes, he had to admit it--just a little bit <u>betrayed</u> by his friend. He himself would never have driven off like that without a warning, without a word.

But there <u>was</u> word. A note pinned to the outside of their door explained that Tom had read Allan's letter and agreed to everything except the haircut. But he wanted some place he could always go to. He was taking the car now to check out a hunters' cabin some farmer had advertised for rent in the *Berkshire Eagle*. Twenty bucks a month, with a wood-burning stove. If he took it, would Allan be willing to kick in for half the rent?

Allan really admired Tom's decisiveness. And he'd happily pay ten bucks a month for more free time with Ann. Hey! As co-renter maybe he could even drive out there with <u>her</u> sometime! Now that opened vast new possibilities! No more night watchmen to hide from, no standing guard outside the bathroom (hmmm, come to think of it, probably no bathroom there at all, but...what the hell?)

He was grinning as he unlocked the door. It swung open, to reveal his suitcase from the car. Tom had hauled it out of the trunk and carried it upstairs. Allan was genuinely touched.

By the time he'd unpacked and was in bed it was well past midnight and still Tom had not returned. Allan wondered if maybe he'd rented the cabin on the spot, then gone up to B-town or somewhere and lucked out. Tom and the girl might even have driven right back to the cabin and be spending the night there--giving the place a trial spin so to speak. He shook his head and grinned in quiet admiration for his friend. Then he turned out the light. Grades or no grades, the guy was no dummy—that was clear!

Chapter 14: *Mezzo Forte*

Next morning, Allan met Ann in the lobby of the theatre building. She looked tired, and a little sad.

"What's the matter," he asked. "Didn't you sleep well?"

She shook her head "no."

"Bad dreams," she told him simply.

Allan nodded and looked wise. But he was really just admiring the way her bright hair echoed and softened the movement when she shook her head. She was absolutely gorgeous, and he must touch her.

"All that driving," he suggested. "I kept seeing headlights and midline stripes for hours before I finally conked out."

Nothing.

He smiled sympathetically and laid his hand gently on her arm.

"Hey. Cheer up!"

Still, she didn't respond.

He took her right hand between both of his, and looked deep into her eyes.

"It's Reuben sandwiches for lunch today at the house. And French fries. Fried potatoes are good for the soul, you know, if not the waistline. But then, you don't exactly have to worry on <u>that</u> score."

He looked her up and down; it must be all too obvious to her what <u>he</u> was hungry for.

Whether it was or not, at least she smiled then, and to his quiet pleasure, put her hand in his. They crossed the street and climbed the steps to the Di-Gamm house linked and swinging arms in approved young-loverly fashion.

From down the block, well before they reached the glass front door, they could clearly hear the juke box in the basement wailing:

> *...caint get n-oh*
> *sa-tiss-Fack-shun,*
> *Ah caint get no*
> *ste-dee Ack-shun...*

"Wouldn't you know," Allan grimaced. "Don't worry; they'll turn that damn thing off before we start to eat."

"I don't mind," Ann assured him.

Allan guessed she was just being brave. In so far as she'd shown it to him, Ann's taste in music lay securely in the 19th century (Tchaikovsky, Mahler, Brahms) with perhaps a little jazz for her dancing and a lick of folknik fun ala The Weavers, or Odetta. Certainly nothing rock-and-rolly with the possible exception of the Beatles. Well, that was no crime. Even he admitted those four hairballs could make crafty music.

The noise inside was louder. The door opened on an elegant curving staircase--the kind Scarlet O'Hara might have glided down to the last antebellum ball. Guys were variously posed upon—or better sprawled across—the carpeted steps, reading mail, or *The Williams Record,* or simply gabbing. More milled about in the living room off left; and between their loud talk and the dish-clatter coming from the dining room even the juke rumble from below ground lost its urgent dominance.

Allan helped Ann off with her coat and noticed approvingly how well the dark patterned stockings she wore complimented her long dancer's legs. How, he wondered, could she be so excruciatingly delectable at all times and in all places?

Fred Mason caught his eye as he turned back from hanging up Ann's coat, and beckoned him over.

"Allan! Got a minute?"

"Sure, Fred." He turned to Ann and made introductions. "Fred's the house president," he told Ann, "and he paints pretty well, too. That landscape on the staircase is his. Recognize the view?"

"Of course. That's Mount Greylock. It's lovely!"

"Not my best," Fred scowled.

"Fred prefers <u>abstracts</u>," Allan explained. "But to me they all look the same--like the paint bucket fell on the floor, and he kicked it around some."

"Anyway," he went on, "I only mention this to show you that not <u>all</u> the brothers here are drunken bums...like me," he added, fishing for a laugh.

None came. But Ann did roll her eyes upward briefly, tolerantly, fetchingly. Then she asked if there were someplace she could go to powder her nose.

This euphemism surprised Allan. It wasn't Ann's style to be so coy—or so inaccurate. He didn't think she even <u>wore</u> powder--just a touch of eye shadow and a little lipstick. Maybe she felt extra nervous today. He steered her toward the downstairs john, around beneath the staircase, then returned to Fred.

"We could use your help with the new pledges," Fred told him.

"I thought initiation wasn't till spring break. Pretty early to be starting with that now, isn't it?"

Fred shook his head. "Not this year. Everybody knows the frats are being forced off campus in a year or two. But I don't want these guys to get the idea we're already dead. We need to get them 'inside' right away. Give 'em the history of the house, traditions—all that stuff. I seem to remember you took to it all fast enough. So I figured maybe you could make <u>them</u> care too."

"How much for how long?"

"After supper. An hour or so. Couple times a week, starting tonight. Go through the ritual with them; why the questions matter, that sort of thing. The prompt book's on my desk upstairs. But you probably remember the responses."

Allan did. He had enjoyed his own initiation, sophomore year--the robes, the weird lights, the surprises, even the fear. Then last year, when he'd been on the other side, helping stage the event, he'd enjoyed discovering how all the technical effects were rigged. Even this year, his last initiation--maybe the last one ever on this campus--the symbolism of the ceremony still intrigued him; that and seeing how the pledges would react to the process, what they might learn.

"Okay. Sure," he told Fred. "I'll be here."

The lunch gong sounded. Knots of talkers unsnarled and moved toward the dining room.

Ann was back. And with her was Sara Mitchum. Sara was officially enrolled at NYU; but she and Fred had been going together since junior high, and the fact was, Friday through Monday most weeks she actually lived here at the DiGamm house, with Fred.

Allan liked Sara. She was short, and loud, red-haired, and Brooklyn-bred. She might have been the waitress at a truckstop diner, or a truck driver herself. She drank beer fast, and plenty of it, danced wild, laughed easily at dirty jokes, and told them better than most guys. Above all, she was Fred's girl, every minute, every day, and damned proud of it.

The two girls sat together, and Allan watched the pair of them talking. How different <u>were</u> they, really? Fred and Sara liked rock music, beer drinking, big frantic parties. He and Ann would rather spend an evening listening to Bach chorales, or old English ballads, or cool jazz, sharing quiet conversation over coffee and liqueurs with a few close friends. But they too would be a pair, united solidly.

He was pleased to hear Ann and Sara already laughing and talking easily about coursework and parents and clothes. He'd never realized how much girls had to talk about among themselves that guys either didn't know or couldn't properly appreciate. Hem lines and colors and what stores were best for particular things had a significance for them he would never comprehend.

Meanwhile, Fred was talking basketball at him. Allan tried to listen intelligently, but he was hopelessly out of his depth. The best he could do was ask a question now and then to keep Fred talking. As a result, he finished his meal first and began to observe Ann eating while Fred dribbled on.

Ingestion was a fascinating process, he reflected. It was oddly funny and a little frightening to follow the mechanics of a human mouth stretching wide to swallow cut up scraps of red pastrami and dark bread with melted cheese and glistening sauerkraut. Ann was carefully dissecting her sandwich, pressing her fork deep into the toasted bread, while her knife held it firmly in place to permit a deep, sure puncture. Only a silvery strand of kraut or an occasional wisp of melted cheese untidied the tight bundle that she lifted from her plate to disappear into the slick-surfaced tooth-framed cave beneath her upturned nose. She caught him staring at her, blushed, and instinctively patted a napkin to her mouth.

"Is something wrong?" she asked him.

"Nope," he smiled. "Just looking."

"Well, don't! It makes me think I've just dropped something down my dress."

"Sorry," he told her. "I'll watch it. That is, I mean I <u>won't</u> watch it, from now on."

After lunch, the couples parted at the door. Ann called goodbye to Sara, standing at Bill's side with her arm around his waist and his arm across her shoulders, for all the world, thought Allan, like a married couple waving from their own doorstep to departing friends. When would it be like that for him and Ann?

Walking back across campus, he told her that Fred had asked him to help work with pledges that night. "That's probably all for the best," she said. "I really ought to <u>study</u> at the library tonight. And Daddy's been asking some odd questions lately."

"So you're still lying to your folks about us?"

She sighed. "Yes. Of course."

"Why do you bother?" he asked, suddenly stopping and turning to face her. "They know we see each other weekends. And they both like <u>me</u>. Why can't I just drive by and pick you up nights when we're going out to 'study'? For that matter, now that we both really DO have to study sometimes, why not just stay there? God knows your living room beats the library for comfort--quiet too, once that sister of yours is out of the way. Seriously."

"<u>Seriously</u>," she mocked him, "it's impossible! You don't understand. My family life isn't what you think. You don't know <u>any</u> of us, Allan. Not even ME."

"Yeah. I suppose you're all vampires or something."

"Who told you that?" she asked sharply.

"Told me what?"

"Said that about my family?"

"Nobody. I was just making a joke.

"Well it's not funny. Besides," she added, letting her eyes take on a scary look, "suppose it's _true_?"

He shrugged. "Then I just hope you have a special fondness for A-positive, 'which is what I'm equipped with'."

"Don't worry. You're safe enough. We only suck each _other_'s blood."

"Come on now, Ann..."

"Oh, mother's all right in her way, but Daddy !" She shuddered and closed her eyes. "Do you know he actually _follows_ me whenever I go out now? You don't believe me, do you?"

She moved closer to him, talking earnestly. "I've caught him snooping in my room. And you should see his face any time he finds I really AM where I told him I'd be. He just turns around and walks out like I wasn't there. It's _comic_."

"Don't you think you're exaggerating? He could just call the librarian up at the front desk if he ever wanted to find you."

"Huh-uh. He knows Miss Brooks would tell him I was in the stacks if I asked her to. She likes me--you too, for that matter. Think I haven't noticed how she winks at us and nods toward where I'm sitting when you come in? I'll just bet we're her idea of perfect well brought-up young lovers."

"Sounds like an apt description to me," he agreed, and started to laugh.

But her glare silenced him. He tried another tack.

"I suspect," he began "the real secret is that we're such good customers. I'm always taking out records no one else has ordered up for years. And what's more I usually bring them back on time. Librarians love that."

"Hmmmmmm. I think what <u>she</u> loves are your big blue eyes," said Ann, wrinkling her forehead to look serious.

He knew she was only playing, being provocative, changing the subject. But still, he was pleased ... and then, much more than pleased.

Ann nodded solemnly. "Yes. And my mother likes you, and so does my aunt. You definitely have a <u>way</u> with older women."

"How about the younger ones?"

"Well, Cindy says.. "

"I meant <u>you</u>."

"Oh...," she shrugged, "you're all right I guess .. ."

"'All right,' Hmmmmm?." Now it was his turn to frown. But she giggled, so he kissed her, quickly and hard.

Her eyes gleamed mischievously, and she purred: "Oh. So it wants to kiss me now, does it?"

"Mmmmhmmm. (kiss) It does (kiss). In fact (kiss), it wants desperately (kiss) right now (kiss) to tuck you (kiss) safe into bed (kiss). Its OWN bed (kiss, kiss).

"But my English class " she parried.

"Cut it (kiss, kiss)!"

"Mmmmmmmmmm. And your roommate... ?"

"Bet he's out. And anyway, if not, he'll see us coming and suddenly "remember" he's got a class or something. Really, Tom's an okay guy. He'll understand how it is."

"Yes," she said quietly. "He will, won't he."

And just that quickly it was gone.

Worst of all: she was right. Letter or no letter, asking Tom to leave was only just slightly less embarrassing for everyone than waiting for him to realize that he <u>ought</u> to.

"Then let's go somewhere else," he pleaded, "even the goddamned <u>snackbar</u>, I don't care "

"But I thought you were so desperate to 'tuck me in bed'--or was that '<u>fuck</u> me in bed?'"

He winced to hear that word from her, with the "using" it implied. More so because, at this particular moment, she was <u>right</u>. It was not tenderness he felt. Hell, no! Right now it wasn't even <u>sex</u> he craved. He'd just like to grab her, shake her; feel her wholly in his power; now, this moment have <u>her</u> begging <u>him</u>!

He was losing direction, but he tried one last time to cover his confusion with wordplay.

"Yes, I did" he growled, "but that's not <u>enough</u> any more! I want to <u>worship</u> you!" He bared his teeth and let a silent movie leer of fiendish passion play across his face, hoping desperately for a laugh to break the tension.

"Well then," she began, "you can worship me from . afar!"

And she was off like a deer running over the lawn toward the library. A stunned second later, Allan was tearing after her, his feet crunching through rotten snow and wet curled leaves. She was running hard, so hard he wasn't sure if she really <u>wanted</u> him to catch her.

He thought of stopping, calling after her, but she never looked back. So he just kept on, and on, spurted harder, till, only yards from the library door, he got close enough to grab her coat sleeve.

Brought up short, she jerked violently as if to throw off his hold. But he yanked her back against him and held her.

Both of them were puffing hard from the run, and he at least was sweating freely under his heavy jacket. He kissed her fiercely on the mouth. He had earned the right by capture after flight. She hung limply in his arms, neither fighting now nor teasing. He was utterly confused.

"Wh-why did you do-o that?" He tried to stop puffing and swallowing, but couldn't.

She didn't look up. Didn't answer.

He asked again crushing her still more tightly in his arms: "Ann, why?"

She looked up at him steadily now, calmly, blankly.

"To see how much you really wanted me."

She was serious. How _could_ she be?

Allan shook his head in disbelief, still panting. "You don't have to MAKE me follow you. I WANT to."

She made no reply.

"What do _you_ want, Ann?" he gasped. "What do you _want_?"

It was his father's question. Finally, he'd asked her.

But she only shook her head and clung to him, rubbing her forehead back and forth across his jacket until he took her cheeks between his hands and turned her face up to his. Her eyes were filled with tears.

"What IS it, Ann? What's wrong? Can't you tell me?"

"Oh, nothing. Everything. You're just...so awfully, awfully... wrong about me. That's all. If you only knew! I can be such a perfect little bitch!"

He stroked her hair consolingly. "Perhaps a very little bitch. More like a puppy, I'd say."

"You don't...you shouldn't...I don't know...I do things. You ought to hate me...you should!"

"Hate you? That's the last thing I want to do, ever! I want to make you happy—any way I can. I'm ready to be whatever you want me to be, whatever you need. Can't you see? I love you. Just tell me what's eating you. It isn't like you to be closed and hard."

"But it is! That's just like me!" She gripped his arms and looked pleadingly up at him. "That's exactly how I am. Hard, and selfish, and mean! How can you always stand there and say it's all right and love me even when I do such awful things? It simply isn't fair! You ought to hate me!"

"I'd rather kiss you," he told her. And he did.

She let her head sink onto his chest once more. And he stood there holding her, shielding her from what he didn't know.

A wind he hadn't felt till now stung his cheeks and sang in his ears. Other people—students and professors—passed by glancing at them or ignoring them. It didn't matter, they were still alone.

He imagined how he must look standing there: like some doomed Resistance hero in a World War II movie, comforting his trembling fiancée in the last few frames before a hail of bullets from some Nazi firing squad came shattering out of the soundtrack to rivet them together in love and history. He set his jaw defiantly, and forced his eyes full open to the wind, letting tears well up unblinked.

But no bullets came; only discomfort. Numbness slowly stole across the rim of Allan's ears and up the bridge of his nose. It was damned chilly work standing out on the snow-crusted grass in the middle of a darkening January afternoon. Still, he hated for the moment to end.

Inside his arms, Ann raised her head and snuffled, a delicate sign that she felt steadier. "Better now?" he asked.

She closed her eyes and nodded. Then she smiled again.

"Sorry," she sniffed. "It's so silly."

"No. Not silly—sexy! Very, _very_ sexy. Any time you feel like being chased again, I'm your man. It's stimulating."

"No," she sniffed, "But I'll nibble your earlobes now and then. They're really quite delectable. You just don't _know_." And rising on tiptoe she nipped him softly once to demonstrate. And they shared another long damp kiss.

Then she pulled away. "I'm late for class."

They turned back from the door of the library, and walked a while in silence, Allan's hand clenched over hers, his thumb caressing the backs of her chilled fingers.

They made a date for that night at the library, and Ann passed through the door into the English classroom building, leaving Allan more confused than ever, but every bit as much in love.

Chapter 15: *Pavane*

The remaining days and nights before Ann left were not easy ones. In spite of Allan's letter, and some not-too-subtle hints and gestures, Tom always seemed to be around when Allan wanted most to be alone with Ann. They would run into him at the snackbar. Or he'd be up in the room working when they got there. Or, he might show up unexpectedly early and catch them just before they could get started making love. It got pretty annoying, Allan had to admit, even for a guy as patient as himself.

Fate played a hand too. Tom would no sooner take Allan's car to drive off somewhere, than Ann would phone to say her father was making her stay in that night, or the family was headed to Pittsfield for communal after-supper shopping, or that some relative or visitor was due and she was expected to help entertain them. This happened three or four times. He began to understand how big a problem Ann really <u>had</u> with her family.

But Tom was different. Tom was <u>his</u> problem and, friendship or not, Allan knew it was really up to him to do something about it. Yet day followed day, night followed night, until it was almost time for Ann to leave for Wellesley, and he had done nothing. Looking back, Allan realized they'd only been to bed together twice in all that time. Not exactly the frantic pre-nuptial orgy he'd been banking on. But... that time would come.

He could sense how uneasy Ann was about leaving for school. Smiles were rare now, glum looks the rule, and tears never far away. He comforted her as best he could, but this was more a job for a parent, than a lover. He knew this would be a whole new life for her, her first extended time away from home. All he could do was try to sympathize.

But sympathy, he knew, doesn't always help; and in this case, it didn't help at all. He wanted Ann physically, touchably near him every minute of the day and all through the night. There was a song. He'd hear it through the walls from next door and sometimes on the radio: "*Girl--I want—to be with you--all of the time--all day—and nighttime, too.*" Honestly, that about summed it up—crudely, but accurately. Somebody—Tom? –once improvised a different lyric, changing the bridge line "*The only time I feel all right is at your side*" into "*The only time I feel complete is at your teat.*" And Allan had chuckled with the rest. So? He was human too.

And it was true. He didn't feel "all there" without Ann. It was an old story--Plato's in fact. Man and woman were a single animal the gods had forced apart, and love was simply the expression of their urge to find again that old lost unity. Just a myth? Maybe. But it made as much sense as Freud.

What if he really <u>could</u> join bodies with Ann, be like Tiresias in Greek mythology, <u>become</u> a woman, feel what it was like for her to live, walk, breathe, make love? Then if, as he feared, men really got more pleasure than women did from sex, he could gallantly let her be <u>him</u> as often as she liked. He would gladly give Ann his own pleasure, if he could. He would give her anything.

*   *   *

The Sunday Ann was due to leave for Wellesley, she phoned him at ten in the morning. She was crying. No one else was home, she said. They had all gone out. Please, please come over right away. She <u>had</u> to see him.

He would have liked to run to her, but he made himself take the car. They had said their official goodbyes the night before. It had seemed so sensible a way to part: a single trembling goodnight kiss at the front door after yet another pleasant family meal. He had felt mature that night, and proud of Ann's and his ability to hide their deep emotions. But then, both of them <u>had</u> known that he'd be driving to see her on the following weekend. So perhaps this tender public parting was really only being "staged" at Ann's request for her family's benefit.

This morning was a new scene, not in the script. He was pleased, of course, and eager, but at the same time he felt unrehearsed.

Even the car seemed too slow, but he knew he could never make it all the way to Ann's house running, or if he did, he would arrive so out of breath that <u>she</u>'d have to revive <u>him</u> instead of him helping her.

Ann stood at the open front door waiting. She hugged him fiercely, then led him by the hand, almost running, up to her bedroom. She flopped down on the unmade bed, inviting him to fall on her. Instead he eased himself gently down beside her. She rolled toward him clinging desperately.

"Oh, Allan. I don't <u>want</u> to go. I don't want to leave <u>you</u>! What can I do? Help me. Please!"

He cradled her, stroked her, wrapped her in his arms.

"What's wrong? You told me you were so glad to get away from home. A week ago you were practically dancing on air."

"It didn't seem real then. But now it's here, and I'm not ready. I don't know <u>anyone</u> at Wellesley, and I just hate meeting strangers. You <u>know</u> I do."

Actually, he didn't know this. He had never thought that Ann was shy. She had responded so warmly to him and had always seemed so ready to smile and be friendly to people they'd meet—and especially Allan's friends, Tom, for example.

"Hey. Relax," he told her. "Boston's not that far away. I'll be in next weekend. I can even be there sooner, if you really miss me. Hell, I'll come down <u>every</u> weekend! You'll see. We'll have more time together there than we ever could here. And more privacy, too. Besides, you can call me every day. Or I'll call you. That ought to impress your dorm mates. I'll bet none of <u>them</u> has a boyfriend who calls them every single night! Hmmmmm?"

"They probably all date <u>professors</u>," she grumbled, "or <u>grad</u> students anyway. And it's so late! Everybody else will know their way around. I'll always be asking people how to get somewhere and they'll all think I'm stupid or retarded."

"They won't! They'll just think you're <u>new</u> on campus--which is true—the same as <u>they</u> were once. And as for waltzing in at midyear, they'll figure you've been doing something far more exciting than <u>they</u> have since September. You'll be a 'lady of mystery.'" Allan ran his right hand teasingly along her thigh. "And <u>that</u>'s true too."

Ann's cheek nuzzled his shoulder as she squirmed more tightly into his arms.

"In a week or two," he concluded, "what do you bet you'll be giving directions yourself--probably guiding campus tours! You'll see."

She slipped her arms around his neck and hung there as if her hands were tied at the wrists. It was a dramatic pose, if not entirely comfortable. Allan braced himself, extending both hands flat against the mattress. He felt awkward. So he lifted slightly, slipped his arms around Ann's back, and lay down on his side, carrying her pressed full length against him. This proved an elegant and satisfactory evolution.

It was time to be practical.

"Are your folks around?"

"Not due for <u>hours</u> yet. They're off somewhere shopping with Cindy."

"Where? What's open on Sunday?"

"North Adams. Spring Street. I don't know. Who cares?"

Her fingers had already teased along his fly, and were now fumbling to unfasten his belt.

"<u>They</u>'ll care plenty if they walk in and find me ravishing their eldest daughter in the sanctity of her own bed! Which is exactly what's about to happen."

"Help," she whispered, "Help!"

He clenched his teeth against the laughter in him. "I don't know what's got into you. But I hope you keep the recipe."

"Why, nothing's 'gotten <u>into</u> me'," she simpered, "..yet."

The front door banged, followed instantly by the thunder of Cindy's feet charging upstairs. She burst in on them a few seconds later. But by that time, Allan had stood up, and Ann was sitting placidly smoothing her skirt.

Cindy's eyes widened visibly and she came to a sudden stop just inside the bedroom door. The news that had left her half-breathless with excitement to tell her sister was forgotten in the instant of this still-more exciting discovery.

"Oh!"

"Cindy " Ann's calm voice held a warning note. "Not a WORD about this. Not <u>one word</u>. Do you understand?"

She voiced no specific threat. But the glee in her sister's eyes quickly faded.

Cindy broke her gaze, nodded, and hung her head. Ann stood up, walked to the mirror at her dressing table, and began methodically to comb and pinup her long entangling hair.

Over her shoulder she told Allan "Your shirt tail's out."

He looked down. So it was. He tucked it in.

Hair pinned up, Ann turned back to Cindy. "What did you come galloping up here for, anyway?"

"Well..." Cindy began, hesitated, and looked sheepishly over at Allan.

"Should I leave?" he asked.

"Stay here," said Ann, decisively. "Go on, Cindy. What is it?"

"It's just...well...I got...that thing you wanted... from the co-op. You know...your..."

Ann relaxed a bit. "Oh. Good. Thanks."

"Want to see?"

"Not now. I'll come to your room in a little while. Where are mother and daddy?"

"Bringing stuff in from the car. Oh, and daddy says for Allan to come on down and help with the heavy bags."

"How did he know ?" Allan started to ask. Then he knew. "Oh, that's right. My car's parked right outside."

Ann scowled. "Why on earth did you <u>drive</u> here?"

"You said come right over. And the car seemed faster. Anyway, where's the harm? Why <u>shouldn't</u> you have me over in the middle of the day?"

Ann sighed.

Cindy slipped from the room, with a parting look at them both that mixed shyness with envy.

Alone now, Ann clenched her fists in helpless fury. Allan expected her to be trembling but she wasn't.

"Damn them," she hissed, pressing the words out slowly between her teeth, "Damn <u>all</u> of them."

She turned to Allan. "Mother <u>knew</u>. I trusted her! I told her I <u>had</u> to be alone with you today. She <u>promised</u> she'd get daddy out of the house and keep him away. But it was just a trick to catch us. <u>Now</u> what do we do?"

"Will you calm down? So what if we're here alone together? I'm practically your fiancé. Your parents have to know I love you. And they seem to approve of me as your suitor, don't they?"

"Oh yes," Ann said savagely, "they <u>approve</u> of you all right. God, you're their <u>dream</u>! They can't <u>wait</u> to get me off their hands, settled down with some nice boy, producing fat pink grand-children for them. They 'approve' of you so much it's <u>sickening</u>. The first night you walked in here they liked you better than they <u>ever</u> liked Cindy or me. We're just trouble for them, but they can be <u>proud</u> of you."

"Hey, don't get so.. "

"They never wanted girls. Nobody <u>ever</u> wants girls really. Everybody wants a <u>boy</u>, and they'll do just <u>anything</u> to have one."

Ann paused for breath, but not long.

"Daddy always thought he could make us into boys if he tried hard enough. He was always throwing baseballs at us, dragging us off on camping trips so we could "rough it;" wanting us to be more athletic, to do the things <u>he</u> can't do any more. Ask him about that limp of his sometime, and what happened to his eye. You <u>do</u> know one of them's glass, don't you? No? I'm surprised he hasn't pulled it out to show you yet. He was always doing that when I was little, scaring my friends. Anyway, he'd be just <u>thrilled</u> to tell you how it happened, how brave and tough he was, what a hero. Only he <u>won't</u> tell you how my mother almost died because he wasn't there, and didn't give a damn!"

It was all too much. Allan grabbed her by the shoulders and shook her.

"Ann, stop this! Look, I wouldn't care if your parents caught us bare naked and climaxing down on the living room rug! I <u>want</u> them to know how much love you. I want the whole <u>world</u> know it! Just like I want them to know that you love me. There's nothing that we need to be ashamed or frightened of. We <u>love</u> each other. Don't we?"

She gave him a look he couldn't decipher—a smile, a tear?

"I...care for you...so much...," she began, then stopped.

Allan drooped.

She hadn't said 'love'. Why wouldn't she? What had he done? Or failed to do? What could he still do even now to make her say that word?

"Say you <u>love</u> me, Ann. Why can't you say it?"

Her eyes closed. "I can say it...but it's such a danger. And I will not be locked inside a trap—not even with you."

He let go of her shoulders. What else could he do?

"Allan, please. You mean so much to me. You do! More than anyone else in the whole world."

"Just not quite enough to call it 'love,' huh?"

"Allan. I've heard Daddy say he loves us all my life, but what it means is that he <u>owns</u> us—mother and Cindy and me. Because he 'loves' us, that gives him the right to do just what he likes with our time and our lives. And if one of us complains he'll just act hurt and say we don't know what we're doing to him. His 'love' makes us helpless. But we're <u>not</u>! I'm not. I won't be! I can't <u>live</u> if I'm helpless. Don't you see that, Allan? Don't you?"

He wanted to, for her sake. But, honestly he couldn't. Not really.

"Ann, love's only a word, you're right. But when two people have so much...share so much together with our words and bodies, why <u>can't</u> we call it love?"

Ann stood silent a while. Then she said: "You'd better go downstairs. Daddy's waiting."

"Do you see what I'm saying? What I'm <u>trying</u> to say?"

"Oh, Allan. I don't know. When I hear you say it, it makes sense. But when I try to think things through alone, it all breaks down and I can't be sure any more. I remember all the lies and trouble here at home. The way my mother lives--I couldn't stand that kind of life, I really couldn't. If that's what love makes happen, then I just won't love <u>anyone</u>. <u>Ever</u>!"

She pressed his hands between her cold ones.

"Why is it so important to you that we get married, or tell people we're planning to? Why not just stay the way we are? Share all we can together and still keep free?"

"Free for <u>what</u>?" he asked. "Free to be alone? To be out of reach when we need each other, or when we could be sharing something good? There's nowhere I want to <u>be</u> without you, Ann. And nowhere I want to go, either. Whatever your mom and dad have it's different. We're not <u>like</u> them. And we don't have to be."

"But they're married, and that's what you want."

"Lots of people are married--and happy together. Look at <u>My</u> folks for instance. You saw them. Aren't <u>they</u> happy? Don't you think they love each other, like we would?"

She sighed.

"Yes...Maybe...I don't know. Part of me wants to believe you're right. But if you're wrong....Just bear with me a little longer? Please?"

Allan swallowed hard.

"Sure," he nodded, and grinned. "I'll hang on. Hey, I'm not that easy to get rid of."

"Like a stray alley cat?"

"Well, I followed you home, didn't I?"

The sound of an automobile horn interrupted their kiss.

"*Vox Pontiac, vox dei*," Allan groaned. "Even <u>sounds</u> like your dad. Any chance of my staying to lunch once the groceries are in?"

"If mother doesn't ask you, I will!" Ann assured him.

So Allan turned and went downstairs to help his prospective in-laws restock their larder.

*   *   *

There was no need for explanations or excuses, Allan found. The Professor seemed entirely absorbed getting the grocery bags into the kitchen and repacking the station wagon with Ann's college gear.

All he said was: "<u>There</u> you are. Here, grab this."

As Ann had predicted, Mrs. Ash invited Allan to stay for lunch. At the table, Cindy seemed quieter than usual. Several times Allan caught her looking curiously first at him then over at Ann, who said little, but seemed calm enough now. The Professor, too, was uncharacteristically silent.

Mrs. Ash did most of the talking, recalling her own years at Wellesley in the 1940s, and how much the school had changed since then, but she was certain Ann would like it just as much as she had. Allan agreed politely. Ann said nothing.

The meal was nearly over when the phone rang. Professor Ash left the room to answer it, and Ann immediately leaned over and whispered something to her mother. Mrs. Ash shot a hurried glance out to the hall where the Professor stood bent over the telephone. Then she nodded to Ann.

Ann reached across the table and took Allan's hand.

"Come on," she said.

She led him quickly through the kitchen, and up a steep flight of back stairs. They emerged in a large attic room. From the line of full-length mirrors and the barre along one wall, it was obvious the place had been fitted out for dancing practice.

There were a couple straight-backed chairs, and a table off to one side holding a tape recorder, a few spools of tape, and an empty take-up reel. Allan would have liked to examine these, but Ann led him straight to one of the chairs, where an open gym bag lay. She reached her hand inside.

"Cindy bought this, but it's for you to give me." She held it up for him to see.

It was a lace-trimmed garter, purple and gold, the Williams colors. And it bore the miniature figure of a cartoon cow (purple of course) with gold horns and a large white "W" on its flank.

"Like it?" she asked, and waved it slowly back and forth in front of him.

It was tasteless, a bad joke. How could she--or <u>anyone</u>--really wear a thing like that? He would never have chosen itfor her, not in a million years. And he almost said so, too; when thethought of her wearing it, high up beneath her skirt, where no one else would see, made him pause.

It might hold up one of those patterned stockings of hers, or it might just cling there tight and unsuspected against her skin, its gentle pressure circling her thigh. She would probably feel it all the time. Then he imagined his own hand sliding up along her leg to fasten it in place, or to slip it off. He thought about that, hard.

"Yes," he said, "I like it."

"Then put it on me. Right now. Hurry."

She seated herself on the chair, raised her right leg, and held it straight out to him, elegantly, effortlessly, a dancer's gesture, instinctively pointing her toe. Her skirt was maybe mid-calf length, and full. But she made no effort to raise it. She was leaving that to him.

Allan took the garter in his right hand and slipped his left beneath under her outstretched leg to support it, going down gracefully on one knee as he did so. Ann broke out in a sudden grin, but quickly regained her composure and remained looking calm and serious.

He paused a moment, gazed into her eyes. Then slowly, slowly he began to slide his left hand up from her heel to her ankle and along her cool unstockinged leg. His wrist pushed up the heavy folds of her skirt as it passed. He slid his hand around so that his palm caressed the curve of her calf. Her skin felt cool and maddeningly smooth. To the knee, and then above the knee.

Just there, the pushed-back skirt revealed a tiny scar, off center to the left, from a bicycle fall she had told him. It took real effort now to hold back. He was much more excited than he had imagined possible. Part of it came from knowing that this stylized caress was not mere foreplay, something to be gotten through and passed beyond. This was all they would have, their last moment of intimacy.

This was why she had brought him here. They were both to remember this scene, that was her plan. She might not wear his ring on her finger, but she would wear this garter, feel its gentle but relentless hug, and recall the touch of his hand there upon her leg, high and secret and desired.

He almost fell upon her, then and there. For just a moment he was sure that any price--discovery, disgrace, even her own rejection of him after--would be worthwhile for the chance to ease in one great whelm this urgent, desperate need.

But the mad moment passed. A better time would come. He was sure of that now. All her delays and doubts were just so many games to be played through. But some night, he promised himself, remembering all she had put him through, he would ravish her wildly--recklessly--in revenge for this torment of long-stifled desire.

"Hold still," he urged. She had twitched, involuntarily perhaps, as his fingers slid along the hollow of her knee. He already knew her ribs were ticklish. Here, too?

When he let go, she kept her leg straight out and her gaze was full on him as he stretched the garter wide with both hands, then began to slide it slowly up. Over her toes...her ankle... Allan stared with rapt attention now at every inch of her skin as it passed within the ruffled circle of taut elastic. Onward, above the knee,...six inches... ten...maybe slightly more. He stopped, and let the garter lovingly contract around her thigh, pressing his fingers softly into her flesh. Her skin was warm to his touch now. Slowly, reluctantly, he slipped his fingers out from underneath the garter's pressure and pulled away.

"There." He stood up and stepped back to admire.

She smiled at him and, without breaking gaze, gently placed her foot down to the floor again, her full skirt falling slowly like a final curtain.

"Thanks," she said.

And that was all. A moment later, she stood up, and moved to the door. She opened it a crack, peered out, then gestured for him to follow. Together, they slipped down the stairs, and back into the kitchen. Here they kissed; only once, but long and deeply.

Allan was flushed in the face, and perspiring freely as they reentered the dining room, where Mrs. Ash and Cindy looked up smiling from their desserts. Ann ignored them both, but Allan nodded and stifled a smile of his own.

From the hall, they could all hear the voice of Professor Ash, still talking on the phone.

Half an hour later, Allan was standing between Cindy and Mrs. Ash waving goodbye as Ann and her father drove away. His position made him feel more like a brother than a future husband. This was another new sensation for him, only child that he was; a sensation, in fact, that he rather enjoyed.

Chapter 16: *Sforzando*

It was Allan's fourth day without Ann, a rainy Thursday, when he decided to straighten up Tom's desk before tackling his own. They were comparable messes, but Tom's was slightly worse, topped off by two half-eaten apple cores going brown, and a bent cigarette butt floating dead-man style in a bottle of flat Orange Crush.

Near the top of the heap, just below a crumpled legal sheet of class notes, which Allan was careful to leave more or less in place for Tom, lay a folded page of letter paper. Allan gave it a casual glance as he unfolded it and noticed that it was carefully typed, and that the signature was Ann's.

He must have dropped it somewhere, and Tom had picked it up by mistake. No harm done, though he wondered how he'd ever been so careless. Still, it irked him to think that Tom must by now have read Ann's private words addressed to him. He decided he would read it over now to refresh his memory, and to focus his annoyance at Tom. It was dated December 24, and began with the words:

"Dearest."

Christmas Eve? Bah, humbug! This time two days ago I was curled up on the couch beside you feeling so warm and cozy and at home. And now I AM at home, and you are miles away, and I feel like a lost dog in the snow--all cold and frightened and confused and miserable....

He read it through, quickly, for what he realized was the first time ever. Then he sat down in Tom's chair and read it carefully again. Then he stood up, refolded the note, and laid it back down on his roommate's desk, where it belonged.

Air leaked out of him. He'd been holding his breath without noticing. He half expected something cataclysmic to occur. But nothing did. The walls and ceiling stayed in place, and the sound of passing cars outside in the rain was no different than a moment earlier. Only <u>he</u> was different.

He sank into his own chair and stared straight ahead. Could it be some mistake? A joke? The letter not really from Ann at all? But he knew better. Her signature, her typing, even her words--words she had said to <u>him</u> almost the same way. It was Ann all right. But not <u>his</u> Ann; <u>Tom</u>'s Ann; an Ann he hadn't known, hadn't even remotely guessed existed. His mouth formed the phrase "Tom-and-Ann," and his doubt turned to certainty.

The next phase was to wonder "why?" He thought back. Had he done something? Driven her away? Or had it all been planned? Had their dating, their laughter, their love-making all been nothing more than a cover to hide from her parents and everyone else what she really felt for Tom?

Allan hauled himself up, left the room for the hallway, walked down the four flights of stairs to the street and went out. He wore no coat, but the rain had stopped now, and, though cold, he felt none of the drenching icy drops he had been counting on to steady and distract him.

He headed for the music building. Downstairs was the small rehearsal hall. He went there, avoiding the solitary practice rooms for once. This place was special.

Someone had set out music stands and chairs for a small chamber group, but all was deserted now. He sank down gratefully on the padded leather stool before the Baldwin grand that held center stage. The space here and the silence were somehow comforting, in spite of the memories they held.

Ann had come here with him, straddling his lap, nibbling his earlobes, making love to him as he struggled to keep on playing the wild last movement from Prokofiev's Sonata <u>around</u> her till they both collapsed in a breathless heap on the floor of this same dark stage. Here their twined bodies had danced together to the beat of their own laughter; their mouths had sung silently each to each; locked tight to one another, they had musicked an hour to eternity. He had sensed the special passion in her then, perhaps imagining an audience was watching. And through her he had shared that passion's rush and echo.

Now he wondered: maybe they <u>had</u> been performing. Maybe Tom had been concealed out there, peering at them, savoring, or just observing, taking notes, to learn what she enjoyed so he could please her even more another time. Maybe Tom had <u>always</u> been there--in the Chapel, in the practice rooms, the library, even at Ann's house!

But she <u>had</u> written Tom, to say how much she missed him. Surely that wasn't possible either?

He raised the keyboard lid and began to play. Just stray chords at first, mostly ninths and major sevenths, but they gradually evolved into progressions as he played them over slowly again and again. Experimentally, he drew them out into lines and figures--nothing tricky, nothing hard, just lyrical and sad. Three-quarter time, he realized, suddenly--his waltz for <u>Ann</u>. And he smiled then, because it felt better to do that than to cry.

He kept at it till his fingers ached, and a little after. He would miss dinner if he didn't leave now. Good! He <u>wanted</u> to miss dinner. How could he possibly face Fred, or Dave, or (God help us) TOM, across a table and make conversation when the only woman he had ever loved had just betrayed him with his closest friend?

And as he thought these words, the full pain hit him. She had <u>slept</u> with Tom. She must have. More than once. Her letter was so tender, so concerned. That was the way she wrote to <u>him</u>!

Ann and Tom. In bed. Together. When? Where? And why? For God's sake <u>why</u>?

He was supposed to visit her this weekend. Two days from now. He winced. How he had longed to share her new world, explore Boston—just the two of them, alone in a city of strangers. He had even prodded Tom for suggestions about places to go, things to do with her there. Oh, that was rich. Him asking <u>Tom</u>! What a fool, what a perfect <u>fool</u> he had been. All this time!

How <u>much</u> time? How long <u>had</u> it been?

He thought back. When had he first introduced her to Tom? Was it maybe that night when he'd had his laughing fit at the library, and Tom had come over to join them in the snack bar? He had actually left Ann <u>alone</u> with the guy, just walked out, leaving her there, hurt and angry. Was it any wonder that she'd taken the nearest means at hand to hurt him back?

But that was also the night when she had come to him, stayed with him, asked Tom to leave them alone all night. He'd never known how she managed that. Had she offered herself to <u>him</u> as well? Maybe <u>Tom</u> had been her lover too, right from the start.

It hurt so bad now, he couldn't manage another smile.

His head bowed low, till it rested gently on the keyboard. The cool slick ivory mocked him with a soft discordant muddled sound. He raised himself, suppressed the echoes with the pedal under his left foot, and began once more to play. His fingers seemed instinctively to find the notes that spoke to him in Gershwin's simple words:

> *I could cry*
> *Salty tears,*
> *Where have I*
> *Been, all these years?*
> *Little wow,*
> *Tell me now:*
> *How long has this...*

No. Damn it! He smashed flat hands to the keys, stood up, slammed the lid closed. He had to know more. He would face Tom, right now. <u>Ask</u> him. Damn it to hell! He had the <u>right</u>!

He stormed out into a night black and starless enough to match his mood. He could ignore the cold, and no walkers crossed his path to distract him. Good!

It would be like a scene from a movie. A show-down—but not like the gunfight in *High Noon*, nothing grand, or public. No. More... he reflected as he strode...more like that Japanese film he'd seen last summer in Tokyo: *Harakiri*—where Tatsuya Nakadai, as the old Samurai, meets his one remaining enemy all alone in a field of wind-blown high grass far from anyone's eyes.

He could remember clearly, even from that single viewing, how those two strong desperate men had slashed and parried, how they sweated, snarled, and occasionally simply disappeared from view (though the sounds of their struggle continued) as the camera turned indifferently away through the waving grasses that were clearly fated to outlive their duel and even their memories. That was how he must face Tom now: aware of how little their struggle meant to anybody but themselves--and Ann.

The room door was unlocked. Tom sat working at his desk. He looked up as Allan came in.

"Fred Mason from Di-Gamm called. Says they're waiting for you. Something about pledges?"

Pledges! With a sudden pang of conscience Allan remembered he'd promised to coach the new pledges tonight in their responses for the initiation ritual. <u>Help</u> them? Yeah. Some help! Feed them all wrong answers, set them up for their big surprise. He shuddered. Not tonight. Hell, of <u>all</u> nights, not tonight!

"I'm not going."

Tom shrugged. "Well, they'll survive I guess. Say, what's eating you? Something wrong?"

"Yes."

Tom didn't lower his eyes or turn away. Instead his face set and a hard, quizzical expression wrinkled his forehead.

"You mad at me or something?"

"I found a letter on your desk today, from Ann."

"So?"

"So why did she write to <u>you</u>? What do you mean to her?"

Tom sighed. "So you finally know, huh?"

"Know what, Tom? What should I know?"

"About us, Ann and me." Tom looked at him calmly, not ashamed, but not defiant either.

"What <u>about</u> 'Ann and you'?"

"That we've been going out. That we like each other. A lot."

"So what does <u>that</u> mean? You been <u>sleeping</u> together or something?"

"If you really want it spelled out. Yeah. We have."

Asking this had been Allan's last faint hope of being told it wasn't so. He'd been almost sure before, but now, to actually hear Tom say it, calmly, casually, not even boasting, took the fight right out of him.

He would have liked to fall, or at least sag dramatically against something. Instead he just stood there by the bookcase looking stupidly at Tom.

"How long?" It was all he could think of to say.

"Christmas break. We spent a couple days in Boston before... New Years."

It sounded as though Tom had started to say "before she came down to see you" but changed his mind. He didn't need to say it. Allan had the picture.

"How many times?"

"Jesus, I don't know. I wasn't 'keeping score'. Does it matter?"

Allan _had_ kept score. It was eight times—nine counting that night on stage in the rehearsal hall. He had wanted to remember every detail: all his thoughts and feelings during and after. What the weather had been like. When she'd laughed and when she'd made moaning sounds that weren't really pain. The ways they had teased and played, or just enjoyed each other. All of these things mattered to him. Why not to Tom? Did he really not remember, or just not care?

"Guess it didn't mean much to you, huh?" Allan sneered. But his throat was dry, and the scorn he intended came out pathetic—like a too-small bandage on a deep infected gash.

"No. Not much." Tom agreed. _She_ mattered. Being _with_ her mattered. But not how many times."

Allan hung his head. Tom was right.

"You should have told me," he offered. "You two could have had... so much more time together."

Tom spread his hands. "Yeah, well, I was ready. Believe me. You don't know how close I came to letting you have it right between the eyes a couple times. Look man, what can I say? I'm not sorry about this, just sorry it happened this way."

What else could he say? What could <u>anyone</u> say? It was over. The big duel. The showdown. The wind in the grass won again. Run the credits. The End.

Tom hadn't tried to deny or explain or apologize; or even blamed Allan for reading the letter on his desk. It was out in the open now and Allan had lost. without even a struggle. What was left to struggle <u>for</u>? Ann was gone. Really, she'd never been. Not <u>his</u> Ann.

"Yes...well" Allan rubbed his forehead and let out a long breath. He walked past Tom and dropped into the armchair; he pulled out a cigarette, lit it, puffed once, twice. He was trying to think and not doing very well at it.

Tom stood up, came over to him, and looked down, like a visitor in a sickroom.

"Want a drink? There's some scotch left."

Allan nodded.

"Me too," Tom agreed. He poured two glasses, not big ones, and handed one to Allan. "Cheers," he said.

Allan swallowed one mouthful; and didn't like it. He breathed in and let the vapors flood his nostrils. That was the best part of scotch as far as he could see. He could feel it burn going down, and the aftertaste wasn't <u>quite</u> as bad as brandy. Still, he wouldn't drink this stuff for fun.

He tried to adjust to the idea of himself as victim. Ann had betrayed him; so had Tom. The two people he had most trusted, and known best. Or hadn't known at all, really. But no. No, he <u>had</u> known them. Cared for them; maybe even loved them both in different ways—Tom as a comrade, Ann as a...wife.

What had changed them? Tom must have done it. Stolen Ann away when she was already pledged to him, Allan. His own roommate, and without a word, without a warning. How <u>could</u> he?

Allan set down his drink, and looked Tom in the eye. Tom caught the look and set his drink down too.

"Now what?" Tom asked.

"You bastard." Allan's voice was quiet. He pronounced each word distinctly, carefully. "You god-damned bastard!"

They were both on their feet.

"Look, I said I was sorry you had to find it out like this. Okay?"

"You fucking son of a <u>bitch</u>!"

He lunged for Tom, wanting only to smash that broad face with its curly black hair, to flatten that big straight roman nose, to blacken those jeering eyes at any cost. His rage was out now. The hate that had been lying coiled tight inside his ribcage all this time punched up through his words like a fist through a glass window.

But Tom was more than ready. He easily parried Allan's badly-aimed swing with his left arm, while his right drove forward, palm first, fingers up, in a shove that knocked Allan backward off his feet and down sharply against the corner of the cement-block bookcase. His shoulder hit, and hurt. The bookcase wobbled, but held. He struggled to get up. But Tom was down on top of him.

It took Allan very little time to realize he was helpless. Tom had studied Judo. Allan couldn't even box. He struggled a little longer, just because he felt he <u>had</u> to try, but Tom's heavy weight on him didn't lessen, and at last he gave up. But he wouldn't talk.

"Had enough?"

No answer.

"Good. Well then, while I've got you here, maybe you'll listen a minute. I'd say it's been a good long while since you listened much to _anyone_ beside yourself."

Allan glared at him but remained still.

"How long have we been roommates? Three years? Well, two and a half anyway. I'd hate to count up all the hours we've spent together talking. That is, mostly _you_'d talk and I'd listen. Did you ever think what it was like for me, hearing you sound off about yourself and just how fucking _great_ you are, huh?

Allan stirred and muttered, "I never bragged to you!"

"No. That's just it. You _don't_ brag. You only smile, or start laughing for no reason. Then, when somebody asks you _why_, you say it's nothing. But you know they'll keep after you; and pretty soon you let them squeeze it out of you that this really clever thought just crossed your mind, or you found this great new piece of music and its running through your head and you've just GOT to play it; or some prof chose your paper to read from in class today, or some big deal just happened, or some bigwig just kissed your ass. But when you cut through all the bullshit Ross, it still comes down to just plain loud-mouthed bragging. And what makes it so pathetic is, you probably don't even know you're doing it."

"You just know I'm successful and you're not!"

"Yeah. You _look_ successful, don't you; down there on the rug with a lump on your head and my ass practically in your face. That's _real_ success, isn't it, Ross?"

"Let me up, you fucker!"

"So you can get knocked down again, and maybe break a chair or push the bookcase over? Huh-uh. We'll just stay like this a while till you cool down."

Tom twisted around enough to reach his drink off the table.

He raised it in the air; "Cheers!" He took a big swallow and went on.

"I used to wonder why you wanted to room with me. You, such a Big Man On Campus--theatre, frat rat, music, you name it. And me: no money, average grades, activities zilch, no girls, no friends to speak of ...or only other loners. I mean it was <u>flattering</u>. It really was. I figured you must see something in me I couldn't. I felt great thinking you were my friend."

"Yeah, you sure showed <u>your</u> friendship. You and Ann."

"Listen, asshole, you think I <u>planned</u> this?"

"Oh, I guess she <u>raped</u> you, huh?"

"You are really asking for it, Ross! And you're a great one to mouth off about <u>friendship</u>! Hell, you only wanted me around to show yourself off better. Once I figured <u>that</u> out it should have been pretty easy to start hating your guts. But you know what? It wasn't. You think Ann and I <u>liked</u> giving you the shaft? Man, you are wrong, wrong, wrong!"

"Bullshit."

"You'd really <u>like</u> me to paste you one in the mouth right now, wouldn't you?"

"Go ahead! What's one more dirty trick to you?"

But he could see Tom wasn't really angry. He was no threat to Tom. Not now. And knowing that hurt even worse. For Tom to hit him now while he was down would be a relief. It would give his hate some solid core to crystallize and build around. But Tom just went on talking.

"I got to admit it was kind of fun at first, watching you kid yourself; knowing how totally off base you were. I'd wonder sometimes if even you could really <u>be</u> that blind. Once or twice I even thought—oh, you'll like this--that you and Ann were working some wild kind of double whammy with <u>me</u> as the victim. Conscience maybe? But later on, I just felt sorry for you. I would have told you right away. But Ann was scared. Figured you couldn't take it maybe. I don't know."

"Why bring <u>her</u> into this," Allan snarled. You're the one who started it. You could have stopped it too, any time, if you'd been any kind of friend instead of the sneaking bastard you are."

"Wrong, man. You won't understand even now, will you? Words don't change what she felt, what I felt, it was <u>there</u>. It was <u>real</u>. All we did was let it out so we could be happy at least some of the time instead of staying miserable because somebody might think that wasn't <u>nice</u>."

"That's crap!"

"Tut, tut. Such language!" Tom took a slow sip of scotch.

It was time for another tack, and Allan tried it. With a sigh he relaxed his muscles and managed to control his voice enough to sound relatively sane.

"Let me up now, okay?"

Tom considered doubtfully. "You sure you're settled down?"

"Yes."

"All right." Tom drained the last scotch from his glass. "But try anything and you <u>are</u> gonna get hurt."

"Okay."

Tom stood, and Allan got up off the floor. He rubbed the places on his head and shoulder where he had hit the bookcase. He could feel some swelling and a little wetness under the hair. Inspecting his fingers, he was gratified to find a few small flecks of red. Tom had drawn blood. Okay. So would he now, one way or another.

Allan walked into the bedroom to get a better look at his head cut in the mirror. No point trying to stick a bandaid over all that hair. It would heal itself in time. Just let it bleed.

He stood a while staring at his face in the mirror. It ought to look different, he thought. But it seemed pretty much the same as always, the way it had looked before ... before he found out about Tom and Ann. And he wondered how much else would ever be the same?

Chapter 17: Partsong

Now that Tom was an enemy, not to be trusted, what would it be like to live beside him? Who else would know about him and Ann? Who knew already? That stopped him again. Could someone else have set this up, Allan wondered? Helped Tom to steal Ann away, or, worse still, been luring Allan himself along, knowing from the start what Tom would do?

Not likely. Few of Tom's friends knew Allan—or Ann. And what reason could Ann have had to pretend she liked him when she didn't? Unless just out of fear of her father. If Professor Ash learned about Tom there could be trouble—but that didn't seem very likely. Still,he realized, Professor Ash's power over Ann was suddenly no longer a hazard to him, but a positive aid—perhaps his ultimate weapon against Tom.

Ann was the real question. What should he do about her? What could he do? Call her; or write? He was supposed to visit her this weekend. How could he do that now, knowing? And yet, he still wanted to go--to be with her again as if nothing had happened.

Once she was really gone, he hadn't missed her much for the first day or so. Even this morning he had put off calling with the excuse that he had no news. But hell, they didn't need "news." They were lovers!

But now, when he had every reason to suppose she was lost to him forever, that she'd never even want to see him, he longed to be close to her...if only with his words.

Best bet was probably to tell her that he knew; ask her straight out what she wanted now. If she still cared, he would go to her as planned, meet her face to face, maybe hope for a touching reunion, another of Ann's tearful confessions. Now he could finally understand that fury against herself the times she had cried on his chest and told him how awful she was. Maybe now at last he could truly comfort her, and they could put this all away.

Or, when he called, she might tell him everything was over. In that case he supposed he would yield graciously to Tom, and withdraw holding tight to whatever dignity he could still muster. He must never lose that, not in _her_ eyes, no matter what.

So he would call her. Now. Tonight. He strode past Tom, out the door, and down the hall to the pay phone. He didn't think anyone could see how much he hated this or how afraid he was. Hell, who was watching him anyway? No one. He looked around all the same, and hesitated before dropping his two quarters in the slot. Would that cover three minutes worth to Boston? Or should he go back to the room to get more change? Tom would see him then, maybe figure out what he was doing. He couldn't stop him, but he would _know_. And then _he_ might call her later.

Could he even _reach_ Ann? She didn't have a phone in her room. She'd given him a dorm number, and so far both times he'd called someone else had answered. The phone was probably out in the hall just like this one. Would she feel too embarrassed to talk about personal things, especially this, in a public place? Maybe better to just write her after all. He could take his time in a letter, say things exactly the right way, not make mistakes or rush into statements he might not be able to finish.

All right. But no. She was expecting him _this weekend._ He _had_ to call her, and now was the best time. He checked his wristwatch. 10:40 pm. Late, but she should still be up. The quarters slipped from his hand and were lost forever as a double bong rose up from deep inside the black machine.

He waited for the operator, then counted the rings. Three times. He would hang up after five. Four ... A girl's voice answered; but it wasn't Ann.

Could he please speak to Ann Ash? No. Ann was out, and the girl didn't know when she'd be back. Would he like to leave a message? No, he'd rather   Wait a minute. Yes. Just tell Ann that <u>Allan</u> called and...and that he couldn't make it down this weekend after all. No need for her to call him back. He'd be in touch soon to explain. Thanks a lot. Goodbye.

He hung up feeling rotten. He'd done <u>everything</u> wrong! First he'd called late when he should have waited till morning when he'd have a clearer head. Then he'd left a message instead of simply saying he'd call back. Stupid! And finally, to top it off, he'd closed out any chance of seeing her this weekend by telling this perfect stranger to pass on the message that he couldn't make it. What a mess! Now <u>she</u>'d be mad at <u>him</u>, on top of everything. And she'd be right.

Of course, his odd message might just worry her enough to make her call him back right away. But if it didn't--and he'd brainlessly said that she didn't <u>need</u> to call--what then? He felt he could put his head right through the phone booth wall.

Suppose he called her back right now? But he'd have to go and get more change first. And anyway, that would more than likely only make a worse mess of things. He'd blundered enough for one day. Unwilling to face Tom again though, he headed downstairs and out.

*   *   *

Not surprisingly, Tom was fast asleep by the time he got back. Allan turned off the lights in the living room and undressed in the dark. He briefly considered sleeping out on the couch, but gave it up as a pointless and uncomfortable form of protest. Tom was snoring fruitily. He would never even <u>notice</u>, much less be pained by, such a gesture. Besides, why should he let the guy steal any more from him? Wasn't Ann enough? Did he have to give up his bed too?

Sleep came slowly to him that night. Every time his mind let go of its numb ache long enough for drowsiness to grow, the head-lights of a passing car or the roar of a late truck seemed to kick him back awake. But finally he did sleep, deeply, without fitfulness or dreams.

His alarm failed to go off next morning. He had forgotten to set it. That made an angry beginning to the day. Worse yet, Tom _was_ up and had gone out without ever waking him. Why the hell _hadn't_ he? Allan was not much inclined to suppose it was any reluctance to disturb. He suspected subtle reasons like a guilty conscious expressing itself in small nastinesses, to be rubbed like rough salt crystals into his already gaping wounds.

He threw the covers off violently, then had to pick them up from the floor. Damn!

So all right. He had missed Markham's dumb class yet again. Well, too bad! _And_ he was too late to go get breakfast. Double Damn!!

How come he felt so hungry? No supper last night, he remembered. And then, in a flash of pain, the details of the night came back to him. God _damn_ Tom Petard! Damn him to _hell_!

Allan dressed. He looked at his wristwatch. 11:45. Should he call Ann again? She'd probably be in class. Besides, what could he possibly _say_ to her? Better at least write it down first. Then he could either mail it, or use it for notes to help him on the phone.

He worked on this letter for most of the rest of that day, working first in the room, then later (after Tom returned and sat down at his own desk without a word), at the library.

Dearest Ann,

Time's a funny thing. It's not a week yet since I saw you last, but right now you seem very far away.

I had a showdown with Tom last night. He told me everything. You both had me fooled completely. I had no idea. You should have let me know. You could have had so much more time together.

Yes, I'm hurt; and yes, I'm angry--mostly with <u>him</u>--for acting like a stranger instead of a friend; and a little with you for sharing with someone else feelings I thought we kept for each other alone.

But my deepest anger is at myself for being so blind to how you really felt, and so positive that what I wanted for us you wanted too. I was a fool.

Maybe what I'm really angry at Tom for is that he actually <u>did</u> what I longed to but held back from--going after you passionately and to hell with everything else. He just behaved like a lover, and I tried to be something more.

I hoped that my holding back, being patient and all would please you and prove to you that I wanted more than just fun. I told myself I was putting your feelings first, that there would be time enough later--a lifetime of being together--for me to enjoy myself openly, completely, as your husband and the father of our children.

Tom was a lot more honest about what he wanted, and a lot more direct. I'd have called him <u>selfish</u> a little while ago. And who knows, maybe he was. But he got results. I wanted you as a woman just like Tom did. But he only asked for your friendship, and pleasure now; I wanted <u>love</u>, and a whole lifetime of being together.

It was only near the end, in those last couple weeks before you left for Wellesley, that I finally began to loosen up some. Maybe I was just smug, or maybe I really did feel sure enough of you at last to think I couldn't frighten you away. Whatever the reason, there were times when I actually could let go, break down, open up, show my need to you instead of always trying to act "mature."

Even now, part of me thinks that what we had was a good thing, and that our feelings for each other are real and deep enough to last, while the passion between you and Tom will pass. Is that just wishful thinking on my part? The ultimate in self-delusion?

What <u>do</u> you feel for me, Ann? Please tell me now. Whatever you say can't possibly hurt me more than the hurt I've brought on myself by not asking you this earlier.

Pardon my foolishness if you can. You seemed so right for me, so practical and silly and appealing and a little sad, and beautiful and comforting. I just had to grab for you and try to hold you the best way I knew. I wish now I could have shown you better how I need you, and that we might have shared our desires more openly and more often. But thank you always, and for everything.

With music,

Allan.

These words didn't satisfy Allan, but he was pretty sure no letter could, and he was finally tired of writing and ready, for now at least, to stop feeling sorry for himself. So he slipped the pages into an envelope, slapped on a cheerful commemorative stamp, just to show he still cared about details, and mailed it to Ann.

Half a dozen times in the next two days he nearly called her again, but chickened out before he finished dialing. Half a dozen times he braced himself for the sound of Ann's voice when he was called to the phone, but it was never her.

Saturday arrived and passed without word. So she must have gotten his letter. By Monday, he was convinced he would never hear from her again. Tuesday morning, her letter arrived.

It was fat, and Allan could see through the thin blue paper of the envelope that it was all hand-written. It bore an ordinary generalissue stamp, and was postmarked Boston. He carried it up to his room unopened, made certain Tom was out, then locked the door, and sat down at his desk to read.

Part of him was wishing this had never come. It had been hard enough wondering what Ann would say; now it seemed even harder to face finding out. Yet it had to be done. He fingered the envelope experimentally. It was thick. Five pages easy. Maybe more.

He reached for the thin brass letter opener that had served him since high school as wrap-slicer, nail cleaner, and, in moments of mock despair, his just-pretend samurai sword for committing ritual suicide. He used it now to deftly slit the envelope's fat belly; and pulled out its folded guts.

Ann's letter was full of details about Wellesley— the campus (enchanting to look at), the dorm (disappointingly run-down), her roommate (from Fairbanks, Alaska of all places), food (nothing special), and classes (much easier than Williams so far). She described her excitement at shopping in Boston, her quiet sadness missing him and how much she was looking forward to this weekend. This weekend?

Puzzled, he turned to the letter's front page again. It was dated last Wednesday. Their letters had crossed in the mail. Just to be certain he checked the address and the greeting. Yes, it did say "Dear Allan," and yes, it had his mailbox number.

He laughed, briefly. What would this letter have meant to him if he had never found out about Tom? He would have treasured it in triumph. It was cheerful, relaxed, very much in Ann's style, more like intimate pillow talk than writing. A lot of what he loved her for was right here. But could he trust it, now that he knew the score? "The score!" God, he was even starting to <u>think</u> like Tom. He shuddered.

Ann's real letter arrived on Thursday, and was thin.

Dear Allan,

You ask me what I feel for you, and I owe you an answer. But everything is so confused right now, I can't find any words that make much sense.

Our letters crossing in the mail seems almost like poetic justice, because so often we have talked past one another when we tried to touch.

I don't know what Tom told you, but I sense a strength and honesty in you that sounds as if you've grown a lot more than you know. Whatever caused it, I like the results very much.

Can you accept the fact that you and Tom are both dear to me in different ways? You are such different people that I never understood how you two became friends. But then I never understood what you saw in me to make you say the things you have or to offer me your love.

I feel very low and solitary today. Will you call me soon, or at least write me? Please say you will. Hearing your voice would mean ever so much to me. Promise me.

Please?

Ann

Allan put down the letter and rubbed his forehead with his fist. No apology. No defiance. No admission of anything at all for that matter beyond simply "caring for Tom". But then she wasn't rejecting him outright or declaring for Tom. This whole letter was an appeal to him to show concern for her, to prove he really meant what he had always told her.

And in exchange? No promises. No conditions. Nothing.

Another anticlimax. There was no ending for him here, not even a painful one, only another start--or better, another turn on a dark and winding trail. He could go on loving her, or not as he chose. But she wouldn't make the choice for him. It was up to him.

He slipped the thin note back inside its cover. Then, taking special care to place this beside the drab brown maple leaf and his other souvenirs of Ann, safely inside the locked drawer of his desk, he went out for a long, long walk.

Chapter 18: *Sonata Rondo*

Snow had been forecast, badly needed snow to create the giant sculptures and patch up the balding trails and ski jumps for the College Winter Carnival. But instead it rained.

Winter Carnival at Williams was always chancy. Here in the "Purple Valley," a January Thaw might easily extend into early March. The event had already been cancelled once in Allan's first three years, and now it seemed about to be again.

He could not have cared less. His trio with Pete and Elroy had agreed to play on Saturday night at the lounge in the New Dorm, but that could happen with or without a full-scale Carnival weekend. There wasn't much for him to celebrate anyway, not without Ann. And Ann would not be coming.

Her reason for refusing, when he finally reached her on the phone, was typical but maddening. It wouldn't be fair for her to go with Allan and ignore Tom. "Fair!" He would cheerfully like to bust Tom's skull for him, for "fairness" sake, or at least his jaw.

To top it off, Tom had another date! Mary Kaplan was finally coming up--direct from Florida.

Allan would have argued more if, when he pointed out this proof of Tom's infidelity, Ann hadn't simply said: "He already told me. And he made that date with her months ago."

If she didn't even <u>care</u> that Tom was seeing another girl, what could Allan do? Her words also confirmed that Tom was in touch with her regularly by letter or phone, possibly even seeing her somehow (though at least he wasn't using Allan's car to do it).

So he'd ended the conversation (their first since the day he'd found Ann's letter on Tom's desk) with a curt: "Well, I'm sorry you can't come. I'll miss you," and quickly hung up on her--a gesture that Allan had never steeled himself to carry out on anyone before.

And now here he was, dateless and bored by the prospect of watching everyone else having fun—in particular <u>Tom</u>—while he sat around steeped in gloom, like a tea bag in a cold pot.

Should he ask some other girl? Time was short but he wasn't entirely without resources. There was Tricia at Skidmore, or Cathy at Wells, or even Kate But would that (to use Ann's logic) be "fair" to anybody? He didn't <u>want</u> some other girl, he wanted Ann! Pretending otherwise would only be a waste of time and emotional energy--and Allan hated waste.

No. He preferred to suffer; to nurture his resentment against Tom, and, not least, hope that somehow word of this self-denial might filter back to Ann. She had spies and allies everywhere on campus, he was sure, from her parents, to Dave Carter—who seemed to know everything about her, even now—all the way to…well, to Tom.

He could make a point of stopping by her house on some pretext and let her family see how he was pining for her and keeping pure. And he would seek out Dave, too, and start him reminiscing about Ann in high school. Even Tom had seen how Dave enjoyed that. And Allan would make the perfect audience, because he really cared.

From his dorm room window, Allan faced the storm. What had started early in the day as sleet, was now a steady dreary rain, turning the gutters into muddy streams, and leeching the piles of snow-plow tailings into gritty black-streaked combs of ice.

Suppose he threw himself from this window, four stories up? Ordinarily, he'd splatter on the pavement of the drive below. But right now, those piles of cleared snow ought to cushion his impact pretty well— that is, if they hadn't hardened into ice already, under the rain.

On a wild impulse, he actually raised the sash. Chill drops splashed in around him, driven by rattling February gusts. He lifted both legs up onto the window seat. He really <u>could</u> do it! The prospect fascinated and appalled him. To fling himself out on the wind, to fly. To sweep down grandly tumbling into a drift that might be soft as feathers, or as hard as stone.

It was the not-being-certain that made this plunge possible!

Suicide without a hope was pointless. And to jump when there was really no danger would be a cheat. But now, his letting go would have some meaning. He would be risking something serious, death, crippling injury, pain, for <u>her</u> sake, and for his own. He would be able to look back and say: "I dared this, when I wasn't sure." Then he could be proud. He stuck his head outside the window experimentally, a blind mole reaching up from his familiar burrow to sniff the free air.

Behind him, the door flew open and banged shut again as Tom stamped into the room.

"Jesus, Ross! Shut the fucking window. Are you <u>nuts</u>?"

Allan pulled back and turned to face him. Tom was wearing a plaid wool jacket and he was drenched. Beaded drops stood out on his tangled hair and face, and his sleeves scattered water everywhere as he shook them.

"Couldn't you do that outside? You're messing up the floor."

"Tough!" Tom grunted.

"Well at least get a towel," Allan snapped as he stood up and yanked the window down again, sealing in safety, and reason, and comfort, and cowardice.

"<u>Now</u> you're making sense," Tom admitted, and went for the towel.

He emerged from the bedroom a few moments later with a thin worn ribbed college towel draped around his neck, prize fighter fashion.

"It's a bitch out there. Fucking wind and rain. Bet the bus is late."

He meant the bus from Albany, the one that would no doubt be carrying Mary on the last leg of her trek up from Florida.

"You got plans for the weekend?," Tom went on.

Allan could guess what he was after, but he wasn't about to make it any easier than he could help.

"What sort of plans?"

"Girl plans."

"I might. Why?"

"Cause I'll be using the room. That's why."

"Sound pretty sure of yourself."

Tom shrugged. "What else is there to do?

He was right. Here was Mary, and hundreds of other girls, trekking up here expecting a real New England winter wonderland, and arriving to find... this! What a letdown. Allan thought of the skiers on the racing teams, and their coaches, and the guys at his house and their dates, at least the ones who weren't on sleeping terms yet. It would be an indoor weekend for everybody if this rain kept up. Oh sure, there'd be dancing, and even more drinking than usual in the houses, but that still might not make it a party if you weren't already comfortable together.

And Tom didn't have that option anyway, not being in a fraternity. He could take Mary to the snackbar, or they could sit in the public lounge of the New Dorm, or visit the art museum for a couple of hours maybe, or they could come up here. Allan knew what <u>his</u> choice would be.

It was easy enough to hate Tom now; but hard not to feel at least a little sorry for him at the same time.

"You can take the car if you want." Allan said, without much enthusiasm.

"You mean it?"

"Sure. Just don't run it off the road. You'll want to pick her up at the bus stop anyway, right?. And drive her to wherever she's staying."

"Well, thanks."

"By the way, where <u>is</u> she staying? <u>Here</u>?"

"I wish! She almost had to, though. I tried all over town, and no luck till I ran into Dave Carter in the snackbar. Seems he had this free room all lined up for <u>his</u> girl, but now suddenly she can't come. So he said Mary can have it. Pretty lucky, huh?"

Allan nodded, but said nothing. Dave, again. Always there to help. Talk about selfless devotion! He introduces Ann to you because she asks him to; then he puts your roommate Tom up for the night so she can go to bed with you; and now, even though he must know Tom and Ann have been playing around, he finds a free room for Tom's other girlfriend! Allan wondered if Ann might possibly have put Dave up to this too, and if so, how.

*   *   *

The lounge was packed that night when Allan sat down at the keyboard, with Pete enthroned among his shining drums and cymbals, and hulking Elroy, beret and shades and cigarette, and all, plucking experimentally at the strings of his darkly gleaming bass.

Here and there, Allan's ears could pick out a familiar voice among the buzzing crowd of revelers and their dates. But he couldn't see an inch beyond the pool of spotlight dazzle.

He held up his left hand for quiet, flexed his index finger a couple times to give Pete and Elroy the beat, then the three of them swung off together into a fairly obscure old tune: *I Should Care*. Allan had chosen this especially to set the mood tonight: light, cool, a little sexy (it was a party weekend, after all), but wistful, too. Ann wasn't here, but he would play for her anyway. He wanted the pain of missing her to show through his music, hoping that it might touch her somehow, even at second-hand.

The set moved on with two Rogers and Hart standards: *Isn't It Romantic* and *My Funny Valentine*. Then they up tempo'd with a double-time romp through Jerome Kern's "*Pick Yourself Up*.

At this point, everybody needed a rest. Allan leaned back, thanked the audience, introduced the group, and began his patter leading into the first original of the night.

"Here's a little number we just wrote, for someone very far away. About two million light years, actually. You'll notice the music goes 'round and 'round, and that's because, you see, this piece is dedicated to...the Great Spiral Nebula in Andromeda; or, as her friends like to call her,... '*M-31* '!'"

A polite ripple of amusement followed his words, and there must have been at least one Astro major in the crowd, because someone guffawed. The piece itself went beautifully. It was basically just a string of steady changes—up the scale in seemingly endless progression, then quickly down again to start all over. Nothing the three of them couldn't handle, but the repetitions could get monotonous and trip you up if you didn't stay alert. Allan was secretly pleased to think how well its form reflected the intricate circles Ann had been leading him in, though of course no one, not even Pete and Elroy, knew about that side of it.

He faded back to comp chords right at bar one of the second chorus, leaving Elroy to plunk out the melody. It was the right move. Elroy's nimble fingers danced around the line like happy cannibals around a crowded stewpot, while Pete's gentle brushes on the cymbals urged the other two along into a sassy stride beat. As they approached the climax, Allan laughed out loud for sheer delight. Now this was jazz! This was what they worked for: clever and complicated, carrying them all away—right along with anybody else prepared to listen with both ears—to venture someplace better than reality, where beauty lived and love was deep and sure.

The crowd responded too. When Allan soloed next with a sad slow version of *Here's That Rainy Day*, he could feel them with him, patient, willing to put off their own enjoyment for a while to share a little of his pain. But he didn't wallow in it.

They wound up the set with a vocal by Pete, who had penned his own irreverent lyrics to that bright but totally unseasonal tune for a wet February: *Santa Claus Is Coming to Town*. Allan introduced this attempt at a musical joke as best he could.

"Finally our drummer here, Pete Jackson, is going to sing for you. But don't be too scared, he doesn't bite. I think you'll recognize the melody, but it's the words that really matter, and Pete dreamed those up all by himself.

"He was thinking about Christmas—must be all the snow we've had around here lately...(loud groans and bitter laughter from the audience)... No, the truth is Pete's been working up this ditty for some time now. And he knew the thing that most guys here at Williams really want doesn't come from Santa Claus at all, but from a very different giving spirit, namely Venus, goddess of love.

"He wanted to write a song about Venus, but he could only think of one word to rhyme it with, and if he used that one, he could be pretty sure we wouldn't get to play it much in public, sooo Uh huh, ...I can tell you're beginning to get the drift so, he needed an alias for this delectable deity. Now, as you probably remember—the

Greeks had a word for her too: APHRODITE. So now, here he is, Pete Jackson, with a song that really says it all: *'Aphrodite's Going to Town'*."

Allan began things with a slow incongruously lush and schmaltzy intro, then Pete leaned across to the microphone beside his high-hat cymbal, and, grinning broadly, started to sing in a voice not unlike Louis Armstrong with a headcold:

> *You figure you're tough?*
> *Figure you're smart?*
> *Get ready, get set,*
> *Hang onto your heart!*
>   *Aphrodite's going to town.*
>
> *She's headed your way*
> *Heavy and hot*
> *Dyin' to know*
> *Who's ready to trot*
>   *Aphrodite's going to town.*
>
> *She knows who you've been sleeping with*
>   *and why you stayed awake.*
> *She knows that you've been bad—but good!*
> *When the bedsprings start to shake.*
>
> *So take your best shot,*
> *And play your top card,*
> *It's hard to be good,*
> *But good to be <u>hard</u>!*
>   *Aphrodite's going to town!*

There were more verses, some of them funny, most of them crude, and just what the listeners tonight seemed to want. The set ended to wild applause, and Pete's lyric was undoubtedly the big hit of the evening.

Allan didn't mind. *M-31* and *Rainy Day* had made the night for him. And Elroy, if he felt upstaged, didn't stick around to show it. As usual, he zipped his shining bass back inside its stained and wrinkled cover, and just walked off, without even a goodbye. Allan shrugged. Funny guy, Elroy. But, well..., so were they all, he guessed, all funny guys.

*   *   *

Sunday morning dawned clear. Still not much to do in town, but the rain had stopped. It was colder, too. Thin free-form sheets of ice lay here and there on the streets and sidewalks, and a crackled glistening skin gleamed from tree trunks and parked cars.

Allan hadn't seen much of Tom since Friday afternoon when Mary arrived. Except for the trio's performance Saturday night, he'd stayed in the dorm pretty much, leaving Tom and Mary the car to search out whatever excitement they could find.

This morning though, Tom approached him right away.

"You were on the trail crew for Outing Club, right?"

"Yeah, two years. What about it."

"So you know the mountains around here. Where do you think we could find some real snow?"

"What for?"

"For Mary. She brought her camera and wants to get pictures of deep drifts to take back to Florida. There's nothing but slush piles in town here."

Allan pondered. How much did he really want to help this guy now: his ex-friend, his tormentor, his faithless companion?

"Well," he began hesitantly, "you could try driving up past Bennington. Or over east."

Tom shook his head. "Haven't got time for that. Her bus leaves at three."

"Well then I'd say your best bet was Greylock or the Hopper."

"Think we'd find snow there?"

"Bound to, up near the top. And the Hopper's so well shaded, you find snow pockets sometimes as late as May!"

"How do we get there?"

"The Hopper? Hike in I guess."

"No; the mountain, Greylock. There's a paved road, right?"

"Well, yeah. But this time of year, the gate's probably locked."

"So what! The trail crew goes up there to keep it clear, don't they?"

"Parts of it, sure. But if you think I'm letting you drive my car up there, forget it."

"Think I can't handle it?"

"No, just not sure you care much one way or the other what happens to something of mine."

"Oh, Jesus, Ross! Are you back on <u>that</u> again? Look, once and for all: I did not '<u>steal</u> your girl.' Ann was never "yours" in the first place!"

Allan had no good answer to this. It was the one thought he had kept pushing down inside himself since the day he first found her letter on Tom's desk. <u>He</u> might be Ann's for the asking, but that didn't necessarily make her his. In a way, she had never betrayed him at all; because she had never promised to be faithful. Nor, for that matter, had Tom.

He thought back on it, and realized he himself was the one who had said he would never fall for a friend's girl. Tom hadn't promised the same. So logically, he had no reason to be feeling hate or rage or even pain. But illogically?

"Yeah, well. That's for her to tell me, not you."

"So you won't help."

"I won't let you run my car over a cliff while you're mind's on the scenery instead of the road, no."

"What if there was some other way?"

"Like what?"

"Like maybe <u>you</u> could drive us."

"Me?"

"Why not? It's your car. It'd be safer that way."

"Why should I, give me one good reason .."

"You got something else to do today?"

"No, but "

"It'd mean a lot to Mary. She's never seen real snow."

"<u>Never</u>?"

"Only at the flicks. Look, I'll even pay for the gas. What do you say?"

"I don't know..."

"Come on. Don't be chicken."

"I'll probably regret this," Allan sighed. "But look, if we're going, let's get started. It'll take at least an hour to drive up there, figure an hour to walk around, another hour back. We'll need to be on the road by eleven if her bus leaves at three."

"No sweat. We'll meet downstairs."

And they did.

Mary was bundled up in an expensive-looking fur-trimmed coat, with a cute fur hat to match. All she needed was a muff, Allan thought, and she could have been a pin-up girl for Currier and Ives. She was definitely pretty. He envied Tom.

He put Mary up front beside him to give her the best view, and because he didn't relish looking like a chauffeur even if he was playing the role. She rolled her window down to poke the camera out. It was a serious instrument, not just a tourist's little box: 35 millimeter, single lens reflex, that was all Allan could tell for sure, but it was enough. Either she took her camera work seriously, or her family was rich enough not to care what they paid for her toys. He was encouraged to believe she was serious by the way she took time to choose her angles and would occasionally pull a light meter from her coat pocket and consult it.

Allan drove south toward Pittsfield. This would give them the classic postcard view of Mount Greylock through the Hopper, and also allow him to drive the longer but easier road up toward the summit. Coming down, they'd take steeper shorter way, which would bring them out close to the bus stop on Route 2. Smart!

Mary was not impressed by the vista of two mountain ridges crossing in the shadow of a central peak, resembling the grain funnel in a flour mill that gave this formation its name: "The Hopper".

"It's a doggone shame ah didn't bring my wide angle lens," she said, "But ah'd jest be wastin' film to try shootin' this without it, don't you know?"

Mary might have the voice of a flighty southern belle, all right, but somehow Allan trusted her knowledge of photography. It would never have occurred to <u>him</u> that anything beautiful to look at would not be equally beautiful when photographed. After all, wasn't that a camera's <u>job</u>?

But he did notice how the summit of Mount Greylock, true to its name, was obscured by clouds. It could easily be snowing up there, he thought, despite the fine day here below. Reluctantly he put the car in gear and pulled onto the access road.

The long winding climb began smoothly enough. The paving was in better shape than he'd remembered, and the gullies on either side didn't look as deep as they had on his last trip up, behind the wheel of the overloaded Outing Club VW minibus. Then they had looked like parallel Grand Canyons yawning to swallow a tire and tip him over if he made the slightest error steering.

They crossed the snow line well before the barred gate blocked the road to the actual summit. Mary was ecstatic, and even Tom seemed impressed. Allan pulled to the side and, after turning on the inside map light to check his pocket trail guide, confirmed that they could reach the summit faster by leaving the road at this point and just clambering.

Surprisingly, Tom objected. He favored sticking to the flat but winding road. They'd made good time so far and weren't in any danger of coming back late, he argued. Why risk their necks or get their shoes soaked climbing?

But Mary couldn't wait to jump into the mysterious white world with both feet; very soon she was laughing and scooping up handfuls to toss at Tom and generally whooping and hollering in a most un-belle-like way. Allan began to wonder if she could have been drinking. But it was pretty early in the day; and besides, Tom looked sober enough.

Eventually they decided to split up. Tom would follow the road, while Allan and Mary hiked straight uphill. It was a rougher climb than it looked at first, and Mary was no hiker. But at least she had real boots, elegant fur-topped and glistening, while Allan slogged along in torn rubber galoshes that were soon so full of snow, he might as well have left them off.

The sky soon clouded over, and the wind bit sharply. But the chill seemed to excite their senses, not numb them. Snow had painted itself on the trees, driven deep into bark and branches by wild lashing gales. The ground, for the most part bare rock outcroppings studded with low bushes and yellow lichens in summer, was now a treacherous incline with a thin icy cover, polished and sanded by the steady wind into a glazed and hard-packed desert that had little resemblance to ordinary snow.

Allan led the way, but lost his footing just short of the summit. He would have slid ten or fifteen feet if Mary hadn't braced herself and blocked him with her body, just in time.

In spite of his embarrassment at falling, Allan was almost glad as he regained his footing and steadied himself with his hands on Mary's shoulders. He liked the feel of her through her heavy coat, the way the wind ruffled the fur of her hat, the shine of her pale blue eyes, and her dazzling grin.

"You just be careful, now," was all she said.

Nothing overtly sexy, nothing provocative really, and yet he was ready to believe southern girls did know instinctively how to make boys wild for them. He watched his own breath puff out white and vanish as it mingled with hers. Her smooth tanned cheek was so close to his own, still pale and stubbly with unscraped morning beard. Did this girl want what <u>he</u> wanted? One way to find out.

Apparently not. His lips had been on hers for a long moment—six seconds maybe, when she pulled back abruptly and slapped him, hard.

"What do you think you're <u>doin</u>?"

"I'm sorry. I.. "

"You leave me <u>alone</u>. Y'hear?"

She turned away and began climbing briskly.

Allan stood for a moment looking after her, flushed and confused. He didn't need to rub his cheek. She'd had her glove on, and the blow hadn't really hurt, only startled him. The truth was he still believed she'd been inviting him to kiss her. Had she changed her mind? Or was she having it both ways--flirting and then resisting him to preserve her reputation?

A few moments later they were both standing silent before the hundred-foot tall granite tower that rose impressively from the summit of what was the highest peak in Massachusetts.

Built as a World War I memorial, this tower, with a glass globe at its top, could be seen for miles on a clear day, and, with its beacon lighted, even farther on a clear night. Now it was sheathed in hoar frost, like the empty trees, and might have belonged to some ice giant out of Norse mythology. It had a door (always locked, in Allan's experience) so presumably there were stairs inside that led to an observation level just below the light. Allan could see the windows, curtained with ice, and wondered what, if anything, one could see from them now.

"What took you guys so long?"

Tom emerged from behind the tower. It looked to Allan like he had been running, and a tell-tale patch of white on one knee revealed that he, too, had stumbled and fallen at some point; but right now he was acting calm and collected.

"Oh, Tommy, there you are. Ah guess we just stopped a dozen times along the way."

Allan listened with disbelief. It was a lie. They had stopped only once, when he stumbled. What was she trying to do?

Tom flashed a brief glare at Allan, who pretended to be fascinated by the tower.

Oh my God, she was _using_ him to make Tom jealous! That was it. Had Tom maybe been watching when they kissed? Then he'd know she had slapped him. But if some of her lipstick was now on his face? Allan stroked his chin while secretly wiping a thumb across his lips. It brought away no trace of red that he could see.

Tom said nothing, but took Mary by the arm and stayed close beside her all the while they remained at the summit. She took a few pictures, including one of Tom and Allan in a buddy-buddy pose beside the locked and rusty door of the frozen tower. Then they walked down, all three together this time, using the road.

It took maybe twenty minutes to walk down the easy way, and by the time they reached the car there was real snow falling. They climbed in. This time, Tom insisted that Mary sit in the back with him. Allan put the key in the ignition. There was a weak electric stutter, but no spark. He tried once more. Same result. And again.

Then he noticed the map light was on. It was only glowing faintly, but it had been on for more than an hour, and that must have drained the battery in this cold. They were stuck.

Mary giggled. But Tom cursed.

"Ross, you idiot! Now how the fuck do we get down?"

"We walk. Hey, I'm sorry, okay? But it's a regular road, no cross country trails or anything. It'll take maybe two hours if we hurry."

"Oh, but ah'll miss my bus."

"Yes," Allan admitted grimly, "you will."

"And besides, ah simply couldn't walk for two whole <u>hours</u>. Ah'm exhausted!"

"Well you can't very well stay here. You'll freeze."

"Not if Tommy stays here with me, ah won't."

"Yeah," Tom agreed. "There's a blanket back here. What's the point in all of us walking out to get help?"

"Well, why the hell should <u>I</u> go if it comes to that? Why not <u>you</u>?"

"That's pretty obvious isn't it? It's <u>your</u> car that's stuck us out here, and Mary is <u>my</u> date."

Allan ran a hand through his hair. It <u>was</u> obvious, even to him. It was also beginning to snow harder now. He ought to get going.

"All right," he told them. "But look, it could take a lot longer than two hours to get back up here with a tow truck. I'll phone from the first place I find, but be ready to spend the night up here. You know, you're both crazy not to come down with me. If this storm gets bad you two could really be stranded."

"Ah won't do it! Ah am <u>not</u> goin' to wear myself out completely and then catch my death of cold. You wouldn't make me do that, would you Tommy?"

"Yeah, Ross. Can't you see she's bushed?"

"Okay then, stay! Just keep one window open a crack and try the engine again every now and then. If you do get it started, drive on down and pick me up. I'll stay on the road."

Tom nodded, and Mary pulled the drab army blanket up to their chins as she and Tom spooned together on the back seat. Allan's last glimpse of them over his shoulder was of Tom nuzzling Mary's neck. The two of them were about to make love, he thought wildly, while he froze his balls off to get them rescued!

For a fleeting moment he considered <u>not</u> bringing help back at all—just walking home, leaving them up here to freeze. It might be days—maybe weeks— before anyone found them. And people said freezing wasn't a bad way to die. Freezing <u>in flagrante</u> should be even better.

On the other hand, it was <u>his</u> car, and someone had probably seen him drive up here. Even worse, his tracks leading down the mountain might not get completely covered by the snow. And last of all (though maybe least) he didn't really hate them all <u>that</u> much. He <u>envied</u> them, if the truth were known—her brass, and Tom's goodluck. One more thought occurred to him, and raised a partial smile. The more intimately Tom and Mary got together, he reasoned the less he would have to worry about Tom and Ann.

*   *   *

Allan was back in under three hours with a tow truck from the Gulf station down on Route 2. It cost him twenty bucks all told for what turned out to be a simple jump start (outrageous!) but snow was falling steadily now and he had known he might need more than just a jump-start, so he agreed and paid.

Mary commandeered a taxi to Albany (which she even paid for), and announced that she would just catch a later train. With a limp handshake she thanked Allan for his rescue efforts. He guessed she'd been somewhat kinder than that to Tom. But while this seemed highly likely, Tom wasn't talking. In fact, he acted sore.

As Mary's cab drove off into the early night, he turned on Allan and said: "You planned that all along, didn't you, Ross?"

"Planned what?"

"You didn't leave that map light on by accident! Nobody's that dumb. You wanted us to be stranded up there, make Mary miss her bus, maybe keep her around so you could..."

"So I could what?"

"Okay, you think you're so smart. But it didn't work, did it? And believe me, you'll be sorry. I'm not going to forget this!"

Allan could have answered, but he was tired. And if Tom was feeling jealous, well, let him. It made a nice change.

"Yeah. Right, Petard."

"Just wait. You <u>will</u> be sorry," Tom warned, and stalked off through the first real snow to fall on Williamstown for weeks.

Chapter 19: Jazz Waltz

Allan's hanging up on Ann must have had some effect, because it was she who called him the next time they talked. But their exchange resolved nothing. He started to apologize for trying to "own" her. She interrupted him, saying she'd never thought that; and she was sorry she'd hurt him. He insisted no, she shouldn't feel bad. How could she <u>help</u> but feel bad, she countered...and so their talk went: tender, awkward, confused.

About all they could agree on was that they both needed time to think, and that Allan wouldn't come to see her for a little while yet. Meanwhile, they would both continue writing letters.

Days followed, full of events and concerns other than Ann.

Classes, seminars, papers, tests—all the routine of being at college—suddenly seemed important again, and pleasing. More so because, as a senior, Allan knew time was running out, that he would soon be exiled into a wider, less familiar world.

Months before, he had applied for several grants and advanced study programs. Now, within a week, he got word that he had won a year-long fellowship to the Sorbonne in Paris, <u>and</u> been accepted into the graduate program in Musicology at Princeton. He decided, with advice from Professors Forrester and Markham, to accept the Sorbonne Fellowship (which included a unique seminar with the music critic for *Le Figaro*) and postpone entering Princeton till the fall of the next year.

So Allan's future looked secure. And from that week on, it was the present and the past that filled his thoughts increasingly. Uncertainties about even the simplest things in life began to creep into his consciousness. He found himself watching other people far more closely than he ever had, listening to their words with greater care, minutely studying their actions and appearance. It was if he sensed now for the first time that these others knew—had <u>always</u> known—things he had never even guessed and must somehow learn.

And most of all Allan began to study Tom—his habits, his clothes, his attitudes on everything from politics to modern art—looking for clues to what about him might have attracted Ann.

There was a careless freedom about Tom, he realized—the shaggy hair, the jeans, the scuffed tennis shoes—the very details he had always looked down on or just ignored. Now, Allan realized, he envied these outward signs of casual easy ways, and always had. There was Tom's language, too—the tough-sounding street slang, the gratuitous <u>fucks</u> and <u>shits</u>, and his seemingly relentless taunting of authority. Allan could see Tom was posing, performing, just as he himself did, but for a different audience—an audience of his own age and outlook. His self-chosen role might not endear him to those in positions of power anywhere, but right now, here, at Williams College, Anno 1965, it played, it played.

Allan even began to really listen to the records Tom put on: The Kinks, Herman's Hermits, even the Rolling Stones. One night alone in the showers, he found the refrain of one particular song running inside his head, and words only half remembered forming on his lips. True, there was not much tune, only a gutsy rhythm, pushing, pulsing:

> *"...I can get no*
> *SatisFACtion.*
> *I obtain no*
> *steady ACtion.*
> *Though I try, and I try*
> *and I try, and I TRY...*
> *I can GET no...*
> *(no, no, no)*
> *satis.."*

Hell! It annoyed him to find himself even <u>thinking</u> such shit, much less mouthing the stuff half aloud, Allan swung the shower dial savagely over to cold. For a full thirty seconds he would mortify this faithless flesh of his. Well, twenty seconds anyway.

*   *   *

"*Merde!*" Elroy White exclaimed mildly, both arms loosely embracing his big mama bass. Swift vibrations of the head indicated his shocked disbelief and sent ash from the cigarette stuck to his lower lip dribbling down onto the stage. "Your conception of <u>art</u> rates a capital F! George <u>Shearing</u>? *Mais non!*"

"Tatum," said Pete Jackson decisively from behind his drum set. "<u>That</u>'s jazz! Art Tatum. Nooobody even <u>close!</u>" He concluded this pronouncement with a quick snare drum roll capped by a rim shot and a <u>tsishhh</u> of cymbal for emphasis.

"I never said Shearing was <u>the</u> <u>best</u>," Allan responded patiently. "I only said I admire his <u>technique</u>. Pete, I agree with you on Tatum. He's unbelievable, truly. But sometimes he's almost got too <u>much</u> versatility. It's overpowering, you drown in it. I admire guys who can <u>under</u>state things. And Shearing can <u>do</u> that."

"Mashed potato music!" Elroy scoffed. "The cat sold out for a fat record contract, hasn't played a note of real <u>jazz</u> in years. *Ce typ ça,* he's nothing but a bop Liberace!"

Even Allan had to laugh at that remark, though he didn't agree.

"All right, you tell me," he asked Elroy, "who <u>does</u> swing?"

"Mingus. Miles. Parker. Monk. Taylor. El-ling-ton...*on continu?*"

"Who's Taylor?"

"Oh, man! <u>Cecil</u> Taylor? Where have you <u>been</u>? *Mon Dieu!* Don't you <u>listen</u>?" Elroy sounded genuinely angry, and Allan couldn't understand why.

"Okay. So maybe I like my own groove too much to dig all the new cats. Is that a crime?"

"Man, the cats I mean you could not dig with a steam shovel! And let me tip you... lay off the jive talk, *comprenez-vous*? Like it's just not your scene. Dig?"

Allan shut up; and stood up too.

"Hey, look, you guys," he said, turning from one to the other, "What's wrong? Am I suddenly playing all clinkers now? You make it sound like I've got leprosy or something."

Pete shrugged. "Don't look at me, man."

But Elroy nodded.

"Leprosy? *C'est peut etre le mot juste.* Yeah. White skin." He leaned across his instrument, blew smoke, and looked toward Pete as if for confirmation.

He didn't find it. Pete turned away from him.

Elroy shrugged and went on. "You got good hands, Ross. Good hands. And you invent—all the time you're thinking, thinking, thinking. But that's not jazz. You've never been where real jazz comes from. You play like it was all lines of notes and slick chord changes. You play like jazz was comedy, a game. You don't bleed when you play.*Merde!* You don't know even how to it feels to bleed. Okay. That's your world. *Bonne chance!* Stay in that soft safe white world of yours—with Shearing and Brubeck and Lenny Bernstein, and, yeah... Darius fuckin' Milhaud. But out here, where Pete and I come from it's cold, real cold, and black!

"Oh man," Pete moaned disgustedly, "get off the soapbox, will you? Save it for those Harlem chicks you like to snow. You're no po' boy off the streets. Your old man's loaded!"

"*Mon pere*," Elroy told Pete, icily, "has learned how to beat Whitey at his own fat money game. But my true heritage is <u>not</u> Lincoln Center or Carnegie Hall. And I am <u>proud</u> of it. But you, you can't make up your mind, can you? You love everything you see up here in Whiteland, everything 'cept maybe when you pass a <u>mirror</u>!"

"Balls!" Pete tossed a drumstick in the air and caught it deftly, as his right foot worked the pedal once and his bass drum boomed.

Elroy turned back to Allan.

"*Ecuté*, man. Around here you pass for real cool, but out there, where jazz is, you are <u>nowhere</u>. Maybe someday you'll wise up and learn to blow some <u>real</u> licks. *Entretemps*, try a few sides of Taylor. Or Monk."

"Elroy, I already <u>do</u> dig Monk. You know that. Hell, you even introduced me."

Elroy shook his head. "Wrong, man. You don't. You only <u>think</u> you do. *Au re <u>fuckin</u> voir!*"

Allan looked at Pete.

"Oh. Give it up," Pete sighed. "It's hopeless, Al. This threesome just ain't cookin' any more. No offense, Elroy, but you're a royal pain in the butt. You know? You act like <u>own</u> jazz, like only <u>you</u> know how to swing."

Elroy took a last puff, dropped his cigarette and ground it underfoot against the stage floor. "Huh uh. We don't <u>own</u> jazz. Hell man, it owns <u>us</u>!"

"Yeah, right! Jazz to the barricades!" Pete called out in a mock-heroic tone.

"Damn straight," said Elroy. And he pulled up his heavy bass and stalked away.

"Damn it, Pete. Why'd you have to say <u>that</u>?"

"Come on, Al. It was <u>you</u> he was putting down."

"Yeah. Well, maybe he was right. I'm going after him."

"Suit yourself." Pete shrugged.

Allan reached the door in time to see a tall dark figure with a man-sized burden striding swiftly off across the gravel parking lot into the night. He called out, but Elroy didn't stop or look back. Allan slowed down to a walk, keeping his distance but staying within sight.

As he walked, he thought back to the night when his own jazz had "gone public" for the first time. It was during a break in a late rehearsal for the class variety show his freshman year. He had sat down carelessly at one of two pianos parked in the orchestra pit of the main stage. He'd begun idly picking out a Bach fugue, but soon gave it up for a little George Shearing tune: called *She* that he'd picked up from an old Bud Powell recording.

He played so softly he thought no one else could hear, but after a few choruses he became aware that someone at the other piano was laying down chords to comp his melody. He looked over and found Elroy White, who grinned, nodded, and said something unbelievably corny like "Go, man go!"

Allan should have felt embarrassed, but for some reason he didn't. He played on, more loudly now, for one more chorus, then gestured to Elroy "Your turn." With a little conscious effort he switched over from melody line to comp chords, while Elroy took off.

It had been good to listen, fun to play. They had gone on and on together, trading off lead and backup for five or ten minutes, until finally the director leaned over the pit and suggested they move it up on stage. And they had!

By the end of rehearsal, they were working up arrangements for half a dozen songs to play as piano duos to cover the set changes between skits in the Review.

Elroy played bass in a college jazz group called "The Purple Hillsers". (Besides referring to fanatic old grads in general, this was a pun on the name of their pianist and leader, a Junior named Jerry Hill).

Elroy made the necessary introductions, and Jerry let Allan sit in a few times at the group's rehearsals. At first, Allan couldn't keep up with their improvised jamming. But he soon caught on, and by the following spring, he could play a modest repertoire of standards, and had even arranged a tune or two of his own for the group— notably his little jazz waltz *Something for Sylvia.*

When Jerry graduated, Allan hadn't exactly planned to fill his shoes. Still, he and Elroy and the old group's drummer, Pete Jackson, formed a trio playing mostly for their own amusement, and now and then even got a paying job.

Elroy didn't exactly need the extra cash. Like Tom, he was a non-affiliate, but for all his hipster image, Allan knew that Elroy's father was a millionaire. So Elroy could afford to do—and be— whatever he liked.

Just now, he liked being a student, and he was good. Better than Allan in fact: all straight 'A's, and had made Phi Beta Kappa in his Junior year. When he left, Allan guessed, he would step straight into his father's business or become a management trainee somewhere important. That would be a sight: Elroy White in a grey flannel suit— and probably still sporting his black beret and shades.

Elroy also roomed in West College, and Allan caught up with him in the hallway on the ground floor. Elroy was breathing hard and grinning widely.

"Well, *mon vieux,* you surely are persistent."

"I live here too, remember," Allan managed.

"*Eh bien!* So you do." Elroy leaned his bass against the door jam and looked around. No one else was in the hall. He stepped closer.

"Uh...*entre nous*, your roommate and I concluded a small transaction tonight for some excellent grass. May I offer you the same?" He looked expectantly at Allan.

"Uh, no thanks," Allan said. "I don't smoke... marijuana."

"*C'est dommage.* You really ought to try it sometime. What you don't know might surprise you. *N'est-ce pas?*"

Allan hesitated, curious, even eager, but wary too.

Elroy made a Gallic gesture with palms upraised close to the shoulders. "Some time when you feel more...daring? *Peut etre?*"

"Maybe." Allan agreed.

He turned from the door and was walking away when he heard Elroy call after him.

"Seeing much of *la petite* Ann these days? One hears she has been *tres occupée.*"

Allan froze for a beat, but said nothing. Then he continued walking. Somewhere, a door closed. But if Elroy was behind it, still chuckling, Allan couldn't hear him.

The guy <u>knew</u>. God damn him, he <u>knew</u>! Tom had <u>told</u> him. The smoldering anger in Allan blazed up again.

He pushed open the door to their room. Tom was sitting in the armchair, smoking.

"Tom, did you tell Elroy White about you and Ann?"

"Maybe. Why?"

"<u>Why</u>? Because you had no <u>right</u> to, God damn it! No right!"

"Hey, since when are you telling me my <u>rights</u>? I'll do what I fucking please."

"Don't," Allan warned.

"You going to stop me?"

"One way or another, yes."

"I can break you in pieces, man. You want another demonstration?"

Allan caught himself. Tom <u>could</u> break him, and he knew it. Still, he couldn't believe they were both saying all this, not after three years of friendship.

"Look, Tom. You're not just hurting me now, you're hurting <u>Ann</u>."

"Oh, shove it, will you? I'm so fucking tired of your straight-arrow crap! You think Ann cares who knows that we were screwing? I sure don't. And if she does, well tough shit!"

Allan glared at him helplessly.

"You don't care about <u>her</u> at all, do you? I don't believe this. First you steal your best friend's girl, and then you brag about it to anyone who'll listen like she was just some whore you picked up on the street."

Tom moved in on him, wavering a little on his feet, Allan thought. But he didn't look drunk exactly.

"Listen, shithead. You want to talk about 'friends'. Well when the fuck were you ever a friend to <u>me</u>? And don't start with that fraternity business. I never asked to join your fucking frat house. For one thing it costs <u>money</u>, asshole, and my folks don't <u>have</u> it. I'll bet you never even thought about that did you?"

Tom took a breath, then went on. "I may not have much, but I've sure as hell got Ann. And she'll take anything I give her and be glad of it! Don't think so? Well, stick around and watch."

"I swear I'll get her back from you!"

"Yeah. You and what army? Go ahead, tell her everything I've just said. Tell her anything you like, Ross. Only don't give me any more bullshit about 'caring' and 'friends' and 'fairness'. Christ, look at you. If you could kill me, you'd do it right this fucking minute; wouldn't you, Ross? Only you haven't got the guts, so you went snaking after <u>Mary</u>!"

Tom bowed low, and made a ridiculous a flourish, then declaimed in a mawkish imitation of a Southern accent: "Suh! Yoo are a scoundrel and a cad! Ah demand SATISFACTION!" He mimed the gesture of striking Allan across the face with a glove. "Chuse yo' wepons, suh!"

"Fuck you, Petard!" Allan turned away, choking with anger.

Yes, he realized, he really <u>could</u> kill Tom. But death was the last thing Allan wished for him, though not the worst, not by a long shot.

For days afterward, alone in the practice room, or at his carrel in the library stacks, or just walking across the campus between classes, his hate for Tom would suddenly rise up to whelm him with blast visions of pure rage. For those few moments he would grind tooth over tooth, clench fists and narrow eyes while his mind filled up with scenes of violence, atrocious pain, and utter degradation centered on one figure, always the same.

Apache Indians might carry out the details, or those Tuareg Arabs out of P.C. Wren's *Tales of the Foreign Legion*, or, better still, one of those cruel and jaded emperors of ancient China, for whom the subtle arts of torture ranked alongside music and calligraphy as refined amusements.

One scene in particular, picked up from some bad dream or inadvertent reading long ago, recurred to Allan, by turns appealing to him and appalling him. A Chinese c r i m i n a l, condemned to death by torture, stands upright and naked in a palace courtyard. His outstretched arms and legs are chained at full extension so that his entire body is stretched tight against the rough black surface of an iron chimney. Inside this iron tube, a huge fire has been laid and is just now being set alight.

At the very instant when the kindling is about to catch and flare, out onto an overlooking balcony walks—the empress herself, the Lady An, swathed in silk robes, and as she moves her many ornaments of gold and jade click and tinkle like cool pebbles in a mountain stream.

The prisoner, about to plead one final time in vain for mercy, or to let loose the first of many, many screams, lifts back his head and meets <u>her</u> eyes appraising him with calm disinterest. Her look is mildly curious as if he were some exotic reptile in a zoo.

Seeing her, the prisoner stiffens in his chains, and bows his head—yes, bows, even though he knows it was <u>she</u> who expressly ordered he should die. Then, with no word, or sign, without the slightest flicker of emotion, slowly she turns and disappears once more inside the palace.

Yes. That would be her way: to turn and leave the one in chains— not really Tom, of course, but <u>Allan</u>, Allan all along—uncertain even in those final seconds before the first fierce agony of scalding metal seared away all reason and humanity forever from his mind, if she had even recognized his face, remembered him, or caught the meaning in his bow of adoration.

*   *   *

Allan wrote to Ann continually, and she wrote back. As March wore on they spoke more often on the phone. At times he felt that everything was healed, that Ann's defection had been nothing more than a momentary yielding to Tom's unconventionality, to his defiant confidence; but she was past that now, and recognized and welcomed the proud secure future that he—Allan—was offering and wanted her to share with him.

Other times, they would argue. On the phone, he would try to stay calm, let her raise her voice and get whatever anger was inside her out into the air. Then he would suggest they hang up and talk later when they were both feeling better, being careful to make it <u>her</u> choice in the end, and to leave her the final word. Or, if an angry letter came from her, he would read it slowly, then, with a red pencil, underline each of the meaningful things she said as opposed to the merely emotional. Then he would draft his answer so as to meet each of her reproaches one by one. Patience and care were his best weapons, he was sure, and time his strongest ally.

Sometimes her letters brimmed with concern for him, and self-condemnation. She hated herself, she told him, she was so worthless, such a bitch. How could he stand to think of her? Why didn't he just turn his back on her? How could he possibly go on caring for her?

Those letters he would always answer with sweet reason, little jokes, funny stories—anything to take her mind off herself and off feeling sorry for him. At times he frankly felt pretty noble about all this. But mostly, he was just doing what came naturally to him.

His own parents seldom argued. But on the few occasions when they did, Allan recalled, his father's approach had been the same one he used with stubborn patients determined to diagnose their own disorders and prescribe their own cures. He would let his wife say anything she liked, and never flatly contradict it, but simply tinge his calm responses with hints of doubt. Over time—most often just a few hours, but sometimes days—these tiny seeds of doubt would grow big enough to nudge her point of view close enough to his own that they would reconcile.

Having witnessed this technique succeed, time and again, Allan adopted it almost instinctively in any argument. It was only now, with Ann, when the outcome mattered so desperately to him, that he could no longer feel <u>certain</u> he would win.

There were too many things for him to doubt now: <u>Values</u>--did his own really make life better than those he rejected? <u>Friends</u>—why had Tom betrayed him, why had Ann given in and not resisted the temptation? Even <u>music</u>—could Elroy be right to claim he lacked the <u>soul</u> for jazz?

Allan's moods swung wildly between panic and determination. He was ready to consider anything. Sure, time would tell, but right now, time was keeping its mouth tight shut. And he didn't like it one bit.

Finally, in a breakthrough of sorts, Ann invited Allan down to Wellesley. In fact, she told him, she had arranged with her parents to let him drive her back to Williamstown for spring vacation. But that wouldn't be till Saturday, the 20th. Until then, their apartness continued to gnaw at his composure.

*   *   *

The Wednesday before he was to pick up Ann, Mrs. Ash phoned Allan and asked him to come to dinner. This surprised him some, with Ann away, but it pleased him too, and he accepted gladly.

As he approached the house that evening, it began to rain, dampening the small bouquet he carried. He had heard this was the proper European thing to bring your hostess, and was already practicing for next fall in Paris.

The front door was open, but he knocked anyway, first shaking off the raindrops from his coat and hat as best he could.

Getting no response, he called out "Hello? Anybody home?"

Mrs. Ash's voice wafted in from the living room.

"Out here!"

She stood beside a loaded tea trolley gazing out through closed French doors that opened, in warmer weather, onto the back lawn, a busy little stream, and the tall trees beyond. Those trees were just now coming into leaf after months of waiting.

Her smile was warm, even friendly, but a bit unfocused.

"Allan! How nice. Won't you join me? I'm having martinis."

She shook a tall glass pitcher at him, three-quarters filled with what looked like ice water.

"Uh, well yes thanks."

"You <u>are</u> legal, aren't you? Over 21? We don't want trouble with the liquor board. Lose my license." She laughed.

Allan laughed.

"No. I mean yes. Twenty-two actually. I started late in school."

"Mmmmm. But you caught up, didn't you."

She handed him a short round-bellied tumbler, practically brim full. A yellow scrap of lemon peel and fragments of ice swirled across its trembling surface.

In return he handed her the bouquet.

"Flowers? How sweet. I haven't gotten many flowers lately. Thank you, Allan."

For a moment, he thought she would kiss him. Instead she turned and shoved the long stemmed blooms, still in their paper wrapping, down the throat of a tall white vase, where they nodded tiredly and wept raindrops from their petals onto the bare wood floor.

This done, she returned to the drink cart, and picked up her glass again.

"I hope you don't mind vodka? I just discovered we're all out of gin."

"No. This is perfect, Mrs. Ash."

"<u>Susan</u>, please. I mean, here we are practically family, yes? Thanks to Ann. So why not act accordingly?"

Allan nodded and took a gulp of his drink to avoid having to answer.

Mrs. Ash sat down at one end of the couch beneath the photograph of the Great Andromeda Nebula, and patted the cushion beside her, invitingly.

She reminded him of Ann, now that he looked at her closely. Yes, they had the same eyes, the same smile. An older Ann, more self-assured perhaps, or was she only more blasé? He remembered other evenings sitting on this couch, with the real Ann.

"You look tired, Allan. Are you?"

"A little," he admitted. "It's been a pretty busy time lately."

"Mmmmmmmmm. Yes. I know."

Did she really? Allan wondered. Ann might have told her. But how much?

He was happy to keep talking, only not about Ann. At least not yet. So he asked: "How's Cindy coming with her ballet lessons?"

"Living in a dream as usual. Still seeing Moira Shearer every time she passes a mirror. In fact my husband just drove off to fetch her home from her class in Pittsfield."

Allan absorbed this information with a thoughtful nod, and sipped his cold sharp stinging vodka.

A large clock somewhere in the house ticked steadily in time with the rain. Allan felt the quiet rise around them. His noticed the photo on the wall.

"That really is magnificent," he said admiringly. "Did the Professor take this."

Mrs. Ash nodded. "Yes, he did. The same day Ann was born."

"Oh, so you were with him, then?"

She laughed.

"Not exactly. He was up a mountain, somewhere deep in the Sierra Madres; and I...wasn't climbing much by that time. Ever been to Mexico? Don't bother. Fleas, sand, chronic diarrhea...sorry."

She tittered; put a hand to her mouth, then took another sip of her drink, and went on.

"The expedition couldn't be postponed, of course, I understood that. Road conditions, atmosphere, star alignments. 'The stars don't wait,' as Wooten likes to say. He went on and I stayed down in Urique. Don't worry, you've never heard of it. It was only a village—though, who knows, by now it might be a city. Back then it was...a dump. Chihuahua province. You know. Chihuahua, like the little yapping dogs?" She sipped her drink again.

"Ann never told me she was born in Mexico.

"No?"

"It's too bad he couldn't be there with you. The Professor, I mean."

Mrs. Ash laughed with genuine delight.

"Oh, I think Wooten was right where he belonged. Do you know," she added in a serious confidential tone, "he'd no sooner taken this photo than he fell off some damned cliff and landed smack in a tree! Clumsy of him, wasn't it? Broke his leg rather badly, poor dear. That's how he lost his eye too. I expect he's told you about that. No? He likes to say it wasn't losing an eye, but gaining a daughter. We calculate that Ann was born at the very moment he fell. Now isn't that funny?"

"Amazing," Allan agreed.

"Naturally, he named her 'Andromeda'. Wooten will tell you he'd have liked to christen her 'M-31' but I wouldn't stand for it, and so we compromised. Not true of course. Sometimes he still calls her 'Em'. His little joke, you see. Like pulling his glass eye out to amuse our guests."

She paused briefly to swallow the last ice from her now empty glass.

"He hung the whole night in that tree before the others could get to him; must have suffered dreadfully, poor dear. I believe I'mready for another little drink. You, too?"

"Uh, thanks. I'm still working on this one. But the Professor, I mean he's all right now isn't he?"

"Oh, yes, yes. We <u>both</u> are. You get over pain in time." She stood and walked toward the cart to refill her glass, then hesitated.

"Allan, would you...do something for me?"

"Of course, Mrs Ash."

"Susan."

"Uh, Susan. '

"Would you . play for me? The way you do for Ann."

He breathed easier.

"Of course. Anything you'd especially like to hear"

"Whatever you prefer."

Allan knew exactly what he felt like playing. At the keyboard he paused only a moment before beginning *Ann's Waltz*—the real one, the tune that had come to him the night he first found out about her and Tom. He had worked it over quite a bit since then, and though it might not be completely set even now, in his mind, it was already hers--<u>really</u> hers, not just borrowed or handed down. He offered it slowly, achingly: three choruses and a long gentle close.

When he'd finished Mrs. Ash didn't speak or applaud, so Allan stayed seated. But at last he turned to look at her. A single tear was trailing down the face of this aging woman who was almost Ann.

Allan felt that she knew everything about him, everything.

After a long pause, she said: "You really <u>love</u> her, don't you."

Mrs. Ash closed her eyes and sniffed.

"I don't suppose," she continued slowly, "that you could love <u>me</u> a little, too?"

Allan stood up and was walking toward her, when there came a crash of thunder and Professor Ash arrived—or you could say materialized in the room.

His bulk filled the doorway, and he held a gnarled walking stick in one hand and his broad-brimmed black hat in the other. The hat was streaming rain from the storm that raged outside, and his Loden cloth cloak swirled theatrically.

"Aha! Caught in the act!" he roared, looking quickly from his wife to Allan. Then his head went back and he laughed loudly, banging his stick on the floor.

"No concerts allowed in here before the whole audience is seated! Heard you from the porch. What was that you were playing, Debussy?"

Allan shook his head, and tried to clear his throat. "Just something new…American."

"Ahh. Not 'commercial', eh? Can't say I'm surprised."

Allan smiled weakly, and continued to stand there, wondering if it would be polite to laugh or move.

Mrs. Ash turned away, refilled her glass, and said tiredly: "Dinner's in ten minutes, Wooten. Drinks are on the tray."

Cindy darted in, her pink chiffon ballet skirt pushing out all around beneath a yellow raincoat. When she saw Allan, she stopped, executed a graceful curtsey then scampered off again without a word. Allan instinctively bowed back to her--she really <u>was</u> enchanting. Aloud he said "Boy, she's growing up fast isn't she?"

"Mmm. Aren't we <u>all</u>?" the Professor agreed.

Mrs. Ash stood there briefly, and, with careful dignity, walked out to the kitchen.

The Professor hung his dripping cloak and hat up in the hall. Then, headed for the martini cart without looking at Allan.

"Son, I don't know exactly what's going on between you and Ann, and I don't wish to know. If you want to marry her and she agrees, it's fine with me. You're old enough, and I hear you've got some talent. But I tell you this for your own good. Don't ever let a woman steer you. Follow your <u>own</u> stars."

"Yes, sir. I think I've learned that already."

"Well, good. One more thing."

He turned with the freshly poured drink in his hand.

"I know my 'little girl' can take care of herself, just fine. But if I ever catch you sniffing around my <u>wife</u> again, I'll rip your balls off." He smiled, and picked up the martini pitcher. "Have another?"

Allan nodded.

The Professor poured.

"Susan and I have seen a lot together through the years. It's not always been easy. We're not "easy" people, either one of us. But whatever happens, I will never let her make a fool of herself—or me. Is that quite clear?"

It was.

*   *   *

Over dinner, Allan asked for news of Ann, but learned nothing he didn't already know from their phone calls and letters. Still, it never hurts to check.

As usual, he had little trouble getting the Professor to hold forth on matters curious and terrible. Tonight's impromptu chat was on galactic radio sources and the final heat death of the universe.

Mrs. Ash asked Allan what he would do after graduation. He told her about the Sorbonne, and asked if she'd ever been to Paris. She said yes, but did not elaborate. He had to bite his tongue to keep from brightly suggesting that they let Ann join him--at least for part of the summer. He realized it was a little premature. Ann might come with him if it was their own idea--his and hers. But no more formal invitations—that much he <u>had</u> learned.

Cindy, freshly showered and changed, sat looking very serious and thin--like the Degas ballerina of her dreams, Allan guessed, eating slowly and as little as possible.

"How's your school?" he asked her, to be polite and because, with her hair pulled tightly back as it was now, she reminded him more than a little of Ann--and of how much he <u>missed</u> Ann.

"School's okay."

"I meant <u>dancing</u> school."

She brightened, and began eagerly describing the new steps her teacher had just been showing them. Allan was quickly lost in a maze of jargon, mostly French, that sounded extremely precise and conveyed no images whatever to his mind. But he smiled, and nodded, and kept Cindy talking just so that he could enjoy watching her be happy, and imagining Ann.

Later, Mrs. Ash confessed that she'd been a dancer herself, before she married. Of course that was years ago. But she did, now and then, still like to practice with her girls.

Allan smiled. That was something he would truly like to see: the three of them together, dancing.

He was ready to talk about Ann now. But when he asked Cindy if her sister's dancing had made <u>her</u> want to learn too, she quickly shook her head.

"That isn't <u>real</u> dancing," she told him, "the stuff Andy does. It's just all she <u>can</u> do; isn't it, mommy?"

Mrs. Ash replied diplomatically, saying that Ann danced beautifully, but simply felt more at home in a less formal style.

"Hell," the Professor said sourly. "Tell him the truth, Sue. He's old enough. So's our little swan maiden here."

"Really, Wooten, I don't think..."

"Well I <u>do</u>. She got to be too <u>big</u>, see? You know, <u>breasts</u>? Some of 'em have more than others? Well she got too much. Made her top-heavy."

"Wooten!"

"And when her teacher told her she could never be the dying swan, or Giselle, or who ever it was..."

"Cinderella!"

"That's right, Cindy. <u>Cinderella</u>...and that she'd always have to stay back in the chorus..."

"For ever and ever and ever!"

"<u>Cindy</u>!"

"Oh, leave the kid alone, Sue. Anyway, when it happened, can you guess who she blamed? That's right, <u>me</u>. It seems someone..."

The Professor rolled his eyes in the direction of his wife.

"Someone told her big breasts came from <u>my</u> side of the family. And of course one look and she could <u>see</u> that it wasn't her <u>mother</u>'s fault. But anyhow, she took the news rather badly."

"Wooten, please stop this."

"No, Sue. I don't think so. Not tonight. What she did, you see, Allan, she snuck down to the kitchen one night and she got this big old knife, and then she tried to cut off her own..."

"Wooten, how <u>can</u> you!?"

"Didn't get very far of course. But, then, I suppose by now you've probably seen the results for yourself, those half-moon scars in a very existential place, hmmmmmmmmm?"

Cindy shrieked and shrieked with laughter.

Mrs. Ash abruptly turned and slapped her daughter's face. Then she stood up and walked stiffly out of the room. As she passed her husband's chair she stopped and bent down just long enough to spit on him.

The Professor never moved, but his eyes closed briefly, and he sighed.

"Sorry about that. Susan's been under some strain lately. You know how they get around that age. Now, where was I? Oh, yes. <u>Ann</u>. Well, after so much fuss the family decided that we ought to make some changes. Seemed a good moment to "make a new start" so to speak."

As it happened, this job opened up and we came here, to Williams. That was five years back. And I'd have to say we've all settled in pretty well, considering. New school, new friends, new... interests."

Professor Ash reached up with his napkin and dabbed his wife's spittle from his hair.

"And now," he sighed," my little girl is all grown and gone away to college."

"I'm your little girl now, daddy!"

"Yes, Cindy. Yes you are."

"Only I'll dance the <u>good</u> way, the <u>right</u> way."

"Sure you will, honey. You dance just as long as you can."

Allan swallowed.

"Well," the Professor continued, putting down his napkin, "I'd say this dinner is pretty well finished. Shall we go and see what's become of our hostess, or must you be going?"

"Uh, it _is_ getting late."

"Right. Well, then let me say good night _for_ her. Susan will understand. You can see yourself out can you? Good."

Allan and Professor Ash stood up. Cindy continued sitting there, beaming up at both of them like a gleeful imp.

The Professor laid a heavy hand on Allan's shoulder.

"Welcome to the family,…son."

Chapter 20: Blues

Could it be that <u>nothing</u> in his world was really what it seemed? The awful ache of doubt in Allan now was intensified by growing curiosity. More talented than some, less so than others, he had always seen himself as a model or at least an acceptable norm for any group he mixed with in classes, at his fraternity, with other musicians, even among the theatre crowd.

But now, he realized, all this time another very different culture had existed all around him here— guys who raised beards, left their hair shaggy, wore dirty blue jeans, and let it be known that they took drugs—not just pot, but other things—expensive, powerful, illegal things that could give you wild hallucinations, maybe even wreck your mind. Before now, he'd dismissed such actions as chemical Russian roulette--dangerous, pointless, dumb. Now he was not so sure.

Tom knew this other world. So did Elroy. And they could lead him there. He'd only go to look of course; and come back safe again. But he could ask them. It was something he should know about— another mystery, one he'd never taken seriously till now, beyond alcohol, or sex, or maybe even love.

He managed, casually he thought, to ask Tom one wet morning what it felt like, taking drugs. Was it like getting drunk?

Tom smiled. "Huh-uh. Booze is a DOWN trip; grass is a HIGH. No hang-over, no conking out, just...I don't know, peace maybe. Y'know?"

"No. I <u>don't</u> know. I can't even imagine it."

"That's right. And you never will, until you try it. Hey, that's it. You <u>want</u> to, don't you? Tell me I'm wrong."

"You mean <u>here</u>? Right <u>now</u>?"

Tom hesitated. Maybe he didn't trust this sudden show of interest. Allan could understand that. If Tom were to admit he kept drugs right here in the room, Allan could always report him to the campus police or something. Naturally, he'd never really <u>do</u> something like that. Still, it would be nice to <u>know</u>.

"Well," Tom coughed, "No. I just mean it could probably be arranged. You got twenty bucks?"

"I could write you a check," Allan offered.

"Huh-uh. Strictly cash."

"Then I'll have to hit the bank."

"Sure you want to <u>do</u> that, Ross? You could get in <u>trouble</u>." Tom made a face.

"No. I'm <u>not</u> sure. I just thought it might be interesting to try getting high some time."

"Yeah. Right. Well, think about it, and when you've got the money I'll see what I can do. Remember we've got the cabin...hey, you've never been there, have you?"

"Not yet." Allan admitted, feeling guilty and pleased at the same time to think he might soon be learning something completely new.

"Okay, how about tonight? That is, if we can take your car."

Allan hesitated. He didn't feel prepared. But how <u>did</u> you prepare? Maybe sometimes just letting things happen to you was preparation enough. He should have done that more with Ann, he realized. He thought of her again, and hurt again. He would be seeing her this weekend--driving in tomorrow afternoon to Wellesley. But she had sent no letter for the past three days.

"Sure. I guess so. Yeah. Tonight's fine. Who's <u>we</u> though?"

"Relax," Tom laughed. "Just a friend. It's <u>better</u> with friends there, especially the first time. So, eight o'clock at your car. Is it set?"

"It's set."

*   *   *

Tom was standing alone by the car when Allan came out.

"Where are the others?" Allan asked.

"Only one. He'll meet us there. You got the money?"

Allan nodded. "You want it now?"

"Naw. I trust you. Let me drive."

Tom headed south along Route 7, then turned west toward the New York line. It was a quiet night and clear, with a few white clouds, a full moon, and many stars. Fields were drenched in moon silver close to the road, and solitary trees stood out like twisted hands against the gleam of frost on grass or painted houses. But the hills beyond loomed black on every side, and closed around them fast once they turned off the main road. Their headlight beams stitched through a tangled darkness suggesting deep woods.

"You must come out here pretty often to recognize that turn so easily at night," Allan commented.

"A couple times," Tom agreed. "Hold on now. From here it gets rougher."

No kidding. Before long the road was so pot-holed and gullied that Allan was glad they weren't going more than five or ten miles an hour. He wondered if Tom drove this carefully every time he brought the car out here. He guessed not. In Tom's place he'd have seriously considered gouging a fender or breaking a headlight just for spite. This thought immediately shamed him, but it wouldn't go away. He still wanted to hurt Tom, to make him suffer, even though there was no point now.

The dashboard lights were dim. They'd need gas soon--only a quarter tank left. But that was probably plenty at this speed. The road turned a lot. Allan thought they were heading back east again.

"Ever checked a map to make sure this cabin of yours really <u>is</u> in New York?"

"What's the difference? We're safe. No cops'll come around. And I can find the place, so who cares?"

Allan shook his head. He wasn't satisfied. Tom's answer was practical, but showed no curiosity, no imagination. That was the difference between them. Tom would rush into things blindly just to see what happened, and then just as quickly rush on to something else. Allan moved cautiously, but he also took the time to analyze and savor each experience. That made him superior to Tom in the long run. He smiled to himself in the darkness as he thought this. The car took a sudden lurch, and he heard the muffler scrape.

"Hey! Watch it," Allan yelled.

"Keep your shirt on. It's okay."

"Yeah, well just remember, it's a long walk back if we get stuck out here."

"Don't sweat it huh? We're there."

At first Allan could see nothing but a thicker darkness at one side of the road. Then, as the car rolled to a stop, their headlights flashed back at them from a dirty shade-drawn window.

The cabin wasn't what you'd call romantic. No chinked logs or field stone chimney, just a tarpapered shack with one grimy four-paned window, a weather beaten door, and a rusty tin pipe sticking up through a sloping tar-papered roof.

"You don't suppose anyone ever really <u>lived</u> out here, do you?"

"You think people don't live in worse-looking places? You should see Roxbury."

"I just meant it's so far away from anywhere."

Tom took a key from his jacket pocket and opened the padlocked door. Stepping in, Allan felt even colder than outside. For some reason he'd expected warmth.

"Home sweet fucking home!" Tom made a sweeping gesture around the room with his free hand. The other held a cigarette lighter up high. By its flickering shine, Allan could just make out a pile of something in one corner, and what might be a table and one straight-backed chair close to the window.

"Isn't there a stove?"

"Of course there's a stove. Jeesus, you think I'd freeze my ass coming out here if there wasn't?"

Allan shrugged.

"See that box by the door? There's some wood in it. Ought to be anyway. Take a look."

Tom snapped his lighter shut and darkness rushed in. Allan felt around inside the wood box. There were a few sticks and some bigger chunks, but they felt light and rotten. He took out a few of each, and was just about to ask what next, when a warm red glow suffused the room. Tom had pulled off his coat, and was bending to adjust the wick of an old red-glass kerosene lantern. Stolen from some construction site, Allan guessed.

Now he could see the stove. It was not the quaint pot-bellied job he'd been hoping for, but a shabby cheap-looking thing made of thin brown sheet metal.

He helped Tom stuff pieces of wood inside—punk and windfall branches, just as he had surmised— together with a few twists of dry newspaper. At the touch of Tom's lighter the mess flared.

"That stuff won't last long," Allan warned.

"Yeah. There's a pile of real logs around back. How about lugging in a couple? That's if you think you can make it."

Allan made a mental note to break Tom in one or two vital places at the first convenient opportunity. Then he stepped outside and brought in three big logs. They were a heavy load, but he made it.

Once the first of the logs was burning well, Tom led him over to toward a pile of three or four mattresses and pillows in the corner (all of them Williams College issue, Allan noted coolly).

"Where's that twenty?" Tom asked.

"Right here. See." Allan held out two ten dollar bills.

"Okay." Tom pulled in the two tens and pocketed them. "So now we're set. Relax. Get comfortable. The stuff'll be here any minute." He sat down. "Meanwhile "

Tom held a can of something like tobacco on his lap, and began rolling some of it inside thin paper. After twisting both the ends shut he passed it to Allan.

Allan looked at it curiously.

"Is that grass?"

"This is grass."

"What does it <u>do</u>?"

"Don't worry, it won't kill you."

"Hold it! Somebody's outside." Allan hissed.

Tom frowned for just a moment, then relaxed. That was a sports car motor they were hearing, not a police cruiser.

"Hey, Elroy. That you?" Tom called out.

"Whom else? You were expecting perhaps *les flics*?"

Elroy entered laughing. He was perfectly dressed for the role of well-heeled hipster: black beret, dark glasses (Allan wondered how he could possibly see anything, wearing them at night, especially in the woods), fur-collared coat, soft leather gloves, and a knitted wool scarf of red, white, and green.

"*C'est si froid, comme la* proverbial witch's tit," Elroy observed.

"You bring all the stuff I asked you to?"

"Safely here."

"What stuff?" Allan asked.

"Tell you later." Tom interrupted. He pointed to the hand-rolled paper twig in Allan's hand. "Go on. Light up and see what that does for you."

"Ah, yes." Elroy grinned. "*Le petit garcon est en train d'essayer son premier* toke *n'est-ce pas*?"

"Okay, okay," Allan admitted. "Yes, this is my first."

He tried to appear nonchalant as he placed the crooked cigarette between his lips, ignited it, and took a first deep draw. He liked the smell. He couldn't quite place it, but it was somehow familiar though. He puffed again. Nothing to it. Easy as smoking.

Tom too, had lighted up. But Elroy had turned away and was walking out the door.

"No, no. Like this," Tom said. "You gotta hold it in. Keep your lungs full like this, see? That's the way."

Allan thought he was catching on. It was beginning to warm up now inside the cabin. The pillows beneath him were comfortable, and the dim red lantern light was soothing. But he didn't like the expression on Tom's face.

Why had he agreed to come here? Why should these two want to help him get drugs? Elroy he respected, in a way; but he'd been acting awfully moody lately; and Tom he had every reason to mistrust. Hell, if they did mean him trouble he'd played right into their hands. They could do anything to him out here.

"How you feel?" Tom asked him.

"Fine, I guess. No different. What should I feel?"

There was a noise at the door, and Allan looked up just as Elroy reentered carrying his bass before him. Tom walked over to join him, or help him. They seemed to be unpacking it, but that was strange, because the bass already leaned against the wall, but the case still seemed to have stuff in it; stuff that wasn't the bow or extra strings.

Elroy and Tom leaned close together, far from Allan. He eyed them carefully. What did they really want from him? Both of them were smiling, saying things he couldn't hear. They were also looking down at something in their hands, something hidden from him by the shadow of the big black case.

He caught himself staring back and forth from one to the next--all three of them--including the case, as if it too were alive. His eyes narrowed. He was really alert now, ready for anything they tried to pull.

Elroy pointed at him, nudged Tom, and whispered some more. Tom nodded vigorously.

"Yeah. I think you're right," Tom agreed.

"Feel anything yet?" Tom asked, moving closer to Allan.

"I don't know. I don't think so. Maybe just tired. This one's about finished. Is there an ashtray?"

"Naw. Just use the table top. Don't toss the butt away though. They get better when you save 'em up. Give it here. See?"

Tom pinched the nub end between thumb and forefinger, held it to his lips and sucked greedily. "This is the best part," he managed to say without letting any noticeable quantity of smoke escape.

Allan was impressed. He wanted to try that.

"Got another?" he asked.

"Yeah, maybe later. Elroy's got something better, something really special, just for you."

"Oh," Allan said calmly, and leaned back into the pillows.

He was not feeling drunk or light headed or in any way strange. He just didn't especially care to move, and accepted Tom's announcement without protest or thanks.

"*Je quoi que trois c'etait assez, mon vieux,*" intoned Elroy, who was suddenly also there at Allan's side. He opened his hand to Allan, who saw, cupped deep inside his Caucasian-pink palm, three small round flattish lumps, like little withered lollipops without the sticks.

"What <u>are</u> these?" he heard himself asking. "Toad-stools?"

"The keys of the kingdom," Elroy replied. "Paradise pills, cactus candy, <u>peyote</u>--considered most sacred by those of Amer-Indian persuasion. *Allons enfant*<u>!</u> Eat, drink. 'This is my body, and this is my blood'." Allan saw a glass of sparkling wine—or was it merely water?—in Elroy's other hand.

"What?"

"Chew 'em up good and swallow," Elroy spoke softly, close to his ear. "The water helps. *Allons!*"

Allan ate. And drank.

The cactus lumps were bitter with a slightly tinny taste, and spongy. As he swallowed, Allan felt a little sick. He was not really enjoying this.

"Attaboy!" he could hear Tom say, as the last of the water went down and he released his breath. But he paid no attention. Something else was on his mind.

He could see patterns now each time he shut his eyes--not swirling and random as they were sometimes when he fell asleep, but long straight-lined regular shapes, sharp and geometric. Not pictures of the day's events either, as sometimes happened after a long drive, merely lines and solids. They would change when he blinked, or when he shook his head without opening his eyes. This was interesting to Allan. He found it was easy to smile. And so, he smiled.

"Hmmmmmmm," he heard himself say.

Tom and Elroy were busy making their own sounds that might have been laughter. But Allan wasn't listening. He was too late to catch their joke, and it would only embarrass him to ask them to explain. He no longer felt anxious. He had no desire to run away, or even stay alert. Instead, he felt drowsy. It was pleasant feeling this way, and he made the most of it.

Not much was happening. But that was fine too. The metallic taste wouldn't leave his mouth, and every now and then he felt a twinge of nausea, but mostly it was simply quiet here, and red, and warm.

He knew the redness was lantern light and not from the fire in the closed tin stove. But it was the stove that held his interest.

The straight lines and flat-edged shapes no longer danced behind his closed eyelids, but the stove seemed somehow akin to them and oddly familiar, a shape he could like, and trust, and smile at. So he did.

The stove had volume, so must be full of light—though he could only see its darkness. This made him think of space—of the vast emptiness between stars and the vaster emptiness between electrons and their nuclei.

Allan could visualize individual particles colliding to form matter. He could see these in turn drawing other particles to join their mass and so on through immensities of time until first wisps of gas then whirling balls of many vapors swirled together ever tighter till they glowed then blazed up into stars.

Yes, and the stars exploded, spewing viscous lumps that cooled and hardened down to planets. Then the solid planets surging, breaking, and reforming, mixing and compounding every sort of matter—heat and cold, water and air, pressing into stone and grinding solid stone again to sand.

The intense clarity of Allan's understanding made him grin and close his eyes.

When he opened them Tom was close by, bending over him, and smiling.

"Feeling good, huh?"

"Yes," Allan said, quite distinctly. "Very clear. It's not like what I'd thought."

Tom grunted something encouraging over to Elroy. Allan picked up only a few words here and there: "You ready? ...check...uh, batteries?...okay, okay."

Allan's planets now were cooling, going green, extraordinarily green, more green than leaves or plankton, emerald green, a fiery green, green blaze. And Tom was talking to him now, and not to Elroy any more. Allan was pretty sure of this. But asked him to repeat that once again.

"I said: How about if I ask you some questions?"

"Okay," Allan agreed.

He decided to close his eyes briefly. There were sounds in the room, like someone smothering a laugh and saying "Oh Jesus!" as if the laughing hurt. But this didn't concern him. He had so much else to think about.

Tom cleared his throat. "Hem, hem. All right, so tell us, Mister Ross: what can you see--right now, this minute?"

"Interesting," Allan nodded. "Well, it's not quite seeing it's more realizing things I never figured out before."

"Like what?"

"Well...evolution, maybe; only <u>all</u> the way back, to before everything. It's all just the same process, really. And I can <u>see</u> it working. Things running every which way and randomly sticking themselves to each other and staying that way or exploding or sometimes just bouncing off. That's it. That's everything. That's even <u>life</u>!"

Bigger noises came out of the dark. Allan opened his eyes. He could see human shapes in the dim red lantern glow, two at least, and one more not so easy to place. And this third one was grunting. Grunting blue! Throbs of indigo and turquoise and sapphire flashed and bled into each other without pain or effort as something he knew but could not at first label—a thing that established itself in his head, entering through his face, or perhaps his ears.

Tom and Elroy were standing together, though not in the same place. By turning his head, Allan could see them both moving their shoulders up and down, and they were both making noises. But Tom was using only his mouth, which made little sense, while Elroy with two hands was choking and pinching a fat-bellied thin-necked third shape, which then uttered its own words in a language that Allan was perfectly sure he could speak if he tried.

He supposed they were looking at him. Tom was closer and held out a small thick stick pointed at Allan's mouth. Nothing threatening, silvery, wired, a flat-headed banana with a long tail.

"Yeah?" Tom was saying. He sounded out of breath. "Gee, wow, that's really something. So, what else do you see?"

It was flattering, Allan conceded, to be asked this. But how could he tell someone outside himself? It's not something you can explain to just anyone. He hadn't even told Ann yet. But she'd understand him, he knew, when he <u>did</u> tell her. And he would do it the next time he saw her. He'd do it for love.

Something prodded him. A very interesting finger. Tom's?

"Hey Al! Don't fall asleep on me now. We want to hear more about uh...life."

"Sorry. I, uh...lost my thoughts for a minute. 's see. D'I mention how living stuff's really just lumps of chemicals acting on other chemicals to make more of themselves as they go along?"

"Yeah. Right. At least I <u>think</u> so. That what you heard him say, Elroy?"

"*Mais ou<u>i</u>!* The boy's sweet wisdom is forever sealed inside My Foolish Heart."

At these words, which reached Allan with a force like that of a soap bubble ripping through steel, the third speaker, the grunter, abruptly and distinctly chimed in "*For this time it isn't fascination / Or a dream that will fade and fall apart../ .It's love, this time it's love... my foolish* "

Allan wanted quite badly to answer in kind, but found his own fingers had nothing to talk with. They were tongue-tied. His fingers were tongue-tied! His mouth laughed instead.

The blue grunts shaded off into violet, and ceased to glow. Allan slowly stopped laughing in time to hear Tom saying something like "Shhhh! Fuck it! Will you shut up! (mumble, mumble) or the tape'll run out. Cool it, huh?"

Then Elroy's voices slipped off into the dark again, too far to trace. So Allan stopped paying attention.

"Any more?" Tom again.

Allan nodded and tried to explain.

"Mmmmm, you see, the neatest thing of all is these life blobs, they just never stop <u>being</u>. That original first blob is <u>still alive</u> even now after billions and billions of years. Sure, it's split up into pieces again and again, but all of it's really still there—just one big animal! Well, okay maybe parts of it we call animal and other parts plant, or bacteria or mountains and oceans or whatnot. But whatever you call it, it's all strung together. It's just that the connections—the strings— have been cut, and the parts move around on their own. Isn't that... wonderful!?"

Tom was shaking and wore a broad grin, but for some reason didn't or maybe couldn't speak; but he nodded. So Allan went happily on.

"Like, imagine a tree full of leaves. If there weren't any gravity, you could just cut off each leaf at the stem, but the tree would keep looking the same from a distance, because no leaf would fall. See, no gravity, no parting, they would all just float there in place. And its that way with us, you and me, everybody!

Babies come out tied to their mothers until the doctor cuts the chord. Only we <u>do</u> have gravity here, so when the chord gets cut—the leaf stem—the baby leaf falls away from the tree. The family tree. See, there really <u>is</u> a tree! And it's not just people, it's all the animals, and plants and everything."

"It means there <u>isn't</u> any <u>death</u>! You see? No final, end-of-it-all death. The old ingredients just get remixed. Old parts slough off, but they just re-combine someplace else and the same old blob keeps moving around and growing—ever and forever!"

Somebody laughed out loud from sheer happiness. It was Allan.

"Wow!" Allan heard Tom say. He sounded honestly impressed. Allan was glad he could impress Tom like this. He <u>wanted</u> to impress him, just like he wanted to be his friend. They had always been friends before. Before Ann....

The name hurt. He would rather not think about Ann.

Allan frowned.

Tom's voice again, up close: "What'sa matter?"

"Hmmmmm? Nothing. I guess. Should I go on?"

"There's _more_? Yeah, sure. Go right ahead."

"Do you know how far away the Great Spiral Nebula in the constellation Andromeda is?"

"The _what_?"

"Two _million_ light years," Allan announced gravely. But on some nights you can see it with your naked eye, if you know where to look. And I _do_ know where. _Ann_ showed me."

That name again. He hurried on.

"But with a telescope you can see out for billions of light years, and radio telescopes can 'hear' even further. Professor Ash'll tell you the details. You and I can't imagine all that's going on out there. But he's seen it! Measured it. He's not just guessing, he _knows_. He can tell you what must have happened in the past for what we can see to be there now, and he can tell what's coming in the future too, in a way. I mean for instance, six billion years from now this place we're sitting on will be vaporized. The sun will expand, and everything we know will melt away. No cities, no mountains, no people, no planet, nothing left of us but dust and gas."

"But then," and here Allan couldn't help beaming with relief and joy, "the whole business will start up _again_! So you see? It's like life, the universe--it doesn't die or stop any more than _we_ do. It just changes form, moves from place to place, body to body, through time. Stars and systems get bigger, explode, fly apart, then slow down, cool off, but then drag themselves back together, get big again, explode again, and so on and on. That means there's nothing to be _afraid_ of. We don't have to worry how things began or will end, because they never really _do_. Things just always _are_!"

Tom may have snorted or only coughed. Allan couldn't tell. But what did it matter? Everything was right and fine, and just as it should be.

He was calming now, slowing down. He smiled over at Tom for support, understanding. But Tom had turned away and was using his hand somewhere. Allan could hear a loud click.

Tom turned back and said: "Yeah. Well that's pretty great all right. How you feeling now, Ross? Still okay?"

Allan considered, and, doing so, suddenly knew that those wonderful blue flashes coming to him from the dark had been music notes, low ones, heavy and resonant, deeper than any he had ever played. He took in a long breath.

"Yess. I'm fine. A little dizzy maybe. I don't know."

Allan smiled. The blue flashes were gone now. Elroy had laid down his bass. That was it. He had been playing. The blues had been real. Allan had witnessed the birth of the blues. His mind accepted this phrase as a pun, but decided it wasn't worth laughing at. No one thing here was more funny now than another.

He felt the cold too, and was briefly afraid he might be sick. The red warning lantern still flickered in the room. Allan wished the stove were closer.

"Are you chilly?" he asked Tom.

Tom nodded. "Yeah. Time to get back. Don't worry. I'll drive."

Allan was not worrying. He felt as though a great stone had been lifted off his chest. He could breathe now. He had been somewhere, said important words, seen interesting things very clearly. He would remember them all again soon, he was sure. But not now, not just now, there was no need.

When Allan next opened his eyes, Tom was stuffing something large into a dark green book bag. Allan's bag.

The front door opened. Elroy stamped in.

"*C'est ça!* So. You two ready?"

"Finished," Tom nodded. "Boy, this should be good!"

"Tom?", Allan asked.

"Yeah. What is it?"

"Am I high? Have I been high?"

"You <u>know</u> it, man!"

"Oh." Allan nodded, pleased. He was not exactly sure if he <u>should</u> be, but he was. He began to examine his fingernails closely, and found they were quite interesting. Still, it would not be polite to exclude the other two. He ought to say something, to make conversation. He wanted to be their friend. After all, they were interesting people.

"How...how was <u>your</u> trip, Tom? Did you get high too?"

"Oh yeah. It was cool. You know, wild dreams and stuff. Just like you, right?"

Allan thought so. He remembered the angular lines and intense blues and thinking so logically and saying something true, something Professor Ash was part of. He wondered suddenly if he had talked about Ann? He hoped not. Tom shouldn't hear. Mustn't know. Oh, but Tom <u>did</u> know. That's right. Tom and Ann had been lovers, before she left.

"Tom," he asked slowly, "did you ever bring Ann out here?"

Tom looked down at him.

"Yeah. A few times. Why"

"Did you...turn her on?"

Tom sniggered. "Yeah, well not like you. But we smoked a few joints."

The words hurt, but not deeply. It didn't surprise him to learn Tom and Ann had been here. Allan just hadn't thought of it. So that meant they must have made love here too, just as he had done with her, in his own bed, and almost in hers too. But never in a place like this, so alone, and so free.

Suddenly, he missed Ann, very much. He wished she were here right now. He said so out loud.

"You and me _both_," Tom agreed. "Think you can walk? It's just outside. Or you could ride with Elroy?"

Allan shook his head.

"You staying here?" Tom said this to Elroy, who stood near the stove rubbing his hands.

"*Mais non*! I shall follow you. If you really believe you can navigate your vehicle. How many joints did you <u>give</u> that poor boy before I arrived?"

"Awww, only one. But the peyote was real, huh? Jeez, where do you <u>get</u> stuff like that?"

Elroy shrugged. "I enjoy a wide and varied acquaintance among the local <u>arts</u> community. And, my musical colleague here," he gestured with his head toward Allan, "has the good taste to appreciate *vrai qualité*—even if he never could dig the blues. *Et vous?* Was the performance <u>satisfactory</u>? Did you get each nuance safely down in highest, highest fi?"

"Shut up. He's gonna hear you."

Elroy yawned. "*Je m'en doubte.*"

"Hear what?" Allan asked, puzzled.

"Tell you later." Tom promised.

Allan nodded. It could wait.

*　　*　　*

Soon after, they were in his car. Allan heard the door slam and the engine roar to life. He could feel the cold of the seat penetrate his legs and buttocks. But his back and head felt warm. He kept his eyes closed and began to think. It was a long thought.

Later, he could not remember riding home, or how he got out of the car. He woke up in the parking lot behind the Di-Gamm house, floodlights in his eyes and frozen gravel under his feet.

As they climbed the four flights to their room, Allan remembered Elroy had been with them out in the cabin, and half expected to see him come grinning toward them. But the halls were empty, and so was the bathroom when he went in there.

In the dark before sleep, he thanked Tom for everything.

"Skip it," Tom yawned. "Maybe we'll do it again sometime."

Allan's head sank slowly back onto the pillow. He wondered what sex would feel like if you'd just been taking drugs? Someday, he thought, he and Ann might find this out together. Then he screwed his face up tight, because he suddenly remembered Ann didn't need <u>him</u> to learn this. She already knew.

Chapter 21: *Da Capo*

Spring break arrived on Friday, and Allan set forth to rescue Ann from her enforced captivity in Wellesley. It would be their first face to face meeting since...well, <u>since</u>.

Tom was off in New York City job hunting. Somehow he had lined up no less than three interviews, including one with a bank. He had not cut his hair or modified his rebel image though, and frankly Allan didn't think much of his chances. But of course he didn't say so. What was the point? He was just glad to have their rooms all to himself for a few days. And he was glad to be seeing Ann. Glad is a relative term though, and Allan was not at all sure, as he drove along Route 2 toward Boston, what he would find.

He wondered how often Tom and Ann were writing to each other, and what they said? He had never seen anything that looked like a letter from Ann or an unfinished draft to her on Tom's desk since that fateful day in January. But all that proved was that his roommate had probably gotten better at hiding.

He set off to classical music from the car radio, but the Albany station crackled out as he veered through the mountains beyond North Adams. It happened right in his favorite part of Brahms' *Third Symphony*, where the string section swings into syncopated life. He fussed and twiddled with the dial for twenty miles, while the narrow two-lane road plunged and twisted beneath him, but it was hopeless. Near Greenfield, he reluctantly conceded defeat and switched to Boston's rock'n'roll station, WBZ.

He promised himself he would listen with an open mind. And it wasn't that hard. He even found himself smiling and toe tapping to a new song from the Beatles, though clearly this "Ringo" had even <u>less</u> of a voice than the other three. Still, it was a catchy little up-tempo number titled *I Feel Fine*, and it made Allan smile, because, at this particular moment, so did he.

Outside Concord, Allan pulled in at the Howard Johnsons for a cup of coffee and a piece of pie. The pecan looked good, but, as usual, came off too sugary-sweet. Would he never learn? He left, picking sticky pecan fragments from between his teeth, and still fondly dreaming of the ideal--the Platonic--Pecan Pie that perfectly balanced crust, crunch, and creamy-chewability. Someday, perhaps,...someday.

He used the restaurant phone booth to call Ann. She answered at once, and sounded glad to hear him. She was ready to go, she told him, but suggested they eat dinner at Wellesley first, before hitting the road. She even offered to do some of the driving because she knew he'd be tired.

Well, yes, he was. But tired or not, sitting on the <u>wrong</u> side of the front seat with no steering wheel and no brake pedal under his foot was uncomfortable for him in <u>anyone</u>'s car. Still, Ann did have her license now, and, for a lot of reasons, he believed he ought to show her he had confidence in her. So okay, sure she could drive.

He made two wrong turns coming into Wellesley through the rush hour traffic. So it was half an hour later than he'd planned when he finally rolled through the campus gates and pulled up to a stop in the parking lot beside Ann's dorm.

She was waiting on the steps, and came running to greet him. Her camel's-hair coat was half open, and beneath it he could just glimpse a jumper and white blouse outfit, that made her look like a proper English schoolgirl. A sudden pang of desire flashed through him. How <u>could</u> she--how could <u>any</u> woman—be <u>so</u> adorable-looking <u>all</u> the time?

He had rolled his window down to ask directions at the gate, and now, to his surprise and pleasure, Ann leaned in across the sill. No words, she just leaned in and kissed him. He was terrifically pleased, but struggled to take this unhoped for display of affection calmly in stride.

"Hey! Not so fast," he countered. "Let me get outside where we can do this properly!"

She waited, but just barely.

He soon lost count of their kisses...*da mi basia millia, diende centum*... sang in his head. Good old Catullus! Right again, as usual: exchange a thousand kisses, then a hundred, then confuse the count, so that no one watching may grow jealous of you, tallying the number of your kisses!

Still she didn't speak, no tears, no explanations, just the pressure of her body on his own, and kisses, still more kisses; wet lips and cold hands, chill dusk of spring, her soft hair fragrant against his cheek, his glasses clicking hers.

Somewhere, far off in this deep twilight, poor King Arthur might be rallying his broken knights for one last desperate charge. But Lancelot the fair stood <u>here</u>, with Guinevere locked safe inside his arms.

Or was it really just old Merlin snared once again by Vivian, his nemesis?

...I ever feared you were not wholly mine....

Oh, screw you, Tennyson! Can't you tell honest love from sorcery? Well...learn today from Allan Ross--Allan the Just, the Rewarded, the Proud!

Whoever Allan was, the time at last came when they all began to shiver.

Ann, who felt it too, pulled back and laughed, "Poor baby. You must be freezing. Where's your coat?"

He nodded toward the car.

"Well put it on and let's go eat. I'm starved!"

*   *   *

They walked hand in hand to the dining hall, exchanging looks and small talk that meant little but said everything about desire, nothing about pain.

"No, I'm not tired," he lied. "It was an easy drive in. They've got Route 2 resurfaced outside Greenfield—or is it Springfield?—I can't remember. Anyway, you'll see. It's a lot smoother now."

"Oh, it's not soooo bad here," Ann confided over dinner. "Only I expected more atmosphere—tradition, something—I don't know. But so far it's been very matter of fact. And the classes are easy compared to those I audited last fall at Williams."

The meal was pretty decent, he thought, for institutional cooking—and, best of all, they had a whole table to themselves. There were maybe a dozen other girls in the dining hall, which echoed gloomily. Wellesley's Spring Break had started the day before, and most of Ann's fellow inmates had already been sprung by loving families or lusting boyfriends.

Allan grinned. "If only Williams were co-ed, huh?"

Ann smiled back thoughtfully, faintly.

"No," she shook her head. "Not really. Oh, it would be nice to have the mountains...and to be near you," she added, just in time. "But I couldn't stand four whole years of it. Not with daddy there, and everybody knowing who I was."

"Well, I admit you've got a special problem. But really, you adm if Williams let in women it'd make the place a lot more interesting."

"Hmmmmmmpf. Interesting for whom?"

"Touché, and grammatically correct," he conceded. "But believe me, it could happen. After all, the fraternities are fading out; and lots of alumni swore they'd never let that happen either."

"How are things at <u>your</u> fraternity?" Ann asked.

"Di-Gamm? All right I guess. Oh, Fred and Sara say hi. They're getting married in June right after graduation," he added.

Ann showed no reaction to this unsurprising news, so he went on.

"And tomorrow night we'll initiate the pledges. I admit, I'm kind of looking forward to it. There aren't many ceremonial occasions left in life—only weddings and funerals; and both of those are probably more fun when you're part of the crowd and not a star performer."

"Probably," Ann agreed. "Tell me, do these pledges of yours go through trials of fire and water? Or have to bend over and get walloped with a paddle or something?"

Allan laughed. "Nothing so physical. That stuff went out in the 1950s. Before the War though, I've heard there were plenty of crazy hazing stunts. For instance, guys would be led out into the woods at night blindfolded, and left standing on a clump of grass in the middle of a swamp and warned not to take a step in any direction till dawn. They'd hear what sounded like the others walking away, only they wouldn't really leave. They'd be right there watching. If the pledge moved a foot or more in any direction he'd fall right into the swamp and they'd have to fish him out before he drowned. And if he took his blindfold off, well, he'd see them, and of course that'd be the end of him as a pledge."

"Sounds cruel to me."

"Tests <u>can</u> be cruel sometimes. But noble too. At least I always thought so. I could tell you more. Want to hear?"

Ann nodded.

"Well, usually the brothers testing the pledge would wait about half an hour. If the pledge hadn't moved, a voice disguised so he couldn't recognize it would call to him and instruct him to take a step forward. If he did, without asking questions and without taking off his blindfold, he'd fall right in the water, but they'd haul him right out again and accept him into the fraternity. If he refused or said the pre-war equivalent of "fuck you" they might leave him standing there for another hour or so. But if he had the presence of mind to ask for <u>proof</u> that the command really came from a Di-Gamm brother, he would be handed an object--I can't tell you what, but he'd recognize it all right. Then, when he took his step forward, he'd find a plank bridge and soon be back on solid ground safe and dry."

Allan paused, finished lifting the forkful of mashed potatoes he'd been gesturing with all the while to his mouth, and swallowed the potato part.

"Naturally," he added after a properly dramatic pause, "that was years ago. We do it all with words now, mostly—words and ritual."

"You take it seriously, don't you? This 'brotherhood' business."

"Yes," he admitted, "I suppose I do. Don't ask me why, but yes. It's a bit like acting in a show, or playing jazz. You get a special feeling for the guys you're with. It's not like <u>friendship</u> exactly, more like a special understanding. You've all been through the same thing, so you know something people outside never do. That's about all a fraternity is--a shared secret, a special event you've been part of. I doubt I'll ever see most of these guys again once we leave school. But I'm glad I met them, and I'm glad to know them now. Does that make any sense?"

"Some." Ann said, and put her napkin down beside her plate. "If you're finished eating, we could go upstairs."

Ann's dorm room was on the third floor. And, since her Alaskan roommate had already left, Allan was hoping they might make love here. But when they arrived, he saw the door of the room directly across the hall was open. Inside, three girls and a bottle of something were attempting (a bit forlornly, Allan thought) to have a party.

The girls were nothing special. One was a dizzy-looking blonde; another, taller, with dark stringy hair and no figure; the third, whose face he couldn't see, laughed too often and too loud. "Wall-flowers Incorporated," he guessed, and then was instantly ashamed of himself for writing off three girls he didn't know at all on the basis of one quick glance. His bad impression might be due to the simple fact of their <u>being</u> there and spoiling his plans for a cozy half hour or so with Ann. He mentally apologized.

Ann was already packed, with one soft-skinned blue suitcase, and one dark green bookbag, just like Allan's own. Allan picked up the suitcase, which was heavy, and offered to take the book bag too, but she said "Don't be silly."

This annoyed him. Was she worried he might break down under the extra weight? For the thousand and tenth time, Allan decided he might like himself better if he managed to get more exercise. He wasn't a weakling, exactly. And Ann had never <u>complained</u> about his looks. All the same, he had to admit he was 'soft' in the tummy. His hands were strong enough, and his fingers; but he wasn't exactly the football hero type with bulging muscles and a rock-hard gut. He should try lifting weights, or work out in the pool a few times a week. Yes. He would really do it. This semester.

As soon as they were seated in the car, Ann leaned over and kissed him.

"A penny for your <u>thoughts</u>, big boy."

She did not sound very much like Mae West, but her words had the desired effect. He grinned.

"I was thinking I should probably exercise more."

"Yes, you probably should." She agreed. " But I like you anyway."

He kissed her, gratefully; then asked: "Want to give your folks a call? Let them know we're on our way?"

"Don't worry," she assured him, "they know when to expect us. I phoned them before you arrived."

"Well then, shall we 'ride off into the sunset?'"

"Let's!"

*　　*　　*

Allan persuaded Ann that they should stop at the Howard Johnson's in Concord for ice cream cones. She chose raspberry ripple, and he got his favorite double scoop: coffee and mint-chocolate chip (which she obligingly sampled and found good). She in turn persuaded him to let her do the driving for a while. He agreed easily and handed her the keys.

It was a clear windless night, not bitter cold, but a long way from summer, and they were both glad Allan's car had a working heater. Ann steered confidently around the funny traffic circle by the penitentiary, and out along the empty highway. This section of Route 2 was a long straight-away, and there were few oncoming lights to blind or distract them.

Allan peered out and up at the constellations. There was good night viewing along this dark road. Orion saluted from a hill some distance to their right, and Cassiopeia's chair hung upside down like a frozen moment from some wild amusement park ride. That much told him where both dippers were. And, while the roof cut off his view of the little one, the other ought to be dead ahead through the front windshield.

But it wasn't there. Instead, all Allan could see was the flat, black unlighted end of a large truck growing rapidly larger.

"Ann! Look out!"

The car seemed to physically tense up, then swerved wildly, first sharply left, then back right. The near corner of the dead truck grazed Allan's-side door handle, then they were past--with inches to spare.

"Pump the brakes, and ease onto the shoulder," Allan directed, not nearly as calm as he sounded, but totally aware of what they had just missed.

A moment later they had stopped, and he had his arms around her.

"You all right?"

"I'm...okay. You?"

"Fine."

He let out a sigh. "That was <u>close</u>!" He squeezed Ann's shoulder gently and smiled. "But you handled it just right. Don't worry. Your driving is fine! I'm not sure I could have turned us that fast without running off into the ditch. You saved our lives! What the hell was that guy <u>doing</u> anyway, parked in the road?"

"Yes, but you <u>saw</u> him, Allan. I <u>didn't</u>!"

"So we make a good team. Hey, we're both still here. That's what counts. Look, you want me to drive for a while?"

"No, I can...well...all right, yes <u>would</u> you? You don't mind?"

"Course not. Gives me a chance to feel all strong and protective. Helps the fragile male ego, you know." He grinned over at her.

She grinned back.

"Okay, then. Out! It's still a long way to Billsville."

But the way didn't <u>seem</u> long now. For the first few miles, they both sat quiet, musing over the deaths they had just missed. Increasingly Allan felt exhilarated, proud—of himself, for warning Ann in time, and of <u>Ann</u> for reacting so coolly and doing exactly the right thing, when another girl might have just frozen in panic or screamed and closed her eyes. They had saved <u>each other's</u> lives.

It was one more shared moment binding them together, something noone now could ever steal away.

It seemed no time at all before they were coming up on Greenfield. Soon the road would begin winding up through the mountains until it crested the Hoosick range and plunged steeply into North Adams and on into Williamstown. When Allan suggested they should stop at the summit to stretch their legs and look out over the valley before driving those last few miles home, Ann said she'd been about to suggest the same thing.

They paused in Greenfield for a long traffic light—the only one in town, Allan guessed, and found there were suddenly two cars behind them, another facing them, and one more in the left hand lane: a traffic jam by Greenfield standards. And yet it was here, here of all places, after hours of driving together alone through an intimate darkness; here, bathed in the glow of street lamps, and store fronts, here where anyone who cared to look could plainly see, that Ann leaned over, draped both her arms about Allan's neck, and began to kiss him long and passionately.

The light turned green. The cars behind them honked repeatedly, then finally gave up and pulled out around them with angry shouts and squealing tires. Dimly, Allan heard, but didn't give a damn.

Once they were recomposed and on their way again, Ann remarked: "It's wonderful how alone and free you are in a crowd of strangers. You can do anything you want and no one cares or notices. It's only people you <u>know</u> who try and hold you down. Don't you think so?"

Allan couldn't argue; and had no wish to try.

Whatever Ann felt for him, it was more than friendship. Any doubts of that disappeared forever along this winding stretch of road climbing in and out among the trees. He knew he was driving too fast, for the sheer fun of it, a thing he never did, and that they were both enjoying every moment. Thrown together by swerving turns, they would rub bodies and exchange quick dangerous kisses ignoring the road, then laugh wildly as the next turn slid them apart once again.

They were linked more closely now than if they had never broken, and what was past, Allan thought, could just go <u>fuck</u> itself. He smiled to hear himself think this. The phrase would have made him cringe once, not so long ago.

At the ridge's crest, they pulled off the road and parked, overlooking North Adams. The sky had clouded up, and mist hid the valley floor. Here and there a light winked out to them, but mostly sky, hills, and valley all appeared equally empty and gray.

Climbing from the car, they stretched and yawned simultaneously, and, catching each other doing this, ended up laughing. The moment woke memories in Allan of summer vacations as a child, scuffing his shoes on the gravel in front of some nameless motel while his father heaved and fitted big family suitcases into or out of their battered old blue Ford.

The hour might be midnight, but the smell in the damp chilly air was a morning smell, tense with the feeling of things becoming possible, about to happen. This was what he remembered, the shared excitement of setting off or arriving, mixed with sleepiness and shivers of expectation.

He shivered now, partly from cold, but more from the sheer joy of being where he was, and who he was, and having Ann to share this with. And it wasn't the night, or the driving, or even the near miracle of their escape from death that most excited him. It was Ann—beside him now, and more than ever <u>his</u>.

The pressure of her hand fitting into his own made him smile, and the sudden unstoppable yawn that sucked in on his cheeks was not weariness but nervous anticipation at knowing for dead certain (but without yet knowing when or how) that they would soon be lying warm and naked and at peace in each other's arms.

"Mmmmm. It's nice here," Ann murmured.

He leaned down and kissed her cheek.

"Are you happy," he asked?

Her eyes closed and she answered "<u>Very</u>."

"Too bad we can't stay here all night."

"Oh, I don't know. It would get awfully cold. And beds are really soooo much nicer."

Allan laughed. "Practical aren't we? Okay, what I <u>meant</u> was it's too bad we can't spend the night together--in a bed."

"Why can't we?" she asked, with a wide-eyed innocent stare.

"Aren't your folks are waiting up for us? You said you called them right before we left."

"Yessss. But I told them I'd lined up a summer job interview tomorrow morning so I'd be staying over one more night, and that you'd stay at my Aunt Sally's in Boston. Oh, don't worry. Aunt Sally likes me. She'll cover for us in case Daddy should happen to call. So you see, nobody expects us back before tomorrow afternoon."

"You little <u>witch</u>! You planned this all along, didn't you."

"Mmmmm. I wanted to surprise you. For being so…nice."

"<u>Nice</u>, am I? We'll see about that."

Back in the car they swooped down through the empty streets of North Adams, and on into dark Williamstown. He parked off behind the infirmary, well away from main campus. Ann needed only her bookbag, into which--being the clever girl she was--she had stuffed a nightgown, toothbrush, and other essentials. No one saw them walking up past the freshman quad toward West College, or heard them climbing the stairs to Allan's room.

The hallway, too, was empty and still, but he stood guard for her outside the shower room in case. While he waited he listened through the door to the sound of running water, and tried to remember what she looked like without clothes. It was a pleasant line of speculation, and his enthusiasm for it was so obvious by the time she emerged that she giggled when she saw him.

"My, my! Impatient, aren't we."

"You just wait!" he promised.

He left her "warming the nest" as she charmingly put it, and went off to shower himself, brush teeth, and generally check over his appearance one last time before he went on stage.

It <u>would</u> be a 'performance', he realized--dialogue and business scripted by Ann out of gratitude to him for his continuing affection, and regret for having ever caused him pain. Tonight would be a formal interchange of diplomatic courtesies disguised as frantic coupling. But he didn't mind. If she was offering, he was accepting, confident now that better times were soon to come.

He toweled himself dry, and sniffed under his arms. Some girls liked the smell of sweat. Did Ann? He wasn't sure but decided against deodorant or after-shave. He was stubbly, too. But his razor was back in the room. Anyway, beard burn was one of those occupational hazards a girl just had to accept—and might even welcome. He brushed his teeth, then breathed out onto the back of his hand. Fine. Ready.

Ann made no sound as he entered, locked the door, turned off the lights, draped his damp bathrobe over a chair, and, wearing no pajamas, slipped under the blanket beside her.

He could feel the stiff light cloth of her nightgown against his body. Its roughness contrasted wonderfully with the yielding warmth of her skin. She turned toward him, pulling him closer, tighter, curled herself up into his embrace. His hand slid gently down her back, found its natural resting place, and cupped her there. She nestled her head against his shoulder. Nothing, he thought, could be more peaceable, more trusting.

He began nuzzling her ear with slightly parted lips, half kissing, half suckling. Then he nipped: once, twice. Each time, she twitched sharply in his arms. He pulled back.

"Did I hurt you?"

"Yes. Exquisitely," she murmured. "Please!"

Instead, he scouted with his tongue the outline of her ear, again, and then again. His hand slipped down and cupped her breast, found the long thin ragged scar.

She twisted free and kissed him full on the mouth.

"God, I <u>love</u> it when you do that!" she said fiercely. Then, when he didn't answer, added, in her English schoolgirl voice, "I'm <u>so</u> glad you enjoy my ears."

He laughed with all his breath, and rocked her in his arms.

A moment later, he was deep inside her, snorting and full. This was reaching her, his body joining hers, completing both of them. Whenever he approached she welcomed; this was true fusion, unstoppable, unending, nothing else existed.

He whispered softly but aloud—to her, to himself, to poor old dead Catullus, to the universe that was no longer there: "*Eis aeona,*— ever and forever *eis aeona, eis aeona, eis aeoooona...*"

Chapter 22: *Dies Irae*

Later, everything came back—tomorrow, and yesterday, Tom and Elroy, and Dave, his parents and hers, the college, music. Allan could hear Ann gently breathing. He would have liked a cigarette, but was afraid to wake her. He hoped she was dreaming.

In the moments of runaway, he'd lost all awareness of her identity as someone to care for and please. He regretted that now. He grinned to himself in the dark: Well, well. So this was 'post-coital depression'! The man's burden. Women and horses, he'd heard, never felt this. And Ann, if she sorrowed at all, certainly wasn't showing it.

Still, his happiest moment of that night came sometime near dawn, when they woke together and made love again. If their first joining had been explosive, solar, this was lunar, tidal, and his pleasure crested like a wave rolling out into ripples as he imagined hers must do.

"You're awfully good at this," she told him, somewhat later. "A lot better than Tom."

He was surprised how little it bothered him to be reminded Tom had been her lover, if, at the same time, he could hear her say that she preferred his love-making style to Tom's. *O vanitas*, he thought, *vanitas vanitatem*--vanity of vanities.

He didn't answer her, didn't have to. It was enough for both of them to lie here now, completed, satisfied.

But the daylight wouldn't go away, kept getting stronger, and at last they had to admit the night was over. Allan padded to the window, pulled the shade up, and faced the day.

"Beautiful, damn it," he grumbled. "Absolutely gorgeous."

"What's the matter? Don't you <u>love</u> bright mornings?"

"I wish it had <u>snowed</u>. Then maybe we could stay holed up here together, and just call your parents and say we were stuck on the road somewhere."

"Fat chance. They know every inch of Route 2. Besides, they'd hear weather reports on the radio."

"Okay, so maybe they'd see through us. What the hell? I could always apologize later for putting you in a compromising position, even offer to make an 'honest woman' of you."

Ann laughed. "No <u>thank</u> you."

"Well if that's too corny, why not just admit what we've been up to. Then your daddy would get down his shotgun, and next thing you know we'd be off to the parson, and.… "

"You don't know my <u>daddy</u>. First he'd phone the Dean and have you booted out of Williams, then he'd give <u>me</u> the licking of my life!"

"Really?"

"You can bet on it."

Allan shook his head, but couldn't disbelieve it now. Not after what he'd seen of family relations Chez Ash.

"Ahem!" she coughed. "Shouldn't we be getting dressed?"

He supposed they should.

*   *   *

Since it was Spring Break, there was very little traffic on the road, despite the fine day. They drove up to Bennington, where they stopped and ate a good big breakfast. Next, they spent a leisurely few hours driving east toward Brattleboro, and then turned south along back roads. They got lost once, but finally emerged in North Adams, got safely back on Route 2, and arrived at the Ash's front door shortly after noon.

Allan stayed to lunch, of course, and found, a little to his own surprise, that he could still enjoy it thoroughly. Ann described in detail to her parents how the job she had interviewed for hadn't panned out after all, and they seemed to believe and sympathize. It truly astonished Allan how smoothly Ann could lie.

She warned him she'd have to stay home tonight; but Allan assured her that was okay, reminding her that this was initiation night at his fraternity, and he really <u>had</u> to be there. She seemed surprised at first, and disappointed, but reluctantly agreed they wouldn't try to meet again till lunch next day.

"How about luncheon in bed?" he whispered to her, when the coast seemed clear.

She grinned, and nodded eagerly. "Mmmm Hmmm!"

*   *   *

Walking home, Allan felt just a little smug. He had lied to Ann. Not in a <u>big</u> way, but he really <u>could</u> have met her earlier tomorrow. The fact was he simply didn't want her to see him drunk or hung-over, and he was pretty sure he was going to be both in the next 20 hours. A wholesale carouse following the solemn initiation was as much a Di-Gamm tradition as the ceremony itself, Allan remembered, and for one last time he meant to be in the thick of it. After all, his bachelor days were surely numbered now. Better make the most of them.

He returned to West College to find signs of Ann all over his room--signs only he could recognize. Her lipstick on a cigarette stub, half a cup of the lousy instant coffee they had made and tried to share before agreeing it was awful, the tousled sheets, her hairpin in the ashtray. It was easy to pretend she was waiting for him in the bedroom. As he changed clothes, he carried on his side of an imaginary conversation with her, just as if they were already married and at home.

He dressed with care but casually (this <u>was</u> a party after all, and why risk spilling beer on a good tie?).

It was past sunset when he arrived at the Di-Gamm house. Supper, a cold buffet tonight, was already on the table. But before going in to eat, he checked out the basement one last time to make sure everything was set.

The meal was unusually quiet, partly because the six pledges weren't eating. They had each been sitting alone in darkened rooms since mid-day, and would stay there for a couple hours more. This was to intensify their sense of isolation—an isolation that joining the brotherhood would end. Allan recalled that in his own case it had just made him hungry and ready to drink more when the chance came. A few of the guys at table looked a little sullen, Allan thought. In a normal year they'd have likely been off skiing or down in Florida tonight. But no matter, they'd all be drunk and happy soon.

Once the table was cleared, 14 brothers (two sponsors for each pledge, plus the chapter president Fred Mason, and tonight's chief inquisitor, Allan) donned black robes and filed downstairs to the basement chapter room. The robes were elegant affairs, representing some 19th century Romantic's concept of medieval monks' garb : made of heavy black velvet lined with scarlet satin and tied round the middle with a silver cord (in Fred's case, gold). A circle of these robed figures, glimpsed by flickering candle light, with their faces hidden in deep hoods, was an impressive sight.

The initiation rites were simple enough. One by one every light in the house was slowly faded out using a dimmer board setup in the chapter room. A small bell was rung as each light in turn winked out till the house was in total darkness. In the chapter room itself, several candles in tall floor-based holders were then lighted, and full length mirrors positioned at intervals on every side. Properly done, this created an effect of endlessly receding lighted corridors, and turned the simple basement room into a baffling labyrinth.

Alone in their separate "cells", each pledge in turn would hear muffled drums and the slow approach of a procession singing a dirge. The door would open to blinding lantern light, and the pledge would be seized by the two brothers who were his sponsors (though these were unrecognizable now in their hooded robes). They would blindfold the pledge and lead him by roundabout ways to the chapter room. During this blind pilgrimage there would be two stops. At the first, the pledge's ears would be covered with sound-absorbing muffs, and at the second, large cotton-filled gloves would be slipped onto his hands, making his isolation as complete as possible.

Once inside the chapter room, blindfold, ear covers, and gloves would be removed, and the pledge would find himself standing inside a circle of the brothers (including those newly initiated), though the candle light and mirrors would make their identities and even their exact locations hard to judge. Only voices would come to him clearly, posing questions— the same ones that Allan and others had been coaching them on for the past several weeks.

But with a difference. The "approved" answers they had been taught to give would not be accepted now. Every pledge would find himself forced to think on his feet, get himself out of a situation he had thought safely mastered. It was a dirty trick, even Allan had to admit that. But it held a useful lesson: never assume things are quite what they seem to be, or that the people around you are telling you all they know--at least not until you've had a chance to test their character.

VOICE: "Who are you?"

(Pledge gives his name.)

VOICE: "That is <u>not</u> what we asked. Who <u>are</u> you?"

(Pledge must answer as best he can.)

VOICE: "Why do you seek us?"

PLEDGE: "To be of your number." (the ritual response)

VOICE: "That is not enough. <u>Why</u> do you seek us?"

(Again, pledge must answer as best he can.)

And so forth. But the grilling seldom lasted long. Two or three exchanges were usually enough to establish the "new rules" and a conscientious pledge would look into himself and answer honestly.

Occasionally though, a really tongue-tied candidate, or one who just resented the whole process or was bored by it, had trouble coming up with answers. In the worst case a pledge might be led back out to sit alone a while longer and meditate before being questioned again.

It happened once that night. A joker named Clem Hartwell, from someplace in Kansas, couldn't stop laughing. He was their third initiate, and when, after five minutes, he still offered only "name rank and serial number" (from his social security card), the brothers who'd sponsored him led him out, and, Allan imagined, told him to straighten up and fly right. Strictly speaking this was against the rules. A pledge was supposed to figure his own way through initiation, or be rejected. But that wasn't likely now; the chapter needed warm bodies too badly. Besides, most of the guys were already anxious to get business out of the way and begin celebrating. Sure enough, five minutes later, Hartwell was led back in, answered all questions easily, and was duly welcomed into their number as "Brother Clement."

Allan wondered how far-flung the great Di-Gamma Koppa Brotherhood really was. He doubted if Di-Gamm brothers from different chapters could truly spot each other out in the "real" world, or, if they did, that they would actually help one another with no questions asked. Maybe once upon a time life had been like that. More likely it never was, but <u>should</u> have been. He doubted if he himself would ever casually use "the word" or offer "the handshake" in hopes of flushing out a fellow brother.

But if someone approached him first, he would do his best for them. And who knows? Perhaps the "real world" when he got there would turn out to be full of secret brotherhoods. Perhaps he would find that all the supposed accidents that made great fortunes and established reputations were really conducted within and between initiates. He would just have to live and learn.

The last pledge was safe inside the Di-Gamm fold by 10:45. At 10:47, the party began. A few of the guys had been sipping "Greek Fire" (150-proof rum mixed with honey and spices) as each new brother was welcomed home. But now it was beer time, and the real drinking began. A keg of Schaeffers and five cases of imported Lowenbrau had been laid on, and there were known reserves equivalent to three or four more cases of various labels in private ice chests and coolers scattered around the house. There was food, too: cold cuts, pizza, potato chips, pretzels, brownies.

The juke box exploded with sound. Those Rolling Stones again, once more bewailing their relentless pursuit of the unattainable!

This time, Allan joined right in. He knew the words by this time. Heck, he was almost beginning to enjoy the way the Stones kept driving home their point concerning *Satisfaction*, how they could not *get* this, no, nor *Steady Action* either, though they tried, and *tried*.

Drum beats hammered out the rhythm of their pain. Now he could sympathize. He, too, had suffered anguish and frustration. But he was past all that now, back sane again and whole.

There was plenty of shouting and general clowning around—the third major source of entertainment at any Di-Gamm stag party (after noise and beer). And on this particular night, a good many beers never made it from the cup to the lip, ending instead on the carpet or poured over someone's head. But no one got really mad and nothing much was busted.

Shortly after midnight, one of the new initiates discovered it was possible to toboggan or "surf" down the curving grand staircase and out the front door perched on a dinner tray. Thus was a new Di-Gamm tradition born. Allan felt pleased and proud to have been present at the event, though he declined to ride himself.

It was past 2:00 a.m. when he finally decided to leave. By then, he calculated, he had personally downed over three quarts of beer on top of the spiced honeyed rum, and smoked three quarters of a pack of cigarettes. He was hoarse from the smoke and laughter, and stuffed with salty, spicy, sweet foods. It was high time to meander home to bed.

He yelled goodbye at the few who could hear him, and stepped out the side door into the parking lot. It was cold on the pre-dawn gravel, and he shivered. But this didn't do much to sober him. He contemplated the long walk dormward. A bitch-and-a-half! Better take it in stages. Stop in at the theatre lobby maybe to warm up en route? Good idea. He smiled and set off.

Crossing Main Street, he observed with some interest that one ground floor window in the new dorm had a light on. The shade was pulled down and the light was a dim one, but it was the only sign of life around. Hard to believe someone would be in there studying this late--and during Spring Break, too.

When he reached the sidewalk again he stopped and pondered. Was there something familiar about this particular window?

At least he thought there was. Then it came to him. That was Dave Carter's room! Dave must be there now.

Ahhh, that made sense. Since his folks lived nearby, in North Adams, Dave would have no special reason to leave campus over Spring Break. Maybe he'd rather stay here than go home anyway. Some guys were like that.

Allan smiled happily and thought about last night with Ann, and about tomorrow noon. With Ann. Should he tell Dave how it had all turned out? With Ann. The guy was obviously still up, so why not?

He could just drop in, say hi, decide then whether to tell Dave or not, and about what, and how much. About Ann! Deep down, he admitted, he maybe just wanted to gloat. Feel superior. Over Ann! Well, why not? He <u>had</u> won, after all. He had Ann! And that gave him a <u>right</u> to gloat, didn't it? Ann! Poor old Dave. Ahhhh, but, mmmm-mmmmm, <u>Ann</u>!

At the moment, Allan was not fully sure what his intentions were. The very act of walking seemed to him somewhat astonishing. One leg swung out before the other, disembodied but propulsive, while he himself floated somewhere slightly up above: like a tightly tethered balloon. He felt himself move up the curving path. He heard the heavy front door clang shut behind him, and then he was moving smoothly down the hall almost before he was aware of it.

He identified the number on Dave's door, and was about to knock, when the sound of a voice from inside made him pause. It was unmistakably his <u>own</u> voice that he heard.

Allan Ross was talking inside that room. And yet here he was, standing outside in the hallway, and with his mouth closed, too. He hovered there a moment, puzzled, listening.

"...there really <u>is</u> a tree! And it's not just people, it's all the animals, and plants, and everything. It means there isn't any <u>death</u>! No final end-of-everything death. The old ingredients just get remixed "

It went on. But this much was enough for Allan to recognize ideas he'd been telling Tom sometime, not long ago, yes, that night out in the cabin. He and Elroy must have taped the whole thing, to play it back and laugh at.

And now he could hear the laughing too, from behind the door. Tom's laugh, yes, certainly Tom's. And he could hear Tom talking in between.

"...that <u>great</u>? See, I told you how completely nutso he got.."

And then another voice.

" Sweetie, stop this. Please. I mean it. I don't think it's funny, it's just mean, and you shouldn't..."

This voice wasn't Dave's, wasn't male, couldn't possibly be any voice but....

Allan lurched back as if he'd been hit. He held himself up with one hand braced against the wall. Then he gagged as a spasm of nausea swept through him.

He peered down the hall for a washroom, but saw only rows of identical wooden doors. He moved off anyway, stumbling, one hand flat to the wall, the other pressed tight against his mouth.

When the next wave hit him full force, he couldn't contain it. His teeth were clenched tight, but his lips and cheeks bulged and gave way. The stuff squeezed out around his fingers, splattered to the floor, dripped down his coat and all over his shoes. Another wave was coming. He felt the next door. It had no handle, no lock. He fell against it and pushed through just as the vomit spurted out once more from his mouth and up into his nose.

Gallons, it seemed, splashed onto the tiled floor before he could reach the sinks, bright and clean, three in a row, beneath a wall-length mirror. More waves came welling up; he spun both taps full open to blast the thick gray-yellow globules out of sight.

When at last he'd finished, Allan sank down to his knees right where he was. He would have liked to sleep. But this was no place for it. He counted to ten, tried to get up, but couldn't; counted to ten again, and this time made it.

He pulled the last brown paper towels from a nearly empty dispenser, then dug in the basket for used ones to wipe up as much of the mess as he could. He tidied himself, then the floor, then the door of the washroom, and even a bit of the hall. Finally, he gave up, staggered out of the building and away to his room.

It took every scrap of his will power not to look back at that lighted window shade.

Chapter 23: Requiem

Allan walked out to Ann's house at noon as they'd planned. He was sober now, horribly clear in the head.

She was waiting for him on the porch. But the smile of welcome left her face as he neared her.

"What's the matter?"

"You were with Tom last night. In Dave Carter's room. I heard you."

Her gaze dropped for a moment. But when she faced him again there was no hint of emotion on her cheek or in her voice.

"Yes."

"Why, Ann? For Christ's sake <u>why</u>?"

"It wasn't fair to be with you and not see him."

"Fair? What do you call <u>fair</u>? Was it fair to <u>me</u> when he started making his play for you, <u>knowing</u> we were...close?"

"He didn't 'make a play for me'. We were thrown together a few times and found we liked each other. No one planned it."

"Do you love him?"

"No." She sounded calm, sure, serious.

"But <u>he</u> must love <u>you</u>."

She laughed. "God, I <u>hope</u> not!"

"Then what is it...why did you...<u>do</u> this? Was it all just to hurt <u>me</u>? Do you...<u>hate</u> me that much!?"

"Oh, Allan. Don't be a child! Nobody <u>hates</u> you."

"You just don't <u>love</u> me, right?"

She hesitated a long time. "I don't know."

He balled his fists in sheer exasperation. "Damn it, <u>what</u> don't you know? Don't you know I love you? Don't you know I want to be with you, to help you, to share my life with you forever? Why can't you just tell me, yes or no, if you want <u>me</u>?"

"It's not that simple, Allan. Why do I have to want <u>anyone</u>? Didn't it ever occur to you that maybe I might like a little time <u>alone</u>? That maybe I don't want to <u>share</u> my life, just <u>live</u> it!"

He could say nothing.

"See? Now you're hurt, because you think I don't appreciate the lovely toys you want to give me. Well, you're wrong. I appreciate your gifts, your gestures, all you feel for me. But I'm sorry Allan, you're asking too much in return! And Tom's no better. You can both be such conceited, self-centered <u>bores</u>!"

"Is that it, Ann? Is this all a <u>game</u> for you--'switch partners after every dance'?"

"Me? <u>You two</u> are the ones playing games. You and Tom. And sometimes I don't know if I'm really the <u>prize</u> or just the ball that gets <u>kicked</u>!"

"When have I ever played games with you?"

"I'll tell you when. Right now. This very minute. You look at me, but what do you really <u>see</u>? Some princess or goddess or something! You don't want <u>me</u>, Allan, you want a statue, an idol, some object you can praise and possess and look after and...yes, <u>suffer</u> for! Oh, Allan. I know you mean it well, and I'm touched, even flattered. But it's not <u>enough</u> to play the artist's muse <u>all</u> the time. Can't you see that?"

He couldn't. Not really. What more was there to <u>be</u> than inspiring, creative, beloved, and praised in ways that were aimed to make you live forever? Besides, she was no mere <u>object</u> to him. What object could <u>begin</u> to be so fascinating or remain so endlessly absorbing? She was always changing and surprising him--moods, looks, desires, ideas--and the fact that she <u>could</u> change, <u>did</u> change, <u>must</u> change, was what he loved her for. He wasn't <u>using</u> her any more than a flower uses sunlight. He <u>depended</u> on her, and he was grateful.

"Look," he said, "I know you're feeling pushed right now. But I'm not trying to take anything <u>from</u> you. Yes, I want to marry you; but not to lock you up or anything. You can still finish school, have a career, do anything you want. You don't have to be afraid. I won't chain you down in the kitchen, or even the bedroom. Unless maybe you <u>like</u> that sort of thing."

Ann smiled, but like someone in pain. "I'll bet Daddy said all that to mother once, and maybe he believed it, too. But look what really happened. She could have done so much; and <u>didn't</u>, just so she could be <u>his</u> wife, his helper."

Ann shook her head, and went on.

"And you know what she found out? He doesn't <u>need</u> her help; he never did. Not really. And it's knowing that she's not needed, not important, that's been killing her inside for years now. I could see her hurting, but I never understand why. Until what happened to me."

"Ann, you don't have to .."

"Oh, don't bother. I know Daddy told you about my ballet dancing, and how I <u>couldn't</u> any more, and what happened. Only he twisted things a little. It wasn't just <u>these</u>. I was too tall, and too heavy, wrong legs, wrong shoulders--all of me was suddenly <u>wrong</u> for the only life I wanted."

He reached out to touch her arm, but she shook him off.

"And yes, I broke down. But wouldn't you? Losing what you cared about most through no fault of your own? Knowing there was nothing you could have done differently? No one you could blame or turn to for help? How about that, Allan? If someone told <u>you</u> that you couldn't make music any more, couldn't play jazz, only scales and finger exercises, how would you feel?"

He shook his head. "Pain, I guess. Despair, maybe?"

"Well it made me <u>angry</u>!"

"That too."

"Daddy told you about the knife."

"Yes."

"None of that really mattered to him. We moved up here because he got a good job offer, not because of me. He always says how <u>proud</u> he is of Mother and Cindy and me, but the truth is, we're just in his way. I don't ever want to be in <u>your</u> way, Allan."

"I'm <u>not</u> your father, Ann. And I'm not like him."

"No, you're not." She looked at him, sadly. "You're kinder than he is. Easier to like and...to hurt. But that only makes you more dangerous. Oh, you just don't <u>know</u>! You shouldn't be allowed to put such terrible temptation in someone's way."

Allan wondered what she meant, and tried not to let her see how much it pleased him to be told he tempted her.

For a long moment they were silent; exploring one others' eyes, while Spring continued patiently to spin its net of sound and sights around them. Sunlight shone bright on new grass, and the air was soft with birdsong. Little clouds sailed by unnoticed. Rain puddles diminished and dried.

"Come on," he offered, "walk with me."

She came down the steps to join him.

Side by side they crossed the bridge. Clear water rippled below them and boiled where stones interrupted the flow and were slowly but inevitably ground into sand.

Since it had rained in the night, they stayed on the asphalt road even after they entered the cemetery grounds. Allan glanced down the long familiar rows of headstones—worn slate and crumbling Victorian marble, crusted with gray-green flakes of lichen. Peace was here.

At the very top of the hill they stopped outside the low-walled plot that held three gravestones side by side. The stones were new, but shaped in the thin head-and-shoulders style of 18th century slabs. Ann sat on the wall and looked out across the valley. Allan seated himself beside her, but looked first at her, then back over his shoulder at the three stones in their low enclosure.

He had read their real inscriptions once, but forgot them now. They _ought_ to be 'Ann Ash', and 'Allan Ross', and 'Tom Petard'. Make a fine opera finale! Triple suicide? Or better still, maybe a double suicide with the lone survivor felled by grief! Or even just the languishing decline of three fine friends who loved each other too well to be parted even in death? How would you go about writing a convincing triple-aria for ghosts?

Hell! Ridiculous! Not even _close_ to true. He loathed the sight of Tom now, and Tom must feel the same for him. Worse! Tom could despise him for his helplessness; while he, at least, had to admire

Tom's unexpected unbelievable success. And Ann? What was Ann feeling? He had no idea.

"Who was your first...lover?" he asked suddenly. "Before me; before Tom?"

She didn't even turn to look at him. She sounded bored.

"Does it really matter?"

"To me. Everything about you matters to me."

"A boy. From North Adams. In high school."

"Was it Dave Carter?"

"Did _he_ tell you that?"

"I just wondered," Allan said.

"Well, for your information, his name was Bill Briggs and he was a senior half-back and I was a sophomore cheer leader. I'd just transferred in and didn't know anyone yet. He could tell I liked him, and seduced me on our second date. We went to a movie. Afterward he said he'd drive me home. Instead he stopped at school, by the football field. He kissed me, and said all the usual things. We wound up rolling under the bleachers. I got grass stains all over my clothes."

"I don't believe it. You were never a cheer-leader."

"You don't think I could do it?"

"I didn't say that. Do you still see the guy?"

"I haven't exactly had much free _time_ lately, have I?"

Allan said nothing. He was sorry now; too late, as usual. But for once, he didn't say so.

"So anyway," she asked, finally, "who was <u>your</u> first... woman?"

Allan hesitated.

"Well?"

"<u>You</u> are."

"Sweet. But I don't think so."

"Why not?"

"Because you <u>know</u> things. And because you take your time with me and don't seem in a hurry."

"That's just <u>love</u>."

"Huh-uh. It takes practice. And you've had some. More than once, I'd say."

He laughed. "No. You <u>are</u> wrong there. It <u>was</u> only once. Last summer. In Japan."

"<u>Japan</u>?"

"I was with my folks on vacation. One night they went someplace without me--I'd told them I was too tired. We were in Tokyo, some little guest house. It's funny, the neighborhood looked a lot like Philadelphia—trolley cars and all. Anyway, I had it all planned. I was going to find the Yoshiwara district, where I'd read the classy courtesans all were, then I would get--what was that great word I found? Oh yeah—"honked" on *sake*, while some Oriental lovely curled my toes with exquisite refinements of erotic sorcery."

Ann rolled her eyes.

"I'd been reading about Japan for months, and had maybe a hundred dollars in Yen notes in my pocket. I felt like a prince. Prince Genji, to be exact--ever read that book?"

"Heard of it. Go on."

"Well, I found <u>a</u> night club district--<u>not</u> the Yoshiwara (that was long gone anyway)--and got lured into this bar by girl in a pink kimono who looked sad and reminded me a little of...someone I knew back home. It was just an ordinary bar, you know, little lamps on all the tables, pretty dark."

"Go <u>on</u>!"

"Okay. Well, nobody seemed to speak English, but I just said '*sake*' and they brought some over. This girl and I each drank about two thimbles full, then she got up and started pulling my arm to go upstairs with her."

"And <u>did</u> you?"

"Yes. I thought there'd be little rooms--all white wood with sliding rice paper doors and tatami floor mats, and no furniture--like in the movies. But it was more like a cheap tourist cabin in the woods of Pennsylvania: stained wall paper and a plain metal bed and a rusty sink--nothing Japanese."

"And...?"

"And <u>nothing</u> much. Her kimono had a zipper. The bed was narrow, like the ones here at College, only thinner; and it squeaked. It was all over in five minutes. Then she said '*fifty dollar*' in good English. I gave her about that in Yen notes, and she got sore because I didn't have US money, and the next thing I know she was pushing me out a side door into the street."

"What did your folks say?"

"They never found out. I was back at the hotel long before they got there. In fact, I've never told anyone about this--not even Tom."

"So you lost your virginity to a geisha! How romantic."

"Not exactly. I <u>thought</u> she would be a geisha, but she was just an ordinary whore."

"Like <u>me</u>, you mean."

"No! That's what I'm telling you, Ann. <u>Not</u> like you at all. She taught me what I <u>didn't</u> want. And that's why, when I realized I loved you, I knew <u>not</u> to hurry. I mean you read that in books about sex, but I never really believed it until you came along."

"Oh, spare me."

"Damn it, Ann! I just don't <u>understand</u> you. And I <u>want</u> to so much!

"Allan, there's nothing <u>to</u> understand. I'm not sick, or crazy, or magical, or...helpless. I'm just an ordinary, standard equipment, production-line American female! It's not something <u>bad</u> to be, it's just not all that <u>special</u>!

"You're special to <u>me</u>."

"<u>Why</u>, Allan? Because I take off my clothes and lie down with you? You can find lots of girls who'll do that. All it takes is a little persistence."

"No! You <u>talk</u> to me, and <u>listen</u> to me, and feel things in a special way and try to share them with me, like I do with you."

"Other girls can do all that. We're very versatile, us females. A few of us can even <u>think</u>.

"Ann."

"It's true."

Her lips relaxed into a smile.

"I <u>like</u> you, Allan. <u>Truly</u> I do. But you just refuse to face reality. You're only really happy when the world is living out your dream of it."

Again, he couldn't answer.

She stood up and said "Let's go back. It's chilly."

They walked back down the hill over the grass among the graves. Partway down, Allan tugged Ann over toward a certain stone--his favorite. It was old, not the very oldest here, but old enough. His finger traced the worn inscription chiseled into the dark gray slate as he read the lines aloud:

> *Stranger, pause as you pass by.*
> *As you are now, so once was I;*
> *As I am now, so you must be.*
> *Prepare for death and follow me.*

"It's sad," he said. "The way that last line spoils the poem. The first three say it all so beautifully simply, but the last is just too vague. 'Prepare for death ' How do you do <u>that</u>? The last line should <u>tell</u> you somehow, but it only scolds. It's sad. Can't you feel how sad it is?"

Ann smiled, but didn't answer.

Then he remembered: he had shown her this stone before, on one of their first dates in fact. He was going over old ground yet again. Typical. Hopeless. Yes, but he felt he must try, if only one last time, to make her see things through <u>his</u> eyes, to feel them with <u>his</u> hands.

"You and I, Ann, everyone we care about, we'll all die someday. It's so hard to imagine <u>not</u> <u>being</u> here, losing hold of everything we take for granted now. But intellectually we know it <u>has</u> to happen.

Someday everything you've ever done or felt will be past and forgotten except by a few people who knew you and who still care enough to remember. And then every year there'll be fewer and fewer of those people, until the last traces of your life disappear. Unless..."

"Unless?" Ann seemed to recognize her cue.

"Unless we leave part of ourselves alive, something beautiful and important we've created. Maybe a child."

It was a maudlin, desperate, stupid line of talk. Allan knew he should never have begun it. But he also knew he meant every word he was telling her, and that he wanted Ann to hear this, even if it only made her laugh.

She <u>did</u> laugh.

"You know," she said, "for a smart guy you have an awfully weird way of romancing a girl. You start out asking her to give up every other man for the rest of her life, just so you can have her handy any time you feel the urge "

"No! Why ?"

"Well that's what marriage amounts to, isn't it? Some judge or holy man gives you a license to use each other, full legal rights?"

"I'm not trying to <u>own</u> you. I told you that! Marriage isn't <u>law</u> for me, it's <u>love</u>!"

Ann ignored this and continued.

"Next thing, you say she'll be dead soon, and unless she marries you no one will care because she couldn't possibly do anything <u>else</u> worth remembering "

"No, that's not .."

"...But don't worry, you'll make some <u>babies</u> for her, and that way she can grab a little immortality. Well, thank you so much! Have you ever <u>seen</u> a baby being born? Maybe you'll never have to. But believe me it's about the most <u>un</u>attractive process imaginable! Embarrassing and messy, and the pain is frightful, and if you think girls who know anything about reality grow up looking forward to it as life's most treasured moment...well, you're...wrong!"

"Oh, come on, Ann. My dad's a <u>doctor</u>! I know <u>something</u> about what goes on. Look, I don't expect you to jump up and down for joy--though even that happens sometimes. But however you feel, I'm not <u>asking</u> you to have children. I'm asking you to marry me. It's not children I <u>want</u>, Ann, it's <u>you</u>. To be with you."

"Let me go," Ann said. "I'm cold."

He stood back, looking at her. "Is that all you've got to say?"

"Well, what do you expect?"

"Some kind of answer. Where do we stand now?"

She sighed. "You tell <u>me</u>, Allan. Where <u>do</u> we stand?"

"Are you going to see Tom again?"

"Yes," she said quietly, "I am."

"Does that mean you <u>don't</u> want to see me any more?"

"Why should it?"

"Why? Because this way is tearing me apart!"

"So you're asking me to choose between you? Here and now?"

He nodded slowly, "Yes, I suppose I am."

"Are you sure that's what you really want?"

His lips formed the damning word. But before they spoke it, he knew it would be a lie. He did <u>not</u> want to make Ann choose.

Hope, even soured by jealousy, and worry, and confusion, was more bearable than the pain of losing her. He wasn't ready even now to face that yet. But what <u>else</u> could he do? Well, he might stall.

"Would it help if you had more time to decide?" he suggested.

"I <u>should</u> talk with Tom," she agreed. "It's only fair."

"Fair!?" He couldn't hold back. "Why can't you be fair to <u>me</u> for once! You lie to me, betray me, laugh at me. I don't <u>believe</u> he actually played you that tape of me rambling on drunk or high or whatever I was. How could he <u>do</u> that? And how could you <u>listen</u>?"

"Daddy spilled <u>my</u> little secrets, why shouldn't Tom show me yours?"

"I'm sorry, Ann. But I had no idea that your father would .."

"It's all right. He's done worse things. And if it helps, I told Tom not to play me that tape. He had no right to trick you that way. When he played it anyway, I said I'd leave if he didn't stop. And that's exactly what I <u>did</u>, too. Ask <u>him</u> if you don't believe me."

"But you went to bed with him?"

"We made love, yes. That was earlier."

"Oh, so he <u>does</u> have a right to do <u>that</u>?"

"Allan, why do you keep on like this? Let me go inside."

"Ann, please. Won't you even <u>try</u> to understand how I feel?"

"I <u>do</u> understand, Allan. Honestly I do. But if you <u>really</u> want me as much as you say, in spite of everything, then you've just got to take me as I am. No romantic image, just reality. Can you <u>do</u> that, do you think you can?"

"What about you, Ann? Can you take <u>me</u> as <u>I</u> really am?"

"It's the only way I've ever wanted you."

Their eyes met and held.

And for Allan, it was all back, instantly. She was <u>Ann</u>, and he... he loved her. She was worth any price, any pain. So long as they could share this look, exchange these smiles, how could he ever turn away from her?

"I'll <u>try</u>," he promised. "If you will."

"It's a deal," she said.

Now <u>he</u> could feel the cold, too. Clouds had closed in silently and again threatened rain. The splashing of the brook as they crossed the bridge together drowned their little silence. But this was <u>spring</u> cold, he thought, with a trace of softness and promises of warmth in it; not <u>winter</u> cold: hard and dead. All around them in the fields and woods, new things were striving upward, being born. And even the old abandoned relics up there on the hill had not entirely lost their worth or influence--not yet!

Chapter 24: *Cadenza*

Five days later, Ann went back to Wellesley, on the bus, and Tom officially returned from New York. Allan had never actually seen him, and supposed he might have been hiding out at the cabin; but he did not ask.

That first night with Tom back in the room, lying only a few feet away from him, was agony. Allan lay awake in the dark, long after his roommate had sunk into sleep. Sometime around midnight, he gave way to a sudden overwhelming urge to do him harm. He got up and moved softly over to the lumpy blanketed shape barely visible in the muted window glow.

For some moments he just stood there, full of thoughts about the mock samurai sword poised among pencils on his desk an easy reach away—the one he used to open letters. Its steel edge was keenly sharp. The feel of its short wooden handle clenched in his hand was very real to him. He imagined how easily its clean point and narrow tapering blade could punch through this woolly blanket and what lay beneath. How many times, he wondered, could it rise and fall, rise and fall, before the thing it struck cried out? It could pierce deep, that blade, easily puncture a lung, maybe even transfix a heart if properly guided. But was it worth the risk of merely glancing against a rib, perhaps snapping the blade off before the job was properly done?

And then, to murder Tom would mean the end of his own life, too. He could never escape, never hope to make things right again with Ann or anyone. There would be a trial, perhaps a last sight of Ann pointing at him from the witness box, before they took him off to jail or the asylum. A death sentence seemed unlikely. There <u>was</u> provocation after all, and he could get plenty of witnesses to his good character.

But he would still lose Ann. Besides, he didn't really <u>want</u> Tom dead. He wanted him alive to triumph over.

So what did that leave? Allan briefly considered burping very loudly in Tom's ear. But what was the point? You might do that to a friend as a joke sometime when you were drunk. Such a gesture had no symbolic force, no justice!

Justice! That was the key. Shakespearean justice. He would trouble Tom's sleep with ghosts and nightmares spawned from his own crimes, like Brutus on the eve of Philippi, or Macbeth, or King Richard the Third the night before Bosworth: *"Tomorrow in the battle think on me, and fall thy edgeless sword, despair and die!"*—that sort of thing. Tom had a make-up midterm in the morning. Perfect!

Allan leaned in close, thought a moment, then began to whisper softly, eerily:

> *False perjured Thomas,*
> *Dark twin, shadow man,*
> *Friend who was no friend,*
> *Poisoner of love,*
> *Remember Allan, cruelly betrayed.*
> *In thy examination*
> *Think on me*
> *And fall thy pointless pen,*
> *Despair,*
> *And fail!*

While Allan was whispering this curse, Tom stirred a little in his sleep, but went on snoring. Finally satisfied, Allan turned and felt his way back across the dim room to his own bed

Next morning though, he was thoroughly ashamed of himself. It had not only been childish to stand there muttering curses in Tom's sleeping ear, it had been cowardly. He made a point of waking Tom in time for him to get a decent breakfast, even wished him good luck as he left for his exam— and meant it.

But this time, repentance came too late. The runes were cast, and Tom flunked miserably. He would still graduate, but only just.

Logically, Allan knew his midnight prattle could not possibly have made Tom blow an exam. But somehow the mixture of remorse and guilty pleasure he now felt made it easier for him to share a room with Tom to the end of term.

*   *   *

The final weeks of college passed. Questions were settled. Plans were made. The Sorbonne confirmed arrangements for the fall, and Princeton agreed to hold Allan's place open for a year. After that, he knew, he'd have to make up his mind about a career--music critic, composer, or something else. And his choice would depend a lot on Ann.

He didn't visit her again at Wellesley. But she came home twice for weekends . Each time, Mrs. Ash invited him to dinner, and then he and Ann went out—once to a movie, and once to bed. Allan was pretty sure Ann managed to spend equal time with Tom during these visits home, but he never inquired.

He seldom mentioned Tom to Ann, and carefully avoided any reference to her when spoke to Tom. Once, a black rainy Wednesday night in mid-May, Ann phoned, and, after a long breezy chat with Allan, casually asked if she could speak to Tom now. Allan choked a little, handed Tom the receiver and went out without even pausing to grab his raincoat. He came back a half hour later, soaking wet, and feeling like the perfect fool he was.

Ann apologized by letter, and Allan at once wrote back saying, no, he understood and really he didn't mind. Anyway, it never happened again.

June arrived. Finals were taken and passed. Tom did better than expected, Allan a little worse. But at this point, who really cared?

Graduation ceremonies would be held on Sunday, June 13th, outdoors if the weather allowed. Allan's parents would arrive at noon the day before so they'd have time to settle in. And they had accepted Mrs. Ash's invitation to dinner that night. But before this family love feast, Allan wanted time alone with Ann.

The semester at Wellesley ended that Friday, and Professor Ash drove in to collect Ann in the family station wagon. Father and daughter arrived home, just in time for dinner, laden with suitcases, boxes, and two antique steamer trunks. Naturally, Allan was on hand to help unload.

It was a fine afternoon, capping a warm, bright day. Long shadows reached across the lawn, and sunlight played among the trees, making every leaf assume a different shade of green.

Emerging alone from the house, in search of a fresh load to carry up, Allan caught his breath sharply at the sudden view of Ann, Mrs. Ash, and Cindy out on the lawn together, hands linked. It was one of those perfect spontaneous groupings no portrait artist or dance master could ever stage. Ann was laughing, and even her mother smiled, as Cindy pulled them around in a circle, her scrunched-up face simultaneously expressing laughter, impatience, and limitless energy.

Freshness, enchantment, wisdom--everything a woman had to offer, Allan thought--was right here dancing on the lawn. And they were all <u>Ann</u>: past, present, future.

With a pang, Allan realized that he <u>loved</u> them--loved the <u>three</u> of them: mother, mistress, child. God help him, what an utter <u>fool</u> he was! He loved them <u>all</u>.

*   *   *

Ann seemed truly happy to see him, which boded well if he could once get her alone. He had planned something special for tonight, a kind of "goodbye-Williams, hello-World" commencement for two; outdoors on the hill behind the Art museum.

It was easily managed. They left right after supper, as usual, supposedly to see a movie (Antonioni's *The Red Desert*). They'd both already seen this one before, and disliked it for similar reasons, so their alibi should stick if they were questioned.

They walked together up fraternity row and down Spring Street, holding hands, while Ann brought Allan up to date on her life at Wellesley and her family's summer plans. He listened to her, caring, but at the same time wondering what it was that <u>made</u> him care?

Could his caring ever really win and hold her? Why, when she obviously didn't love him only, did he go on caring for her? Who knows? he told himself, you care. Stop asking why. Accept the fact and see what happens.

He squeezed her hand so tightly that she turned and smiled.

"Think we're alone?" he asked her.

She looked up and down the crowded oblivious street. "Uh huh."

They kissed, right there, beneath the lights of the cinema marquee. Then they walked on past and around the corner to the spot where Allan had left his car parked, safely out of sight, several hours earlier. They drove the long way around to end up in the parking lot behind the closed, dark, Art museum.

The low white marble building shone warm pink in the evening light, but not a car or a light or any sound suggested other people near. Allan opened the car trunk and took out a canvas bag that held a blanket, a thermos of hot coffee, a box of Oreo cookies, and some more mundane preparations.

Seeing all this, Ann nodded approvingly. "My favorites!" she said. And from the way she smiled he really couldn't tell whether she meant the cookies or the condoms.

Suitably loaded down, they started up the gentle pasture slope. Stars noiselessly winked into place above them, as the sun-glow dimmed. In the absence of a moon, the sky was up for grabs--a vacant place, awaiting occupation. Stars were still too few, too scattered, to be taken seriously.

Allan led the way stooping carefully to sandwich himself through a smooth wire fence. Once safely past, he spread the wires wide to help Ann through. Cows were sometimes pastured in this field, he knew. He warned Ann to watch where she put her feet.

He pointed to a lone tree on the brow of the hill. They reached it, and set down their things. But instead of spreading the blanket right away, he proposed a short tour of inspection to measure the ground and admire the view.

The stars were shaping up now, assuming relative positions he could recognize, and the air was busy with approaching summer. Birds communed, branches swayed, leaves rustled.

Something dark, that was thicker than shadow, smaller than a tree, but bigger than a man, moved slowly as they neared the clearing's edge.

"Allan, what _is_ that?"

"I think..." he began.

Then the dark shape mooed.

"Answer your question?'

"Yes," she tittered. "But what'll we _do_?"

"Just what we were planning, I guess. That cow won't interfere with us if we don't with her--which I don't suggest--unless you're feeling _really_ depraved tonight."

"Al-LAN! You're awful!"

He wondered how awful he <u>was</u>? If pressed, he would have had to admit that the vision of Ann squirming and squealing with delight as she was ravished by a bull held a certain appeal for him, especially as <u>he</u> identified with the bull. But the corresponding image—of himself in human form humping a cow--held not the slightest allure. Cows smelled so foul for one thing. And all those flies!

Ann beckoned. She had found the perfect spot: level ground out of sight of the road, but near the hill crest with plenty of long soft grass and a large flat stone that could serve them as table, or pillow, or edge-of-the-bed as occasion might require. Allan unfolded the blanket, shook it out, and spread it on the grass. They were home.

Ann lay down at once, smoothed her clothes, and looked up expectantly. Before kneeling to join her, Allan took a moment to scan the horizon. Nothing stirred, but just above the trees to the east was a faint pale glow not at all like sunset. Could that be North Adams?

He came down to her then, gave her kisses, caressed her face and hair, but offered no words. She allowed him against her, not inviting him, not refusing, simply being there.

He looked up in time to see the upper rim of the moon disc risen, cold white, above jagged tree crowns. The beauty of it made him shiver. Suddenly, he wanted warmth, felt movement, looked down, and there was Ann, faintly smiling, her eyes open wide, gazing at him without promise or fear, while her fingers slowly, deliberately, deftly, unlocked her thin blouse: button, by button, by button. She wore nothing underneath.

When her breasts were bare to moon-and star-light, she lay back and closed her eyes, leaving him alone with the gift. She was so utterly perfect. He could laugh; he could cry.

Instead, he stripped his own shirt off, unbuckled, removed trousers, then his shorts, leaving only socks and shoes. He clicked open the clasp of her skirt and rolled her, unresisting, out of it.

And now they were both completely nude, except for their shoes—and, yes, the purple garter she still wore. He took her hand into his and lay down beside her: Adam and Eve with their boots on, he thought, shameless together, in the sight of beasts and the turning stars.

They lay there unmoving, aware of each other but watching the sky, long enough to lose track of before and after. Allan floated upon the earth, hearing only Ann's breathing and his own. He was aware of the tension in his groin, the insistent ache of a rising that would neither subside nor crest, but seemed to pant, keeping time with the pulse of his heart. Before his eyes, the stars began to weave and circle, flicker and fade, all confused and desperately far off, without a sound.

Then he sneezed, and both of them burst out laughing.

"Oh, poor baby. Is-ums cold?"

"Ummmmmm-hmmmm," he snuffled.

She swung herself up, straddled him, her heavy breasts swung free, then nestled down, became his blanket, his warm heavy robe. Her hand grasped him, guided him into her.

Her face leaned closer, dazzlingly bright. He strained upward desperate to reach her. Her long hair curtained him, the stars were tangled in it, held in place.

Again and again she rocked back then leaned down, but never came quite close enough to kiss. Again and again he strained upward, never fully meeting her lips, yet never quite losing touch. She was teasing, tormenting him with joy. For an instant then he paused, ceased to struggle, sank back and saw: the moon, now wholly perfect, floating free above the jagged tree tops.

He adored the moon. Adored Ann. Lacked nothing. Wanted nothing more than this. For ever and forever.

Where was Tom? Hidden up a tree somewhere spying on them at this very moment? Where was Dave Carter? Leading a posse of campus cops and her horse-whip toting father to catch them bare-assed and red-handed? So what if they were, how could it possibly matter now?

Allan's hands slid down along Ann's cool bare flanks, her hips and thighs. <u>Bare</u>? Yes! She must have taken off her stockings at the house before they left. How had he failed to notice? How could he possibly have guessed? What a marvel she was!

He felt her shiver as his fingers closed around her. She might be cold. He asked her with his eyes if she wanted time? But <u>her</u> eyes were shut tight; her teeth clenched as if against some pain. He was killing her. Now she would kill him, too. They would die together here. There <u>was</u> no more time.

He twisted back his head and cried out wordlessly. His own eyes had closed focused on Ann's face; they opened now to see the bright full moon. The images converged. In that one helpless all-powerful moment, Ann's long hair <u>became</u> his sky, her face <u>was</u> the moon, her lips and closed eyes frozen stone, bathed in a glow too warm to be silver, too pale for gold.

Allan gave her everything he had; and thought nothing at all.

*   *   *

"Dwell on her graciousness, dwell on her smiling,
    Do not forget what flowers
The great boar trampled down in ivy time.
Her brow was creamy as the crested wave,
    Her sea-grey eyes were wild,
But nothing promised that is not performed."

—Robert Graves

Notes And Discography

As a guide to readers, here are brief definitions of the musical terms used as chapter heads and, in a few cases recommended LP recordings of specific works of music mentioned in the text.

Chapter 1: *Introit* 1

NOTE: "Introit" (pron. in-TRO-it) = 1) The action or act of going in, entrance   2) An antiphon or psalm sung while the priest approaches the altar to celebrate mass or Holy Communion.

Lulu's Back in Town (A. Dubin)

Thelonius Monk Quartet on IT'S MONK'S TIME (Columbia CL-2184)

Satisfaction (Jagger-Richard)

The Rolling Stones on OUT OF OUR HEADS (London LL3429)

Chapter 2: *Spiritoso* 19

NOTE: "Spiritoso" = In a spirited manner"

Chapter 3: *Andante* 32

NOTE: "Andante" [pron. ahn-DAHN-teh] = "Going, moving." Generally used today of a moderate tempo, inclined to slowness rather than actually slow.

Chapter 4: *A Capella* 44

NOTE: "A capella" [pron. ah-cah-PELL-lah] = "In the church [style]." Applied to choral music performed without instrumental accompaniment.

[Allan's jazz improvisation on a Bach Chorale has no recorded source, but compare John Lewis (of the Modern Jazz Quartet) whose recording THE BRIDGE GAME works jazz variations on Bach Inventions and Fugues (Phillips 826698-1).]

Chapter 5: *Musique Concrète* 53

NOTE: "Musique Concrète" [pron. mu-zeek cone-CRETT] = Music incorporating sounds produced not by voices or instruments but through electronic means. Examples from Allan's student days were often produced with the help of reel-to-reel tape recorders. See for instance Henk Badings /Dick Raajmakers—ELECTRONIC MUSIC (Epic BC 1118)

Piano pieces from Allan's repertoire mentioned here and elsewhere include

Ballade in G minor Op. 118, #3 (Johannes Brahms)
    Walter Gieseking (Angel 35027)

Etude Opus 25 #5 (Frederic Chopin)
    Guiomar Novaes (Vox 10930)

Le Tombeau de Couperin (Maurice Ravel)

Robert Casadesus COMPLETE PIANO MUSIC OF RAVEL Vol. 3 (Columbia ML 4520)

Sonata #7 in B flat Op. 83 (Serge Prokofiev)
Vladimir Ashkenazy (Angel 35647)

"*Bewitched*" and "*Spring Is Here*" (both Rodgers & Hart)
e.g. Ella Fitzgerald THE RODGERS AND HART SONG BOOK (Verve VE2-2519)

"'*round Midnight*" (Thelonius Monk)
Bill Evans CONVERSATIONS WITH MYSELF (Verve CD 82194-2)

"*Something for Sylvia*" [see NOTES to Chapter 11 below]
"*I Got Rhythm*" (Gershwin)
e.g. Ella Fitzgerald THE GEORGE AND IRA GERSHWIN SONGBOOK (Verve VE-2-2525)

Allan's "*Musica Coeli*" has no recorded source, but compare the "Neptune the Mystic" movement from *The Planets* by Gustav Holst performed by Leopold Stokowski and the Los Angeles Symphony (Capital SP-8389)

Chapter 6: Counterpoint..67

NOTE: "Counterpoint" = "The combination of two or more independent melodies. "

Chapter 7: *Crescendo*.. 81

NOTE: "Crescendo" [pron. creh-SHEN-do] = "Increasing" i.e. getting louder.

CATULLI CARMINA (Carl Orff)
Eugen Jochum conducting the Bavarian Radio Chorus & Soloists (Decca DL9824)

NOTE: "Pas de deux" [pron. PAH duh DEW]= a dance or figure for two persons.

NOTE: "Accelerando" [pron ah-tcheh-leh- RAHND-o] = "Quickening" [the tempo]

NOTE: "Cantabile" [pron. cahn-TAH-bee-leh] = "Singable" Applied to instrumental music to indicate that the player should make the music sing.

Serenade in A (Igor Stravinsky)
    Charles Rosen on (Epic LC-3792)

Four Excursions, Op. 20 (Samuel Barber)
    Andre Previn on (Columbia ML-5639)

Piano Variations (Aaron Copeland)
    Frank Glaser on F. G. PLAYS AMERICAN MUSIC (Concert-Disc CS-217)

Three Preludes (George Gershwin)
    William Bolcum on PIANO MUSIC BY GEORGE GERSHWIN (Nonesuch H-71284)

"Something for Sylvia" [=*Waltz for Debby*] (Bill Evans)
    Bill Evans on NEW JAZZ CONCEPTIONS (Riverside OJC-025 [RLP-223])

NOTE: "Recitative [pron. reh-sih-ta-TEEF] = A vocal passage which is more closely related to dramatic speech than to song.

"*The Old Hundredth* [Psalm]"
Try the choral setting by Ralph Vaughan Williams on CD (Nimbus NI-5166)

"*St. Louis Blues*" (W.C. Handy)
e.g. Bessie Smith originally on 78 (Columbia G 30818) reissued many times on LP, and available on THE SMITHSONIAN COLLECTION OF CLASSIC JAZZ (P6 11891)

NOTE: In Allan's day, the bells in the Williams chapel tower were operated mechanically to chime the hours, but could also be played from a pounding board (or "carillon") for special occasions. This provided qualified music majors the occasional opportunity to perform scheduled concerts of hymn tunes and suitable college songs.

NOTE: "Tremolo" [pron. TREH-mo-lo] = "rapid alternation of two notes on one string" a technique often used to create tension and excitement.

Shep Fields and his "rippling rhythm" (achieved by blowing through a straw into a cup of water) was a popular big band from the mid-1930s on and made many radio broadcasts and recordings. Music-snob Allan might look down on this as a mere "gimmick," but his parents would more likely recall it fondly from their own 'flaming' youth.

NOTE: "Mezzo forte" [pron. MEH-dzo FOR-tay] = Half strong (moderately loud)

Satisfaction (see Chapter 1 above)

NOTE: "Pavane" [pron. pah-VAHN] = A slow and stately court dance of the 16th century. In more recent times its "hesitation step" has been employed for music that sounds downright sad (e.g., *Pavane* by Gabriel Faure (1887), and Maurice Ravel's *Pavane for a Dead Princess* (1899).

All Day and All of the Night (Ray Davies),
     The Kinks on THE KINKS GREATEST HITS (Reprise R-6217)

NOTE: "Sforzando" [pron sforr-TSAHND-o] = "forcing" i.e. giving sudden strong accent to a single note or chord

How Long Has This Been Going On? (Gershwin)
     e.g. Ella Fitzgerald w. Ellis Larkins (piano) ELLA SINGS GERSHWIN (MCA 215)

NOTE: "Partsong" = A short unaccompanied piece for two or more voices.

NOTE: "Sonata Rondo" A rondo is a form of instrumental music with a recurring section. In this case three sections corresponding to the exposition, development, and recapitulation of a sonata movement.

I Should Care (Cahn-Stordahl-Weston)
     Bill Evans Trio on HOW MY HEART SINGS (Riverside 9473)

Isn't It Romantic (Rogers and Hart)
     Bill Evans Trio on B. E. TRIO AT SHELLEY'S MANNE HOLE (Riverside 9487)

My Funny Valentine (Rogers and Hart)
Bill Evans and Jim Hall on UNDERCURRENT (Blue Note CDP 7 90583 2)
[but I prefer Take #1 available on CD version only]

"M-31" [=*Orbit*] (Bill Evans)
Bill Evans Trio on A SIMPLE MATTER OF CONVICTION (Verve MGV8675)

Here's That Rainy Day (Van Heusen/Burke)
Bill Evans solo on ALONE (Verve V6-8792)

"Aphrodite's Going to Town" [=*Santa Claus Is Coming to Town*] (Coots/Gillespie
Bill Evans trio TRIO '64 (Verve MGV8578)

Chapter 19: Jazz Waltz

She (George Shearing)
Bud Powell on TIME WAS (CD only)
(RCA 6267-2-RB)

"Ann's Waltz" [=*To Bill Evans*] (G. Shearing)
Marian McPartland on ALONE TOGETHER (Concord Jazz CJ-171)

"My Foolish Heart" (Victor Young, Ned Washington)
e.g. Bill Evans Trio on
WALTZ FOR DEBBY (Riverside 399)

NOTE: "Da capo" [pron. dah CAII-po] = "from the head" i.e. returning again to the start of the piece.

SYMPHONY #3 in F (Opus 90) (Johannes Brahms)
    Bruno Walter conducting the Columbia Symphony Orchestra (1960)
    [reissued on Sony Classical CD as ASIN: B000002A7Y]

NOTE: The bit Allan likes so well is the second theme of the fourth movement.

I feel Fine (Lennon/McCartney)
    The Beatles on
BEATLES '65 (Capital T-2228)

NOTE: „Dies Irae" [pron. DEE-ace EAR-ay] = "Day of Wrath" This is one part of the Requiem Mass (see below) whose text concerns the final judgment of souls.

NOTE: A special Mass of remembrance for the dead, and from which two sections of the ordinary Mass (the Credo and the Gloria) are normally omitted.

NOTE: "Cadenza" [pron. cah-DEN-tsah] = An improvisation added just before the close of a piece. Such "improvs" were especially popular in the Romantic Era. The player was expected not only to display virtuosity but also to allude to thematic material from the entire movement.

About the Author

Lane Jennings worked for over 40 years as a writer and editor for the World Future Society in Bethesda, MD, and recently retired as managing editor of the scholarly journal *World Future Review.*

In the mid-1960s Lane attended Williams College, where he majored in German and graduated cum laude in 1966. He won a Fulbright Scholarship in Theatre Arts to the University of Munich, and went on to earn his MA and PhD from Harvard University, and later worked as an escort-interpreter for the Department of State.

From 1984 to 1990 he wrote scripts and did voice-over narration for SAI, a company producing television documentaries broadcast on PBS and throughout Europe.

From 1992 to 2019 Lane directed a weekly poetry program for Seniors at Friendship Terrace in Washington, DC; he also served as a translator and consultant for the Goethe Institut, helping set up websites and produce poetry-related projects in English, German, and Chinese. In addition, he has read aloud the English translations of works by numerous poets and writers from German-speaking countries at live readings in the DC area.

He lives in the new town of Columbia, Maryland.

www.ingramcontent.com/pod-product-compliance
Lightning Source LLC
Chambersburg PA
CBHW052025220726

48293CB00015B/279